The

FATE

of

OTHERS

The

FATE

of

OTHERS

STORIES

RICHARD BAUSCH

Alfred A. Knopf · New York · 2025

Published by Alfred A. Knopf, a division of Penguin Random House LLC, 1745 Broadway, New York, NY 10019.

Knopf, Borzoi Books, and the colophon are registered trademarks of Penguin Random House LLC.

These stories have appeared, sometimes in slightly different form, in the following publications: "In That Time," "The Fate of Others," "Isolation," "Donnaiolo," "The Long Consequence," and "A Local Habitation and a Name" in *Narrative Magazine;* "Three Feet in the Evening" and "Broken House" in *New Letters;* "Blue" in the *Idaho Review;* "Forensics" in the *Missouri Review;* "The Widow's Tale" in *Ploughshares;* and "A Memory, and Sorrow (An Interval)" in *River Teeth.* "In That Time" also appeared in *Pushcart Prize Stories.* I am deeply grateful to the editors of these publications.

Library of Congress Cataloging-in-Publication Data
Names: Bausch, Richard, [date] author.
Title: The fate of others / Richard Bausch.
Description: First edition. | New York : Alfred A. Knopf, 2025.
Identifiers: LCCN 2024022624 (print) | LCCN 2024022625 (ebook) |
ISBN 9780593801451 (hardcover) | ISBN 9780593801468 (ebook)
Subjects: LCGFT: Short stories.
Classification: LCC PS3552.A846 F38 2025 (print) | LCC PS3552.A846 (ebook) |
DDC 813/.54 — dc23/eng/20240517
LC record available at https://lccn.loc.gov/2024022624
LC ebook record available at https://lccn.loc.gov/2024022625

penguinrandomhouse.com | aaknopf.com

Printed in the United States of America

The authorized representative in the EU for product safety and compliance is Penguin Random House Ireland, Morrison Chambers, 32 Nassau Street, Dublin D02 YH68, Ireland, https://eu-contact.penguin.ie.

This book is dedicated to Lisa and Lila.
And to my firstborn daughter, Emily Chiles,
for her always heartening attention to new work.

CONTENTS

The

FATE

of

OTHERS

IN THAT TIME

Back in late June of 1949, when I was twelve years old, I spent a morning with Ernest Hemingway. This was shortly after I had been hauled down to Cuba, deeply against my will, by my parents, whom I had begun to think of as the Captain and his wife. The Captain had retired from the navy after twenty years' service, and was following a friend from his time on a destroyer in the Pacific during the war. They were planning to begin a charter fishing business. The friend, who had left the navy as the war ended, was already living down there, and the charter fishing idea was his. My father had wired him funds toward getting things set up.

His half of the investment; it was a lot of money.

The friend's name, all I ever knew about him, was Coldrow, nicknamed Cookie. He was supposed to meet us at the harbor in Havana. The Captain and his wife sold things and gave away things and packed things with a kind of unspoken urgency, and the three of us boarded the SS *Veendam* Holland America Line on the seventeenth of June. When we arrived, the morning of the eighteenth, Cookie wasn't there. So, the Captain rented us rooms a couple of blocks from the Floridita, in a place called Pepe's (I think the building is still there, under a different name), a big house with a double-decker porch, and a café on the first level. There was no sign of Cookie, and no word from him, either. The address he had given my father turned out to be a burned-out cottage at the edge of the Canal de Entrada. Someone told my father that a man fitting Cookie's description had lived there, but no one knew what became of him after the fire. He had just gone. There was supposed to be a boat, but there was no boat — there was a little dock, but no boat.

So, we stayed at Pepe's, and the long days went by. The Captain spoke Spanish, but his wife and I did not. They had been married only a little more than a year. They were either going to get used to each other, or they never would (they never did). By the fourth day, he was ready to give up trying to locate Coldrow — he had stopped using the nickname by then — and instead of looking anymore for a place where we could set up house, he spent the next three days mostly in bed. The wife was restless and irritable, though she told me bravely that what he required now was rest, that we all must take time to acclimate. Money wasn't an immediate problem, even with the loss of what he had sent to Coldrow: he had sixty-eight days' retirement leave, a navy pension after twenty years' service, and income from an inheritance his first wife, my mother, left him.

Of course, I had nobody, and nothing to do. Nowhere to go. I was just *with* them: the Captain and his wife.

"Clark," she said to me somewhere around the tenth or eleventh morning, "go out and get us a newspaper and some bananas. Go busy yourself, be useful. You make me nervous."

Sitting on a sofa under the one tall window looking out on the city, with a book open on her lap and a cigarette between the index and middle fingers of her left hand, she put me in mind of a picture I'd seen on a paperback cover of a lady of shadows, though there was really nothing mysterious about her. She was a young woman who grew up in Virginia and had never been anywhere, and came from a family that catered to her whims in ways the Captain never did. No doubt she found this exciting about him at first; now she was too far from home, and fairly disenchanted. But she looked chic anyway — nails painted dark red, like her lips; hair in a natural blond perm. She was very pretty and she had what I'd heard people call Betty Grable legs.

The cigarette sent its winding strand of blue smoke to the ceiling. I'd been trying again to get the radio tuned to something other than static. "They'll have newspapers at the Floridita. Go on, boy. Get."

My own mother died having me. I'd known this for as long as I could remember. And I'd spent most of my life with women my father hired to watch me. He was almost always gone in my growing-up years. Duty tours. The war, of course. But even when he was stationed where I could be with him, regularly I had governesses (his expression) attending to me. It was easy enough to think of him as the Captain.

"Give him some money," he said now from the other room.

"Really?" she called. "I'm stunned. You need money down here? We have to pay for things down here even though we already *sent* money?" Then, low, to me: "There's some in my purse, over there on the table."

I brought the purse over to her and she rummaged through the mess inside. A lot of little tubes, cigarette case, billfold, tissue paper and compact makeup. "Here." She held out a ten-peso note, folded so tight it wasn't much bigger than a postage stamp. "And get yourself an egg or something."

The Captain coughed in the other room. "Bring some fruit. Any kind of fruit."

"Bananas," she called to him. "I *said* a newspaper and bananas."

"I hate bananas and you know it. Jesus Christ."

"You *said* any kind of fruit, Dwayne. And don't use that language. It's common."

"Screw you, how about that?"

"Your father," she said to me, "is a common, uncouth, low-life person."

"What're you telling him?" came from the other room. "It's not even nine in the morning. A lot of people are in bed at this hour on a Saturday. Christ. Any kind of fruit!"

That last was louder, meant for me.

I heard the strain he was under in his voice. He had more to worry about than losing money to a supposed friend, and though I was too young to understand it fully, I knew enough: He'd been duty officer when James Forrestal, former secretary of defense, jumped from a high window of the Naval Medical Center in Bethesda, Maryland. Two in the morning of May 22; he was found on the roof of the third-floor cafeteria, wearing only pajama bottoms. I'd heard my parents talking about it the day it happened. I was in my bed, supposed to be asleep, and the Captain's voice came low, down the hall: "The indignity of it. Pajama bottoms. He was a man of dignity. Something just doesn't add up."

And then her voice: "You're saying — ?"

"There was broken glass in his bed, Abby. I was there. I saw it. Broken glass, and his room was across the hall from the window where he went out. Or was thrown."

"Thrown."

"They know he and I formed a bond."

"A what?"

"That's what *he* said. I even heard him say it over the phone. That's what he called it. He made a big deal about it. He said he felt a bond, that we'd formed a bond because we were navy men, and were against helping the Zionists. And the Zionists, and the government, they hated him. This goes all the way up to the president."

"Stop it."

"Forget I said that about the glass in his bed."

"You're kidding. Poor baby, you're imagining things."

"I was there in that room at six this morning. I came in and he wasn't there. Broken glass in the bed. Forget I said anything. I didn't say anything."

"Who would *I* talk to about it, honey?"

"No. Right."

"Dwayne. The man jumped. Come on. He was crazy."

"Explain the broken glass."

I heard the shrug in her voice. "He broke a glass."

According to the papers and the radio news, Forrestal was quite outspoken about his anti-Zionist sentiments. My father did not like the Zionists, either. I wasn't too sure, at the time, what Zionists were. I knew they had to do with an ancient homeland restored by partition in the Middle East. I had an idea, anyway. All that business about the Arabs and Israel was hard to miss with the radio on every evening and the papers that piled up on the coffee table in the living room of our apartment in Rosslyn. The Captain believed the Zionists might have killed Forrestal, and that there was a chance they'd be coming after him, too. He didn't speak of this, but it was in the air, in the disquiet you heard in his voice. He and Forrestal formed the bond (he kept using the phrase) while Forrestal was hospitalized. Now Forrestal was dead. The facts kept troubling him, and her. I was in the middle of it all.

Zionists, suicide, theft, murder. Cuba, where we knew no one. The uncertainty of everything. The sad Captain and the sad Captain's wife.

I had all this in my head as I went out to get a newspaper. I didn't want to be near them anymore. When I came down the stairs from the top deck, there was Hemingway sitting in the café, a newspaper open on the table, coffee at his elbow, with a squat brown bottle of something on the other side of it. Right away I knew who he was: I had been obsessed with lions and Africa, and the Captain had a magazine with pictures of the author-hunter that everyone called Papa. I knew the face, and now I heard the waiter say, "*Otra cosa,* Papa?"

"A couple more fried eggs, Alejandro. With chorizo this time, please."

"*Subiendo.*"

Hemingway looked at me and smiled. "And what's yours this morning?"

It was really a wonderful smile. There was coffee in his beard, which still had some darkness in it close to the skin, and his mustache was ash colored. He wiped the back of his hand across his mouth. He had on a black T-shirt; ragged, stained white shorts; and rope sandals. I saw the hair on his legs, his big knees. I stood there gaping.

"Why're you crying?" he said.

I hadn't known I was. "Nothing," I told him.

"Okay." He drank, and went back to reading the paper.

"Can I have that paper when you're finished?" I was being a brave unhappy boy.

He gave me a long, evaluative look, then poured into his coffee the last of whatever the clear liquid was in the bottle, and drank. His eyes were red, irritated looking. But friendly. "You had breakfast?"

I shook my head.

"Is that what you're crying about?"

"No."

"You want the paper that bad?"

"No."

He smiled again. "Tears from pain, or from pique."

I stared.

"Pique," he said. "You *mad* at somebody? Where are your people? Your parents."

"Upstairs."

"They mad at you?"

"You killed a lion," I said. I felt stupid. It was all I could think to say. I wiped my nose with my hand and then wiped my hands on my own dirty white shorts.

"You mad at *me*?" He put his fingers against his chest. "It was self-defense, I swear."

"I wish I could hunt lions," I got out.

He took the other chair at the table and turned it. "Sit down, partner."

I did so. He turned a page of the paper and took a drink from the coffee cup. "Alejandro," he said to the waiter. *"Tiempo para el vino, amigo. Un blanco frío."*

"Sí, Papa."

"I'd like to go to Africa," I said.

He shook his head very slightly, remembering something. "Haven't been there in years. I did kill a lion, a big gazelle, and a charging buffalo — water buffalo. You know what that is, right? A great big thing with horns. Black as outer space." He put the paper down and extended his arms into what looked like an embrace of something large. "Massive and ill-tempered. Kill you out of meanness." Then he reached into the pocket of his shorts, and brought out a clean white handkerchief. "Wipe your nose."

I did.

"What's your name?"

"Is a water buffalo fast?" I said.

He nodded. And there was the smile again. "Had to finish one with my bowie knife. Ever see a bowie knife?"

"No."

"Cut you in half. A man named James Black created it for Jim Bowie — you've heard of Jim Bowie."

I wasn't certain, but I nodded. It did sound familiar.

"Created the thing just for knife fighting, way back in 1827. Jim Bowie used it, too, in a big duel called the Sandbar Fight, where he would've died if it wasn't for that knife. It saved him. Damn near as big as a broad-blade sword. And this bull, I got him in the neck as he was coming over me. Just missed getting trampled."

I was speechless for a few seconds, trying to imagine it all. "I saw a picture of you," I got out. "With a lion."

Alejandro brought a bottle of white wine in a bucket of ice, and one glass. He set the glass down, opened the wine and poured a little. Hemingway just nodded, so Alejandro poured a little more, and then set the bottle into the ice. He picked up the squat brown bottle and the coffee cup. "Would you like something to eat?" he said to me in completely unaccented English. I think he was intentionally not noticing my sniffling.

Hemingway lifted one hand at me, palm up. It looked like it might weigh ten pounds, that hand. "Well? What do you say, kid? It's on me."

"Eggs?" I managed, wiping my nose with the handkerchief. "And bacon."

"You like the yolks soft?"

"Yes."

He said to Alejandro, "Three, sunny-side-up, amigo. And five strips of bacon, and do the eggs in the bacon fat. And an English muffin." He looked at me. "You like orange juice?"

I nodded.

"Tell us your name."

I said it, looking down.

"Big glass of orange juice for Clark."

Alejandro wrote it down.

"That all sound good to you?" Hemingway asked me.

"And a waffle?" I said.

He gestured to Alejandro with that smile.

"Sólo pasteles de plancha."

"Only pancakes here, partner. That all right?"

I nodded.

"Coming right up." Alejandro walked off. I noticed that he had a crooked back, and a slight limp. He moved slowly.

"He speaks good English," I said.

"Better than we do. For some reason, he doesn't like to speak it. But he's good."

"Sí," I said.

He nodded, that smile. "Feeling better, I see."

"I'd like to go to Africa."

"I was there way back in '33. Alejandro a lot more recently. He fought against the Desert Fox, a brilliant German general. You ever hear of him?"

"No, sir," I said. The world was full of color now, and interest. Desert foxes and bowie knives and duels, lions and charging water buffaloes.

He looked me over again. "How old are you?"

I told him.

"Your daddy never told you about the Desert Fox?"

"No."

"Great general. His name was Rommel. Erwin Rommel. He was forced to take cyanide by Herr Hitler toward the end. What were you, seven or eight when the war ended?"

"Yes, sir."

"You know about Hitler?"

"Yes, I do, sir."

"How come you don't like your name? A minute ago, you looked like you were ashamed of it."

"No," I told him.

"I think it's a good name."

"Yes, sir."

"You know it comes from the English word *clerk*. They still pronounce *clerk* there as 'Clark.'"

I simply nodded.

"I didn't like my name, either, when I was your age. Ernest. Ernie. That's what I *really* didn't like. Ernie. I thought it sounded puny."

"I think it sounds friendly," I said.

He nodded. "Are you gonna be a writer?"

I shrugged.

"Still not sure, myself." He made a little scoffing sound. "And you know about Hitler. What about Mussolini, and Stalin?"

"Yes," I said.

He lifted his newspaper and held it open, probably in some way intending to compliment me by being unsurprised that I knew the other names. On the other side of the page I saw Forrestal's picture. My heart jumped.

"My father *knew* him." I pointed.

He turned the edge down with his heavy fingers to look, then folded the section to the page with the article, holding it in one hand and sipping the wine. "That's right. The paralytic's navy boy. Your father knew him, huh?"

I repeated the phrase: "Paralytic's navy boy." I thought he might be referring to my father in some way.

"Franklin D.'s boy. Secretary of the navy. Franklin D. was *assistant* secretary of the navy before he got to be president. And Forrestal was our first secretary of defense. Did you know Franklin D. was a cripple?"

Nodding, I said, "You knew the president?"

"Sure."

"My father was in the navy," I said. "He was stationed at the hospital where Forrestal — " I didn't finish the sentence.

"Ah, right. Bethesda Naval Hospital."

"Yes, sir."

When Alejandro brought the orange juice, I said to him, "You were in Africa, too."

He glanced at Hemingway, who returned the gaze, grinning now. It was like some kind of joke between them. Then it seemed suddenly serious from the expression on Alejandro's face.

"Just that you were there," Hemingway said quietly to him.

"Oh, *sí, jovencito,*" Alejandro said to me. Then: "I was there all right, young man. I was there." He went on back to the kitchen.

Hemingway leaned close, and I saw the sun damage on both sides of his nose. "The war," he said, low. "Doesn't like to talk about it. He's a bloody hero, though. Served in a tank battalion. You know what that is, a tank battalion?"

I had enough of an idea of it to nod that I did.

"Were you in the war, too?" I asked him. I remembered seeing a picture of him standing with some soldiers behind some kind of truck or jeep. I wanted him to tell about it.

He looked serious for a moment, the index finger of his left hand tapping lightly on the table. "I've been in all of them," he said. "In this century, anyway." He straightened and stretched, arms up, fists at his ears. "With this latest one, I liberated the Ritz Bar, in Paris. You ever hear of the Ritz Bar?"

I nodded, and smiled at him for the first time.

"There," Hemingway said. "Good. You *are* feeling better. You never heard of the Ritz Bar."

"No, sir."

He laughed. It was a surprisingly high-pitched laugh. When he took a sip of the wine, the sun from the far window sparkled in the straw color of it. "I have two sons, myself, you know. Grown men. You'd like them."

I nodded, but he was looking at the paper, reading the article about Forrestal. The silence lengthened. For a minute, it was like we were old friends, used to being in each other's company and not needing to talk. But the time went on, and I thought maybe he'd forgotten I was there. I still had his handkerchief, so I put it on the table. He looked over the paper at me, saw the handkerchief and put it back. "Says here that his family claims he was just exhausted. Not crazy."

"Does it say anything about broken glass?"

He looked back at the paper and then at me again. "Broken glass?"

"They found broken glass in his bed. It's a secret. My father said not to tell anyone."

"You just told *me,* kid."

"I know. I'm sorry." For a second, I thought I might need the handkerchief again.

"Don't worry, partner. I won't tell anybody."

I nodded, and put on a smile.

"So, your father and he were friends."

"They spent time. Every day, while Mr. Forrestal was in the hospital — yes, sir."

Hemingway combed one heavy hand through his thinning hair. "Did your father know him before the hospital?"

I hesitated, trying to decide exactly what the truth about it must be.

"Your father's navy. This guy was navy, too."

"They formed a bond." I was just using the Captain's phrase.

"Well, what brings all of you down this way?"

"The Zionists may be after my father." I did not understand why I felt the need to lie, just then. And I think this was when I realized that it might not exactly *be* a lie: certainly the Captain was worried about the possibility.

"Do *you* know who Forrestal was?" Hemingway asked.

"Not really. The Captain's friend."

"The Captain."

"My father."

"You call him that?"

I shrugged.

"Does *he* know you call him that?"

I shrugged again, feeling caught out.

"Well, it's none of my business — no need to worry about it now, partner." Hemingway turned the newspaper over and laid it flat, so the article about Forrestal was up. He smoothed it with both hands. "Forrestal was important in the government. But you knew that, right? So what about the feds? They after your father, too?"

"Yes," I told him. "I believe the feds are, too."

"So, he's in hiding." Now Hemingway's smile was broad, stretching all the way across his wide jaw. "Down here. In the lion's den. Not a good place to hide from the feds. There's feds crawling all over the place down this way, kid. That's why I'm here instead of the Floridita."

I looked around the empty room.

"I'd like to talk to your father." His eyes narrowed. I felt that he was looking deep into me now. We just sat staring at each other for what seemed a long time.

Presently, two men came into the place and walked directly over to our table, as if they had an appointment with us. I shrunk back at their approach, and Hemingway reached over to steady me. His rough hand was on my arm for a second. No one had touched me in a long time. It got me sniffling again. The taller of the two men was bald, with thin strands of black hair combed over from a part just above his left ear. He had a camera on his chest, secured by a little strap hanging from his neck. "I'm Ed Volker," he said, and then tilted his head toward the shorter one with him. "This is Tye Blazedall. We're with the *Washington Star-Tribune*." Blazedall had a blue baseball cap on with a red W. He looked way younger. He was rubbing his hands together oddly, shifting his weight from side to side. It came to me that he was excited to meet the famous author and hunter.

The one named Blazedall saw the paper open on the table and read the name aloud in the headline: "Forrestal. What a thing."

Volker took a picture of Hemingway, who just sat there while he took two more.

"I know someone who covers politics in DC," Blazedall said, "and he swears you could see it coming a mile away. Guy was a suicide waiting to happen."

Hemingway took a drink of the wine, and simply gazed back at him.

"I can't imagine jumping, though, can you?"

"Evidently there's some question."

"Oh, that's thinking like a novelist," said Volker.

"No," Hemingway told him. "That's what this article's about. Family says he wouldn't do that to himself. Says he was terrified of heights." Then, looking at me: "What do you think, there, partner? That sound true?"

I gave him a look that I hoped communicated the need for secrecy. He nodded slightly and looked back at the man. "About jumping—not much of a way to go, I guess. I think drowning or freezing to death. I think you just go to sleep freezing to death."

Volker snapped another picture, then stood back and muttered, "Anyway, all that time falling. And from that height a body would break open like a watermelon."

Hemingway reached over again and lightly patted my arm. And when I looked at him he winked. "I never liked watermelon."

"I guess if you've gone crazy, you don't really care how you do it."

"This young man's father knew him," Hemingway said, indicating me.

"That so," said Blazedall. But he seemed to brush this aside. "Well, actually, we do have a reason to be in Havana. Your wife said we'd find you here, but that you'd probably be working."

"I'm being lazy this morning," Hemingway told him. "Miss Mary knows quite well I'm not working. I've just finished the best thing I've ever done. And I'm thinking of hunting big game with my partner here." He indicated me again, and winked. "What say we go to Africa, partner?"

Volker said, "What's it like spending time with Gary Cooper and Ingrid Bergman?"

"I haven't seen those two fine people in a while. Supposed to see Coop soon enough, though. Do some hunting in Idaho. Fine fella."

"What're they really like?" Blazedall asked. "What's Marlene Dietrich like?"

"She's as sexy as you think she is."

"And Coop?"

Hemingway smiled and nodded. "Coop's sexy, too."

"No, really."

He stared. After a beat, he nodded, muttering, "They're fine people."

Blazedall took off his baseball cap and moved to stand next to Hemingway's chair. "Take another picture, Ed."

"Actually, we're about to eat," Hemingway said.

"Won't take a second," said Volker, focusing. He snapped it.

"Thank you so much," Blazedall said. "Listen, I know it's ridiculous, but the paper actually sent us to ask what your opinion might be about the Nobel committee not awarding a prize in '48."

Hemingway sipped the wine, and gazed at the shifting sunlight in it.

The two men glanced at one another. "Goddammit, Tye, it's too soon," Volker muttered.

"What did Miss Mary tell you two? She tell you to get me talking? Have a drink with me?"

They were silent.

"She didn't say I'd be working. I know goddamn good and well she didn't say that."

"I can't drink at this hour of the morning," Volker said.

Hemingway's annoyance was obvious now. "No opinion."

"Seems odd, don't you think? No prize?"

"I just told you what I think."

"Can you say something more about your new book?" Blazedall asked.

This changed things some. Hemingway took another drink of the wine. "You should try this in the morning sometime. Very good for the spirit. Like fuel for an engine." He looked at me. "Isn't that right, partner?"

"Yes," I said.

"Alejandro," he called. "Isn't that right, *amigo*?"

Alejandro was standing in the entrance to the kitchen. "*Sí,* Papa," he said.

Hemingway looked at the two men; he was still holding the glass of wine. "*Otro, amigo.*"

Alejandro went on into the kitchen.

"Twenty-five years old and wounded at El Alamein. He took out a panzer single-handed with a sticky bomb laid into the tread."

The others said nothing.

"So. You boys want to talk about the new book."

"Man, yes we do," Blazedall broke forth in an enthusiastic tone that even an unhappy twelve-year-old boy could see was embarrassing.

"It's got everything I know in it," Hemingway said. "And it's built solid as the hull of a ship."

Alejandro brought the second bottle of wine, already opened. He filled the glass and set the bottle in the bucket as he removed the empty one.

"You sure you don't want some of this?" Hemingway asked them.

"Across the River and into the Trees," Volker said. "Great title."

Hemingway smiled broadly. "You saw it in the magazine?"

"Do you want to tell us more about it?"

A woman came in, then, and walked over to the table. "Volker," she said. She was blond and wiry, with perfect skin. I thought of the Captain's wife, upstairs. The same long legs, the same dark lipstick. "Mr. Hemingway," she said. "Are you liberating this place?"

"You know that story."

"Doesn't everyone?"

"Well. Paris wasn't all fun and games. It was the end of the war, but it wasn't all fun and games. We saw plenty of fighting on the way in."

"I heard you had a sidearm. Against regulations."

Hemingway's jaw tightened. "I had a brigade, madam. At a place called Rambouillet. I was with a group of partisans. We had head-quarters in a bombed-out hotel."

She said, "Can I quote you?"

"This is already out there," he said. "I'll tell you this, though — I saw action. I had a hundred twenty-two sures before I got to Paris."

"Sures."

"Kills. Nazis. You remember the war?" His smile was fleeting. "It was in all the papers."

"Quite," she said.

"You with these two?" he asked her.

"We're in the same business," said the woman. "I'm Helen Talbot. I'm not averse to having a glass of wine."

"Did my wife send you?"

"I don't understand the question. *Vanity Fair* sent me."

"And you want to know what I think of the lack of a prize recipient in a certain award."

"That, and a couple other things. I didn't know about these kills."

"I don't talk about it. Already been in the papers several times."

"Will you write about them? About death?"

"I've been writing about nothing else. My whole life."

"How does it feel to be a legend?"

"How do *you* feel about it?"

She left a pause.

"I don't have an opinion about the '48 Nobel, all right? I never think of it. Nor of anything like it or near it."

"And about the new book? Can you talk about that?"

"Did you see it in the magazine?"

"Yes. But I wondered what you meant to say with it. The old soldier and the young girl."

"You remind me of somebody," he said. Then: "There's nothing else to say."

She stayed silent.

"What I have to say is *it,* itself. That. The book."

"I see."

"You'll excuse us." He gave her another brief smile. "Quite probably you're nothing like who you remind me of. But let's call it a morning's work, all right?"

Alejandro brought our breakfasts out on a big tray. I felt an almost unreasonable sense of relief. I remember that I thought we could go back to talking about lions.

Volker was muttering at the woman, and Blazedall took hold of his elbow and was trying to move him toward the door. "We could stay and order breakfast," Helen Talbot said.

Blazedall said, "Can't you see he's having breakfast with his grandson?"

They all went out and along the street, away. We were quiet, watching them go. Alejandro poured more of the wine.

"They were up early," Hemingway said. "Didn't she look like somebody to you?"

"*Ninguna ex esposa,*" Alejandro said.

"You sure? Not an ex-wife? You didn't think of her?"

Alejandro shook his head, walking away.

I had begun to eat the eggs. I said, "She reminded me of my stepmother."

Hemingway laughed.

"Upstairs," I said.

And he laughed again.

It made me very glad. I sat happily eating my eggs. I thought I had never tasted anything so good. He forked the chorizo into his mouth, chewing and looking off. "It seemed like they wanted the movie stars," I said, chewing.

He laughed again. It thrilled me. We were compadres.

"Tourists," he said. "And they're supposed to be journalists."

"Pah," said Alejandro, from the doorway. He waved one hand across his face and turned into the kitchen.

"Alejandro worked at the Floridita awhile," Hemingway said to me. "Known him a couple years now." He drank more of the wine. Then: "Journalists. Christ."

I said, "Goddamn them." I had heard the Captain say that about journalists. I was merely repeating it, to please Hemingway.

"I started as a reporter," he said. "They disgrace it. I know some very good journalists." He watched me scrape the eggs from the plate. "You read the papers?"

I nodded. I had turned to the pancakes. "I wish I could see a lion."

"Yeah. Lions. You should hear the sound they make at night."

"And you killed one."

He nodded, grinning.

"And water buffaloes," I said.

"Yep."

Because I wanted to keep talking about the lions, I offered what was the full extent of my knowledge about the buffaloes. "They're even bigger." Then I added, "But lions kill them."

"Hunting in concert," he said. "Maybe some. But the water buffalo has no real enemies. The other animals don't bother them." He drained the wineglass, and poured still more. There was no effect of it on him that I could see. "Want a taste?"

"No, thank you." I drank my orange juice, and thought about how the Captain and his wife would be falling-down drunk splitting one bottle.

"The water buffaloes travel in herds," Hemingway said, suddenly. "And they'll fight for each other. The lions stay away, mostly."

"You killed them."

"Killed one each."

I waited for him to go on. Then he was just watching me eat the remainder of my pancakes. Alejandro stood there watching me, too. I began to feel self-conscious.

"Dawns on me I like to watch someone eat who's really hungry," Hemingway said, pouring the last of the second bottle of wine. He held the glass up. "To us soldiers."

Alejandro said, "Soldiers." But he just nodded.

Hemingway drank, then belched soundlessly and put the glass down. I saw his eyes, the light in them and the way they moved, taking everything in. He kept watching the door; I hadn't noticed that earlier. "Those journalists, as they'd call themselves, thought you were my grandson."

I said, "Funny."

Suddenly I wanted to ask him if the things he had told me were true. I knew that I would not do so, but I also understood that there had been no stabbing of a charging water buffalo with a bowie knife, nor any killing of a hundred krauts. So, then I was sitting there with my full stomach wondering why a person of his size and fame and fortune would lie to a boy like me about such things. Also I recall the sense that there was something to learn from him in the fact of it, to have an advantage as I went on with the Captain and his wife. I mean I thought it was part of being a grown-up.

But then, too, I remember hoping, with a guilty ache, that no one would ever catch him out in his lies. I said, "Thank you for the breakfast, Papa," and he clapped his hands together and leaned back, smiling that smile.

"My pleasure, Clark. My pleasure."

In the next minute, the Captain was there, in Bermuda shorts and a sleeveless undershirt. He scowled at me until it registered with him who was sitting across from me. Quickly, he offered his hand. "Very *very* excited to meet you, sir."

Hemingway looked at me. "This your papa?"

I was ashamed, nodding.

"I'm his father," the Captain said quickly. "I hope he hasn't been bothering you."

"Not a bit of it."

"Get up, boy." He cuffed me lightly, painlessly, on the back of my head, though the fact of it hurt. "Don't overstay your welcome. Do you know who this is?"

"He's not bothering me, sir," said Hemingway. "We're talking about going on safari together, isn't that right, partner?"

I had stood out of my chair, fighting tears. Alejandro had come back into the room.

"Come on," Hemingway said gently to me. "Sit down. It's all right. Finish your breakfast. You've still got half a muffin left."

The Captain, uninvited, pulled another chair over, and then seemed to think about it. "Excuse me, would you mind if I just brought my wife down? I — I have to put a shirt on."

Hemingway turned to Alejandro, and indicated the bottle. *"Uno mas, amigo."*

"Sí."

"I'll be right back," the Captain said, backing toward the stairs. "Won't be a second."

"Good. We can talk about Forrestal."

He paused, straightened slightly — which was when I realized that he'd been hunched over, like somebody cringing in the cold. "Yes, of course." Then, looking at me: "Wait here." His voice was full of displeasure and suspicion. He turned and was gone.

I looked at Hemingway, who smiled that smile and then leaned toward me and, with his hand on the paper with the article about Forrestal, said, "Partner, really, it's all right."

I don't remember now how much time went by. It seemed long. Alejandro brought the wine, Hemingway downed a glass of it, then asked for a daiquiri, and Alejandro brought that. Another journalist, a slack-looking wiry man, came in and also wanted to know what the lack of a prize for '48 meant. Hemingway dismissed this with a smirk and said, "Is that all you want to talk about?"

"My boss wants to know."

"You want a drink, some coffee? The price is we don't talk about that shit."

The journalist muttered that he had a job to do, and left.

"Did you notice," Hemingway asked me, "that none of his clothes fit him? They all looked a size too big."

At last, the Captain came down, dressed, and alone. "I'm so sorry," he said. "She'll be right down. She just needs to freshen up a bit."

"Did you see this?" Hemingway asked him, indicating the paper lying open on the table.

The Captain stared at it for an awkward few seconds, while Hemingway and Alejandro and I watched him. It occurred to me that he was reading it. He sat down slowly, still staring at it.

"Coffee, *señor*?" Alejandro said.

The Captain nodded absently. "I'm not supposed to say anything, but we found broken glass in his bed."

Hemingway glanced my way, while feigning surprise. "You don't say? You knew him well?"

The Captain looked at me.

"Clark, here, says you were his friend."

"Well."

Now Hemingway leaned back, clasped his hands under his chin and smiled broadly. "Tough to be a real friend to that sort of character."

"You knew him?"

"Met him in France, during the war. To me he seemed like an unpleasant little son of a bitch. But very efficient, and very smart."

The Captain was quiet. Alejandro brought him his coffee.

"And you liked him," Hemingway said.

"Well."

"He seemed to me like a doubled-up fist," he went on. "The type who would depopulate a country to get his own way."

"He was very strict," my father said. "And, really — yes. Not very pleasant."

I couldn't believe it. The man who had formed a bond. I looked at him, at the folds of his white shirt, the collar, the one button that was undone halfway down the front. Suddenly I knew Hemingway was lying about knowing Forrestal, as he had lied about everything else, toying with the Captain, for my benefit, and that the Captain was suffering, and that this morning was all part of the badness from a suicide and fear and flight to a country none of us knew, and a friend who had lied and taken money and disappeared. In that moment, for the first time in my life, I saw my father as a person. I saw a man down on his luck. And I wanted Hemingway to stop. He had bought me breakfast and was supposed to be my friend. But I wanted him to let my father alone.

I said, "We think the Zionists might've killed him. And they might be after us."

My father looked at me, and all the years of my little journey to twelve years old, when he was far from me and I was alone with one woman or another — all that time away shone in his eyes; I had the sense that he saw me suddenly as a stranger who was being kind. He leaned forward and took the last piece of my English muffin and put it to his lips. "Nothing to worry about, boy," he said, nodding at me. "Really. We'll be all right."

"But that's why you're in Cuba," Hemingway said to both of us.

My father explained about Coldrow and the charter fishing idea, the money, the burned-down cottage. It was as though he were a boy talking to a big grown-up.

"So what'll you do?" Hemingway asked him, grinning.

"Oh, we'll probably head back north."

He leaned forward. "This place is crawling with feds, you know."

The Captain shook his head.

"Crime bosses own Havana. Everything goes through them. And the feds can only watch."

And then they were talking about that. For a while they were just two older men trading news accounts and rumors about Meyer Lansky and Lucky Luciano and the others.

I sat there.

Hemingway began to tell about his war, drinking the daiquiri, and the wine. My father had some of the wine, staring wide-eyed at the famous man going on about "sures" and his new book, the mistakes and incompetence of the military men he had known. It was all dull to me now, and I wanted to go back upstairs. I had found out that we were going to head back north. The blank future was ahead of us.

That future contained, of course, Hemingway's own suicide, and the Captain's divorce from his wife (who returned to Virginia and raised a family), and his remarriage to a woman named Mavis — my now dear friend Mavis — who gave him years of unexpected happiness; there was my own time in the catastrophe of Vietnam, and years in a kind of careful friendship with the Captain, which included his eventual adoption of that form of address, himself. Actually, I called him Captain through those last years, with great affection. Now and then we would talk about that time in Cuba when we met Hemingway.

It was noon before my stepmother walked into the café, wearing a crisp red sleeveless dress with a steep V in front, and high-heeled shoes. Hemingway was getting ready to leave. He glanced at her as she came in, then sat up a little and took her in. Alejandro had brought him another coffee. My stepmother said, "Good morning," to the room and sat down, arranging her dress over her thighs.

"This is Abby," the Captain said. "My wife."

"Hello, Abby," Hemingway said, smiling widely. "You're quite a bit younger than the Captain, here, aren't you?"

"Fourteen years," she said.

It was clear, even to me, that he had only meant to compliment her youthful appearance. He hesitated only slightly, and went on: "Well, Abby. I always liked that name. And you remind me of someone." His eyes were cloudy. He drained the coffee, building up to say something.

But she interrupted him: "We don't want to keep you." Reaching into her purse, she brought out a fountain pen and a piece of notepad paper, leaned forward and offered it to Hemingway. "If you'd be so kind."

He smiled the wonderful smile, and gave a little sighing shrug, and I had a sudden sense of what the whole morning had cost him, the strain of being who he was in that place and at that time, the world as it was then, keeping up with his fabrications. And I'm convinced that I knew, somehow, sudden as a spark and a dozen years before it happened, how his life would end. Because I thought of Forrestal, and the newspaper man's political friends saying you could see his suicide from a mile away. At the time, it seemed only an importunate thought, random, having nothing to do with us. Hemingway took the pen, his hand trembling very slightly, and signed his name.

THE WIDOW'S TALE

For Stephen Goodwin

W HEN SUSAN BRIDGE heard friends or family talk about inklings from the other side or being watched over by a lost loved one, she inwardly dismissed the idea even as she strove to be loving and attentive in the circumstance. She felt sorrow, of course, but considered that in each case bereavement was dictating to the senses. Yet now here was her younger sister Moira claiming visits in her sleep from Susan's husband, killed nearly a year ago in a one-car crash on the Brooklyn-Queens Expressway.

"I'm telling you, Susan, he's himself, and it keeps happening. Last night was the fourth time. He says quite clearly that he wants to talk to you. There's a red dial phone and he hands me the receiver looking sad but there's interference in the line. And I think the interference is your refusal to take this seriously."

"But it's been ten months. What do I do to take it more seriously than I have? I know it's troubling you and I take *that* seriously. But I mean, really, what more can I do?"

Her sister shrugged and then showed her irritation. "I don't *know.* Hell. *Some*thing. You don't even allow the possibility that it might have significance beyond just being a recurring dream."

"Well, it *is* a recurring dream. And recurring dreams're pretty common."

"But these are dreams with my sister's dead husband in them. And they're like visitations."

"Oh, please, honey. You're obsessing about it. You didn't even like Victor. Victor annoyed you. And why would he visit you in your sleep and not me in mine?"

"Because you don't believe."

"Oh, come on," Susan said. "Leave it alone, can't you?"

In the days and weeks just after the accident, she'd found herself addressing him with an almost inaudible sigh. "Oh, Victor," as if uttering a prayer, though there was an unacknowledged trace of reproof in it, too, for him to have been killed in that fashion, going ninety on that highway. Anyhow, she'd forged past all that now. She'd loved him, and she would say she cherished his memory. But he was gone, and there were no dreams about him, nor any shift in her daily reality. The only sounds in the apartment were hers. She'd always been the one who kept up with birthdays and paid the bills and taxes and all the rest, and she had dealt with the galleries and his dealer (she'd even sold the incomplete panel triptych he'd been struggling to finish). She was going on with things, as you were supposed to do. You honored his life by living your own life to the hilt. She'd heard him say that very thing himself more than once. She'd even been on dates with a couple of other men (one seemed oddly, surprisingly, repellent in the first five minutes, and the other simply bored her). Life alone was her inclination now, at least for the present. She was at peace with it. But Moira, with her propensity for jumping to wild, ethereal conclusions, would not stop about the dream.

Perhaps it was being married to Owen Sisler that had helped stir this up. Only last week, during dinner at their house, he lightheartedly repeated to Susan the famous line from *Hamlet*: *There are more things in heaven and earth, Horatio, than you have dreamed of in your philosophy,* actually calling her Horatio. Susan thought at the time that he was humoring his eccentric young wife. But he had called her by that name twice since as an endearment. Plus there was the fact that Sisler, the novelist, eighty-four years old, had turned to a spiritualizing, speculative stance in his latest work. His new novel, *The Deaths of Friar Dominic,* was about the spirit of a sixteenth-century English abbot haunting the monastery where he was murdered in order to educate and then exact a kind of hereditary revenge on the descendant of the monk who committed the crime. The book had all sorts of incidences of the ghost moving through interstices of air and light, and included theories about the meaning of unseen presences in lone places, the many gothic solitary horrors of extreme religion. Moira had already read it twice; it was a favorite of hers among his books, all of which she had admired since college, and which were nothing remotely like this latest. The others had been lavish, prosy realistic portrayals of, well, Sisler, and his six marriages.

Moira, at thirty-seven, was his seventh wife.

The marriage had in fact been fine with Susan and Victor because Sisler was well-off, and he *tended* to Moira, notwithstanding his late forays into the supernatural. (He called it the ultima-real, or the outré-natural, meaning aspects of natural *and* supernatural existence that we can't consciously perceive.) And finally, he was interesting.

"What does Owen say about this dream?" Susan asked one afternoon over the phone.

"You *know* what he thinks about it. He calls you Horatio."

"But that's just to entertain you."

"Well, I can't help what I feel. I feel strongly that Victor wants to tell you something."

"Yes, but how exactly would that work? Really."

Moira began to cry.

"Oh, God. Come on, sweetie," Susan said. "Stop that. Really, I accept it. Okay?"

"Was there anything unspoken between you two — you know, over the years?"

"What kind of question is that, Moira? No. There wasn't anything."

"I'm thinking of going to see a psychiatrist."

"Let's just — not talk about it or think about it for a time."

"But you accept it, as being — what it is."

"Yes. I do."

Moira sighed, and Susan changed the subject, talking about Owen's novel of modern revenge for an ancient crime.

The following night, they were to attend a reading and celebration of Owen and the book. Susan was secretly uninterested. She had only read the reviews, and listened to her sister's talk. In fact Owen's prose always seemed a bit too discursive for her: page upon page of subtle intellectual distinctions about modern life and culture, and the arguments between men and women; lovers, losers and cheaters; unhappy academics and artists, all of them failing at love.

He himself had failed six times before Moira.

But Moira, as Victor had remarked once to Susan, possessed stamina, having already spent a year married to Sisler's friend Eliot Glass, a poet, and the single dullest human being he had ever met. Susan agreed. Glass's poetry was well thought of in some circles, and his normal speech had about it a distinct air of proclamation. Victor had characterized him as someone who could snatch pomposity from the jaws of any English sentence, and, when Susan laughed, added that being in Eliot's company was like sitting all day through a C-SPAN broadcast. The very fact that Owen charmed Moira away from him was to Owen's lasting credit: he'd spared Moira a lifetime of mediocre poetry and numbing talk.

Before the reading, they gathered at Saveurs for dinner: Owen, Moira, Susan, and Eliot, who — in his own faintly baroque expression — "endured in steadfast friendship" with Moira. He was accompanied by another young woman, quite beautiful, with dark blue eyes and shining dark hair. He introduced her as Lana Sharp, and she offered her hand to each of the others in turn.

"Oh, how are you," she said, as the names were said to her. "Oh, how are you." Her smile was white as a lily. And very soon after this introduction, she volunteered to everyone the fact that she had met Eliot at a lecture he gave in Soho, and that he had already written over thirty poems to her.

Susan thought of Scott Fitzgerald's line in *Gatsby* about a woman who was "shrill, languid, handsome, and horrible."

They were joined by a man Owen introduced as Bill Perry, an old colleague from his days at the university. Perry was tall, scarily thin, with a face that showed forth the contours of his skull — deep-set eyes; bony, sunken cheeks; and a smile like a rictus. Susan could only glance at him. His eyes were piercing. Lana talked vaguely about moving out west and asked Bill Perry if he had ever been to San Francisco.

"Actually only for two short visits," he said. "Regrettably."

"I'm headed that way, soon. And maybe Eliot will come along."

"Lana's a medium," Eliot Glass said. "She told me about a dead boyhood friend I haven't thought of in thirty years."

"Eliot, stop."

Perry offered, "A medium, huh?"

"Yes."

"This boyhood friend drowned a month ago in Miami Beach," Eliot said. "And Lana — my divine new lady — divined it some way. I only knew the boy in elementary school in Milwaukee."

"Oh, I want to hear about this," said Moira. "Really, tell us, Eliot."

"Well, in midconversation and completely apropos of nothing she brings up Miami Beach. Says someone from my past was coming through."

"How do you — how does it work?" Moira asked his companion. "How do you bring it about?"

Lana shrugged. "I'm not sure. Sometimes it just happens."

They were all in a half circle, in a thickly padded leather booth.

"Anything coming through now?" Moira asked.

Lana blinked and smiled. "No."

"Well," Owen said. "Speaking of spirits, there's Perry's latest book. *The Far Shore.*"

"A shadow," Perry said. "Pay no attention."

"It's a good book of poems. A rarity these days. Hell, any good book. Gore Vidal once said novelists and poets in America are at the same level as ceramists. And that was thirty years ago."

"Well, not quite so much a shadow," Perry said, low, with that skeletal smile.

They were all quiet a moment.

"Thanks, Owen," Moira said. "Now we're all depressed. Was it your intent to put a damper on the evening before we even get started?"

Another moment passed. They were all looking at menus. Susan glanced briefly over at Moira, admiring how casually and confidently she'd chided her famed husband.

"I only meant to applaud Perry's book," Owen said.

"You meant to hold forth about it," Moira told him, patting his wrist. "Come on, Mr. Sisler, sir. We know you."

"Who was Gore Vidal?" asked Lana Sharp.

"A ceramist, from the last century. So, tell us. Eliot's dead friend's spirit spoke to you?"

Lana nodded doubtfully. "In a sense, yes. It's not really speaking, though."

"I have an idea," Owen said suddenly. "Let's each order a different whiskey, and pass them around for tasting like people pass food around in a Chinese restaurant."

Susan, feeling bad for having been so shaken by Bill Perry's features, said, "Actually, I'd rather talk about the shadow that isn't quite so much a shadow."

Perry turned to her and said, low, with an air of gravity, "Thank you. I am one of those whose name is writ in water." Then he laughed. There was a note of self-derision in it.

Lana leaned toward Moira and with a bright smile said, "And do you write, too?"

"I teach dance," said Moira. "I used to be in ballet, but the grind exhausted me."

"And do you travel with your grandfather often?"

Moira, having hesitated only a second, drew herself up, glaring, and pronounced, "For your information, I am *Mrs.* Sisler."

"Oh, I'm so *sorry*." Lana gave Eliot a displeased look. "No one told me. I never dreamed . . ."

"And you're a — what is it again? A medium?"

She nodded, glaring again at Eliot.

He spoke for her. "I'm sorry about the faux pas, but you know, Lana actually lived and worked in a place where everybody's a medium or knows one. Almost four years. People come from all over to see these — "

"Wait," Moira broke forth. "I just read somewhere about this place. Lily Dale, right?"

"That's right," Lana said. "There are several — "

Owen Sisler spoke over her. "I like my whiskey idea."

" — cottages, with signs outside. I mean, anyone can walk in — "

And he broke in again, with a bad imitation of an English accent. "I say, chaps. Let's order."

"You don't want to talk about anything but you and your book," Moira said to him.

"And how does whiskey figure into that assertion, darling?" His voice was affectionate but the words had come from a thin, brittle smile. He signaled the waiter, who had a mustache so thick you couldn't see his mouth. The waiter took out a pad as he approached.

"I am just so awfully sorry," Lana said, low, to Moira. "About that grandfather thing."

"Forget it," Owen broke in again. "Really. That's exactly what it looks like."

Shortly after they'd ordered their entrees, the tray of whiskeys in gilt-edged shot glasses arrived: scotch for Owen, bourbon for Moira, sour mash for Eliot, Irish for Lana, Canadian for Perry, rye for Susan. They all held their drinks out, as if to show what was in them to everyone else, and Owen said, "Now, instead of a toast, let's say something we know or learned that's attached to a memory. Like where we were, or who we were with, or what was going on in the given day that we learned it."

They waited.

"In my case it's something I learned while honeymooning with my second wife, Beverly, in Africa. I witnessed it. A safari guide who swore he was with Hemingway on his last Africa journey showed me this species of moth that congregates on a twig in such a complex way that it looks exactly like an exotic flower. You shake the twig and they fly up and out in all directions, and then very slowly reassemble exactly as they were, becoming the flower again, right before your eyes. And that's the most vivid memory of that honeymoon." He smiled.

"Imagine," Moira said. "The invisible forces that make a thing like that happen. And then think of the forces that make a man talk about a memory involving his second wife and a species of moth."

Owen Sisler patted her shoulder, smiling. "All part of the great mystery, dear."

"I want to talk about the visitations I've been getting in my sleep. And we have a medium here who can maybe help us talk about this."

"Oh, I wouldn't presume," Lana said.

"You already did presume."

She bowed her head. "I did apologize."

"No, I'd *like* you to presume — *we'd* like you to presume."

"Moira," Susan said. "Please."

"No, really," said Moira, looking at the others, each in turn. "I've learned recently that a dream can recur in exactly the same shape, and so, in the years from now when I have the memory of this time, it'll be attached to this exactly replicated dream, four nights in nine — no, ten. Ten days. I see Susan's Victor with a red dial telephone that only gives interference."

Owen explained quietly to Perry and Lana about the loss of Victor.

"And I've been seeing him in this dream," Moira said. "He talks to me."

Lana said in a small voice, "Do you remember what he tells you?"

"He's got something he wants to tell Susan."

"Can we please talk about something else?" Susan said. "Please?"

"She doesn't believe in ghosts," said her sister. "Or in life after death."

"I don't believe in ghosts either," Owen Sisler said. "I *speculate*."

"You believe in them. Come on. Presences. The ultima — the outré-natural."

"Yes, well, my real interest is in the epistemology of it all. Our experience. What we make of it." He looked from her to the others at the table. "What my lovely wife makes of her dream." He held his glass up again. "Remember — small sips because we're going to be passing them around."

Susan wanted to find a way to get out of all this and go home. "I guess my palate isn't educated enough to appreciate the subtleties," she got out.

They had sole meunière or canard rôti avec gold leaf. Owen ordered two bottles of Bordeaux and a sauvignon blanc. After the sips of whiskey, Moira drank two glasses of the white and took the rest of Owen's first glass, then started joking about his earlier marriages, calling his ex-wives his "other girls." The marriage before this one had lasted only four months. And another had dissolved after a year. "We're at more than three years," she said. "I guess I'm standing the test of Sisler time."

Owen changed the subject. "What does Victor look like in this dream you've been having?"

"He looks like Victor."

"No chains or winding sheets or sifting smoke?" Susan added.

Lana laughed into one slender palm.

"You're making fun of me," Moira said. "I told you. It's Victor, and he wants to talk to you. He wants to tell you something."

They were all quiet.

Lana started to speak: "This red telephone — "

But then Eliot laughed. "Jesus Christ. A red telephone. Isn't that the hotline to Moscow?"

Moira threw her serviette down and turned to Susan. "Now you see what your skepticism does."

"That's enough," Owen said. "Really, dear."

She picked up the serviette and seemed to fluff it, then folded it and put it in her lap.

"I'm sorry," Susan said to her.

Perry said, "I think there was a red dial phone at the front desk of the Hilton."

"Listen," Owen said, ignoring them both. "Why don't we have a séance." He looked at Lana Sharp.

"Well, as far as that goes," she said, "I don't leave until early next month."

He said, "I've got a flight out at noon tomorrow. But I'll be back Sunday."

"We could arrange something for when you get back?"

"What would you need?"

"Eighty dollars an hour."

"Equipment. Setup. Chairs. Ambience."

"Oh. A table. Some quiet. Who'd be there? I'd need three or four sitters, we call them."

"Susan won't do it," Moira said.

Susan, feeling trapped, decided that to resist would seem stubborn, even narrow-minded. "I will," she said. "If it'll help."

"Sunday night, then," Owen said. "At our apartment in the Village. Moira, you take care of the arrangements."

The bookstore was near Washington Square, a block from the Sislers' apartment building. They took two cabs from the restaurant. Susan rode with Bill Perry and Lana Sharp, neither of whom had read the book. Lana Sharp asked Perry about his poems, and his dreams. Susan stared out at the sparkle of the city, the going-by of the streets with their sidewalk stores and their grime. There was already a crowd gathering at the store. Seats in the front row had been reserved for Owen and his companions. Patrons stood along the bookcases and between the bookcases. Susan sat with her sister between Lana and Perry. In those close quarters the air seemed insufficient, full of the sounds of coughing and the clearing of throats and sniffling.

The reading was long, and something in Owen's slow baritone delivery seemed narcotizing, especially after half a bottle of Bordeaux and several sips of whiskey. When it ended, there were questions. As she was pinching her own neck while seeming to support her chin on her fist, she saw Victor back in among the people behind the table where Owen sat talking. It was Victor. He was staring directly at her with a passive, detached, stone-cold objectivity. She shifted in her chair and looked away, feeling the moment as a rushing under her breastbone, and then, slowly, brought her gaze back to the place where he had been. It was a blank space, giving off to a lamp on a small table, and a far window. She breathed, glanced over at Moira and saw that Moira was staring at her own hands in her lap.

Owen went on about invisible nature and "the unseen world that is far more peopled than we imagine." "Even we," he went on after a dramatic pause. "Here, now, all presently trying to imagine it." Susan looked back at the space. It was a vacant space. Owen answered another question. Nothing seemed real. Her lower back ached. She couldn't swallow. She folded her hands in her lap, and looked back at the empty space where she had seen someone who looked like Victor. Reminded her of Victor. She had read about the phenomenon. She told herself everything was as before — it was the wine, the heat, her weariness, fighting sleep, Moira's talk, the woman who was a medium, sitting to her left and exhaling audibly with a high, thin whistle in one nostril.

When at last the reading and talk ended, everyone lined up to buy the book and have it signed. Susan made the excuse of a headache, and stepped out into the night air. Perry followed her. It had grown cooler; a breeze was stirring. "Would you like to walk a little?" Perry said.

"I'm a bit tired," she told him. "No."

"I sometimes feel that I myself am a ghost."

She made no answer to this. She felt weak, shaken. She wished he would go back inside.

"Forgive me." He coughed, once, then sighed. "How long have you known Owen?"

"Since my sister married his friend Eliot."

"I'm sorry about your husband."

Again, she was silent. They stood there, and soon people began slowly to file out. "Do you ever feel invisible?" he said. Then: "Hello, 'I'm nobody! Who are you? Are you nobody, too?'"

She looked at him.

"That's from the great Ms. Dickinson," he said.

She said, "I'm very tired."

"Tired, yes. That's been the condition of my last fifteen years." He gave a little ironic grin. "Sorry."

"No," she said, determining to put away the bad moment of hallucination in the store. "*I'm* sorry. I think I had too much to drink."

He nodded without quite looking at her. She had never seen anyone so epically ugly, and the thought made her feel bad again: he was just a kindly, sickly-looking, elderly man. And a poet. That was interesting about him, even vaguely appealing.

"What are you working on?" she said, forcing it.

He gave a small scoffing smile. "Not much lately."

"So, in your mind, then, what is the far shore?"

He paused, then put his head down. "We don't have to talk about it."

"I'd like to. I said so at dinner."

"Well, thank you for that. In the title poem, the far shore isn't so much a destination but something beyond. Something — anything presently *missed.*"

He wiped the back of his hand across his mouth. The storefront light was greenish and made him look almost dizzily unhealthy. "But the farthest shore," he went on, "is *Meaning,* itself. We *embody* meaning, and so the only meaning is what we ourselves make. Merleau-Ponty, the French philosopher. The concept, as I recall, is summed up as 'Man, the meaning-giver.' But I fear it's only Man, the absurd whirligig of blind fears."

She stared.

"Of course, these days, you can't really talk about such matters, and maybe you never could. Maybe only in a college dorm room. Forgive the philosophizing." He gave forth a small, breathing laugh. "But you asked."

"Yes, I did," she said.

He kept the faint smile. "One spends so much time trying to make sense of things."

She shrugged. "Well, you'd know. I'm a former college dean. I teach history."

A moment later, he said, "Your sister's recurring dream — " But then he stopped.

"Go on," she said. Abruptly she wanted to talk about it. About dreams in general. "On the way over here you said something to our friend the medium about fearing your dreams or not liking your dreams."

Two young people walked out of the store squabbling about what they would serve for guests at a dinner party they were evidently planning. It occurred to Susan that they were a married couple to whom nothing serious had happened yet. She watched them go on, and felt suddenly guilty again, petty and bitter, and she turned to him, forcing another smile.

"Well," he said. "I started to tell you that I don't think I've ever had a recurring dream."

"Never?"

"Not that I remember. I have types of dreams, scenario dreams. Daily — daily-goings-on dreams, where I'm doing something quite terrifyingly ordinary. Or commando dreams, where I'm blasting an AK-47 at troops of killers. Or illness dreams, where — " He stopped. "Like that."

Moira walked out of the store and came right to them. "It's gonna be tonight," she said. "Owen wants to do it before he leaves. We're going straight home with Lana and Eliot. Owen started talking about it and decided he wanted to look into this dream about Victor."

Susan said, "I should just go on home, then."

"No, you *have* to come."

"But you yourself said — "

"Lana told me as long as you keep quiet, and try to have an open mind about it."

"Am I to come, too?" Perry asked.

"Of course."

He looked at Susan. "I'm with you, then, about trying to keep an open mind."

The others came out. Eliot had his arm around Lana. Owen made a little bowing motion. " 'Oh, do not ask, "What is it?" ' " he recited. " 'Let us go and make our visit.' "

Susan had never quite felt at ease in Owen and Moira's apartment. There were books on every surface and all around on the walls, and in three carousel bookcases opposite the long couch with its two end tables, also crammed with books. Of course she loved books, and had a lot of them herself, but the closeness of these rooms made her think of dust, and, often enough, rather oddly, of Egyptian tombs: all the earthly belongings of a pharaoh piled for his journey to the other world. The dining room was high ceilinged and spacious, though what would've been crown molding on three sides was a shelf lined with more books.

Moira and Owen brought chairs from other rooms and set them around the circular dining room table, which was made of heavy, dark cherrywood and shone like a piano. Moira opened a linen tablecloth and spread it. Lana Sharp helped. "We'll need three candles, and a food offering," she said. "And I'll need a pencil and piece of paper."

Owen supplied pencil and paper, and the candles — there had been two tall ones on the side table, and Moira found a short one in the kitchen junk drawer. She brought from the refrigerator a large plate of crackers and cheese with plastic wrap over it, which she had put together in case Owen decided to have people over after the reading. She removed the plastic wrap and fretfully crushed it into the pocket of her blouse. Susan saw his adoring smile at this. Moira smiled back. It was a confidence, exchanged in the middle of a room with others around them, a glance that showed their tolerating affection for each other. It occurred to Susan that she'd been worried about them as a couple. Moira now went to the side table, wrote a check, turned and handed it to Lana, who nodded and put it in her purse on the floor.

Owen dimmed the lights in the chandelier. Lana held her hands out, palm-up. Susan sat across from her, next to Perry. On Susan's other side, Owen took his place. To his left, Moira sat, her hand in Lana's. Eliot was on the other side of Lana, to Perry's right. They were all quiet now in the dimness, watching Lana, while sirens sounded in the city streets outside, two floors down.

"Will the noise interfere with things?" Moira asked.

"Not if we all concentrate," Lana told her. "Now, let's join hands."

Susan was thinking about what Victor would make of all this. What he might say. And abruptly she felt the strange sense of surprise about his absence, the feeling that used to bring forth the prayerlike sigh, "Oh, Victor." In her mind she saw again what she had seen in the store.

Lana Sharp closed her eyes and said, low, "We welcome any spirits who care to join us here. We ask you to make yourselves known to us."

They all sat still, holding hands.

"Any visitors from the other side, you are welcome. We mean no harm."

They waited.

Susan saw the crackers and cheese, the candle flames in their perfect little helixes, and the other faces in the shadowy half dark. It was another bad moment, Perry's hand clasped with hers, dry, almost like a leather glove over bones, while Owen's was clammy. The room was quiet now.

Lana said, "Keep hold, all. I'm getting something." She let go of Moira and Eliot, took the pencil, held it for a few seconds over the paper, and then suddenly commenced indiscriminately scribbling, fast, almost as if trying to color the page — quick back-and-forth strokes, which graduated into circular motions. Still quite fast. "Who do you wish to talk to?" Lana said. A few seconds later, she nodded irritably. "This spirit likes grammar. And has a sense of humor. All right, to *whom* do you wish to speak." She kept making the scribbles. "You," she said. "Need." She kept the scribbling. "Yes, I hear you. A friend to answer. Your call."

Something dropped in Susan's chest, and as she tried to pull her hands from Owen's and Perry's grip, she saw the shadows on the wall of the room, her own part of the shadow and Perry's, a single shape, a distortion, heads and shoulders, monstrously elongated, only vaguely human. She blinked. It was just the shadows in the dim candlelight.

"Yes. Tell us," Lana went on, breathing deep and fast. "With whom do you wish to speak?" She went on with the pencil. The page was almost black.

Moira broke forth, "Are you Victor?"

"Shh!" Lana said harshly. Then: "I'm listening." She looked at Moira and nodded, and went on. "We're here.

"You want, yes. You want someone here to know. You're okay." Lana paused and frowned. "Horatio?" She took a breath. "Tell. Horatio. You're okay."

Susan pulled violently away from Owen and Perry, standing so quickly that her chair overturned. "This is ridiculous." She looked at Moira. "You planned this. You and Owen."

Moira, ashen faced, sat shaking her head, staring. "I swear," she said.

"There was definitely a connection," said Lana. "I felt it strongly."

Owen said, "Did you feel a cold touch of air? Was it suddenly cooler in here?"

Susan took herself out into the hall and down the two flights of stairs, Moira following her, calling her back, saying her name. Perry had also followed. "I swear," Moira kept saying. "Please. You have to see the reality of it. You shouldn't've broken the spell."

Susan turned around on her. "I don't want to see you for a while, okay?" She felt the tears coming and ran the back of one hand across her eyes, sniffling. "Just please, let me be. Can you do that? Can you please please just let me be?"

"But it wasn't *me*. Why won't you believe me?"

Perry said, "The things the lady said were fairly general, though, weren't they?"

"That Horatio thing!" Moira shouted.

"That was you and Owen," Susan said. "Wrong number, okay? Wrong number, Moira."

"I don't know what you're talking about. You heard what he wanted you to know. He said he was okay and he called you Horatio."

"But he's *not* okay, Moira. You know? He's *dead*!" She pushed out into the night, walked to the end of the block in the glare of the passing cars, then stopped and raised one hand for a taxi.

Perry approached her. "I'm so sorry about all that."

"Yeah." She paced away from him.

"I enjoyed talking with you."

She could think of nothing to say.

"I'd like to see you again, perhaps?"

"No," she said. "God."

"I understand completely." He started away. She saw the crook of his back and his slow, halting gate, going away.

"I'm sorry," she said. "Really. I'll be happy to see you again. But give me some time."

He had stopped and turned. He lifted one hand, looking ghostly in the shadow of the building with the streetlamp behind him. "I will, thanks."

The cab ride home was fast, with the smell of the driver's open fast-food sandwich on the front seat. He was of Mideast origin; his name was Kamir. He said nothing through the whole ride, and drove rather recklessly above the speed limit, weaving in and out. The fare to her building was six dollars and forty cents. She gave him a ten, and said, "Keep the change."

He took the ten and drove off.

The now chilly street seemed deserted. She went inside and up the one flight of stairs to the apartment. As she was turning the key, she stopped and suddenly gasped, once. She hadn't expected it; the sound erupted from her throat like choking. She got the door open, went inside and turned to close it. The hallway seemed too dark. Briefly she looked for the line of light at the base of her neighbor's apartment. The neighbor was an old woman named Greta, who used to work at *TV Guide,* but who seldom left the place now, and was often up very late at night. She thought of knocking on Greta's door. It was only ten o'clock. But Greta wouldn't know what to make of that, since they'd never exchanged more than a few words, coming and going.

"Christ," Susan murmured, closing and locking the door.

She was too agitated to sleep. She got into her pajamas, poured a glass of wine and switched on the TV. But it was all pointless chatter, or quarrels, or murder. She thought of Perry, that face, and of Lana Sharp. And she saw Eliot with his earnestness and Owen Sisler, toying with everyone, and Moira, with whom she had never been angrier. Yet she worried about Moira again now, and resolved to call her in the morning. A moment later, something else began to rise awfully in her soul: Whatever the evening had meant, *this* was what the evening had given her. This. The sudden, helpless apprehension that nothing was done, nothing accomplished, no "going on," really, but only, all along, a mere semblance, an absurd show, a role she had played for herself and for everyone else — and the full, actual force of her sorrow was only beginning. It was welling up in her now; it was coming. She went into her bedroom, using the wall as support, and got to her bed.

"Oh," she said to the empty room. Then again, "Oh." She lay down on top of the blankets, folded her hands across her chest, steeling herself, trying to gather all her remaining strength. She took one long, sobbing breath, and waited.

THE FATE OF OTHERS

For Adam and Emily Chiles

T HEY SPENT EARLY AFTERNOON talking about literature and history and the currents of American life, all with that guarded conviviality of new in-laws — Billy Jordan, and his wife Michelle's father, the distinguished poet Thomas Fearing. Because Michelle had to complete her midterm exam in musical composition by that evening, she couldn't do much more that first day than take a coffee and sandwich break with them. This was the third stop on the thirty-two-city tour for Fearing's new volume, *A Faltering, a Rising: New and Selected Poems 2008–2018*. The plan was to spend three days with Michelle and Jordan, and then head back to Phoenix, to catch a plane west to Los Angeles, and then San Francisco, Portland and Seattle. He had driven down from Phoenix in a rented Honda, and brought with him a bottle of Glenlivet and six bottles of wine as a gift.

After sitting with the men for an hour, sipping a glass of white wine while they drank St. Esteph, Michelle went on with her studying. She had seemed relaxed, anyway, talking about life with her father, and managing to avoid — without seeming to — the subject of her mother's mental troubles. But she was quite casual and firm about staying behind in the little house on Coral Street, while the two men drove over to the college in the Honda.

At the college, there would be a reception, followed by dinner, the reading, the after-reading party and finally, of course, the inevitable bar-hopping.

"I'm not going because I don't go to his readings," she said to Billy Jordan as her father showered, getting ready. "Did we just meet? I've told you this. All the way back to before Mom started losing it. I hate the literary-lion persona. Even when I thought they were happy and she was okay, I thought it was bullshit. And as you know I don't read him much, either. Feels like prying. But think about it, baby. You'll be the guy that brought the famous poet to the campus."

"That was Eckhart and the other writing faculty," he said.

"Eckhart wouldn't've been able to interest him if it wasn't for his wanting to see us, and you know that."

"His wanting to see *you,* baby. He doesn't know me from Adam's housecat. I only saw him Christmas and he was sick with that bronchitis that scared everybody."

She shrugged. "You seemed to hit it off just fine, today."

"It was work. And now it's my turn to ask you: 'Did we just meet?' You do know, right, that I'm not comfortable with strangers one-on-one."

"You're not strangers."

"Two brief conversations, Christmas. Come on."

"Well, you were fine today."

"A gift to you." His smile was mirthless.

"A gift to me. You're talking about this morning and not that I had to study."

"I'm saying it was a gift."

"Poor baby. And now we've made peace and you'll go to the dinner and the reading, and then out drinking, as the guy closest to the famous poet. The envy of everyone."

He simply stared.

"Come *on.*"

After a slight pause, he said, "What do you actually think of me, Michelle?"

She frowned. "Hey. We made up enough to tease each other, right? Please. Right?"

He looked down.

"Okay, okay, teasing, come on."

Silence.

"Don't get in another mood. I *was* teasing you."

"Didn't sound like teasing. It sounded like sarcasm."

"Teasing. Sarcasm. What difference does it — hey, again: *'Did we just meet?'*" She smiled at the joke.

He decided to change the subject. "How come you say prying? He's never been considered a confessional poet."

"Yeah, but you know, as he likes to say . . ." She straightened and seemed to gather herself, and when she spoke her tone had shifted to a kind of sardonic high seriousness. "It's all from the *deeps* of him." Then she sighed, still grinning. She was really quite beautiful. "And I still feel like it's none of my business."

"Are you gonna be that way about me and *my* work?"

"Maybe. When was the last time you listened to my music?"

"I hear every note you put in and take out." He couldn't keep the irritation out of his voice. He smiled back at her, trying to soften it. An unspoken area of tension for him lately had been the persistent cacophony of her electric keyboard while she decided for or against notes or passages that he, being tone deaf, couldn't distinguish one from another. It grated on his nerves; it sounded like noise to him. Indeed, it sounded like noise to her, as well, these days — she who had been blessed with perfect pitch.

She gave him a little scoffing wave of her hand, then touched his cheek. "You know I'll read your work — you do the work, and I'll read it."

"I'm between," he managed. He had two unfinished stories, thirty-six pages of typed prose, and he had wasted a lot of the past few weeks hanging out with friends, drinking wine and smoking dope. "You'll see."

"Yes, I guess I will."

They had been married only fourteen months, and life was hard: since the middle of February, her mother had taken to calling several times a week to complain that Thomas Fearing was trying to poison her by putting dust from the moon landing in her tea, and certainly everyone knew that moon dust was lethal; the woman's name was Madeline, and she went by Maddie, and Michelle had taken to calling her Mad. "Mad for short," she would say to Jordan, with a regretful smirk. Her mother maintained that she did not know how Fearing had got ahold of the moon dust, but she could not be disabused of the conviction that he had. And she wanted Michelle to know about it, so she could tell the authorities if anything happened. Michelle dealt with these fretful calls as if she were talking to a frightened child, but finally she would end up taking part in the hallucinatory panic.

"Maddie, just don't drink any tea. Thank him for the tea but don't drink it."

There would be the rushed undistinguishable syllables on the other end.

"Then don't drink the wine, either. Make your own tea and open your own wine."

The fact was that Jordan had fears for his own sanity, which were amplified whenever he heard Michelle's end of these bizarre conversations. He would say to himself, *You're not insane, if you're worried about going insane.* He worried about it all the time. In truth, lately, to be half-drunk or stoned was the only relaxed time he knew.

"Mother. You know he loves you. We both love you. He wouldn't do anything like that. He has to be away to give his readings. That's his work. He only met Neil Armstrong at an NEA festival, in DC, Mother. When he got that medal for his poem about the landing and met the president. He only shook hands with Armstrong."

Of course, afterward, it took days for Michelle to put it all in its place — that province of the long heartbreak that she and her father had been living in for almost ten years. It seemed that her mother had always caused pain. Except that this latest psychosis had gone some to intensify their problems as a newly married couple, still learning about each other. The conflicts about money and time — Michelle's work, his work — had worsened. She wanted to write in long forms, film music, opera, or symphonies. And as her worry over the late-night calls, the horrors as she called them, had practically silenced her, some unexplored region of his soul rejoiced, almost as if it were autonomic, like his heartbeat — because he was not producing anything, either. He had not accepted the intimation that this evil secret might be true, because he loved her and wanted her to succeed. Of course that was the truth. Yet everything felt darkened with anxiety and the feeling of fraudulence that hounded him continually.

This was how things were at the time of the visit by the famous poet.

"We're going over there now, with no female supervision," Thomas Fearing said, fresh from having showered and changed into a tweed sport coat and bow tie. He seemed to loom over them. He had at least four inches on Jordan, who was more than six feet tall himself. The two men stood side by side while Michelle snapped a picture, with the poet holding his book, face out, at his waist. The book's cover was a black and white photograph of Thomas Fearing with an expression of serious contemplation on his face.

"Two words," Michelle said to them, as they started out. And she made the two syllables of the word *behave* sound like separate words. Be *Hayve*.

"Oh, Missy," Fearing said to her. "You'll be with us in spirit. How could we do otherwise?"

She kissed his cheek, and then turned to her husband and gave him a peck on the lips.

"That was a bit chilly," Jordan said.

She put her arms around his neck and really kissed him. There was something showy about it. Her father stood there and watched. "Bye," she said, with a suggestive lilt.

"Talk about behaving," Thomas Fearing said. "Do your homework, little one. Write me a pretty melody."

Two of Billy Jordan's friends in the program, Mark Gaucher (fiction) and Tim Hall (poetry), were along for the whole afternoon and evening; they were especially happy about the bar-hopping, getting to be on such familiar terms with the famous poet — who was, by habit, by temperament and by self-description, on the far side of too much of everything. Early on, he called himself an excessive, and he used the word to describe all four of them: "Excessives, like us," he kept saying, "always require more."

His inclusion of them in the carousing was in its own way intoxicating, though the three younger men were mostly just witnesses. Thomas Fearing did most of the talking.

And the misbehaving.

Which began rather suddenly at the second establishment they visited, just after the bartender announced last call. Fearing produced a fifty-dollar bill from his wallet, slapped it down on the bar, and shouted that if he could not recite all of Dylan Thomas's "Lament" as Dylan Thomas himself would do it, he would donate the fifty dollars to the bartender's favorite charity. The bartender was a woman of some size, taller and wider than any man in the place except Fearing, and before she could say anything or decide about it one way or the other, he launched into the thing at the top of his voice. It was Dylan Thomas, all right. There were still quite a few people present, and they all sat and observed the performance. Perhaps not surprisingly, given the accuracy of the impersonation, they applauded even as he trailed off on the last lines. He bowed deeply at the waist, reached over and put the fifty-dollar bill in the bartender's blouse pocket, his hand trailing down her ample chest. "Sorry," he said. "Didn't mean to cop a feel, there." He stepped around the bar and took her wrist, dancing a little jig, holding her hand high, dipping slightly and smiling at her. Jordan saw the color leaving the flesh around her mouth; he leaned toward her and said, "Our visiting poet. At the university."

"Hello, visiting poet," she said to Fearing, with a brittle smile. "Let go of me or I'll kick you in the balls."

Fearing stepped nimbly back, performed a gallant, sweeping, bend-at-the-waist bow, then straightened, took out his wallet and offered her a credit card. "Madam," he said. "For our liquid rentals."

She took it, gingerly, unwilling to come into any kind of further contact with him, and he flounced away, toward the center of the place, turning in a tight waltzing circle and singsonging "A Refusal to Mourn the Death, by Fire, of a Child in London." It was as if he were making fun of the poetry itself.

As she was ringing up the tab, she said to Jordan, "What's his damage, anyway? What was all that shit about windy boys and sheep? And what the hell's he doing now? Synagogue of corn? I'm Jewish. What the hell?"

"They're poems by a famous Welsh poet. Dylan Thomas."

"Bob Dylan's Jewish."

"Dylan *Thomas*. Welsh poet. We're writers, from the university."

"Okay. Then, you want me to give the fifty back? I really don't feel right taking it from a drunk. Especially an old guy wearing a bow tie."

"He's just happy," Jordan said. "He's my father-in-law. Keep the fifty."

The poet took the check and signed it, bowed deeply again, and led the three friends out and down the street. As they were making their way across campus to another establishment that would be open into the early morning hours, he climbed up on the bordering wall of the library fountain, stood unsteadily, pulled down his zipper, and urinated with epic copiousness, like a horse, into the water.

"Jesus Christ," Mark Gaucher said.

Two hours later, coming back for his rental car to drive to the little house, they passed the same fountain, and he did it again. There was something almost forlorn about the second time, as if he were discouraged by his own compulsion to go ahead with it.

Now they were relaxing in the living room of the house. Michelle had gone to sleep hours before they came in, and had closed the door of the cramped bedroom beyond the kitchen, which meant that they were not to wake her. She taught early morning undergraduate classes as part of her fellowship. And she had her exam. The men were being quiet, sampling the poet's gift of Glenlivet and sipping coffee.

"Smooth," Fearing said about the whiskey. "Huh?"

"Very fine," Mark Gaucher said. "Super fine. Throw the cap away."

They all drank. At least two hours earlier Jordan had experienced that woolliness behind his eyes that always signaled that it was time to stop. He had not stopped. No one had stopped. And Fearing had driven the rental car in that condition. Even Michelle, before she closed the bedroom door, had apparently drunk the rest of the bottle of pinot gris that she had opened that afternoon.

"Here's to all us excessives," Fearing said.

Jordan was beginning to dislike the word. The thought had

slipped into his consciousness, doubtless through the lubrication provided by the alcohol he'd already consumed, that Michelle's highly honored and distinguished father was not a very nice man.

And this had not much to do with pissing in the library fountain.

In the visiting poet's often one-sided conversations, he had eloquently described, with vicious wit and cruel severity, serious fault lines in the work and character of his supposed friends. His colleagues. Anybody and everybody. He had been holding forth. About the novelist who had been his colleague for two decades, he said, "Ah, Michael, he's always there when he needs you. And the poor man is congenitally unable to say one interesting thing."

About the current poet in residence, who had brought him to this college, he said, "I can't remember what Eckhart's saying *even while he's saying it.*" This after he had hugged the man and waved him off into the night.

To start his reading, he had described himself as a quintessentially American poet because he was basically running faster, reaching out his arms farther, borne back ceaselessly into the past, and his reputation was far smaller than his own conception of it.

This was said for the laughs, of course, yet Jordan sensed that it was also calculated to make the audience aware of the magnitude of that reputation, because the reputation was no joke, and Fearing was keenly acquisitive about it: there were several important prizes, the presidential medal, and healthy sales of books, and the new collection had received serious and admiring treatment.

"Great night, boys," the poet said now. "A toast. To four great writers."

A few moments later, he put his head back and was silent, and finally they saw that he had drifted off to sleep. The three young men quietly went outside to have a cigarette. They all stood smoking for a time, standing in the thrown light from the living room window. They thought the night was over. They would smoke their cigarettes and drink some more black coffee and then Jordan would take them home. Jordan's father-in-law could simply stay where he was, sprawled at the end of the couch.

They began talking in low tones about him, because Michelle was sleeping just on the other side of the window and the wall.

"I saw him read at Illinois when I was there as an undergraduate," Gaucher said. "I thought he was terrific. Never dreamed I'd go out drinking with him one day. He was terrific tonight."

"Terrific at drinking and carousing, or reading his poems?" Hall asked.

"Dude, the reading was terrific."

Jordan felt subtly patronized. He said, "Michelle's pretty cool about things. I never saw him like that."

"What about your wedding?"

"What wedding? He was somewhere out on the road. We got married by a justice of the peace before we came out here in the fall. I saw him at Christmas but he had a terrible cold and was in bed drinking tea and having soup, and Michelle made him a toddy each night we were there."

"Must've been a big toddy," Gaucher said.

"I guess it's easy enough to like the poems," said Hall, "but I think they're a bit facile, too. A bit too smooth."

Jordan gazed at him, the thin shadow he made under the streetlamp. There was a severity about him — Gaucher, who was large and often loud and expansive, had said once that you could easily imagine Hall as some sort of ascetic monk with an obsession, an abbot with a scrupulous conscience and the will to punish. It seemed that something was always agitating him, and he had a tendency to find everything facile. He used the word a lot; it was almost like a tic.

Gaucher's appearance was piratical, with his beard and his long hair and his size. He was barrel shaped, with heavy arms and large hands. He said, "I think they're powerful poems, facile or no."

"Making the lines sound like you breathed them is a good thing," Jordan put in. "I mean, it's hard to do. Getting the worked-on quality out of it, as James Dickey used to say. The lines sound like the most natural speech. A superior form of speech that nevertheless *seems* simple."

"The guy's your father-in-law," Hall said. "Of course you like it. And James Dickey hardly ever wrote rhyming poems."

"I liked the poetry before I met Michelle." Jordan flicked his cigarette away, and brought another out of the pack.

Gaucher pulled a joint out of his shirt pocket. "Anybody?"

"Not now," Jordan told him.

"The guy's poems are too orderly," Hall continued. "I'm after chaos — I want to give the fullest feeling of the confusions of life. I'm looking for a deeper realism."

Jordan had felt, without saying so, that Hall's poems were in fact more like schizophrenic word salads. In truth, no one could convince him that his search for a more intense realism was actually just a kind of rebranding of surrealism, and that surrealism was passé. The joke among the other students was that Hall's first book of poems would be titled *Keep Out, This Means You!* And some scoffed at the exclamation point. Yet Jordan also suspected that they might contain something that he, Jordan, was too thick to see.

Gaucher put the joint back into his shirt pocket, and looked into the house. "Maybe we should just adjourn. I don't need more coffee. It'll make my heart race."

"I'll need some more to drive," Jordan said.

"I thought the old man would kill us for sure, coming here."

"I thought he was amazingly straight-seeming," said Hall. They heard Fearing stir, inside. "Hard to figure Michelle coming from that."

"You sure hung on his every word," Gaucher said. "For somebody who isn't into him."

"I just said it's hard to believe Michelle comes from life with that."

Billy Jordan broke forth. "Her mother, boys. No shit." He was appalled by his own words. They stared, and he heard himself go on. "Life with *that*. Believe me."

"I think I read something," Gaucher said. "Somewhere."

"In and out of the bug house, man. And she's been calling Michelle."

"Oh, Christ. Tell us."

"It's — she thinks — no, it's bad. Leave it at that."

"But I wasn't talking about Momma," Hall said. "I was talking about big Daddy in there."

"Hey," Jordan told him. "She idolizes him, okay? Guy can do no wrong. She's been bummed about having to work on her midterms with him coming. And she's seen the shit and is getting the shit with her mother. Believe me. She's Daddy's girl, and thank God. And even so, you know, she doesn't read him. Says it feels like she's prying."

"She's told you that?"

"She's told *him* that."

Again they heard movement inside.

Jordan could not help remarking, "Guy's basically got two questions about every single day. 'When do I eat, and what do we have to drink?' I'd like to accomplish that, somehow."

They laughed quietly.

"Oh," Hall said, "and his other question of each day has to be, 'Who can I mess with?,' right? I thought that barmaid was going to coldcock him."

"It all sounds quite familiar," said Gaucher. "Um, we have met the enemy, boys, and he is *us*." He lighted his second cigarette, and made a show of blowing smoke rings.

"Actually, the critical shit is balls," said Jordan. "I hate that steady evaluation of people."

"We're pretty much doing that all the time, aren't we?" Hall put in. "I think it might be in our genetic makeup as writers."

"It's certainly in our distinguished visiting poet's genetic makeup."

"Wild night," said Gaucher.

Jordan felt abruptly dejected. The night had become little more than an embarrassing exhibition. He caught himself wondering how he would live it down.

"Well," Gaucher said, "I like the poems. Of course I'm not a poet."

"I thought Eckhart would come to the after-party." Hall crushed his cigarette under his shoe. "And, you know, his intro did seem a bit tepid."

Gaucher smiled. "Not to say facile?"

"What?"

"Teasing you, dude. Go ahead. So you think the resident poet hath damned with faint praise the distinguished visiting poet."

"The resident asshole."

"You don't like Eckhart?" Jordan asked.

"Can't stand him, his work, or his teaching."

"Jesus Christ, Tim."

"Only writer I can stand in this program is Marilyn Sing. She's a brilliant poet."

"'Cause she's the bomb," Gaucher said. "As beautiful as brilliant."

"Okay, sure — that, too."

Jordan said, "I like what I've seen of her poetry, and I like her. And she's good-looking, okay? But I like Eckhart's stuff, too. A lot. And he looks like a leprous butcher, to quote our visitor. So it's not just looks. I like him, and I like that he's not afraid of rhymes."

"Oh, fuck rhymes." Hall sounded a little as though he was still saying everything to be heard by the visiting poet snoring on the couch thirty feet away. "The world doesn't rhyme."

"Oh, but it does," Gaucher said. "You just don't hear it. It most assuredly does. Just think of all those molecules and electrons circling like tiny solar systems."

They were quiet a moment.

Gaucher went on. "I like the ones about his little lost boy, and the fate of others. Think of it. That it comes back to *his* fate. To lose that boy."

"But it comes out of the boy's fate," Jordan said. "That's what the poem's about."

"How'd the kid die, anyway?" Hall asked.

"Fell off a balcony," Gaucher told them. "Five years old. Rail broke. Twenty-five feet. Eckhart was sitting right there reading."

"Christ," said Jordan.

"But rhyming about it cheapens it, somehow." Hall blew smoke with the words. "Takes away the spontaneity of it."

Jordan said, "All right. You're a cabinetmaker, trying to make a cabinet to honor your dying father. You want it to be *spontaneous*." He emphasized the word. "So you throw a lot of wood up and see where it falls, right? For spontaneity. So you have a random pile of wood."

"The analogy doesn't hold."

"Sure it does. Sure it does. And so what do you do, cabinet-maker? You make exact measurements and calculations, all that un-spontaneous stuff, and you build a beautiful cabinet. If you're a poet, you take the trouble to write something like Dylan Thomas's 'Do Not Go Gentle into That Good Night.' A fucking villanelle, man. The most extremely difficult form to write in English. Out of love. And respect. Respect. My wife writes music. You think I like every note? But I know she's taking care — that kind of care, man." Suddenly he was near crying. He stepped back, and looked off. Then, breathing slowly, feeling the necessity of finishing, he got out, "Eckhart writes poems like intricately made cabinets, solid as oak, about his lost boy."

Hall smirked. "I don't think your father-in-law agrees with you."

"Well, then we'll have it to discuss as the years go on," Jordan told him. "I'm not a poet. But I do love it and I think I know what's good." Immediately he distrusted the remark, and he repeated, "I'm not a poet."

Their vegan feminist/Marxist neighbor, whose name he could never remember and who, according to Michelle, had no sense of humor, now looked out the bedroom window of her shed, not ten feet away, and pointedly closed the curtain.

"Keep it down, guys. I think we woke my neighbor."

Gaucher stepped on his cigarette, then picked it up and began field-stripping it. "I thought that was a tool shed."

No one moved.

"Gotta get home, anyway." He turned to Jordan. "It's curious. Just shooting the shit, you know, how much his talk is like — like *arranged*-feeling. Statements like pronouncements. Feels like some revelation's coming. And then sometimes it does. Guy knows so much about everything. You sounded a little like him just now, in a good way."

Jordan felt quite unoriginal, having heard his father-in-law say something similar that very afternoon. He was spared from having to respond, because the famous poet stirred loudly inside, clearing his throat, and getting to his feet. They saw him standing there in the living room looking around. "Hello?"

They went in. He stood there rubbing his eyes and scratching the back of his head, then turned and made his way into the bathroom. They heard him clearing his throat again, hawking and spitting. When he came out, he had brushed his thick hair back, and straightened his bow tie. "How about we go get some breakfast."

Jordan looked at the others.

"Okay with me," Gaucher said.

Hall shrugged. "Protein and caffeine."

Jordan wrote a note for Michelle in case she woke while they were gone. Her father watched this approvingly. A hulking presence. The odor of alcohol was all over him. Jordan thought of Michelle drinking the whole bottle of pinot gris. Well, they had all been drunk. Scribbling the note, it occurred to him that Fearing's seeming sobriety now must be some kind of stunt. Folding the note, he turned, and there the man was, standing steadily, no apparent dizziness at all.

"Ready?" Fearing said. The voice was gravelly. He made a deep throat-clearing sound.

They went out and joined the other two. Fearing drove a little slower than the speed limit, and Jordan told him where to turn. They went straight down Fox Road three miles to the Western Eatery. As they piled out, Gaucher said, "Man, I feel positively sober."

They followed Fearing in. A short, compact-looking young woman smiled a pearly smile at them and said, "Anywhere you feel like sitting, guys."

"Where're you from?" the visiting poet asked her. "I hear New England."

She kept the smile, looking up at him. "Maine."

"Ever been to Bar Harbor?"

"Not yet."

"Got a house up there and a boat. You'll have to come visit sometime."

"Oh, I haven't been back for years, sir."

She put big, laminated menus down as they took their places in a half-circle booth. Jordan's father-in-law picked his up and raised his head slightly, as if looking through bifocals. The young woman said, "Can I get you all some coffee?"

Fearing said, "Actually, I'm ready to order. I'll have this big bowl of tater tots, fried to a dark brown. And a glass of tomato juice."

She took out her pad and pencil.

Jordan and the other two ordered eggs, bacon, toast, and coffee. They sat and talked about the evening, the reception and party, and Fearing held forth still more about the failings and deficiencies of his contemporaries and friends. Jordan recalled Michelle's dislike of circumstances like these, and then he caught himself woolgathering about how certain aspects of Fearing's egoism were reflected in her, were a part of her being, exactly as helplessly mirrored as the sharp blue of her eyes and the way she could turn every hour of a day into something about herself. The meanness of this thought struck through him, and he sought to expel it. She did not make the hours about herself. She was his love. Her mother was insane, and making her life a trial, day by day.

His own mind alarmed him.

"American poetry is in a fix," Fearing was saying. "I never sit down to write it that I don't think of Scott Fitzgerald's comment about it. 'These thin-skinned poets moved by everything to exactly the same level of mild remarking.'"

"Well, but hey," said Hall, "you can't really be blowing trumpets all the time, right? And what may seem like only mild remarking to someone like — well, like me — might be earth-shaking to someone else, like — like, say, our pretty waitress."

"You read about a tragedy in the newspaper," Jordan said, aware of his father-in-law's eyes on him, "and it's something that happened to somebody else. Your response by the nature of it is only intellectual."

"The personal life," Fearing said. "Knowing *who* it's happened to. Then it's no longer some stranger's bad luck. And that's Eckhart. His whole thing. The personal life. Pious Eckhart. But it's *his* personal life. Now, think about it. You read *Anna Karenina* and you're partaking in the trouble of somebody you never knew. And what's more, somebody that's actually *never been.* A made-up somebody, from Tolstoy's imagination. Send not to know for whom the bell tolls, boys."

"Exactly," Jordan got in.

But now his father-in-law leaned close to the table, and his smile looked oddly as if he was leering at them. "There's evil in this world — " He paused, then nodded slowly as he went on, also slowly. "And it . . . perr-sists." He sat back, still nodding. "It persists." Then he leaned forward again. "But, you have to remember that the good things persist, too. People are killing each other all over the world, yes, and it's savagery every day, and perfectly sweet people going batshit, but also there's others playing Beethoven and performing Shakespeare and painting pretty pictures and singing and going to garden clubs and luncheons and readings, too. All that's always going on, too. And no matter what anybody says, it's the most gorgeous thing ever conceived. You've just got to try showing both sides, you know? All of it." He seemed to hesitate — no, it was a kind of full stop: something had gone through him. He looked down at his hands, flat on the surface of the table. "Michelle's mother was a teacher all her adult life."

"You — you say *was,*" Gaucher said, with great tentativeness.

"Yeah." The poet's face seemed to have fallen. "Was."

The waitress brought their coffee and his hand trembled as he poured cream into his. Gaucher and Hall watched him intently, and then they looked at Jordan.

Fearing spoke slowly, sorrowfully. "She's in a mental institution. Alcohol and drugs."

An awkward quiet followed.

"I think it's prob'ly from living with me. And, hell, I'm prob'ly crazier than she is."

Jordan said, "We're all carrying our own troubles, right? You're not insane if you're worried about it."

The old man clapped his hands softly twice. "Bravo, William. You're a good guy."

Billy Jordan felt suddenly quite stupid. He had said only a platitude followed by a self-interested attempt to reassure himself in his own fear of coming undone. It was as if this were a seminar and he were the professor's pet, in need of encouragement. The other two must surely have been seeing it that way. The idea nagged him as he sipped the coffee.

"About this personal life stuff." Hall was trying to force the conversation back to the realm of ideas. "Are you guys saying an intellectual response is all that's open to me concerning that pretty waitress I don't know?"

As if summoned, the waitress brought the tater tots in a bowl big enough to hold a basketball. Fearing thanked her, and watched her as she set down the platters of eggs, bacon, and toast. "How come you haven't been back to Maine?" he asked.

"Oh, my husband and I moved here. And my parents moved to Boston."

"No friends back there? No former beaux?"

She shook her head. "I brought my beau with me."

"Lucky lady."

"Well, enjoy."

"Don't let anybody in your life go," Fearing said almost tearfully as she went off.

Jordan thought of the wine and the whiskey, even as he felt the reality of the frantic phone calls and the sorrowful facts.

"We know *her* now," said Hall. "So now we'll take personally whatever happens to her."

Fearing evidently had not heard him. "Ah, tater tots — crisp on the outside, soft on the inside, like me. Dig in, boys."

They said little while they ate, the poet devouring the potatoes as though he hadn't eaten in several days, wolfing everything down. They drank their coffee, and Jordan was sopping up the last of his eggs with the toast when the waitress returned. "Can I get you all something else?"

"Yes, madam." Fearing spoke with officious dignity. "I would like a lightly browned cheese donut and a sexual." He gazed at her, back straight, head erect, with all the seriousness of a man his age, sixty-seven years old and quite straitlaced looking, with a bow tie, a white shirt and a vest.

"Excuse me, sir?" She glanced at Jordan and the other two.

"My dear young woman," Fearing said. "I've heard from reliable sources that the cheese donut and sexual here are the finest available in the Southwest. Now, off with you and bring forth the dish with all possible dispatch."

"I don't understand, sir." Her smile looked like work now.

"Am I misinformed?"

"You must be, sir."

"Well I should tell you that the local resident poet at the college — a Professor Eckhart, I believe — recommended it to me as the specialty of the house here."

Now she laughed, and tilted her head to one side. "You're messing with me. Or he is."

"I'm frightfully serious. Please fetch it forth with all speed."

Now the smile went away. "You've had too much to drink."

"Indeed I have, and forgive my brusqueness. But I think you haven't had enough."

"Do you not know who we are?" Jordan said to her, winking so as to soften it. "We're Thomas Fearing, famous award-winning American poet. And we'd like your famous cheese donut."

He heard Fearing laugh with that hawking cackle, and yet mingled with his pride in that fact was a feeling akin to regret for the bullying sound of the words. He smiled at the waitress, who somehow brought back her own smiling expression. She quietly put the check down and said, "I hope you all drive safely. Thank you," and walked away.

"Good sport," Fearing said. "I love good sports." He got up, and it appeared that he meant to follow her, but he veered off and went to the restroom.

"Jesus Christ," Gaucher said.

"Good thing she *is* a good sport," Hall added.

Jordan went up to the front, where she was ringing up someone else, and when she turned to him, he gave her a twenty and a ten — all the money he had in his pocket. "I'm sure he'll tip you big, and this is extra, for the aggravation."

"Don't worry," she said, with that wonderful warm smile.

Fearing came out of the restroom, walked over and paid with cash, tipping her another thirty dollars. Jordan winked at her as they all went out into the night.

"Where you guys live?" Fearing said. "William and I'll take you to your doors. Right, William?"

"I can walk," Gaucher said.

"I'll walk with you," said Hall.

"Naw, come on. Take you to your door. I'm full of tater tots and coffee. I'd pass any drunk test in the land."

"That's all right."

The old man hugged them, first Hall, and then Gaucher. There was something obligatory about it all.

"Thanks for everything," Gaucher said. Hall just called, "Good night." They walked away.

Fearing hauled himself into the Honda, behind the wheel. "Which way now?"

Jordan had got in on the passenger side. "Straight for a while."

They rode along slowly. "Nice guys."

"Yeah. Hall's a little intense." He realized that he was doing what his father-in-law had been doing all night. Criticizing a friend. "But I love the guy," he added. "And he's a good poet."

"Is he?"

"Sure is, yeah." And now he was lying. He felt very weary of everything.

His father-in-law started talking about the night, how good it had been to let loose for a change. "These tours're the strangest combination of too many faces and loneliness."

"We're glad you could come this way," Jordan managed. Another lie.

"Been a rough winter. You know I wasn't as good a husband as you've been."

"Well. It's only a little more than a year," Jordan told him.

"You seem real good together."

"We are," Jordan said. "We are good together." He thought of Michelle crying only an hour before the poet's arrival in the rented car — the look of sadness mixed with anger on her face as she accused him of assigning her to second fiddle in everything, and wept out that she feared losing her ability to hear notes in all the academic work and the steady distractions, meaning her mother, on top of everything else, meaning him and his recent aversion to serious effort. "We have our squabbles," he got out.

"Sure," his father-in-law sighed. "But you know, in our case — in my case, I should say — I think I really — agh. I really did drive the poor girl nuts. Woman, I mean. She was breakable, and I probably knew it from the start. And I broke her. Because I could, you know. I had the power. This sweet little girl — woman — from Covington, Tennessee, with parents who were elderly before they got out of their thirties. Two people so scared of every goddamn thing in the world. You never saw a pair like — straight out of *American Gothic,* that pair. And she was this sheltered kid, pretty as the *idea* of pretty, and completely unready for me." He sighed again. "But still there's always, through all these sad passes, for the two of us, in some strange way, a kind of enduring love — that keeps us going, anyway. Enduring love, boy. No other word for it."

Jordan thought he heard a tremor in the voice.

"One of the reasons I like to keep moving. Sometimes I like the lonesomeness."

"You gave a great reading tonight." He meant it.

The old man looked over at him, not quite smiling. "I pissed in the fountain." He heaved a long, slow sigh. "Twice."

There seemed absolutely nothing else to say. Jordan concentrated on the road ahead.

"Your wife gets her strength from me, old son. So she's not nearly as brittle."

"I'm thinking," Jordan said, "that between Michelle and me, I might be the brittle one."

Fearing brushed this off with a peevish sigh, but said nothing.

"True," Jordan told him, believing it.

"Don't be glib. There's nothing brittle about you."

He was silent.

"Well," Fearing said, in the tone of someone changing the subject. "There's different kinds of brittleness. Every egoist is delicate as a fresh egg, isn't he." He went on about some French critic of his acquaintance, and Jordan, recalling Michelle describing her father's literary-lion persona as bullshit, thought about how only a moment ago the real man had shown through. But now the thread of what was being said had been lost. ". . . what the man responded with," Fearing continued, "turned out to be a question to the lady, and I think — well it's what I call *the* essential kind of insight for our time, you know. He said, *J'aimerais savoir quand l'ego commence à puer.'* Which translates, 'I would like to know when the ego began to stink.' Isn't that great?"

At a stoplight, a police car came from the right, crossing through very slowly. The cop behind the wheel looked at Fearing. It was almost four o'clock in the morning, and the whole town looked abandoned; they were the only two cars.

"Go on, boys," Fearing said, low. "Nothing of interest here. I don't know a thing about the urine content in the water fountain."

The light turned green and he pulled through. Four blocks down, Jordan told him to take the right that would lead to Coral Street and the house. As they made the turn, he saw that at the end of the first block, which was a railroad crossing, the lights had begun blinking, and the gate was lowering.

"Oh, sorry," he said.

"I'm having a good time, old son."

They pulled down the shallow declivity to the gate and stopped. The train was going through at a glacial pace. It was a long freight train, and the cars went on back yonder as far as you could see.

Suddenly, Fearing said, "Whaddaya say we jump this son of a bitch."

Jordan looked at him. "What?"

"Let's jump it."

"Yeah. Right."

"You never wanted to? Jump a train?"

"I guess, when I was a kid. Sure."

"So let's jump it."

"Really?"

"Why not?"

Jordan looked at the older man, who seemed simply to be day-dreaming, eyes following the progress of the train through the crossing; he felt a kind of woozy amazement. Yet there was an excitement running under everything now, like a current, synapses firing up his spine. "You're not kidding, are you."

"What th' hell. Why not? Right?"

"You really are serious."

"Come on." Fearing got out of the car, so Jordan followed suit. They left both doors open. "This is gonna be fun, William."

The train seemed gigantic as they approached it, a tremendous shape like a moving row of buildings, heavy as the world, clacking across their vision at about the speed of an escalator in a mall. But it was so big. The whole night seemed to be dragging along with it.

Fearing went up to one of the cars and grabbed hold of the handle to the right of the door; Jordan, a few seconds behind him, did the same to the one on the left side. The handles jutted out from the metal, and there was a rung at the level of their feet. Jordan had a moment of being impressed with the design of the cars, the utility of the handles, for climbing up. He and the older man held on, half-running, at either end of the one car, and then pulled themselves up. They were moving through the cooling night, into the dark, holding on. Jordan's father-in-law looked back at him, and called out, his voice several registers higher than the younger man had ever heard it. He sounded like a kid. "Hey, it's the thirties, man. It's the Depression."

They hung on, and they were both laughing, moving away from the light of the crossing. Jordan heard his own howling and felt the rush of adrenaline in his veins, his father-in-law's shout, "We're hobos," seeming to come from a great distance, somehow inside the general metal-crunching massive sound of the big thing's motion. He looked back and saw the little rented Honda, headlights on, both doors open, where they had left it with the engine running, and, beyond that, the big fragmented gleam and endless shadow of the train, a dark outline still extending far into the trailing distance.

"All the way to Phoenix," the visiting poet yelled, and then whooped — a sound from all the cowboy movies Jordan had ever seen, of the raiding Indians.

But the train began to pick up speed.

Jordan shouted, "Gotta get off now," and he let go, hitting the ground running, nearly pitching forward into the gravel, but somehow keeping his feet.

He saw his father-in-law still holding on, gliding away. "Get off now," he yelled. And Fearing seemed to step back on air, not facing forward, but putting his leg back as if to let himself down from a stationary perch. His right foot touched the gravel, and jerked suddenly with the going-by of the ground, and he went down, tumbling like some farcical figure in a slapstick comedy, head over heels, pitching and bouncing, until he came to a sudden sprawling stop.

Jordan ran to him. "Man, you took a tumble."

Silence.

He stood over the prone shape of the big man. The visiting poet was still and quiet. One leg seemed bent at a slightly wrong angle. The very shallowness of that wrong angle in the leg was awful. "Thomas?" Jordan said. He knelt in the soft gravel and reached to touch the side of the face. Fearing's head was turned, as if he were lying there watching the prodigious solidness of the train still moving by, enormous, too close — its acrid metal and coal odor leaching all the oxygen out of the air. "Thomas."

Nothing.

Jordan got up and ran stumbling back to the rental car, falling once in the gravel and scrabbling to his feet, turning to look at the unmoving shape lying beside the tracks. It looked like a big thrown rag doll. He got back to the Honda, crying, and pushed the passenger door closed, leaned on it for a few seconds trying to gather his wits. Then he went around and got in behind the wheel. He turned the engine off. The train had at last hauled the end car through the crossing, and the gate suddenly shook to life, beginning to rise. Its motion brought a startled cry out of him. It went up, and the lights stopped blinking; the bells ceased. With the sound of the train lessening in the distance, the night had become a vast stillness.

He started the car and, pulling it off to the side of the road, shut it off again and got out. The train was gone, and it seemed that there had never been a night as devoid of sound as this one. He made his way unsteadily back to the fallen man, and once more he knelt down, not quite close enough to touch him. "Thomas. Please," he said, crying.

He reached over and put one hand on the shoulder, moved it slightly. Nothing. "Thomas, come on, you can't — this can't — " He stood, then bent down and pulled the shoulder, felt the heaviness of the body, and looked into the dim whiteness of the face. The eyes were open and unseeing.

"Oh, Jeee-sus!"

There wasn't anything to do or anywhere to go or anyone to call, though he stood there screaming out into the quiet night. "God, not this. Please. Pleeeeeease not this."

Finally, he went stumbling and running back to the car, and got in. He had no phone. He had no idea where a hospital or a police station might be. He drove fast, back the way he had directed Fearing, to the intersection where they had seen the police car, and on. Speeding. At the first gas station, he pulled in, brakes squealing, got out and ran to the entrance. A dark, turbaned man with a thick black beard and bad skin stood behind the counter. "I need an ambulance," Jordan said. "Where can — where is the emergency room. The emergency room!"

The man held his hands up as if to express helplessness.

"An ambulance!" Billy Jordan shouted. "Where's your — I need to use the phone."

It took another moment before the man allowed him to use the one behind the counter, and it took still longer to punch the number in, and then to get through to someone. "A man's been — a man's been killed. Fell off a train. A train! Goddamn it. Yes. Climbed up on the train through here a half hour ago and fell off. He's — he's dead! Oh, Jesus!"

He did not know the street where the crossing was, so he had to spend more time getting the man in the turban to give the address of the gas station.

Then he was waiting, standing outside in the chill, sober now, and trembling in the knowledge that Thomas Fearing had been killed jumping a train in Arizona, at a small college, with his son-in-law. That would be the story; that would be the story of the end of Thomas Fearing's life. He sobbed, and uttered the word, "Help."

He thought of Michelle — and another sound came out of him, a keening into the flicker of the gas station lights. He saw quite suddenly and clearly the fact that he had been standing there considering only himself; so he consciously imagined her, now, and told himself the confused self-absorption was the result of the shock and terror he felt. He made himself picture her down to the smallest detail. "Oh, honey." She would be awake now in the predawn, sitting up in bed in her white nightgown, wondering where her father and her husband were. "Oh, baby. Oh, God. God."

He heard sirens. There were still no cars, no signs of life down the long flat street. On the other side of the shadows of the mountains he could see the beginning of dawn, a faint glow like a smudge under a strand of moonlit cloud.

How could he find the words to tell her?

The ideas he had entertained about her replayed wordlessly through the nerves in his psyche, that she was the spoiled favorite child of the indulgent savage outrageous poet, with his legendary escapades and his fame. He had indeed furtively doubted her talent, as she had said, while being overweening about his own — his own, that had produced such trifling work in nearly a year — and none of this had anything to do with the one immense fact that her father was dead. "I'm so sorry, honey," he said aloud.

Their marriage could not possibly survive this.

The full force and weight of that probability came over him now, a breathless pressure across his chest, as if something had struck him there.

He could not stop crying.

The ambulance came blaring into the lot, and he got in and directed them to the place, sobbing through his speech, coughing and sputtering. "The end of everything," he heard himself say, sobbing. "Oh, God, everything." The pulsing of the red and blue lights flashed all around them as they sped to the crossing.

They found Thomas Fearing, visiting poet, with a makeshift cane he had fashioned from a windfall pine branch, standing and leaning against the base of the crossing gate. He had a little blood on his shirt collar, and he had untied his bow tie.

"Where th'fuck did you go, boy?" he said, slapping Jordan on the shoulder.

"Let's get you some medical attention," one of the paramedics said.

Everybody was quiet while they helped him into the ambulance. When they were all inside, one medic in back with the old man and his son-in-law, and the other driving, Fearing closed his eyes and seemed to pass out. The medic took his pulse, and then listened to his heart and lungs. They had pulled away from the crossing, and were headed to the hospital. Jordan muttered, "I thought he was dead."

"Excuse me?" the paramedic said. He did not look much older than Jordan. He had small bulging round eyes, and a wide mouth, and he wore a black baseball cap with the emblem of the college on it.

"I thought he was dead."

"How'd he get there?"

Jordan told him the whole thing.

"So you too, then. You jumped off."

He nodded.

"People lose limbs pulling shit like that. And they get killed, too."

"I thought he was dead. His eyes were open."

"That's not inconsistent with somebody passed out. Really. It happens."

"God, I thought he was dead."

Suddenly the poet sighed out a muddled syllable, then sobbed once, and said the name. "Madeline." His eyes were closed. "Christ."

The paramedic looked at Jordan. "This happens, too."

"Madeline, I never liked those other girls."

"His wife," Jordan explained. "They're — she's — they're not together."

"Aw, hon," Fearing said brokenly.

Jordan thought of the man and his wife, staying together through the years of faltering and sorrow; he thought of her madness and of the poet's sad talk of love that endures.

"What?" Fearing said suddenly. "What?" He opened his eyes. "I'm dizzy."

"You got a bump, sir," the paramedic told him. "And a hurt leg. We're gonna make sure nothing's broken."

"I thought we lost you," Jordan said.

The old man closed his eyes and was out again.

"I thought he was dead," Jordan repeated to the young man in the baseball cap.

The distinguished visiting poet had a mild concussion, and a sprained knee, a few cuts and bruises. He would have to take an extra day before he drove back to Phoenix, and he would have to change his flight to Los Angeles. Jordan thought it best that Fearing be the one to call Michelle with the news of his mishap. He did so with a cell phone one of the nurses loaned him.

Jordan stood there next to the gurney while his father-in-law made the call. Her voice on the other end was frantic, full of tears, and the words were garbled.

"I know," he kept saying to her. "I know."

Her voice went on.

"It was my fault," he said. "Listen. My idea. You know how I get, Missy."

More crying.

"It's fine. Everything's okay." Fearing looked at him and shook his head. "He's right here. Uninjured."

But William Jordan was not uninjured. He almost spoke the words aloud. He saw the scraped places in his father-in-law's cheek, the bruise on the hand that held the cell phone, his wife's voice still issuing forth in unintelligible distress, and everything of their lives together, the whole bad year, played through him. He understood without words that even if he managed to keep her, to find some livable existence beyond this artificial school-centered life with its apprehensions and the insanity coming through the phone lines, the wild bad father out in the nights, this night would stay. Wherever they went together, he would still come awake in the dark and think about this particular hour, this darkness that was now done — light pouring in through the windows, like unpalatable fact: he had been so petty, so selfish and wrong. It was as if he should warn her, confess to her, find some means to express, in some overwhelming, all-embracing way, his regret. Yet he knew he would only stand and take her puzzlement and displeasure, and he would suffer the jokes that would be made, and the trying to live down the whole thing over the hoped-for years. "Can I talk to her?" he said.

Fearing handed him the phone.

BLUE

It was already dark. It would soon be night.

— "Gusev," Anton Chekhov

ERNEST AND MARION HART spent nearly the whole month of January 2020 in Rome. They visited the Piazza Navona, and St. Peter's Square and the Vatican, and marveled at the great art everywhere they looked, but they also made time to frequent the wine shops and cafés, where they had veal chops and pasta, sampled osso buco, arancini, Italian ice cream and pizza, and tasted Brunello and amarone and Barolo, and they came to sense something of the daily rhythms of life there. On the last day, they went to the Spanish Steps and actually threw coins in the fountain and then spent an hour at the Keats-Shelley house, where the poet died. They saw his death mask, the delicate, aquiline, nearly feminine features in that profound repose. Gazing at it, Hart experienced a strange sweet quelling effect in his soul, and evidently his wife sensed this. The next day, flying home, she remarked on it; she'd thought about it overnight, and had come to believe that seeing the mask had somehow softened his normal inclination to gloomy deliberations (for years she'd told friends, teasingly, that this darkness was his nature, and her challenge). "Well, it looked like such pure deep rest," he told her. In any case the whole experience had been so intensely satisfying for them both that as the havoc of Covid-19 subsequently passed so heavily over the world, the Eternal City became something they preserved in happy memory like a kind of mental bulwark. And now that the pandemic was waning, they'd commenced talking about finding a way to go back.

As things stood, they would have to incur more debt.

She was a writer of children's books — their best friend Joan illustrated them — and though three had been published in the last five years, sales had seriously fallen off since the pandemic, as had so much else. The children's book business had been slow to recover. He was a watercolor portraitist who specialized in family pictures, usually of children for their parents, and the recovery there was progressing a little faster. Even so, their finances were such that for supplemental income he manned the reference desk three days a week at the county library, while she taught a writing class at Midsouth Community College. She loved her work; he sometimes felt that he must tolerate his. Plus, her mother, Daisy, had moved in, and was helping to pay the rent.

Another impediment.

Daisy had fallen into the habit of shedding unwanted advice and at times she unwittingly made them feel as though they were her tenants. So Hart began walking out in the mornings — at first just for time alone. Yet the pattern had become habit and the habit pleased him.

Marion, as always, took things in stride. She considered that their irritations about her mother's small trespasses were temporary; even in moments of annoyance, she could joke about it. That was Marion. Finding a way to season the facts with her usual wit. "My mom," she would explain, "is a well-known pianist deprived of public performance by plague and my father is a bastard, but his alimony payments provide support beyond what she's been able to make during the shutdown, so the three of us are sharing our wealth."

This about alimony was only partially true: Daisy had indeed invested those payments and was receiving meager interest from them, but she no longer collected alimony as such and she'd been through several relationships since — as she liked to say — Edgar Clayton went over the wall. The old man, whom Hart had never seen face-to-face, was well-off by inheritance and lived in Madrid these days, involved voluntarily in some vague capacity with the State Department. An undersecretary of something. He hadn't given Daisy one cent after the first two years, though they were still in touch occasionally. "They've got me between them," Marion had said more than once. "I keep it interesting."

Hart would say that *she* made *everything* interesting.

After nine years, he still liked watching her move through the rooms of the apartment — lissome, elegant, even in plain slacks and tan blouse, hair up, or held in a bandana — simply keeping up with what she gave herself to do. She was an arranger of things, bringing flowers into the house, or a lamp or vase she had found while thrifting; there were a lot of antiques in the rooms, and periodically she would change the order of where things were. When she was writing, she'd whisper low and he would hear it, and smile. Usually she sat at the dining room table for work, though Daisy's presence had caused her to move everything into the little nook in the window of their bedroom. A happy arrangement, really. He could lie awake watching her, watching the light play across her features as she concentrated.

His memory was image-oriented after all, and that was probably the core of his gifts as a painter. He didn't consider himself a true artist, since all his paintings were from photographs. Marion and Joan, in his estimation, *were* artists, Joan creating images from Marion's created stories.

The three had met in an art class at the university.

Back then, he was a member of the university football team. Marion had been put off by this — she didn't like the sport — and at first it seemed that he and Joan might become a couple. But consecutive knee injuries had put an end to football, and it was Marion who helped him through all that.

Now the library provided a quiet place to sketch when he was not helping people with their reference questions; he liked his workmates, who were all readers. Interesting people. And his clients had always been happy with the results of his work. Indeed, he enjoyed the whole process: taking the photographs either in the studio at home or out in various parts of the city, and then choosing the ones from which he would make the portraits. Marion took pride in the perfect accuracy of the work, and she would remark about how fortunate it was that the children were all beautiful. They were ordinary little citizens, of course, but so pretty to look at, each of them. And thank God, because Ernest Hart always painted what he saw. Recently, talking to Joan about the sweet time in Rome, she spoke of the dozens of sculptures they'd seen of the empire's citizens. The artists for those had been honest, like Ernest. "These were perfectly rendered busts of wrinkled, ugly members of wealthy Roman society. God knows where the handsome ones went. Maybe they all gathered in Pompeii just before Vesuvius erupted."

Joan shook her head, grinning.

"Too soon?" Marion said.

This particular morning, *this* one, begins quietly enough. Daisy goes out to the grocery store, and Marion begins preparing breakfast. It's their weekly big breakfast morning. Joan is coming over with new sketches for their book. Hart kisses Marion's cheek and sets out on his walk. Daisy has decided kindly to spare him the grocery trip. Perhaps she's becoming aware of how her presence is affecting things. "I hope she knows we love her to pieces," Marion says. "No matter what else."

"She's a great lady," says Hart, meaning it in spite of his suppressed annoyance, heading out with a book.

It's a hot morning, already past eighty. He walks down to Bradford Avenue and goes right, holding the book out so he can use his peripheral vision to keep from tripping on anything. He's become quite adept at this, keeping an even pace, reading as he goes. It's a paperback from the *Brief Lives* series, about the life of Sitting Bull. The two-and-a-half-mile point of the walk is the intersection of Bradford Avenue and Converse Street, perhaps fifty yards past a steep rise and descending slope. The routine has been to turn back at that intersection, for the immediate strenuousness of walking back up that slope and on home.

This morning as he reaches the crest he sees two ambulances, a fire truck and a squad car ranged at various angles near a rusty Volkswagen minivan with a tree standing inside it.

The emergency vehicles are blocking both Bradford and Converse. Lights flashing, but he was reading the book and, in the brightness of the day, hasn't seen them until now. He can't recall sirens, even as ambient noise. Three EMTs have gathered tightly in the space where the minivan driver's door would be. Two policemen stand signaling traffic coming down the crossing street to turn around. A woman from one of the neighborhood houses is nearby. She's wrapped in a white terry-cloth bathrobe, shivering even in the heat, holding the robe tight at her neck. Beyond her is a man in a seersucker suit who appears dressed for work. He's talking low, without looking at her. Hart approaches them, feeling the need to talk. But the man's murmuring a prayer.

The woman turns to Hart. "I heard it happen. It woke me up." She puts her other hand over her mouth. "Oh, God."

"I didn't even hear sirens," Hart manages.

The man says, "I just pulled up."

The three EMTs at the driver's side mutter commands back and forth. A bloody shape is partially revealed and then obscured as they work. It looks like they're trying to pull back twisted steel.

A teenage boy with shoulder-length hair bound by a red bandana emerges from the house that stands in the tree's shade. Hart has seen him on these walks. The boy approaches the minivan on the passenger side and pauses warily, looking in. One of the EMTs waves a warning at him, but the boy reaches into the crushed space and lifts out a shoe. A cop steps around the wreck to examine what the boy holds, and then, reaching in, brings out another shoe. Hart sees the cop's thick, rounded, muscular shoulders through the tight gray shirt. The man in the seersucker suit says, "Ach — no — can't do this," and steps away. He gets into his car and actually guns the engine; his tires screech as he turns around and heads fast back up over the hill. Hart thinks of leaving too, but the woman breathes a small frightened moan, and, absurdly, he feels it would be rude to leave her. The muscle-bound cop and an EMT are now looking through the shrubs fronting the house.

"My God," the woman says suddenly.

And Hart sees what she sees.

A tall, lanky man with his head slanting awfully to one side wobbles toward them along the sidewalk, wearing jeans and a T-shirt with a dragon's head emblazoned on it, and no shoes. Hart looks at the bare feet. The man's black hair is cut so short it looks as though the stubble on his dark jaw becomes his sideburns and runs up over his scalp. Hart calls out to the EMTs and police. "Over here!"

The man sits down suddenly on the curb, perhaps twenty feet away. His head turns very slowly toward the smashed minivan and the tree, and then back to where Hart and the woman stand, fixed. The man stares at them, seems to take them in, then looks beyond them. His face shows no cuts or broken places; it's one night-dark shade of blue, the skin itself a purplish midnight blue. He sinks back slowly on the grass.

"Here!" Hart calls to the EMTs, who are already rushing over.

"Christ," the first EMT says, bending down over the man as two others arrive. He pushes on the chest, then bends down to listen. Two more EMTs run over with a defibrillator and they quickly set about putting it to use. Hart watches the spastic jolts and sees the violet hue of the flesh. The dirty soles of the feet. There's nothing else anyone can do. Still another EMT rushes over, an elderly looking man with a spray of liver spots across his forehead. "I guess add this one, too," he says. "Jesus."

"But he — he was walking," the woman exclaims, pointing shakily at the stilled shape on the grass. "He walked — he was *walking*. He *looked* at us. Didn't he *look* at us?" she says to Hart.

The muscular cop has also stepped close. He stands with hands at his hips and stares. "Sailed through the windshield, right out of his shoes." He stoops slightly and indicates the face, the neck, the exposed chest. "Bleeding everywhere under the skin. Every single blood vessel, every — what do you call them."

"Capillary," the blond EMT says.

"Yeah. Capillary. Every capillary." He shakes his head, bends down farther, lifts the body slightly and brings a wallet out of the back of the jeans. He straightens, opens the wallet and reads the driver's license: "John Stahl. With an H. S-t-a-h-l. Born 1992. July. So, just — what — thirty-one years old?" He shakes his head. "Talk about dead man walking. Never seen anything like it."

They're all quiet. Hart thinks of mourners at a funeral.

The woman finally whimpers, both hands now clutching the collar of the robe, her knuckles whiter than the cloth. She keeps nodding slowly, staring at what's there on the grass. "I'm sorry," Hart says to her, as though apologizing for the fact that her life has brought her to this pass. And indeed he *is* sorry for it. For exactly that. He reaches to touch her shoulder but stops himself. Around them is a blur of activity. A TV van pulls up, people emerging willy-nilly from it as if spilled, with cameras and microphones.

Others are approaching now from the neighboring houses. A very old dark man with close-trimmed white hair and a pointed beard approaches. "Lawsy, Miz James," he says. "I thought it would surely blow up. God help us."

Hart walks back up to the crest of the hill and hurries on, try-ing not to look at any of the stopped or slowing cars. At length, he reaches his part of Bradford Avenue, and his own little road, Mills Court. Here is the familiar peaceful block: the yellow sign that reads *No Outlet,* the houses with their manicured lawns on the left, and, opposite those, his wide, low-slung, red-brick apartment building with its white-bordered windows, flowers in planters and smooth lawn dotted with stone nymphs and cherubs. He stands still for a while trying to call up full recognition of it all, then turns to gaze once more at the houses across the way, the trees flanking them and rising behind them, tall, slender pines with their tops show-ing sharply green against the pale summer sky. It's a warm, sunny morning on Earth.

He feels displaced.

As he steps into the apartment he breathes the aroma of the bacon Marion's been frying, and hears his own voice say, "None for me." He sets the book down on the end table next to the sofa.

She says, "What were you expecting to see out there loitering like that?"

In that moment he decides not to say what he's seen. "Just appre-ciating our street," he manages.

"You weren't waiting for Mom?"

"Such a pretty day," he gets out.

But she has spoken over him: "That's you, all right. Appreciating things. I wish you could do that while you're walking. I'm always afraid you'll trip and fall going along with your head in a book."

"Peripheral vision." His own voice sounds strange to him.

"Anyway, breakfast is almost done."

"I'm not that hungry." He lets himself down on the sofa, and watches her through the open entrance into the kitchen. She's setting the cooked slices of bacon on a plate with a paper towel across it.

"Well," she says. "Daisy won't eat all this."

Forcing a light tone, he says. "You're my perfectly lovely girl."

She pauses and smiles. "Sweet."

This is an ordinary morning for her. He hauls himself in to sit at the table. "Not now for the bacon," he says. "Really. Maybe in a little while."

His hand shakes when he reaches for the cup of coffee she sets down for him.

"Should we turn the A/C on?" she says.

He makes his way to the thermostat in the hall. As he reaches to adjust it, he receives an intensely distressing awareness of the moment itself as being one of many separate meaningless others; he looks at his own hand and feels scarily on the verge of something.

Back in the kitchen, he tries to keep his attention on her features, which he loves in any light. She's wearing gray slacks with a white tank top, and she's pinned back her soft, ash-blond hair — the light from the window shines in the perfect waves of it. *Oh, my darling.*

There have been so many and such sweet times.

She continues preparing the breakfast, and when she opens the oven to keep things warm, he sees the dark blue of the inside. He quickly puts his hand up to his face, index finger and thumb squeezing at the top of his nose.

"You really not gonna eat?" she says.

"Prob'ly have something when Daisy gets back."

She checks her watch. "Daisy should be back by now. And where's Joan?"

He waits.

"Billy's giving her hell," she says.

Joan's estranged husband is living in a rented room in Shelbyville and has actually taken out a protection order against her because she has been calling him demanding payment of money he owes her. It's a lot of money. He's a cop and he has friends in the precinct, and twice these friends have visited her after nightfall. Since they know her, too, they call the visits "friendly reminders" about the protection order. But for Joan it's exactly like those old depictions of mobsters visiting store owners peddling protection, and it terrifies her.

"Who's the one who actually needs a protection order filed," Hart says now.

Marion waves this away. "She's never gonna get the money back unless she files for divorce, but I think she still loves him in some obsessive way. It's like an argument they both want to win without really changing anything. But he's living in that upstairs room on Pond Street and she's afraid to stay in the house."

Hart sits back, feigning calm, clasping his hands at the top of his head. "I wish she didn't have it to deal with." His mind presents him with the figure of the woman clutching the terry-cloth bathrobe closed at her throat. "I wish everything was all right." He almost loses his voice.

"Daisy'll want scrambled," Marion says, as if to herself. Then: "Joan'll prob'ly stay the night here." She breaks three eggs into a bowl.

He folds his hands in his lap under the table. "I gotta set up the studio."

Marion nods. "I know. The twin grandchildren. Mrs. Lessing, who insists on *Mrs.*"

"They'll be here in an hour."

"Just time for us to eat. Joan'll bring new illustrations. And after I look at the illustrations and decide which ones we'll use, we're all supposed to go thrifting."

"You think Joan'll move in with us?"

"Nobody else'll be moving in, Ernest." The faintest note of vexation sounds in her voice.

"Hey," he manages, evenly. "Everybody's welcome." As he draws in the breath to go ahead and, without being too graphic, start talking of the morning's horror, Daisy arrives carrying a bag of groceries. "My God," she says, setting the bag down. "There's been a terrible accident over on Bradford. I wanted to pick up some donuts and I couldn't get through. Must've been five or six ambulances and police cars."

"It was two ambulances, a fire truck and a police car," Hart hears himself say.

They stare. A long silence, no one moving. And then, in a strange rush of letting go, he's telling them everything. He's appalled at how it all pours out, and at the increasing tremor in his own voice. "Never saw a blue that shade, that *deep*," he says finally, putting his hands to his face. "And it was — it was someone's *face,* this guy's *face.*"

Marion hurries around the table to embrace him. Then both women are near.

"The guy looked right at us."

"Oh, baby," Marion says.

He closes his eyes and sees again the lurching man, the terrible unsteady gait, the head so badly awry and the face, that ghastly dark tint. He looks at Marion, and at Daisy. All the words for the color begin running through his mind, words in a nightmare. Obscene words.

"I can see if Joan can go to her mother's," his wife says out of the silence.

"No," Hart says. "Don't do that. Let's just — I've got this photo shoot." He wipes his eyes. "It just shook me. I'll be all right in a bit."

"Should we forget breakfast?" Daisy says. "We should clear all this away."

"I've got it, Mom," Marion says. "He's gotta eat."

He manages to try a joke. "Where's the donuts?" And feels the effort of drawing up his courage.

"Don't be brave," Marion scolds. "You don't have to be brave."

Her mother says, "Oh, honey, he can be brave or not, it's up to him."

"I've just gotta get set up for the shoot," he tells them.

. . .

By the time Joan arrives with her sketches, he has gone into the studio. He's having to fight the images that keep rising, and when he hears Marion and Daisy start telling it, he puts Chopin on the player, and fixes his gaze at what's directly in front of him. Mrs. Lessing has asked for inside sets, no fake countryside. She wants bookshelves and drapes, and perhaps a wing chair. He puts together two different small sets, one involving a light gray plush scrap of curtain partially veiling two rows of books, the other with a lamp and a wing chair in soft pink light. The title letters on one book's dust jacket are lined in pelagic blue, and he takes it off with a shaken agitation, fumbling with it, almost dropping the book. He pauses, the crumpled dust jacket in his fists. He looks around the room and finally closes it up in the bottom drawer of his desk. As he's setting up the scene with the wing chair, Joan comes to the door. "You all right?"

He turns, looks into her dark eyes. "Guess so," he says. "Yeah."

"Maybe try to think of it as a bruise. One big, awful bruise."

"*Bruise* doesn't cover it. The guy looked at me."

"Yeah, but he wasn't really seeing you, Ernest." She stands there, one hand on the frame of the door. Only the day before he confided in her that his mother-in-law's almost continual presence has been getting on his nerves. And here is poor Joan dealing with Billy's depredations. A marriage coming apart after fifteen years. He remembers thinking that Joan and Billy were solid as a couple — sometimes even suspecting that they might be more passionate when alone than he and Marion were.

"Anyway," he says, forcing a small smile that turns into a sob. "*Bruise* — sounds too trivial."

"Oh, God," she says. "Poor Ernest."

He sits down in the wing chair. It's almost a collapse. "I can't get it out of my head."

She walks in, bends and put her arms around his neck. "You poor thing. Try not to let yourself dwell on it."

They hold tight to each other for a moment. She's his dear friend. When he took her out that time back in college they ended up in bed together; but there's nothing remotely erotic in this embrace. Even so he feels the darkness of it, as though it's a transgression, a defection. Everything seems to be caving inside him. When she lets go and steps back, he pulls up out of the chair, making an effort to seem strong, an infinitesimal part of him expanding with self-disgust, as if all this is an indulgence, something he should be able to control. "Hell," he manages. "It's done. I mean I just walked up on it. Christ."

She glances back into the hall. "Any improvement with Daisy?"

"Wishing she'd go on tour for a while." He hears the querulous tone and tries to walk it back. "No, she's fine. And she *is* helping."

Joan says, "Well, Marion feels exactly like you do about it."

He glances at the wall with its photographs and paintings. None of it carries any weight now; it seems trivial. He can't find himself in the web of things. He thinks of Marion and her sense of humor as if it's a curiosity of nature, somehow not connected to him. When he looks back at Joan, it's as if he's just discovered her there. "Joan," he says. "God."

"Well," she says. "We just have to put one foot in front of the other." Now she seems faintly confused. After a brief pause, smiling, she says, "Cliché saves the day." Then she turns and goes on back into the living room. He hears the three women talking indistinctly. They're having mimosas. He hears Joan laughingly say *self-medicating.*

A little later, he joins them, and has one, too, then pours himself a coffee. The breakfast is strewn on the table; several strips of bacon remain. He eats one, and almost retches.

"Maybe it'll be in the newspaper," Joan says.

"Oh, let's stop," says Marion. "Let's put it behind us."

"Heard from your dad this morning," Daisy announces. She's standing at the sink, where she has rinsed her plate. She smiles. It seems almost genuine. She steps over, puts the end of her index finger on the shiny surface of the table and makes a slight circle. "It's my pleasure to report that he's had a minor operation to remove a boil from his right buttock."

Marion says, "Come on, Mom."

"No, really. So there he is. A short shit with an extra hole in his ass."

Marion and Joan laugh, a little more heartily than the remark merits. Hart understands that Daisy has meant to distract them from the terror of the morning, and he loves her for it. He walks over and kisses her cheek. "Thank you," he says.

Mrs. Lessing is a thickset woman with leathery olive skin and large white straight teeth. Her smile is odd. Her eyes and hair are a shade of light brown, and the twins' features don't reflect her at all. They're blond, pale, slender, so strikingly identical that Hart can't keep from continually glancing from one to the other. Their grandmother has them wearing the same outfit — red plaid skirt and pink blouse. Marion's mother says, "Hello, I'm Daisy."

One twin gives a quick curtsy and says flatly, "Carla."

"Cissy," says the other. This time the curtsy is exaggerated, with obvious mockery. She says to Joan, "You look like our math teacher at school."

"Oh, I hope she's good-looking."

"She's *mean,* and we don't like her."

In the same instant, almost as if intending to speak over any response Joan might have, Mrs. Lessing says, "What have I *said* about negative speech."

Marion hurries to say, "Sorry for the mess, here. We've had a strange morning. Ernest saw an awful accident on his walk."

Mrs. Lessing says, "There was a lot of traffic coming down from Poplar."

"We had an accident last year," Cissy announces. "A complete and total wreck."

Hart says, rather insistently, "Well, we're set up for our photo shoot. So, if you'll just follow me, please."

In the first setting, the girls argue over who'll sit where. Cissy wants to be on Carla's left, repeating the demand. "Her left. I want her left side." Their grandmother seems merely to be observing them as they squabble. They look nearly translucent in the studio light; their very hair seems virtually diaphanous, wafting in the stirrings of air like filaments of white haze. Their pale cheeks show tiny blue veins. Hart finds that he can't concentrate, can't adjust the camera or their poses. Mrs. Lessing suggests several, and gets them to understand that they'll have the opportunity to sit on either side of each other. "We'll have one of each pose, sweeties."

"Yeah, but what'll he *paint*," Cissy whines.

"I'll paint what you agree is the one you want," Hart tells them. The tiny forking of a vein in Cissy's cheek shows even darker as the two girls keep on about how they should be posed. They're so pretty, so delicately slight, so fair with their soft features and hazel eyes. So rude.

Somehow he manages to get them sitting still and takes a few shots of them in each setting. His stomach's upset, looking at the color in the white cheeks.

When they've left, he goes into the bedroom and lies down. Marion, Joan and Daisy have gone thrifting, and are probably having lunch somewhere. His stomach hurts. He takes three chewable antacid pills and goes out to sit in the shade of the balcony off the dining room. He looks at the woods spanning that end of the building, the almost cloudless whitish sky above them. The day's heating up. He closes his eyes, wanting sleep, but the face of the walking dead man jars him awake.

That evening on the local news there's a report about the accident. The two newscasters, a young, movie-star-pretty brunette woman and a late-middle-aged man, go through it rather quickly. Behind them is a photograph of the wrecked minivan in its awful embrace of the tree. "Tragedy early this morning," the young woman says, "when a high-speed chase ended in a crash that claimed the lives of two men." Her partner picks up the story. "Martin Dupee, sixty-three, and John Stahl, thirty-one, of Collierville were killed instantly. Mr. Dupee, the driver, died behind the wheel and Mr. Stahl was thrown from the vehicle."

There's no mention of the macabre walk.

"Apparently," the pretty young woman adds, "both men were intoxicated."

The two newscasters turn then to local sports and weather.

"Why wouldn't — what reasoning — " Hart begins. The TV screen now shows a green map of Memphis and surrounding areas.

Marion picks up the remote and shuts off the TV. "Think of it, Ernest," she says. "What would a relative feel, hearing about a thing like that?"

They're all quiet a moment.

"God," Hart says, low.

But Daisy and Joan are agreeing about how ghoulish it would be to report such details in a public broadcast.

In their bedroom, the Harts don't speak about it. He brings up the lovely late afternoon light in the Piazza Navona. And the luminous twilights, how the shadow of Borromini's church, Sant'Agnese in Agone, falls on Bernini's Four Rivers Fountain at that time each day. "Remember," Hart says, "the guide telling us Borromini designed the building to do just that because of an ongoing spat between him and Bernini. Imagine, a four-hundred-year-old daily insult."

"What made you think of that?" she asks.

"Rome," he says, and brings her close in the bed. "I'm thinking about Rome." He feels the urge to tell her, as the thought occurs to him, that this day casts a shadow that will always be there now, like the twilit shadow of the ancient church, but then she sighs, and says, "Maybe we can go back in the fall."

"Oh, yes," he says. "Oh, let's do that."

He sleeps so fitfully that it feels like wakefulness, like no sleep at all. Finally, turning the small reading light on, he tries to read the book about the man called Sitting Bull, whose literally translated name, according to the book, was Buffalo Bull Who Sits Down.

The morning paper has more about the accident, surprisingly as part of an article about alcohol and its effect on one family: it turns out that Dupee was the late-life son of a former Tennessee congress-man, Wildcat Tyrus McGill, from the 1920s.

The Harts sit side by side at their kitchen table and read this, sipping coffee, Daisy and Joan having gone out to get takeout for brunch. The article says Dupee had been working as a handyman and Stahl was his nephew, helping him for the summer. The two

had spent a long night drinking at a celebration of another nephew's impending marriage. They were weaving in traffic and had no
headlights on, and when a state patrol car attempted to pull them
over they fled at high speed. The article says they were going a hundred and ten miles an hour when they hit the tree. The article writer
posits the theory that the alcoholism could've been inherited, just
as recent studies have suggested that suicide or the depression that
produces suicidal ideation might be. Both men were divorced; both
had been in several different kinds of difficulty involving alcohol
and drugs and the itinerant lives they'd lived in the delta. For the
nephew, there was also time spent in the Mark H. Luttrell Correc-
tional Center, after a violent altercation at a movie theater, two years
before.

"No surprise," Marion says. "Forgive me."

Hart wants to know more. It can't be that simple. "Why would
they *run*?"

She shrugs. "Why worry about it now? We don't know them."

He stands and leans on the back of the chair. "But I can't stop *seeing* it, honey. The guy looked right at me. He could see well enough
to walk and he looked at me. And he was dead. And I — I can't
shake the memory of the particular shade of — of the *color*. I saw the
deepness of it, its — its *totality*, just as I was beginning to know he
was — what the situation was."

"It's done now, though. It's over, honey." She begins to clear away
the coffee dishes. He watches her and reaches for a paper towel to
wipe the table. "Let's leave it," she says. "Okay? We'll just have to go
over it again when Daisy and Joan get back."

He gathers all his breath and sighs the words out slowly. "God,
Marion. This is the blue planet. It's mostly blue. A blue stone in the
center of space."

She's silent, staring. Then she seems to draw herself up. "What're
you saying?"

"I couldn't look at the sky this morning," he tells her. "I started
my walk and came back in. Marion, I couldn't bring myself to look
at the sky. I have this feeling: it's like this is our — this — going
along this way — living the minutes of the day, this is something

not us, somehow, a chain of events unfolding in time and leading to some — fate. I can't explain it."

"Fate."

"I can't help but sense that this is the beginning of something."

"Stop it," she says. "You're scaring me."

He says nothing for a moment. They're simply staring at each other. Finally he looks down. "I feel strange, honey. I have this awful dread just now."

She steps over and embraces him, and they remain like that for a few moments. "We just have to get past this next few days. It'll fade."

He doesn't answer.

She continues. "Joan and I are supposed to have lunch with this woman who wants to be our publicist."

"I've gotta try to paint." The words sound troublingly beside the point.

"The cute twins," she says. "They should go to Pompeii."

He manages a smile and leans over to kiss her hair. "Keep joking," he says. "And I'm sorry."

How do you completely exclude one of the primary colors?

In the studio he sets out the photo Mrs. Lessing has picked — since, she told the girls, who were audible in the background with their arguing, the portrait is for *her.* He looks at the faces, and is confronted immediately by the new difficulty about shades of blue, and there are in fact hints of the color in all the photographs he has taken of them — he sees it in the light green, faintly cyanic drape and the blond walls of the room itself, and he sees it in the girls' hair and pale cheeks, with those traces of the veins, and he can see it while anticipating all the necessary touches even to deepen some shade of gray; it's all brutal distraction.

He backs away from it, experiencing again in memory the breath-stealing aghast horror of the tottering figure lurching toward him. He paces a little, still seeing it, and thinks of trying again with the walk. Go out and look at the lovely summer world. He puts sunglasses on, to mute colors. He fears now for his sanity. In the living room, Marion sits with her pages on her lap, penciling in changes.

She looks up. "Good idea with the sunglasses. You look cool."

"Let's do go back to Rome," he hears himself say suddenly. "Now. Let's find a way."

She frowns. "Baby."

"Maybe this is tied up with the pandemic, somehow." The thought surprises him. "Can't we — let's find a way to go back this week."

"Ernest," she says. "Stop it. Everything's all right. We're all right."

"I feel separate from you."

She pauses, staring.

"From everything. And I think Rome — " he begins, but doesn't finish.

"It'll be fine." She frowns slightly. "You're just upset. It's trauma, seeing a thing like that." She seems to give a small half shrug, stepping toward him. The light from the window casts a bluish tint onto her white blouse, and he sees it above the frame of the sunglasses as he bows slightly to accept her kiss. The thought seizes him again that this is all one thing, part of something ongoing. There have been the depredations of the shutdown and the scares and climbing horrors of Covid, and Daisy's moving in, and the increasing scarcity of funds and having to work the library job, and even Joan's estranged husband with his friends in the police department — and Joan now, Joan, too — and through everything he, himself, making the effort to be decent and loving. Here *this* is now, like a pitiless last straw coming from the very chain of all circumstance. He recognizes the absurdity of the notion, yet *feels* it under his heart like truth. He stands braced against the counter, just beyond the bath of light from the window, as his wife approaches.

"Well?" she says. "C'mon — kiss me. In honor of our trip to Rome."

He kisses her, holding on, eyes shut tight.

A LOCAL HABITATION AND A NAME

WHEN DARCEY SHIPMAN and Marie Ward decided to be among the first to avail themselves of the Supreme Court's ruling about same-sex marriage, Marie's father, a devout Catholic, refused to have any part in it or even to acknowledge it. In fact, he would have nothing more to do with Marie, since she was defying all the years of growing up in his house. From the minute the marriage was official, he said, she would be dead to him. He used that phrase in a level, low, fiercely disdainful tone, and then almost immediately apologized, nearly in tears — you could hear it over the phone — begging her forgiveness. But in the end he was unable to accept the fact of the marriage, and Marie was therefore exiled, as it were, consigned to outer darkness, like Cordelia in the old play. No phone calls answered or returned, no communications of any sort acknowledged, and that was that. In the first few weeks, Marie, with her customary wit, called Darcey her French king as an endearment. Nashville she called France, across a channel (212 miles of asphalt: Interstate 40). But the banishment continued.

She felt the long pain of it of course, but went on being herself in the hope that it might change, the way the country had changed. Her father's silence became essentially like the silence after the death of a loved one. Darcey, who had lost her parents in an auto accident when she was nineteen, spoke of how the world itself seemed an awful increment quieter then, lacking their voices. Marie could recall feeling that, too, about her mother, without ever putting it into words for herself. Now, to a degree, she felt it about her father. She and Darcey were alone in the world, and they were together, which, Marie insisted, was what mattered. And though she had been at odds with her father about other things when she was in her teens, and was still battling an opioid addiction, and though Darcey was a recovering alcoholic, none of that, she would hasten to point out, was the true reason for the old man's renunciation: it was solely *Obergefell v. Hodges.*

She would say this as though it were the punch line of a joke.

She sent birthday cards to him anyway, and a yearly Christmas letter describing visits from friends and new arrivals in the friends' families, and even some words about the struggle to stay clean and managing to stay clean.

Darcey, through this time, was always careful not to say anything negative about him, though she did not understand how anyone could deprive himself of a daughter in that way, over an abstraction, a religious bugaboo. She and Marie loved each other with a complete passionate consideration, and they were happy together, though they did not step back to look at it or examine it much. Life was hard and they remained mostly cheerful in it, holding on to each other.

When the pandemic hit with its attendant terrors and shutdowns, they got laid off within a week of each other — Marie from her job as a receptionist at Union Trust, Darcey from her substitute art history seminars in the county schools. The plague weeks, as they called them, turned into plague months, and their meager savings dwindled quickly to nothing. They found themselves on the dole, drawing unemployment and taking emergency payoffs from the government. When it became clear that they were about to be evicted from their apartment, Marie — having heard from an old family friend that Henry was barely able to get around anymore — decided to make one more call to him. "The last call," she said with fake cheer, her voice giving forth the faintest note of old humiliation and sorrow. She put her phone on speaker and punched in the number.

To the astonishment of them both, he answered, and almost immediately assented to Marie's hint about returning home. "I haven't been myself," he told her. "For a long time."

"Yes," Marie said. "We *know* that." She smiled and winked at Darcey.

"How do you know?" he asked.

"I talked to George Myers."

"I don't see him much anymore," Henry Ward said.

"Well, I heard," Marie said. "Okay?"

His voice as he responded was halting, almost penitent, unsettlingly ameliorative, as though he were the one who had called and was asking Marie to come home. "I've been having trouble getting around. I'm very weak now. I don't drive much anymore, you know. To church and back. Usually I can get a ride. It's hard to walk, really. I'm eating a lot of cereal."

"Well, then we'll come," Marie said.

So the two women packed up and left Nashville for Memphis and the house where Marie had grown up. They took up residence with the old man — to help, and, they could admit this to themselves, be helped.

Their first days in the house felt like a sort of game with no discoverable rules. Darcey had been spooked by what she saw as the bizarre décor, with its crucifixes on the walls in the kitchen and the living room, and the print of Jesus — effeminate hand to his flaming heart — in a frame atop the television. They both yearned for other minds and hearts, and there was a deal of confusion, at such an unfortunate and fatal time. They could not go out; they'd often had to order in. When they took walks along Almond Street, people coming the other way would step out into the street, or Marie and Darcey would, depending on body language. Everyone wore a mask, even outside. They would walk with the old man once or twice a week, but he had a walker and did not like to be seen using it. Life in the house was usually quiet enough. They both learned to ignore the old man's occasional lapses concerning his undiminished indignation about their status as a married couple. For his benefit, without having consciously decided to, they kept a platonic tone between themselves in his presence; it was simply the air they breathed. Mostly they refrained from speaking directly about it. He would quietly say grace at the meals Marie or Darcey made, and he would kneel by the side of his bed to pray before being helped into it. Marie performed every tender task without complaining once about it, even to Darcey in the privacy of their room, lying in the bed where she had slept growing up. "We went through so much when my mom got sick," she murmured. "And his faith helped him get through it all."

"And you?" Darcey asked. "Did it help you?"

Marie gave a little helpless shrug. "Of course."

"Come here, my darling."

Outside the sweet secrecy of that room, they behaved like affectionate siblings.

Darcey thought of it as something to which they were accommodating themselves, like an unmentioned illness or handicap. In the evenings they watched movies, or played cards, or read, but they seldom even mentioned anything about the silent years. Three or four times in the first week, he expressed regret about the missed time without referring to the actual source. And Darcey saw Marie's efforts to endear herself. The first morning, Marie said proudly as he sat at the kitchen table with his newspaper that Henry still liked the morning papers. No internet for him.

Darcey wondered what the old man really felt in these instances; he was so infirm.

But he and his daughter were very sweet with each other, and she saw how they took the trouble to skirt things. Once, in the middle of a card game, he paraphrased the line from Robert Frost about how home was the place where, when you have to go there, they have to take you in. Marie laughed, though Darcey felt it as a dig. To her, several times, he called himself Marie's failed widow-father.

Now Darcey, too, was a widow.

Ten days ago Marie had driven in her mask to the Banksville Piggly Wiggly to store up in preparation for what was predicted to be the first winter storm of the season. She was waiting in the long checkout line there, everyone keeping to the social distancing signs on the floor, when a diminutive, freckled teenage boy wearing a camouflage jacket walked into the place, pulled a pistol out of the side pocket and began shooting. Marie was hit first. The pistol was a Glock 21 Gen4, with fourteen rounds, and all fourteen rounds had been fired, thirteen into the crowd of scattering innocent people buying groceries, and one into the mouth of the shooter — who, according to everyone possessing any knowledge of him, had been a normal kid from a good home.

Darcey, a day later, still crying, researched the gun online, its aspects. The sites she looked at all had a pop-up question: *Are you eighteen years of age or older?*

The boy was sixteen.

No one knew where or how he got ahold of the gun. And no one seemed to know what must have led him to his final act. The media called it the Banksville Rampage.

Rampage.

There really were no words to describe it adequately except simply to use the nouns and verbs that gave the clearest picture.

The fatal shot had gone through Marie's carotid artery and severed her spinal cord. She died instantly. And while her father wanted very much — needed very much — to think that her death must have been a painless blackout, there also persisted his helpless, unwanted mental images of her in the eternity he believed in. Darcey had watched him struggle with this. She felt sorry for him, had even suggested that he speak to one of the parish priests about it. But he was far from able to take that step, even as he kept receiving visions of his daughter in hell. The muttered laments about the "waste of a soul" and "dying without being reconciled" — the nodding motions of his head as, looking away from Darcey, fighting tears, he talked about his one daughter and his great failure — all showed the nature of his thoughts and of his anguish. Yet he denied it all. Kept saying his rosary and holding on to the assurances of his faith. And Darcey, being kind, and suffering herself, had decided to remain here, at least until she was asked to leave.

In any case, she herself could not imagine going through it all alone.

This morning, waking from an absurd dream of needing to be somewhere and talking fruitlessly to someone about airline flights, she reached across the empty expanse of the bed and remembered everything again. She had gone to sleep thinking about the room and the bed as Marie's room, Marie's bed. Now she heard the old man moving around in the other rooms. Picking up her cell from its charge plate, she lay back and looked at the screen. Since the predicted ice storm had turned out to be nothing but a little rain and wind, she went past the weather — she would never trust another weather forecast. She swiped through other screens, seeking possible subjects for talk. In the news she saw articles about the Ukraine war, the strike in Hollywood, the Tesla automatic pilot accidents and an opinion piece about the CDC's announcement that mass shootings constitute an actual health crisis in America.

"Jesus, you think so?" she murmured to the air.

She lay crying a little, keeping quiet as best she could. Finally, closing the phone, she got out of the bed and pulled her robe on, then stepped into her slippers to go into the bathroom. In the mirror over the sink she saw an unrecognizable, bleary-eyed, wild-haired, glowering woman. A woman years older, in grief. She cleaned her teeth and brushed and pinned her hair, and put on some makeup, like someone preparing to go to work. She heard him in the kitchen making the unpleasant glottal sound that she had come to know did not come from his throat, but from a small hernia or pocket in his esophagus, which caught food particles sometimes after he swallowed. He could not eat chips or seeds of any kind, and was confined to soft foods and liquids. Now he coughed, and the cough continued, a harsh tubercular sound. She waited, pulling the robe tight around herself. It was awkward for him to have her in the same room when these physical problems occurred. She could see how it embarrassed him. When it was finally quiet, she went in there. He was at the small table facing the doorway. Light streamed in from the one window, which was open a crack at the sill, chilly air coming in as if blown that way by a fan. She breathed the aroma of the coffee he had made; it filled the room. He held his cup in both hands, staring down at the day's open newspaper.

"Morning," she got out.

He glanced up with his sad eyes and seemed to consider, then nodded, as though to agree with a simple assertion of the time of day.

"I meant, good morning. Like wishing it." She paused. "For you."

"Thanks." He sipped the coffee. "Sorry."

"Do you wanna try to walk today?"

"We could."

She turned to pour herself some of the coffee. "How did you sleep?"

"Like the dead."

"Good."

A moment later, he said, "You?"

"Bad dreams," she told him. "Busy dreams." She sat down opposite him with her coffee. Outside the window, crows circled and seemed to protest in the trees that lined the street. The sun shone through the branches. "Looks like it'll be a clear day."

"Yeah," he said. "Those bad dreams, though. Don't we all . . ." He paused.

The coffee warmed her. She took another sip, deciding to say nothing.

He continued, low, as if to himself: ". . . have bad dreams."

This, to her relief, did not seem to require an answer.

Presently he said, "You planning on looking for something to do, soon?"

The question surprised her. The dynamic of their recent days was of simply getting from one moment to the next. "It's Sunday," she told him.

"Lord." He put a napkin to his mouth. "I got the paper here in front of me and didn't think about it. Don't even know what day it is anymore."

"It's okay."

"I have to go to Mass," he said.

"What'd you have for breakfast?"

After a moment of throat-clearing and spitting into the napkin, he said, "Nothing, really, a little Cream of Wheat. Coffee." He looked at her. "You gonna eat anything?"

"I'm not hungry."

"But you don't want a drink." He had not yet, at any point, mentioned anything about her old trouble.

"I don't want a drink," she lied. "Why'd you ask that."

"Because I need one." He began clearing his throat again, and she kept her gaze out the window at the crows in the yard. She had a bad moment of recalling that the term for a group of crows was *murder*. A murder of crows.

"Oh, me," he said, after another cough. He called it his smoker's cough, though he had not had a cigarette in more than forty years.

"They're saying Putin's in trouble with his own people about Ukraine," she managed.

"Really."

"You haven't seen it there?" She indicated the open newspaper.

"Not yet," he told her. "I didn't even see it was Sunday." He looked at the paper. The entry was on the first page.

She watched him, glad of the pause. Then: "What do you think?"

"Haven't given it much thought." His face still had the stricken look of the first hours of knowing what had happened in Banksville.

A moment later, she said, "The eleven o'clock Mass?"

"Only one left, isn't it?" he said.

"I'll drive you."

"I'm sorry. I guess it's gotta be you, yeah."

Marie had been the one who drove him each week, and she even went in with him, and sat quietly at his side as she had when she was a girl, her mother gone, with a wordless sense of his devoutness as sustenance. To Darcey, alone in their bedroom one night, she'd murmured, "It can't do any harm, and it cheers him."

"Of course it did harm, sweetie. It robbed you both of eight and a half years."

"But there's nothing to do about that. And I don't care about it if it eases things for him now. I mean we don't talk about it, and I think that's a courtesy he gives me. Us."

"Did you actually go up and have communion?"

"No. But he doesn't say anything about that so it's fine."

Last Sunday, last week, at the funeral, three days past the shooting, the force of his grief had nullified his senses.

Indeed, it had nearly finished him.

He stood by the passenger door of the car and waited for her. With a jolt she recalled that when his daughter had driven him, he required help getting in. So she helped him sit and then lifted his surprisingly heavy legs in and closed the door. Walking around the car, she said, low, *"Introibo ad altare dei."*

On the way to the church, he held his "trusty rosary," as Marie had called it, but seemed only to be gazing out at the traffic and the scenery. He was a man who had lost his wife and his only child to the world and death and change, and again Darcey felt sorry. The church looked like a school — red brick, a portico, very modern. When she pulled up in front and walked around to help him out, he said, "Please come in with me."

She was holding him by the ankles, bringing him around so he could manage it.

"Please?" he said.

"But can I? I mean, I'm not Catholic."

"Everyone's welcome," he said. "Really."

She helped him out of the car and stood uncertainly while some people who knew him walked up to express their sympathies. None of them seemed aware, or even curious, as to her purpose or situation. One or another of them nodded at her, even smiled slightly in hypothalamic politeness. Inside, there were some others. Henry Ward was a well-regarded member of the congregation; he had served as an usher on occasion, and headed various diocesan committees, a man whose involvement had been curtailed by health problems, and now by tragedy.

Everyone was kind, even loving. Several women hugged him, or kissed his cheek. Darcey smiled and nodded and made her way graciously through it all, and sat next to him in the pew like a daughter, and when the communion ceremony began she watched him struggle out and get into line to receive the host. It took a long time. He came back slowly, and did not look at her, kneeling carefully and bowing his head. She watched this, thinking of Marie and the eight and a half years.

In the car, after it was all over and she had again helped him into it, and she was driving them away, he said, "Was that so bad?"

She took a moment to respond. "Nothing quite feels good to me," she got out. It was the exact truth.

He still held tightly to the rosary.

"How could it?" she added.

Perhaps a full minute passed. "I know you had a lot of feeling for each other," he said at last. "I know you're grieving, too."

"Oh, yes," she said, feeling the tears come. "I not only loved her. I *admired* her."

He said nothing, staring out the window at the houses and lawns, and the cars gleaming in the sun.

Ten days, ten days.

In the first hour of knowing, they had actually held on to each other and wept. Neighbors brought food and condolence, and there were calls from reporters — they were going to name the victims, to establish the reality of each person. He fielded the calls, saying Marie's name, her age, where she went to school, what she studied. Explaining that she had lost her mother to ALS. Yes, that was it, amyotrophic lateral sclerosis, Lou Gehrig's disease. Yes.

Darcey stayed in the room that had been hers and Marie's. She looked at pictures on her phone, and spent herself in tears, all those photos of laughter and busyness, the smiles and silly poses and views of places they had been, and of the creative ways they had learned to spend time during the plague weeks — the many hours they spent looking at all the Shakespeare they could find online, and the many old movies, lying in bed together with the laptop open on Marie's lap or Darcey's, and a tray of buttered English muffins with hot chocolate nearby. Or a plate of fried chicken, Marie's favorite. And the cooking together, coming up with new dishes from the cookbooks Marie liked to order online.

Darcey had undergone the awful practicalities of the immediate aftermath: identification of remains, funeral arrangements, dispensing of belongings and personal effects. He could do nothing. At the funeral, she had to help him remain upright, and later he had stood weeping, unable to remove Marie's clothes from the dryer. Darcey put things away. Her dead wife's journal notebook was folded into her own larger one, on the dresser opposite the bed where they had slept.

When she and Henry returned from Mass, she went directly to Marie's room, and he put the television on. Some western on TCM. They had said nothing else on the ride back.

She lay in the bed and realized that now she could not think of this little space as anything but Marie's room. She read for a while from one of her own books of Shakespeare's plays — an introductory essay about *A Midsummer Night's Dream*. The prose was fairly academic and specialized, and she drifted off to sleep with the book on her stomach. The sleep was as it had mostly been since the shooting — fitful and full of a kind of gray, unrestful drugged-feeling miasma, an emptiness so vast the fact of it seemed to bludgeon her where she lay. Most wakings from these lapses were attended with a dull headache.

She sat up, surprised, dazed, and looked at the window. Dark already outside. And a whole night to get through. She wondered if he would be hungry, or if he, too, had gone to sleep.

She found him in the living room seated in his chair, while a dark-haired pretty young woman stood before him with an open notebook and a pen. "Oh," the woman said.

"This is Darcey," said Henry Ward to the young woman.

"I'm Norma," the woman quickly said.

"Norma's just here about Marie and what happened."

Darcey waited for him to say more.

"I'm writing an article about it," Norma said. "This won't take long."

"We were just starting," the old man said.

Darcey did not want to talk about it now, or hear details about it anymore. They both seemed to be waiting for her to do something. "Well," she said. "Can I get you some coffee?"

"Oh, no thanks," Norma said, again with a kind of haste.

"Why don't you sit down?"

"I'm okay."

Darcey went into the kitchen and made herself a sandwich. She heard Henry deflect a question about how losing his only daughter had affected him: "This isn't about me. Nothing about me's of interest to anyone. Please, let me tell you about Marie."

"I understand," the reporter said. "I'm sorry."

Darcey sat at the table, and, picking up the sandwich, decided that she had no appetite. She put it down and went in and sat on the couch, as Norma asked about recent life and what had brought Marie back home after years away. This person, Norma, had apparently talked to others, neighbors, friends of the family. Darcey saw her quick hands taking notes; she looked very young. Ward disregarded the question and began describing Marie's years as a high school student and cheerleader for the football team, captain of the girls' basketball team, top of her class. Straight A's. It was all as though Marie had just graduated. "People knew she would go places," he sniffled. "And when she lost her mother to ALS, oh, her courage was — something." He paused, and took a deep, sighing breath. "I was always impressed by her courage." Then with a worried glance at Darcey, he began speaking more generally of his daughter's knack from earliest childhood for getting up again when life knocked her down. "I remember, she had shoulder surgery for a torn rotator cuff her last year of school, while she was the high-scoring guard on the girls' basketball team — what a difficult procedure, that particular surgery. But she came through it like a champion. She always — you know — " His voice cracked. "Always wanted to be the best at everything."

The young woman, Norma, concentrated on her notebook, scribbling while he coughed and then seemed to break down. He wiped his whole face with his handkerchief, sighing.

"I'm sorry," Norma said. "I know this is painful."

"No, *I'm* sorry," Henry Ward said.

Darcey knew it was Marie's rotator cuff injury that had caused the years of chronic pain, and that the chronic pain was what had set Marie on the path to being hooked on the opioids: her doctor kept prescribing them; the whole medical community was awash in testimonials about their efficacy.

" — and her self-reliance." The old man looked up, going on, holding a hand out as if he were addressing a crowd, but then sniffling, wiping his face with the handkerchief. "She moved to Nashville, to college, no scholarship, just a kid, alone with almost nothing in her pocket. I mean a person with such — such great qualities." He blubbered again, and again put the handkerchief to his face. Through it all he withheld any eye contact with Darcey.

At last, Norma looked at her. "And you're a friend of the family? You live here, right?"

Darcey waited a few seconds. She saw his pleading gaze, not to say it, not to go on. "Marie was my — my friend," she got out. "I loved her."

The other waited a beat, evidently expecting more.

Henry Ward hurried to say, "And such a friend to you. A wonderful, loyal friend to every friend she ever made."

"Yes."

"And this thing," he added, "this thing that happened — it's — you know — just one more of the almost daily slaughters we have these days."

The words seemed somehow almost out of context.

Darcey stood. "I loved Marie very much," she heard herself say. She had not intended to divulge anything. Ward took a quick inhalation, giving her a desperate, sad look.

"Excuse me?" Norma said.

"Marie was my wife," Darcey told her. "And it's — "

He interrupted. "Oh, please. You don't have to *say* it like that."

Darcey kept her gaze on Norma, and felt herself giving in to something, her voice rising along with all her feelings for Marie, an exquisite someone, a human so full of love, who had suffered everything this man put her through with his goddamn god. "I loved her exactly the way anyone loves a wife." She turned to Henry. "And you're my *father*-in-law, for Christ's sake. And you lost *your* wife when Marie's mother — "

"I won't *hear* this," Henry broke forth. "God forgive you for bringing it up here." He folded his hands together in an attitude of prayer. "God forgive you."

She turned to Norma, gathered herself, and continued. "We were married six years ago, right after the Supreme Court said we could do that."

Norma stood there, holding the notebook.

"Now *listen*," Ward said through his teeth. "I do not want that printed. I will not allow that to be printed."

"Oh," Norma sputtered. "Well, of course. If you feel — "

Darcey broke in, "Print it."

The old man started to say something, but she raised her voice and stopped him. "Marie was my wife, and I demand that *that* be printed. I *require* that it — that it be part of the record. I lost my wife." Now she was crying, and she glared through her tears at the old man, who was not looking back. "Goddamn it. I lost my wife."

"Yes, I understand," Norma said, closing up her notebook. "Yes, thank you both. I'm so very, very sorry for it all. So — so very sorry." She opened the front door, pushed the screen and was out.

"Print it!" Darcey cried after her, moving to the screen. "And when you have questions, if you'd like to tell people what Marie was really like, what the actual person went through right up to the minutes before she was taken from me . . ."

The other woman had hurried out to the end of the sidewalk. And Darcey pushed out, the screen door slamming behind her. "Listen. I mean it." She went down the stairs and approached the other, crying. "If you want to know the woman far more deeply than those fucking high school memories — he's remembering a *girl*. Because he *has* to. Do you understand me?"

"No," Norma said. "Yes I do. Please. I'm sorry."

"But that is not the person who was *killed*," Darcey said, wiping across her nose with the back of her hand. "That person, is the one — the one *I* knew, okay? Call *me*! Ask *me* about her."

"I'll call," Norma said. "But listen — " She held the notebook up as if to demonstrate with it. "This is a very small paper — not — not general. I don't even know if they'll print it."

Darcey stared at her for a moment. "What?"

"I mean — listen, I want to be a reporter and I promise I will do my best but this is a — this is a — not a real — like, newspaper." She took Darcey's wrist lightly, leaning toward her. "It's a very small town paper. But I'll see — I'll see what I can do."

"*What* paper," Darcey said.

"It's the — it's *Faith West*. I should've said. I should've told your father."

"What's *Faith West*?"

"The — the diocese's magazine. Catholic magazine. They probably won't print any of this. They don't — they haven't — I was gonna see if I could — oh, I'm so sorry. I meant to sympathize."

Darcey took a sudden step toward her and stopped, appalled at the way the other had lifted her arms to her face, wincing. "Okay, listen," she managed. "Norma. Okay? Just listen, Norma." She took a breath, still crying. "If they'll print anything, please call me. It doesn't have to be that Marie — that she was my wife. It should be about what sort of person she was." She sniffled. "And — and how brave and funny, and kind."

"Yes," said Norma, beginning to cry. "Oh, yes. Of course."

"But — you mean — but they didn't send you. *Faith West* didn't send you."

Norma did not return her look; she stared off, and slowly nodded. "I — I thought if I did a good story about a longtime member, parishioner, you know — "

"Okay," Darcey told her. "I want you to *think* about what you *did* tonight, and for *what* reason. Think about how selfishly *predatory* this was."

"Please — please forgive — "

"Get away from here."

Back in the house, she heard Ward break into a sobbing cough; it sounded terrible. He was in the kitchen. She called to him. "It was just some kid."

"What did you think you'd accomplish," he said, walking unsteadily in to take to his chair again. "What in the world — "

"No one will see it. Okay? No one."

"What're you talking about."

"She was just some kid. Probably from the high school. She wasn't *sent* here by anybody."

He was silent, sitting there clutching the handkerchief with both hands in his lap.

"Hear me? Nobody sent her. She was just — freelancing. She was going to present her article to this — magazine. Thinking she could *sell* it."

"I don't know," he sighed. "I don't know anything anymore."

"I think I'm going to move out now, Henry. I think it's time I went on my way."

"Please don't," he said, low, not looking at her. "Can't we — I'll change, I swear." He sat there with the handkerchief up to his face, sobbing, and she saw the veins standing out along the side of his head. "Can't we go on a little while?"

She could think of nothing whatever to say to him. She made her way into the bedroom and took out one of the suitcases she and Marie had used for the move. They had sold so many things and given up so much to come here, carrying the few books and clothes and personal items, photographs, trinkets, cards, little gifts they had treasured enough to keep and travel with. Such a meager collection of effects. She remembered how strangely hopeful that little journey "across the channel," as Marie put it, had been. And she had an image of Henry and his daughter holding on together, grieving the loss of Marie's mother. She put the suitcase back, sighing. She murmured the name: "Marie."

In the living room, he was still in the chair, hands to his head under the light, the one hand still clutching the handkerchief. He looked helpless. A sick old man with no one but the pitying congregation, none of whom knew him well enough to really help with his pain. And Marie had loved him. Marie had hurt all those years he was not answering letters or calls, and she had forgiven him, too. She had somehow understood how her father could believe to his very heart that no other choice existed for him, and she loved him anyway and kept her humor and her kindness and her marvelous way with people.

He brought his hands down, revealing his aghast, sorrowing face. "I hope you won't go. For a little while, please, Darcey. I know you're hurting, like me."

She looked at the walls, the sconces, the pictures, the strip of faded wallpaper above the window on that side. It was such a sad place. She thought of Marie growing up here, being who she was, possessed of all that vivacity and intelligence, all that appetite for living, with only this kindly, devout and lonely man to care for her.

Oh, girl.

"There's a sandwich on the table," she said to him. "You should have something to eat."

DONNAIOLO

I. The Magdalene

Tonight Benjamin Halliford is remembering the trip he and his wife, Rachel, took to Italy, six years ago; indeed, he's been seeing it all, reliving it, really, like some kind of visual earworm. The one journey to visit their daughter, Angela, and her new husband, Gino Venza Jr., at his parents' commodious lakeside villa at Livorno, in Tuscany. This was not quite a year after the wedding, which, following the tensions leading up to it, had been a travesty: the priest, a friend of Angela's from Durham, got drunk at the reception and made a pass at the maid of honor. The maid of honor poured champagne over his head and stormed out of the hall, and Junior's best man, a wholesale liquor salesman from Chicago, knocked the priest down. Several awkward, narrowly civil exchanges then took place between the Hallifords and the groom's family, all of this essentially arising from the fact that when Angela decided on Junior in the first place, it was through a net of her father's objections. Some hard things had been said. Indeed, by the time of the wedding, the Hallifords and their daughter were scarcely speaking, and the business with the priest only provided a kind of parenthetical emphasis on the unfortunate facts of things. The bad feeling remained through the first months of Angela's married life.

Six years ago. And the marriage has recently broken down.

Angela's come home, now, staying in her old room, which is unchanged since she left for college, her mother having kept it all these years like a shrine (the birthright of an only child, Angela has always called it, a long-standing family joke).

It's difficult for Halliford to imagine joking about anything these days.

Now his wife straightens, stretches, turns toward him, settles and begins the soft snoring again. He looks over at her. In the faint white light from the full moon at the window, her face, even in repose, appears distressed, shows the perplexity of the hours in her day, Angela back home, a twenty-nine-year-old divorcee "behaving," as Rachel has put it, "like this is a teenager's endless weekend."

The faint snoring subsides, then stops, and, sighing again, she turns away to the wall. She's quiet, suffering her own form of restlessness.

"Honey?" he whispers.

Just the slow sleep breathing. He thinks of getting up, finding something to do, and a moment later, hearing the racket of the night bugs in the trees outside, he imagines himself getting out of the bed and closing the bedroom window. But soon he's back in Florence. A dog barks and is answered by another dog somewhere in the neighborhood. No, he'll try, again, to fall asleep.

Though the Italian trip was presumably a chance for Halliford and his wife to become better acquainted with the groom and the groom's parents, it was in fact an effort to make peace. Summer was near, early June. For Benjamin Halliford, at the beginning, each hour spent in the family villa required much appreciation of weather and landscape, family portraits and architecture, furniture and the balmy breezes, along with polite and diplomatic attendance to every nuance. Matters still felt quite strained. On both sides, it seemed.

On the sunny morning of the third day, to his great relief, Angela offered sightseeing in Florence with the newlyweds.

The four of them went to the Piazza della Signoria, and stood before the replica of *David,* and they spent an hour in the Cattedrale di Santa Maria del Fiore, the Duomo — they actually went up to walk around the high base of the dome, which Rachel, with her fear of heights, was brave enough to do (and how Halliford admired her for it!). After the Duomo, they looked at Ghiberti's *Gates of Paradise,* and then strolled around to the small galleria behind the basilica (it was adjacent to a wine shop), where they saw Donatello's *Magdalene.* And while the day's experience had put Halliford in a susceptible frame of mind about the profound *otherness* of ancient life — an existence filled with the sort of religious fervor that had resulted in these marvels, and that oddly made him feel dimly discouraged (he thought of peasant and slave labor) — the *Magdalene* was another matter altogether.

The statue was in a room with a thirteenth-century plaster crucifix on one wall, and a cabinet full of relics at the far end. But the central thing, under a soft cone of white light, was the life-sized, burnished wooden figure with its troubling, almost quizzical and aghast expression. Walking into that space was like coming upon a profound, startling *present moment.* It amazed him. It stopped his breath. And he realized in the next instant that this was because, apart from its timeless quality as sculpture, he saw something of the bone structure of his daughter's face in it. The resemblance reached deep into him, and caused an eerie sense of foreboding as if he had been given a vision of Angela in harrowing old age. He found himself glancing over at her, involuntarily seeking the reassurance of her then happiness.

He kept this to himself, of course.

Outside, the other three spoke briefly in the quiet tones inspired by what they'd seen, but they seemed already to have put it in its place in memory, something they would tell people about, seeing Donatello's beautiful wooden sculpture. They all walked down to the Mercato Centrale, Rachel remarking how hungry she was, and Angela saying excitedly how much they would enjoy the quality of the fruits and cheeses there. But Halliford kept seeing the face of the statue. And when his son-in-law showed them an enormous wheel of Parmesan that looked as if you could break it up into panels and pave a sidewalk with it, he put his hand on the younger man's shoulder to show his acceptance and approval. He felt himself trying to give Angela the best chance at forgetting all their earlier trouble, and he kept looking at her and marking her smiles, her charming bursts of laughter. She seemed very happy.

A little later, they went into the unfinished-looking, old stone church of San Lorenzo, with its basilica ceiling by Meucci, and subsequently down into the sacristy basement, where pencil drawings of Michelangelo were on display. They stared at the drawings in awe, and when Junior murmured, "It's like the closest thing to touching him," Halliford had the pleasant thought that perhaps Angela would be fine after all, living in Italy with the Venzas and this young man so sensitive to wonders. Yet he kept glancing at the bones of her face.

As they came out into the light and headed across the piazza, she was accosted by an old, old woman with a dark child lovely as an angel who held a plastic bag full of money and wallets. The woman lifted Angela's purse, and Junior shouted, *"Polizia!"* until she dropped the purse and gave him the thumb-thrusting-from-under-the-chin evil eye, moving off, pulling the child with her. Angela chuckled nervously about it, but for the instant of the theft she had appeared terror-stricken. Benjamin Halliford moved to her side and put his arm around her.

"I'm all right, Dad, jeez," she said with a measure of old annoyance.

Later, over the too-quiet dinner at the Venza family villa, Halliford broke the silence by talking about the afternoon's foiled theft. "To think of it — there we were in the sublime presence of the sketch work of one of the greatest artists of the ages, and right outside was this ridiculous corrupt old lady with her bag of loot and her poor grandchild or whatever that kid was."

They were all seated at the family table on the broad veranda overlooking the lake. The table was arrayed with the feast that Junior's mother, Carmella, had prepared. Her husband, big and barrel-chested, bald as a stone but with coal-colored thick hair on his arms and the backs of his fingers, sat at the head, eating with the steady, quick efficiency of someone dispensing with a task. He was a man who had been all over the world, by his own account, and he spoke four languages — also by his own account. But if his English was inconsistent (he occasionally lapsed into Italian, or French, and then apologized), it also left no reason to doubt his claim. Plus, there was little accent in it. He sounded very cosmopolitan, as Rachel put it, and his son sounded American all the way. Venza Sr. kept pouring Brunello di Montalcino and offering it by holding the bottle out. Halliford, looking again at his daughter's cheekbones, said about the child with the old-lady thief, "I wonder what that poor little girl's life is like."

But Angela was talking to her new mother-in-law, who made a joke about her son being a *donnaiolo*.

"What's that mean, *donnaiolo*?" Angela asked.

"Womanizer," the old man said, chewing, without looking up from his plate.

Carmella touched Angela's wrist, and with a smile, said, "But you will settle him down. You will give him no reason to — "

And Junior spoke over her, addressing Halliford's comment about the child thief: "So many of the poor in the streets these days are refugees from the wars in Syria and Afghanistan."

He looked like a thinner, smoother version of Venza Sr., who now directed his gaze at Halliford and said, "Gypsies. All thieves. It's in their blood."

"Now, Papa," said his son, frowning.

"*Non farmi la predica,* Junior," the old man said. "*Nemmeno in inglese.*"

"I'm not lecturing you. And we all speak English. That's one of the reasons you sent me to school in America. May I respectfully request that you not be rude."

Halliford, impressed by Junior's willingness to stand up to the old man, quickly broke in to express admiration for his quick reaction about the thief.

"Well, he's a good boy," Venza Sr. said with an odd air of grudging admission.

Putting this to the back of his thoughts, Halliford proposed a toast, feeling that perhaps they could indeed all be friends eventually. He could make it happen, for Angela. "To our one family," he said. The day ended with everyone sipping Montenegro as the sun went down over the calm waters of the lake.

Toward dawn, now. He turns in the bed and pictures the lovely fluidity of the colors on the water that long-ago evening, a perfect, subtly undulating reflection of the ancient city, like moving shimmers of starlight. He sees again the image of the *Magdalene,* persistent as a memory of trauma. All that is over — all that worry about how his little girl would fare in that family so far away.

Today, there are other worries.

Music comes from her room down the hall. She's up early, but she'll listen awhile, and then turn the music off and go back to sleep. It's the pattern. She has said it must be that she's still on European time. It's been almost fourteen weeks.

Rachel stirs, turns once more. He looks over his shoulder and sees her pull a pillow over the side of her head, sighing.

"You awake?" he whispers.

Nothing.

The last evening of Angela's one brief visit home, three years ago, they had a little too much wine, and she spoke cavalierly about the dreariness of being the little wife in an old-world family, even in a villa four times the size of this house. But she didn't refer to it again and when she spoke to Junior on the telephone, planning her return, she seemed cheerful and comfortable.

He gets carefully, soundlessly out of the bed and dresses. Rachel moans and then rolls over on her back and begins to snore again. He knows she has the alarm set for seven o'clock, and that she'll probably keep pressing snooze until seven thirty, as she does most days. He passes Angela's door, where some baroque-sounding violin piece he doesn't recognize is playing, and makes his way downstairs to the kitchen, to put coffee on. It's not yet six o'clock, still dark.

As he's pouring the coffee, Rachel comes in. She moves to the breakfast nook and sits. Her reflection shows in the dark window to her left — a weary woman in a flannel robe.

"No snoozing this morning, huh," he says. "Can I make you something to eat?"

She waves this away, but gives a slight smile. "Too early."

"I've been going over our Italian journey all night it seems."

"Why?"

"I can't get it out of my mind. I'm worried that some part of me — a big part of me in the beginning — wanted it all to fail. Her life over there. With those people."

"You sound like a racist."

"I mean that family. Come on, Rachel, they never really wanted any part of us."

"Or we, them."

He sets his coffee down and sits opposite her. "I guess I will have some," she says. "Sorry."

He gets up and pours it, and places it in front of her. She says, "I wonder if it might have to do with a prejudice against the rich. I never liked them."

"The rich?"

She nods absently, then says, "No — the Venzas. Well, hell. Both, sure. The Venzas and the rich."

"We're comfortable enough. Some people would call *us* rich."

"You know perfectly well what I mean."

"You remember when we saw the *Magdalene,* that day, after the Duomo?"

"Oh, let's not do this," she says with a dismissive wave of her hand.

"I'm talking about last night's insomnia."

"All right."

"I keep thinking about the *Magdalene.*"

"I don't want to talk about Italy, Benjamin."

He sits down, putting his hands around his cup, and gazes at her. The soft roundness of her eyes is nestled in lines now, and the eyes are bloodshot. She looks exactly as tired as, in fact, she is. He says, "I just wanted to say it did something to me."

She waits, blowing across the surface of her coffee, and then sipping it.

"You remember the statue," he says.

"Of course I remember the statue. Lord, Ben."

"Well, I never told anybody this — but — "

"I don't want to talk about it, sweetie. Please? Italy's over. It's done with. And the whole time she was over there, all those years, I lost sleep. I worried and felt scared every minute. I kept thinking I heard something in her voice on every phone call. Now she's home. She's out of there — out of that. And I'm afraid the whole experience has done something to her. I mean, what happened to her over there? I don't know this person."

He shakes his head. Then: "I was just gonna say I saw something of her face in the face of that statue, and it rocked me."

"You told me that when we were there." Her tone is impatient. She reaches over and touches his wrist. "Sorry. Or maybe the plane ride home."

He searches for the memory. "I must be slipping."

"But what about it, anyway? Why would that be important now? What if there *was* a resemblance?"

"I don't know. It kept me up most of the night."

The faint sound of the music upstairs stops.

Rachel sighs. "Time for the brilliant morning nap."

"Oh, Angela," Halliford says, like an exhortation, as if the girl were standing in the doorway. "Aw, God. My girl."

"She's not your girl anymore, Ben."

Rachel was pregnant with her when they moved into this house. Angela was born here, in the upstairs master bedroom, their bedroom. The house is a two-story Craftsman on Young Avenue in midtown. Having begun as a self-taught carpenter and electrician, Halliford built a contracting business, which he sold at a healthy profit last May to become a man of leisure and a bibliophile, as he describes it. Rachel has worked intermittently as a nurse, mostly in home care and hospice. That first month of retirement, he changed the landscaping out in back, putting in a gravel path and building a bamboo-roofed structure he calls their Hawaiian gazebo at one end of a little flagstone patio area.

Angela loves it, and spends hours reading out there in the late mornings, and most evenings under the tiki lights.

They do not talk about Italy, or her childless time there.

Halliford unhappily recalls jokes he made about the in-laws during those first years of her time away. Comments about gangsters and how Angela flew off to Tuscany as the wife of a cologne-smelling, thick-fingered Italian with ties to the underworld. The

Venza family business, he would say, was olive oil and extortion, with side investments in bootleg whiskey, gambling and, occasionally, a soupçon of homicide.

In truth, the Venzas do own some shipping, a small airline and a bank with branches in Florence, Rome and Milan, and there are widespread other interests, vague as whispering in another language. But it's all completely legitimate. Venza Sr. spends a lot of time in Monte Carlo. He likes to play roulette and blackjack. He's evidently always been lucky at roulette, and highly skilled at blackjack. In fact, everything he does makes money.

Just as everything his son does has lost money.

When Angela and Junior met, back at Duke, he was learning to keep the books for two of the American franchises owned by the family — a Fiat dealership in Florida, and a sporting goods store in Toronto — and when those duties didn't pan out (funds kept disappearing or being misapplied) he ran errands.

Angela finally sought the divorce because he turned to drugs, and was always in a haze of marijuana or alcohol. Or both. Several times she found him snorting cocaine in their bathroom. The marriage had become farcical. She's told her parents that much. How she grew tired of worrying about the carabinieri, and her husband's recurring strife with his perpetually displeased father, with whom, in fact, she herself got along quite well. "But we were living on the dole from the old man after the third year." So she sued for divorce. Drunkenness, drugs, abandonment, verbal abuse. The settlement is extremely handsome, paid for by Venza Sr., so it hasn't been necessary for her to think about finding something to do. Hence, the long hours in the gazebo when the weather is good. Otherwise, she's living in her old birthright. Home from Europe and taking time to acclimate and chill out. *Free at last,* she said to her father in the first week. *Free at last. Thank God almighty I'm free at last.*

Nearly four months.

Each day, she remains in bed until the late hours of the morning, and, after a walk around the neighborhood, fixes herself a sandwich or some cereal, and either goes to "Hawaii," as she sometimes calls it, with a book and a glass of iced tea, or back up to the room. About the divorce, she won't elaborate further than she already has. "It's over and that's that," she said not long after her arrival. "I want to have some fun now. With my folks. I mean, is it okay if I stay here awhile?"

"Oh," Halliford said. "Of course. How can you think it wouldn't be?"

She gave him a soft, simpering look as if to say there were reasons she might suppose otherwise.

———

She's taken them to dinner several times. The conversation is almost exclusively about the idiocies of the sociopath in the White House, the uselessness of the Twenty-Fifth Amendment, and Russian interference with the election. The decline of respect for America in the world. "They're laughing at us over there," she says about her erstwhile place of residence. She's heavily into CNN and MSNBC, and she loathes the "bloat president," as she calls him, and all his minions. She does a good imitation of New York's crazy former mayor. There have been enjoyable moments in her company. The matter of Junior's antics, the drinking and drugging, never comes up.

She herself loves wine, as her parents do, and has ordered several superb bottles of it. "For the house cellar," she says. The wine has arrived in gift boxes, three to a box. More than a thousand dollars' worth, each time. "They're all for you guys," she says. Now and then she takes a bottle alone up to her room.

She's been spending more and more time there.

And she can't be counted on for any help with the house — the meals, the cleaning, the laundry, even her own. Each day, whatever she uses, she simply leaves behind: dishes, glasses, clothes, pillows, boxes of snack crackers and cheese, bags of potato chips, empty cartons of ice cream, half-empty bottles of Barolo and amarone and Margaux. It's all debris. If she takes a plate or a glass up to her room, it stays there. And the room is in utter disarray.

She seldom goes out, and usually that's only to buy more supplies for lying around. She almost never sees old friends or has anyone over. When she does accept an invitation, she shows her parents by every gesture what an unpleasant duty it is for her. Halliford has remarked that she's living off interest in several categories: materially, intellectually, spiritually, psychologically. He worries about depression. But Rachel thinks that's absurd. "Come on," she says. "I never saw anyone happier or more content."

It's true. When Angela's in her room listening to her music, or cruising on her iPad or phone, or laptop, you can hear her humming, or laughing. At dinner, she stares, nodding, as if consenting to some agreeable memory. She seems to be entertaining herself with her own thoughts. They haven't seen her frown once.

This morning, after their coffee, the Hallifords drive out to Brother Juniper's for breakfast. They greet the owner, a compact, round-faced man whom they've known for years. He doesn't mention Angela. It's as if he knows not to. Saturdays in Memphis are always vibrant and busy, and the place is crowded with families. It's been unseasonably warm for the first week of November.

"I'll need a nap today," Halliford says after their yogurt with berries arrives.

"Me, too."

Presently, she adds, "Maybe she really is depressed, and we just don't see it."

"She's got an awful lot of money in the bank," he says. "It might be hard for her to remain steadily gloomy, wouldn't you say?"

"She's like somebody in a witness protection program."

He smiles, admiring the aptness of the analogy, eating, saying nothing, thinking again of the *Magdalene.*

"Doesn't she get lonely? How can she not be lonely?"

"Maybe she is. Maybe this is how she deals with it."

"I won't ask what she plans to do with the money," says his wife. "I don't care about the money — I never have."

"Good thing." He smiles.

"I mean it."

"My true companion."

"Oh, what is she thinking, Ben? What in the world is she thinking?"

"I wonder how much money it is."

"I don't even want to know. But it's knowing she has it that makes things all that much harder when I have to pick up after her like she's a junior in high school."

"Talk to her again."

Rachel tilts her head and does a very good imitation of their daughter's voice and manner. "Oh, of course, Mom. I'm sorry. I'm such a klutz. I'll take care of it just as soon as I finish my room. Just leave it. I promise. Oh, Mom, I'm such an ass."

Halliford reaches across and touches the back of her hand.

"And then I end up taking care of it," Rachel says. "*Again.* Or *you* do."

He sighs, his appetite gone. "I don't want to lose her again."

Rachel's lower lip trembles. "You think I do?"

II. Half of All Marriages

Almost a week later, the idea occurs to him that they might throw a small party celebrating the divorce and the homecoming. Perhaps that might provide a kind of closure: if the divorce can be put behind her in some ceremonial way, she might take hold, and decide to seek a graduate degree, or get a job. Something to occupy her. Anything.

Rachel's skeptical. "Like you said, Benjamin, she's not sad. She's rich. Living on interest. And paying no rent."

The two of them are lying in bed, whispering — though the Sturm und Drang of Mahler's Sixth is coming from down the hall.

"I've thought of introducing the idea of rent," he says.

"You'd think that might've occurred to her," says Rachel. "But that wouldn't change a thing."

"Well," he says. "She's reading the existentialists now. And she told me she might try writing a book."

"While we slave picking up after her and cleaning."

He says nothing.

"She never remembers to flush the toilet, for pity's sake. I bet the existentialists all knew enough to flush a damn toilet. Was she having that done for her in Italy?"

"I saw no one waiting around to flush toilets when we were there." He means this as a joke.

She hasn't really heard him. "Every morning, there's the cutting board with fruit scraps all over it. Like I haven't *begged* her to please for Jesus's sweet sake clean it up after she's through. I'm sick of it. Let her mess up her own place."

He sighs. "I was truly sorry about the divorce, but I was also thrilled she was coming home. I hated to think of her suffering alone on the other side of the world."

"Are you *listening* to me, Ben? Here I am working my tail off at almost sixty years of age and she's living the life of a queen."

"Well, maybe if we mark it, you know. The end of a bad marriage. The happy homecoming."

"That'll only be more mess to clean up."

"There's got to be some way through this," he says, "without losing her."

"I think," Rachel says, fighting tears, "maybe we already have lost her."

Late morning the following day, after another mostly sleepless night, he stands in the doorway of her room, taken aback by the suffocating effluvium of stale cigarette smoke, body sweat and days-old leftovers. It's a wintry, cloudless day. Almost Thanksgiving. She's decided to forgo her walk, and is lounging on the floor in a T-shirt and pajama bottoms, with her laptop open, smoking a cigarette and looking at YouTube. "Your mother and I thought we might throw you a little party. Celebrate your freedom. What do you think?"

"Really?" she says.

Several plates with remnants of food hardening on them litter the dressing table and the chair by the bed; clothes are strewn on the floor and piled to overflowing on the wicker basket that's supposed to be for dirty clothes. The whole room looks like a hamper with garbage thrown in. Aside from the ashtray at her elbow, there's another on the book-crowded nightstand, both of them overloaded with cigarette butts and ashes; beer cans and empty wine bottles are ranked all along the baseboard and on the windowsill.

He finds that he can't contain himself. "Jesus God, kid, you've really gotta clean up in here a little. This is ridiculous. This is a fire hazard."

"I know, I know, you're right. I'm such a slob. I'll get to it," she says. "But please don't remind me of it." She gazes with serenely fake remorse up at him, and then, seeming at first to be indicating the clutter, she goes on about the room. "This is my birthright, remember."

"Yeah, but you don't want to burn it up and the house with it, right?"

Her gaze is faintly sardonic, though not unfriendly. "What am I, a teenager?"

He affects a disbelieving, slow look around the room. "That might be my question exactly."

"Okay." She smirks. "I'm sorry, Dad."

"Were they this sloppy at the villa?" he can't help asking.

"Carmella was meticulous."

He sees something in her gaze. "Go on," he says.

"Everybody had to stand inspection."

"Really."

She grins, remembering. "No. She was just — busy. I got on her nerves, I think. But she was always pleasant. And Junior and I kept her laughing. We laughed a lot."

He leaves a pause, believing she might go on.

"Anyway," she says. "That's all over now."

"Well, what about the party idea? Mom and I thought we'd celebrate your being home. Might be nice to mark it. Like a milestone."

"Is that really necessary?"

"I just thought it might be fun."

"We're pretty well past the sell-by date, though, don't you think? It's been months."

"Look, sweetie," he hears himself say suddenly. "Do you have any plans at all?"

She offers a whimsical little maddening shake of her head. "Not really, just now."

"Well." He moves to close the door.

"Don't be mad."

"I'm not mad. But if you want to talk about it all, you know."

"There's really nothing left to say."

"But maybe it'd be good to have some kind of closure."

"There's a whole lot of closure in the bank." Her smile is sarcastic.

After a pause, he says, "But you don't mind if we have a celebration."

She shrugs, and smiles again. "It's your house."

"Good," he says. Then: "I love you."

Still smiling, she tilts her head. "I love you, too. And there's literally nothing you have to do, Dad. I'm closured, really. Completely closured."

"What's that mean? I don't think I like the sound of that."

"Nothing to worry about. Really."

"Well," he says.

Walking away after quietly closing the door, he receives a sudden sense of the absurdity of the whole thing. Part of him wants to go back and hit the door and when she opens it, demand that she clean up the fucking mess — that she please muster a little goddamn self-respect and a smidgeon of consideration for her poor mother.

In the afternoon, he sits in the sunlight through the window of the breakfast nook and calls to invite several friends who have known her since childhood. The Bransons and the Caulfelds, and the Millards (Jane Millard was there when Rachel's water broke at a barbecue in her backyard). Angela comes down while he's still on the phone. She seems both surprised and curious at his talk of the celebration. She watches him for a time, standing in the doorway of the kitchen. When he ends the call, she says, "What's up?"

"That was Jane. Everybody's coming."

"Oh." She saunters over and sits opposite him. "It's a sweet idea, but I don't know."

He says, "Well, I've already got the ball rolling, honey."

She taps her fingertips on the table surface and then stands and moves to the counter. There's something of nervous restlessness in it. She pours some of the coffee he made, and sits down again. "I have to go out tonight. Remember Claudia?"

"She's the one who poured wine on Father Rolfe's head."

"That's her. She wants to meet me at Henry's."

"Is that place still open?"

"She's been working there a couple years."

"Why don't you ask her to the party? Like to see her again. It's for close friends. Friday. The Bransons, the Millards and — "

She sighs, "It's your house."

"It's in your honor, baby. Ask Claudia to join us."

"I don't think divorce is something to celebrate. It's a failure, isn't it."

"But you're happy about it. *We're* happy about it."

"Well. Relieved, maybe. I don't know about *happy*." She considers. "Surviving, you might say. Making the best of a bad situation, you know." Her hand comes up swiftly. "Not you guys, of course. But, you know, if I had a chance to relive those years, I think I would." She stares, waits for him to respond, and when he doesn't, she goes on: "Just seems funny to celebrate having to get out of a marriage."

"That's how fifty percent of them end," he says. "It's no shame. You got the money. That's happy, right?"

"I can't believe you mention the *money*."

"*You* said you have a lot of closure in the bank. I just mean to say it's not *only* about failure."

She seems to ponder this a moment, but then she simply shrugs and says, "Feels like failure to me." She takes her cup of coffee and climbs the stairs to her room. He follows, but she closes the door, as if unaware he's behind her.

III. What's There to Do in the Middle of the Night?

Rachel, whom Halliford in all seriousness calls the love of his life, is an attractive, petite woman with light green eyes and a perfectly oval face. She wears her hair in a tight ring of blond curls that frame her soft cheeks, and her daughter looks nothing at all like her. Angela's much taller, very thin, has a long, slender neck, and a kind of narrow-jawed angularity, with high, prominent cheekbones, like those of Donatello's famous statue. Where family resemblance is concerned she bears only a faint likeness to her father, with his bladelike nose and deep-set, sad brown eyes. In Angela, these features add up to exquisiteness. She made a dazzling bride. As she goes out the door to go meet her friend Claudia, Halliford notices that she's gaining weight around the middle.

He thinks about this, but holds it back as he and Rachel finish their dinner and put away the dishes. Through this, they say nothing, really, about anything. He turns on the TV in the living room, and after a few minutes she appears in the entrance and looks at him. "I didn't like the way his father was with his mother. I was afraid he'd be like that with Angela."

"What if I apologize again for the way I was when she married him."

"You think this is retaliation of some kind because you didn't like Junior? *Or* Senior, for that matter? *She* doesn't like them now. And she's pleasant enough with you. No, she just doesn't care. She can't be bothered."

He's silent, staring at the TV without really taking much in. A show about police procedure and detectives.

"I'm going to bed," she says. "I'm exhausted."

A few minutes later, he turns off the TV, and follows. He finds her sitting at her dressing table with the coffee. She brings the cup to her lips. Coffee's always the first thing she has in the morning and the last thing she has before going to bed.

"Should we ask her to leave?"

She thinks a moment, then gets up and goes back downstairs, and he comes along behind. "I'm stalking you," he says. She smirks.

In the kitchen, after emptying the coffee into the sink, she gets a cocktail glass out of the cabinet and pours a shot of Maker's Mark. He does the same. "Feel like finding a movie to watch?" he asks.

"I'm gonna sit here and sip this, and then go up and do the crossword for a while. I don't want to talk anymore about Angela, or Italy. Or the party."

"I hate the idea of fighting with her," he says. "I'm afraid this all has to do with the divorce. Then I wonder if it has to do with that dreadful wedding reception and the stuff that went on before."

"Please, Benjamin."

"But think of this: in order to keep her in our lives, we have to let her do what she wants."

"What the hell are you talking about?"

"It's true. If we ask her to move out, we'll lose her. She'll go live somewhere else because she has the wherewithal to, and she won't come back. She won't have to come back. She only came back that one time when she was in Italy."

"I do not wish to discuss this any further," Rachel says. "You're going on the idea that our daughter has no love at all for us anymore. Please." She inhales sharply, almost as if startled, then fixes him with a fierce look. "Oh, Christ, Benjamin. I know where we stand. You think I don't know where we stand?"

He drinks his own glass of whiskey sitting in the lounge chair in the living room, with the newspaper open on his lap. The whole world is one disaster after another, according to its pages. When she comes through on her way back upstairs, he says, "I'll be up in a bit. I'm gonna have another one."

"You're gonna wait up for her."

"Good night," he says.

He pours the second drink, and then sits sipping it, reading the newspaper and nodding off to sleep.

Much later, in bed, he listens for the car, a Camry he bought two years ago. It's in need of some routine maintenance he's been putting off. He waits for its uncertain rumbling sound. The sleepless hour passes. Finally he goes into the bathroom with his cell, and calls hers. No answer. He calls it three times. Then he tries two hospitals, and the police. As of two thirty, no reported accidents or incidents. He tries her cell again, thinking of the noise in Henry's. But Henry's has surely closed. He returns to the bedroom and gets in next to Rachel as soundlessly as he can. More sleeplessness. He lies there building up possible catastrophes. Briefly, he drifts, then wakes and listens again. Near four a.m., he rises and goes to the window. The Camry isn't there.

Rachel's voice from the bed startles him. "I looked half an hour ago."

He gets back in, pulls the blankets over his shoulder and in the lengthening quiet wonders if she's fallen back to sleep.

"You thinking something might've happened?" she says, suddenly.

"I called her cell. Called it several times. Then Saint Francis and Baptist Memorial, and the police station. As of two thirty-five, nothing."

They're quiet for a few minutes.

"You want me to try them again?"

She says nothing.

Sirens sound, far out in the night, and then a train horn, long and mournful. The familiar Memphis night sound.

He sighs. "She's probably at Claudia's."

"Wonder if she's flushing the toilet *there.*"

More silence.

"At least she's not hunkering in that room," he says.

"I did some cleaning in it," says Rachel. "There were cobwebs across the closet door, Ben. Spiderwebs across the fucking closet door."

They're quiet for another moment. It's as if they're listening for a sound in the house.

"Spiderwebs," she says again. And then she actually laughs, or he thinks it's a laugh. But he realizes quickly that it's closer to crying. She's laugh-crying into her hands.

"I'll make the calls again," he says, getting out of the bed.

"Probably at Claudia's," she says.

At the window, looking out at the empty street, he makes the calls, with the same results. No accidents, no automobile incidents.

He has a moment of understanding his own relief as a measure of the anxiety the whole night has caused. He gets back into the bed and props himself on one elbow, gazing down at her as though this is some new chance. He thinks of happier times, when he would've leaned over to kiss her. "Maybe she'll take the hint when she sees what you did in her room," he says.

"I spoke to Jane Millard this morning, and she wondered why we're letting her stay. Said she was so glad her three adults — that's how she put it, Ben: her three adults — are living elsewhere. Is there something wrong with us?"

"Our one daughter's just gone through a divorce. This isn't permanent."

Rachel snuffles, and says nothing.

"I don't know," he says. "There's something morbid about it all, though, I admit."

"Morbid."

He's silent.

"God, Benjamin. Morbid."

"All right. Macabre? Weird? Do we believe — finally, honey, the thing that worries you so much. Do we believe she feels anything for us? Why is it we think she won't come back if we ask her to get a place of her own. I mean, what is that?"

"That's *reality*," Rachel says. "She's spoiled. And we spoiled her. That's what it looks like and feels like."

He sighs, and receives an image of Angela with the glad smile when they all stood before the *Magdalene.*

"See if you can sleep," his wife says. "You've been up all night."

But sleep won't come. He keeps seeing the lake at Livorno, the streets in Florence, the famous statue with its craggy, appalled countenance. But then he does drift off, and the image dissolves, becomes clouded. Abruptly, he sees his daughter as the brown figure in the cone of light, and comes suddenly awake, heart beating in his ear on the pillow. Looking at the luminary little window of his wristwatch, he's dismayed to find that he's been asleep for only six minutes. And he remains wakeful. Toward dawn, he hears the car, and gets up to look. Angela sits in it for some time, listening to the radio; it's so loud that he hears the drums and bass. He puts a robe on and pads down to the living room. He's standing there when she comes in.

"What're you doing up?" she says.

"Couldn't sleep."

She puts down her purse, removes her coat and drops it on the couch.

"Could you please hang that up?" he says.

She picks it up with a small exhalation, hangs it on a side hook in the coat closet across from the front door, then goes into the kitchen. He sits on the couch, elbows resting on his knees, feeling old, crotchety, oddly slighted. "Want a whiskey or something?" she calls from the kitchen.

"It's morning," he says. In the picture window to his right he sees the reflection of himself sitting in the light from the lamp, with the ghost shapes of the trees outside showing through. He sits back, and sighs, then calls, "I guess you could say it's still night for me, since I haven't been to sleep. Maybe a whiskey."

"Neat, as usual?"

"As usual."

He remembers something that happened when she was in middle school. A fresh September morning, the child she once was prancing downstairs wearing a Scotch plaid skirt and white blouse, so pretty, so much the girl turning into a woman. They stood talking, and he went with her to the door. They shared a few minutes standing out on the porch in the cool, dewy breeze. She talked about her dream of becoming a movie star, and then they were talking about the chess lessons he was giving her, how he was such a poor player and knew so little about it that she wouldn't really learn much. Just the moves and the general ideas of strategy. They lost track of the time, and her school bus pulled up like the sudden intrusion of facts. Racing toward it across the yard, she caught her foot on a jutting tree root in the lawn and went sprawling headlong, her books flying, papers jerking upward and taken by the wind, all of this in plain sight of the others on the bus. She got to her feet with a mortified alacrity that cut him to the heart. He felt as though something had been irrevocably harmed, hurrying out to help her and seeing the horror in her eyes, because he was still in his pajamas, and had only contributed to the general humiliation of the scene. She hurried to pick up the books and flying papers, and he helped anyway, rushed around anyway, chasing the ones still lifting in the breeze, until finally he had to stop and signal the bus driver to go on.

He let her stay home. He canceled an appointment at a construction site, and they spent that whole day watching movies, Angela in the lounge chair with her traumatized dignity, and with her sore knee wrapped in a cold compress, and him sitting on this very sofa where he's presently sitting, as the light of this day begins to stream in the windows. He feels the sting of that other time all over again.

She walks in from the kitchen with the whiskey, hands him his and sits down across from him. They're quiet for a few moments. "I'm beat," she says. "But I had a lot of coffee. So, this should help me sleep."

"Where'd you go?"

She looks at him. "Henry's."

"We got pretty worried."

"I figured you'd call if you were worried."

It occurs to him that she was willing to let them *get* worried enough to call. The thoughtlessness of this glares at him. "I did call, as a matter of cold fact. Over and over."

She reaches into her purse, brings out her phone and looks at it. "Oh, hell. Sorry."

He sips the whiskey. "I also called the police station and the hospitals, darling. Twice."

"Oh, God, so thoughtless, too. I'm sorry. What a clueless jerk. And I wasn't even having that much fun. Can you forgive me?"

"I forgive you." He can feel the whiskey after only two sips.

A moment later, she says, "Anyway, Claudia and I ran into a guy we knew in high school. We went and hung out with him and a couple of his friends. Weird couple getting engaged and all they can talk about is video games. But then, just as we were leaving, guess who called me?"

He sits there rubbing his eyes, waiting.

"Why can't you sleep?"

"Don't know."

A moment passes.

"I will after this whiskey."

"Yeah. Me, too."

"Who called you?"

"Oh," she says, as though it's a trivial thing. "Junior."

Halliford waits.

"Of all people. And he's clean. So he says. And he's in New York."

"He's in the country?"

She nods. "New York. Got in a couple weeks ago."

Halliford can't speak for a moment. He feels suddenly sick to his stomach.

"Says he's clean, too."

"What're you telling me, honey? You're divorced."

She nods. "Weird, huh. We talked a long time."

"What's he doing here?"

"Sobered me right up."

"Angela — what's he doing here?"

"He got sick of being under his father's thumb. That's how he puts it. Strange. I like his father, and he liked me. When it was allowed."

"What's that mean?"

"Carmella didn't like it."

He says nothing for a beat, watching her ruminate. Then, "What's going through your mind right now?"

"Junior and his father."

"That's not your problem now, though, right?"

She sips her whiskey. The increasing light from the window shines in her hair.

"Angela," he says.

She takes a breath. "When I have trouble sleeping, you know, I don't even try."

"Do you have something else to tell me, honey?"

She has a little more of the drink. "I'm the sort of person who hasn't got any patience about not being able to sleep. If I can't sleep, I just get up and get busy."

Evidently, she won't discuss her former husband's presence in the country. And she's developed the habit of speaking about herself in that defining way: *I'm the sort of person.* He has a moment of exasperation at his immediate inclination to search for words with which to discourage it, as if she were still fourteen. Of course, now, there's nothing he can say, because this — this — is who she has become, the sort of person who talks like that. "You get busy doing what?" he manages to say.

She shrugs, looking off.

After another moment of silence in which she seems to lapse into another daydream, he says, "Angela. So you get up when you can't sleep. It's the middle of the night. What do you do?"

She considers. "I don't know. Read." Another moment passes. "Mostly reading, I guess. Watching old movies."

"Is there anything else you want to tell me about Junior?"

"Seemed like still the same guy."

Another moment of contemplation.

Presently, he says, "Any plans today?"

"Sleep, I guess."

"What about tonight?"

"Haven't given it any thought." She puts the empty glass down on the table.

"Could you rinse that and put it away?"

She picks up the glass and takes the last drop from it.

"So, where'd you leave it with Junior?"

"Oh, we just talked. Mostly I listened to him complain about tyrant Daddy."

"What's he doing in New York?"

"Getting away from tyrant Daddy."

"Are you — are you gonna start seeing him or something?"

"Not much chance of that, I guess."

"You guess."

She shrugs, then starts out of the room with the glass. "Night," she says, yawning. "I'm gonna sleep on the sunporch."

"Night," he answers. "Put the whiskey away, too?"

"I might want a little more. But I will."

"I love you," he says.

"I love you more," she answers.

A little later, lying in bed again, with Rachel beginning to stir behind him, he drifts into a dream of an enormous predatory bird swallowing other birds whole in a blue, blue sky. In the dream he thinks of the processes of predation and survival as though they're part of an intellectual concept, a thing arrived at through some exercise of will. There's someone else with him in the dream, a stranger who laughs at the eating bird. Halliford says to this someone, "No, wait a minute, this is serious," and wakes up with a start. Rachel's propped on pillows, reading.

"Nightmare?" she says.

"What time is it?" he asks.

"Almost ten thirty in the morning."

Since his retirement, he has kept to a fairly strict regimen of exercise in the late mornings. But today he lacks the energy, and he's still feeling the whiskey. He reaches for his own book, then decides against that, too.

"Restless," she says. "Me, too."

"Junior's in New York."

She puts her book down on her knees and stares at him.

"They talked on her phone last night." He sits up, then stands up. "For a long time, to use her words."

"Oh, what else is there to say, Benjamin? 'We love you — leave.'"

"But you don't want her going back to that cokehead any more than I do."

"Okay, 'We love you, pay rent.' She can afford to pay rent."

"I don't understand why she'd — " He stops.

"And we have this — party," she says.

He begins to dress. They hear Angela climbing the stairs. They wait, hardly breathing, as if hiding from her, expecting some reaction to the changes in her room. The door closes with its little click, and there's only silence for a few moments, then music.

IV. German Philosophers

He makes the calls and cancels the party. Angela says nothing about it, and she doesn't go out. That evening, as the sun sinks at the windows, she eats the salmon in dill sauce Rachel cooked, and drinks two glasses of amarone, talking about Nicholas of Cusa, learned ignorance, Renaissance humanism and then humanism, as if conducting a seminar. "You can sum it all up about humanism with something Percy Shelley said: the essence of beauty and morality is the ability to look at and appreciate anything other than ourselves." She dabs her mouth with her napkin, sniggers a little and says, "I find it all so totally fascinating. I'm sure I've just bored you both nearly to death."

"Why'd you say that?" Halliford asks. "I always loved Shelley."

"Well, *I'm* bored," Rachel says. "And nearly to death is about right."

"I'm sorry." Angela grins at her. "I guess I'm the type of person who thinks, *If it fascinates me it'll fascinate anybody.*"

Halliford hears himself say, through the quickening at his heart, "Maybe that's because we stopped and listened to you every time you opened your mouth to speak, even in company." He takes a breath. They're both looking at him. "We taught you that. I taught you that. I — we did that to you."

"You mean, you spoiled me."

"Ben," his wife says.

Angela smirks, softly. "I think we've had this conversation, Dad, a couple of dozen times over the years. Haven't we? Some version of it anyway."

"I was trying to apologize," Halliford says.

"What did you make of your room this morning?" Rachel breaks in.

Angela frowns, considering. "Oh, right. What an idiot. God, Mom, I'm sorry. I meant to thank you, really."

"Really," Rachel says. "Well, really, you're welcome."

"Are you planning on doing Thanksgiving with us?" Halliford asks.

"Sure."

"Anybody you want to invite? Like Claudia?"

"She's got her family."

He opens another bottle of the amarone and pours a glass for himself, thinking of its usually tranquilizing effects. The two other bottles on the counter look like the essence of promise. "Anybody want another glass?" he says, as if more than two people are sitting there.

"I'm done," Angela says.

"Maybe you'll invite Junior to Thanksgiving," says Rachel.

Angela turns to her father. "You told her."

"Of course he did," Rachel says. "Why wouldn't he?"

"Was it a secret?" Halliford asks.

Angela simpers. "Well, Mom — as a matter of fact, no, I haven't talked to him today. He's left the family business, though. And it looks like he'll stay in New York."

"And you?"

"And me what?"

Rachel throws her napkin down and rises from her seat. "Perhaps someone else will clean this up." She strides into the living room. Halliford remains where he is, sipping the wine he poured, and waiting for his daughter to say something. She wipes her hands, takes a last sip of water, then goes back upstairs, leaving her plate with its smears from dinner, her empty wineglass and her silverware. It's as if she wanted to make a point of it. He quietly cleans the mess, loads the dishwasher and wipes the counters. The house is unnaturally quiet. He pours another glass of the wine and drinks it alone, not really tasting it, sitting at the freshly wiped kitchen table. When Angela leaves, perhaps twenty minutes later, calling, "Gonna meet Claudia again at Henry's," he assumes it will again be for the night, and he doesn't think of waiting up. Tomorrow, Sunday, he'll go out and buy the turkey, the potatoes and the vegetables for Thanksgiving, only four days away. He and Rachel talk a little about that, quietly planning the dinner for three people, and as they go on talking, he's aware that they're avoiding the subject of Angela and Junior.

Monday morning, he prepares eggs Benedict for Rachel, and opens a bottle of prosecco for mimosas. She makes toast and coffee, and the two of them carry their breakfast out to the Hawaii gazebo. The weather's perfect: flowery soft breezes. The tumult of the interstate beyond the neighborhood seems less. A lovely cloudless morning, and as they're enjoying the quiet, Angela comes downstairs in her bathrobe, walks lazily to them from the back door, carrying her cup of coffee. She sits on the edge of the shaded step-up into the gazebo, leans back on one hand, sighs and says, "I talked to Junior most of the night. Almost the whole time about Heidegger. Imagine. He's reading Heidegger, and wanted to talk to me about it. All excited. You guys know Heidegger?"

Halliford raises his hand, as if in school. "A little, yes, ma'am."

"I bet he's an existentialist," Rachel says with a leering little smile. "Right?"

Angela hasn't noticed. "Isn't 'thrownness-into-being' the best and truest expression of what it feels like to be alive? You're here but you can't really say how you *got* here beyond the biological facts."

"I think I know how I got here," Rachel says.

"I prefer Schopenhauer," Benjamin Halliford gets out.

Angela smiles, excited. "Happiness is negative."

He pauses, attending to the agitation he sees in Rachel.

"We talked about Schopenhauer too," says Angela. "Junior's always been big on him. And Nietzsche."

"Oh, well, Christ. Of *course* Nietzsche." Rachel's tone is pure ridicule, which her daughter, somehow, also fails to notice — or perhaps has decided to ignore.

"Anyway," Angela says, "he's getting on a plane about now and he'll be here by four thirty this afternoon."

"Nietzsche?" Rachel says, still being withering.

"Mother." Angela laughs as if at a casual flippancy. "Don't be silly. I'm serious."

Halliford and his wife simply stare at her.

"They've disowned him. And he's clean. He's like before."

More stillness.

"He's free."

"What the hell," Halliford hears himself say.

"Think of it," Angela goes on in a rush. "The family can't touch us now. I've got the money they paid in the divorce settlement and now they've disinherited *him*. He's cut off. So, the settlement's all our free money. Almost a million."

"But wait," Halliford manages. "You're — they gave you that much?"

"Carmella thought I was bad for him — not producing bambinos or learning the language."

The Hallifords say nothing.

"It's perfect. We'll camp here a little while until we decide on a house, either here or in New York. He's clean now."

"Angela," Benjamin Halliford says.

Her eyes narrow slightly. "What."

He searches his mind for something to say.

"There's a place I've looked at for myself over on Walnut Grove. Maybe we can take that. We'd be close anyway."

"When did all this get decided?" Rachel asks, very softly.

"I couldn't sleep," Angela explains as if it's something anyone would suppose. "So, I called him. We talked a couple hours at least. He's got some money, too, that he took when they kicked him out. He's not doing the drugs anymore and he's pretty much quit the alcohol, too."

"He — he took — " Halliford sputters.

"It's his. It was in some trust or something."

"Angela."

"We'll only stay until we can settle on a house."

"He can't stay here," Rachel says. It sounds almost like a question.

"It'll only be for a while. Really. I'll pay for whatever we eat or drink, you don't have to worry. Most of the time we'll spend in my birthright."

"I'm not picking up after him."

"No. Of course not." Angela seems surprised.

"And I'm through picking up after *you*," says her mother.

After a brief pause, Angela says, "I know I'm a complete slob. I'm so sorry."

"Sorry only counts if you *do* something about it."

"I — of course I — "

"And you'll have to pay for him here," Rachel goes on. "That, too. I'm not doing the cleaning and cooking and all the rest of it for this — this person whose own family — "

"Of course, I'll pay for him. How much do you want? Let's agree on a figure."

"Rachel," Halliford says.

But his wife has already begun to speak. "Let's say four hundred fifty a day."

Angela looks at her.

Shrugging slightly, Rachel adds, "S'what he'd pay for a hotel room."

"Well, maybe we'll just go to a hotel."

"What a good idea."

"Wait," Halliford says. "Let's not start fighting over Junior again. Come on."

"We won't stay more than a week," Angela says. "Do you want me to write you a check? Fill out a contract?"

"Come on," Benjamin Halliford says.

But his wife speaks over him. "Cash," she says, "In advance." And she walks back to the house and in.

"You have to understand," Halliford says low to his daughter.

"I thought you'd both be happy for me."

He watches her walk away from him.

While she's gone to the airport, he helps Rachel go over the house, making it as right as possible for company. Rachel remains silent, brooding, moving in a controlled, tight-lipped fury. When they're finished, she opens one of the bottles of Margaux, and pours a big glass. "We don't even like him," she says, offering it to him.

"I liked the way he carried himself when we were in Florence. Maybe we can come to some sort of understanding."

Rachel takes a drink of the wine. "I think I'm gonna be in bed with a headache. All day. Starting about now."

V. Saharas

Halliford can't believe the change in Junior since that visit to Florence. The man looks strangely flaccid; there's a doughy texture to the flesh around his thick jaw and slack chin. The whole appearance is rounder somehow, and his dark eyes look like little buttons, too small for the face. He sits next to Angela on the sofa, upper ankles showing between gray slacks and black socks, cradling a glass of pomegranate juice over his rounded stomach, talking about starting up as an agent in the music business. "And, as you know, Memphis is the place for that."

Angela seems completely at ease. Yet her father thinks he sees something of the strain this is. Her features have a kind of uneasy, postulating, wide-eyed aspect, and once more Donatello's statue comes to mind. "You know," he can't help but say to her, "when we came to visit that time — "

But Rachel breaks in, addressing Junior: "So you're planning on living here. In the States."

"Well, yes. My green card's good for another two years."

"Never seeing your family again."

He seems momentarily at a loss. Then: "I don't think they'll — it's not like they won't ever speak to me again. It's not like the church."

"The church," Rachel says.

"He's not excommunicated," Angela puts in.

Rachel says, "Did Angela inform you of the conditions for your staying here?"

"Yes, ma'am."

"Oh, you needn't 'ma'am' me."

"I'll make sure we get everything right," Angela says, turning to Junior. "Right?"

Halliford looks away, having seen something else in her gaze, this time far from the Donatello — a wistful, loving expression you might see in a puppy's eyes.

A little later, the two of them go off together in the Camry, and in an hour they return, Angela in the Camry and Junior in a red Mazda MX-5 convertible. They pull into the driveway honking both horns, wanting to show off the new car. Angela excitedly talks about how Junior bought it for her, and paid cash for it. She desires to take each of them for a ride in it. Rachel demurs, holding her hands to the sides of her head, claiming her headache. Halliford gets into the front seat, hoping to speak to Angela alone, but instead of Angela, Junior gets in behind the wheel. Angela stays back with her mother. The car's engine roars, and Junior guns it to the end of the block, then speeds to the entrance onto Sam Cooper Boulevard, where he really opens it up. For all the warmth of this late November, the rushing air stings.

"Zero to sixty in less than ten seconds!" Junior yells.

Halliford yells back, "Too fast, man."

His former son-in-law shifts down.

"They patrol this road a lot, son."

Junior shifts up again, but keeps the car at sixty. "Smooth, right?"

Halliford simply nods, looking over.

"You want to drive it?"

"No, thanks."

Junior swerves suddenly to exit onto North Graham Street. He pulls over and comes to a chugging stop, shifting down. "Come on, man. Be fun," he says.

Halliford, his forehead prickling from the suddenness of being out of the chilly rush of air, says, "I'm fine."

"Come on," says Junior, "you won't believe how good it feels."

"Let's just go back," Halliford says. "Okay? Christ."

"If you say so."

They get back on Sam Cooper, headed the other way. Again, Junior speeds, the engine roaring. There is one other car on the road, and they go by it as though it's parked.

At the house, Angela stands with arms folded on the top step of the porch, leaning on the post. "How do you like my new car?" she says as they approach.

"Fine," Halliford manages. "It's fast."

"And sporty," Junior says. "It'll take years off your age."

"Mom's got another migraine," she says. "Went up to try and nap a little."

They go into the house, and almost immediately she and Junior go up to her room. Music starts. Drums, horns. Something from the swing era. Halliford finds his wife lying on their bed, one arm across her face. Without moving, Rachel says, "Oh, God."

Thanksgiving Day is very quiet. Angela insists on letting Junior cook lasagna, and Rachel lets him do it. Halliford puts the turkey in the freezer, and spends the afternoon watching football, which he has to explain to Junior when the younger man comes in to relax, waiting for Angela to finish making the homemade pasta, her part of the project. He's already prepared the sauce, mixed the ricotta and shredded mozzarella and fontina; he's seasoned and seared the ground beef. She'll mix the vegetables. Rachel spends most of the afternoon in their bedroom, napping.

The meal itself is unremarkable. And so is the lasagna. Junior talks about how soupy it is, and apologizes. "Too much ricotta," he says.

"It's delicious," Halliford manages.

Angela begins talking about the new fascism, and Junior interrupts her with a finality. "I do not wish to talk about politics, darling. Politics and religion are the two subjects we always avoid. Let's talk about something else. Anything else."

"You just sounded exactly like your father," she says.

"Well. Anyway, no politics, please."

Halliford has a moment of believing he's witnessing a hint of how things must have been in Italy. He looks across at Angela, and says, "Do they call it the new fascism in Tuscany?"

She glances at Junior, shakes her head and pours more wine.

Halliford says, "You don't mind a little talk about our present mess, do you, Junior." It was a statement.

"I'm sorry about the lasagna," Junior says, and sips his wine.

"I agree about politics and religion," Rachel says suddenly, surprisingly, to Junior. "I don't want to talk about any of it. It's all bull, as far as I'm concerned. But I wonder how your parents are doing."

"Moth*er,*" Angela says.

"Oh, they never change," Junior says. "Nothing ever seems to affect them, really. They're like a — a trackless expanse inside, empty, with random winds." He smirks, pleased with his figure of speech. "A vast interior desert, you know? Nothing ever really gets to them because there's so much money. I mean so very much of it."

"Millions," Angela says.

He glances at her. "Thousands of those, sweetheart. Thousands of millions."

"Thousands?" Halliford says.

"*Billions.* So I don't worry about them, and they've given up worrying about me."

Rachel looks over at Angela. "Do you feel like that about us?" And suddenly begins to cry.

"Hey." Angela gets up and moves to her mother's side, bending to put her arms around her. "Of course not. Gosh, Mom."

"Rachel," Halliford says.

"I'm sorry, Mom."

"It's all right," Rachel says. "I'm sorry. I still have this migraine."

Angela steps slowly back to her seat. "I hate those. I haven't had one in a while."

"Well," Halliford manages. "Let's talk about what we have to be thankful for."

"I'm thankful not to be a trackless desert inside," Angela says.

"Oh, I meant no disrespect at all about Gino and Carmella," says Junior. "I think they might describe themselves in a way that would make you think in those terms. They like big spaces between other people and themselves." He gives a small, sighing laugh. "They've always had a special bond no one can break through, you know. They don't want to let anyone in because they're so happy where they are, the two of them. And they'd love my talking about trackless expanses, endless dunes. They'd tell you themselves that nothing reaches where they really are together. Sometimes I think they can read each other's minds. It's uncanny. It's love, too. And some kinds of love will shut you out as quick as paranoia."

For a moment, they're all silent.

"I was just stating a fact. Like describing weather."

"I'm thankful for closure," says Angela. "My happy closure with the new surprise."

Junior turns to her. "That's an odd thing to say."

She smiles at her father.

"I'm just — thankful to have my family here," Halliford manages.

Rachel begins to cry again, excusing herself. "I'd be so thankful if the dishes were done."

Angela stands and begins to clear the table. Junior helps her.

Black Friday, Angela and Junior drive off in the red Mazda, and come back within the hour. She's bought a briefcase, and the briefcase, it turns out, is full of cash. She comes downstairs and cheerfully hands Rachel thirty-one crisp hundreds, and one fifty-dollar bill.

Rachel stares, astonished.

"That's the correct amount, for the week, right?" Angela says.

"You're staying a week?"

"Is that okay?"

"All right." Rachel folds the bills. "But I hope you understand this is not a salary."

"What're you talking about?"

"It's pretty clear, isn't it? This does not amount to a salary."

"You want a salary?"

"No — *listen* to me, Angela. It's rent. Okay? Not a salary. I won't be your employee for this or for any amount of money."

"Oh, okay. I never thought otherwise. Jeez."

"It's for the room. And for the food you'll consume here."

"I get it, Mom."

"And there's no laundry or cleaning service."

"Not even clean sheets? We'd at least get that in a hotel."

Rachel shouts, beginning to cry, "Then go to a hotel, why don't you."

"Hey," Angela says. "I'm just kidding. I understand the arrangement." She leans a little to kiss her mother's cheek, and then turns and goes upstairs.

The young couple spends most of each day that week in her room. Halliford and his wife hear laughter, and music playing and then long silences that become more disconcerting the longer they last. "I'm not a prude," Rachel says. "But Christ. It's just — intolerable."

They lie awake in the nights and hear the loud talk back and forth, and more laughter, without quite being able to distinguish words. In the late afternoon or early evening Angela and Junior go out in the little red Mazda, with the top up, because the weather's turned cold. Twice they've come back with supplies, food for the house, more bottles of expensive wine, and also Armagnac and whiskey. Angela explains that they've had dinner at Andrew Michael, or Tsunami or Iris. They've bought cheeses and cartons of milk and fresh vegetables, the best cuts of meat. Junior loves lamb. Angela says she'll make her lamb chops with pomegranate reduction for him. It's as if they've all planned an evening. But very quickly they find reasons to retire to Angela's room, and the meat goes into the freezer, where it remains. Several nights they're out late, to concerts, or schmoozing on Beale Street in the cafés, "looking," Junior says, "for connections." But the nights are getting too chilly for the outside life on Beale.

Afternoons when they bother to go anywhere, Rachel goes into Angela's room. Halliford can't bring himself to do so.

"You should see it," she says, coming downstairs, wiping her eyes with the palms of her hands. "It smells like booze. Cigarettes and booze. I can't stand another day of this."

But the days go on.

They're both in a kind of daze, waiting to see what will happen. Angela seems to have forgotten them. They have no evenings of talk or games or movies. The ex-marrieds, as Rachel calls them now, come and go — from Angela's room to the city center and back. Halliford thinks of it as a kind of desperate stab at her former life. He remarks an aspect of amazement in her features, but can't bring himself to speak. He supposes something of amazement must show in his own. At his computer, he looks up the *Magdalene*. There it is: that strangely quizzical, almost stunned expression.

He and Rachel spend their evenings much as they did when Angela lived in Tuscany. They eat alone. Then they watch a movie or sit reading, and finally they go up to bed together or separately. Neither is in the mood for socializing, and Halliford comes to see how their lives all along have been tending to this: how rarely they ever saw anyone, especially in this retirement that is now a kind of prison. Sometimes, in the middle of the night, he hears the couple's arrival, the carefree hilarity — the stumbling ex-marrieds, and the laughter, and then the door to the room opening and closing, sounds of water running in the upstairs bathroom, the mingling of the two voices, excited, talking over each other, through music; it's quite clear they're getting drunk most nights.

This morning, Junior sleeps later than Angela. She comes downstairs smelling of booze and cigarettes. The smell of the cigarettes is all over and around her. The whole house has begun to reek of it. "God," she says. "I'm a mess."

Benjamin Halliford's at the table in the window seat. He's been up all night. "Honey," he says. "What's the plan, now?"

"I'm gonna make some coffee and go back up to bed. But here." She brings cash out of the pocket of her robe.

He looks at it.

She waves it slightly as if trying to decide what to do with it, and then, with a shrug, drops it on the table.

"Have either of you heard from his family?" he asks.

"Not a thing. They really are kaput. He's changed his cell number. Which I think is a *little* strange." Her tone is half-teasing.

"Any luck with the music agent idea?"

She seems puzzled. "The what?"

"Can we talk?"

"Later," she says. "I'm too bleary-eyed and headachy from lack of sleep."

He stands. "No. We need to talk, Angela. Jesus Christ, kid. This has to stop. We can't keep this up."

She looks askance at him. And then indicates the money. "There's next week's payment. Just one more week."

"I can't believe you'd do this, honey. The whole house smells like an ashtray."

"Oh, I'm sorry. Well — we'll stop smoking in the house. We'll go out on the porch."

"I don't mean — that's — I mean how can you keep doing *this*?" He indicates the robe she's wearing, and then makes a waving motion toward the upstairs.

"Doing what? We're looking for a place." She indicates the little wedge of folded bills on the table. "And there's the rent."

"Are you going to get married again?"

Her eyes narrow. "Is *that* what this is?"

"Aw, Jesus," he says. "Baby. I'm just trying to figure all this out."

"Oh, but please," she says. "Not now, Dad. Please. I've got such a headache."

"I can't believe you," he says. "Think of your mother."

"What does *that* mean? Doesn't she want me to be happy?"

"You're not hearing me."

"Oh, can we just please, please talk later? There's the money. Just like she asked for it. There isn't anything else to say right now. Okay? No smoking except out on the porch." She turns and leaves him standing there.

VI. Donnaiolo

The Friday before Christmas, early in the afternoon, Gino Venza Sr. calls. Halliford has been nodding off in the lounge chair to a movie on TCM, the sound turned low because Rachel's asleep on the sofa across the room, a news magazine open on her chest. Angela and Junior are out in the Mazda, ostensibly shopping for gifts. Benjamin Halliford is so surprised to hear the voice on the other end that he can scarcely muster the phrases of polite greeting. "Everyone is there?" Junior's father asks.

"Well, yes." Halliford switches off the TV.

"Are the children there?"

"Children."

"Yes, *signore*. Are the children there?"

"I'm afraid I — "

The other man interrupts. "It comes to my attention through his New York friends that the children are staying with you."

"You mean Angela and — "

"Yes. *Oh, cazzo! I giovani!* The younger ones."

"It's a temporary arrangement," Halliford manages.

"Temporary arrangement. *Cosa è* — what is that? How so?"

"It's not permanent."

"Will you please put my son on the line."

"He's not here just now."

"Ah. He will not talk."

"No, he's out. Not here. He and Angela went Christmas shopping."

"I will seek justice in law of your land. *Je suis furieux.* Awp. Forgive me. I am so upset I lose my English. *Mio figlio. Ce cochon.* Pig, my son is. I will make him return. I find a way to do it in your law. I have resources. God*damn* I can't talk this. Speak this. He runs away."

Halliford resists the impulse to say *calm down.* "I'll have him call you, sir."

"Are you in this? There are — we have *leggi sull'estradizione.*"

He looks for words. "I don't know anything about the money."

"Money!"

"I don't even know what the settlement was with Angela."

"Money. What do you talk about money? *Cazzo. Fuck.* What money?"

Halliford says, "Can you tell me what this is about, sir."

Rachel sits up on the sofa and looks at him. He puts the cell on speaker and holds it out from his head.

"Estradizione," Venza Sr. says. *"Leggi* — *estra* — extradition. Laws, *signore.*"

"I don't understand," Halliford says. "You'll have to talk to him."

"I will bring him back to face this."

"I'll tell him to call you as soon as he gets here, sir."

"You do not want me as an enemy, Signore Halliford."

"Well, just a minute, now — look. You need to talk to your son. This has nothing to do with me. My daughter has taken him in here and she's paying for it."

"She pays for the pig. He uses her."

"He's your son, sir. Christ."

"C'est un — Agh! *È un fottuto maiale* — a fucking pig. A rotter. He is a stink!"

"Sir, if you could — "

"He cannot be with your Angela. Angela would not do this."

"Do what, sir?"

"She is not his. She has left him. They cannot be — she would not be so bad like he is. Not evil like that."

"Will you please tell me what this is?" Halliford says. "I have no idea what you're talking about. If it's not the money — "

"Angela must not take him back. *La sta usando.* He uses her."

"You'll have to talk to her about that, sir. Or them."

There follows a long, breathing silence. Halliford hears crying in the background on the other end. Carmella? He wants to ask. But the other man begins to talk again. "*Ha un problema serio.* A serious trouble. This will not go away."

"Maybe you can call back," Halliford says, then adds, "Gino," using the name out of a rising, nerve-pulsing sense of disaster, as if, sitting here in his own living room, he's actually hurtling through space toward some sudden stop. A wall. He takes a breath. "Why don't you call back, sir," he says.

"I must speak to Junior," Venza goes on. "I must — I explain to you. You must — a girl. *Una ragazza.* A girl. I have sorrow for the badness. A little girl — *minorenni.* Forgive me. *Con bambino.* You understand? *Da lui.* From him. With child. Forgive me, my upset makes me stupid in the language. *Parlare* — to — to speak. With child, *signore.* This girl. A *minorenni.* Minor. He runs away."

Halliford stands up, now looking at the cell as if speaking into Venza's face. "Let me understand this. You're saying a girl — someone *there,* is pregnant — by your son?"

"*Minorenni, si.* A minor girl. *Quindici fottuti anni.* Rosetta. Fifteen fucking years old."

He looks at Rachel, who has gone white. She gets up and moves quickly to his side. She stands very close, hands clasped tight at her waist. "I'm so sorry," he says into the phone. "I can't — I don't know what to tell you."

"*È un fottuto donnaiolo!*" Junior's father shouts. "*Dannazione!* Goddamn! Fucking womanizer. Now *questo bambino.* This girl, fifteen. *Bussare!* Knocked up. Fifteen fucking years old!"

Halliford says, quietly, "I wish there was something — " He's unable to utter another sound. He waits, nearly sobs.

They hear Venza draw a long breath, sigh deeply and struggle to master himself. "I seek — extradition. *Coupable. È colpevole.* Guilty. You do get me, Angela's father. Angela does not get pregnant. But this — you understand. He breaks the law. *Hanno il DNA. Prova.* Proof."

"I'll tell him to call you — what time is it there. I could — "

Rachel interrupts. "Mr. Venza, this is Angela's mother. Do you want us to tell him about this girl, Rosetta?"

Another sigh. "He knows of her. *Lui corre.* He runs. *Fugge.* Es — escape. He flees. You must tell him there will be extradition."

"We'll tell him to call you," Halliford says.

"You do not let him stay with you in your house now. Not good for your Angela."

"No," Rachel says. "No, we won't."

"I am so sorry to be unpleasant."

"No apology necessary," Halliford manages to say, and hears the connection being broken.

Rachel begins to cry, heading toward the bathroom off the front hall. He can't move for a moment, alone there in the blinding sunlight from the picture window.

The ex-marrieds get in well after midnight. The long day has been spent trying to call Angela, trying to get through somehow. Neither of them can sit still. Rachel talks for a long time to Jane Millard, who suggests talking to the police. So she does that. But it's hard to explain it all to the dispatcher, hard even to decide who she should talk to. So she gives up. She sits on the sofa and cries, and he tries to console her. Neither of them has any appetite. Finally dark comes to the windows. Rachel, looking older than her years, eats two slices of toast and drinks a whiskey, and then wanders slowly, as if trying to find her way in her own house, up the stairs to bed. "Wake me up when they get in."

"Are you sure?"

"I think I should talk to the police."

"Apparently, Venza's already done that over there."

"Wake me."

"You can sleep?"

No answer.

But when the roar of the Mazda sounds on the street, she calls from the top of the stairs. "Don't say anything, Ben. Let me."

So he waits. She hurries down and reaches the foyer just as they come bursting in, laughing about something, both surrounded by the mingled odors of the cold night and the alcohol they've had.

"Oh, God," Angela says to her mother. "Did we make too much noise?" She can't suppress a laugh.

"Sorry," Junior gets out, laughing.

Halliford closes the door behind them, and, with Rachel, follows them into the living room. Angela flops down on the sofa, and Junior kneels at her side and then sits back on the floor.

"There's something we have to talk about," Halliford says.

"Oooh," Angela says. "This sounds serious."

Rachel stands close to him and squeezes his arm. "Not tonight," she tells him. "In the morning."

Angela sits up, pulls off her scarf and hat. Junior has lain back, hands clasped over his chest, feigning sleep or actually having gone to sleep. "Y'kick'n us out," Angela says.

"No," says Rachel. "Go to bed. We'll talk in the morning."

"What is't?" Angela tries to stand.

"Not when you're like this. Go on to bed. Get him up and go to bed. It'll keep till tomorrow."

"You c'n raise th' rent," Junior says, from the floor.

Halliford hears himself say, "You're gonna have to go back home, boy."

"Y'kick'n us out?" Angela says.

"Not now!" Rachel's voice is shrill, and for a second the room is deathly silent. Then she pulls at her husband's sleeve. "In the morning."

"Call your father," Halliford says.

"M'father."

"When you wake up."

"M'father called here?" He seems suddenly serious.

"He wants to talk to you. Probably be a good idea to sober up first."

"I don' have thing say to'im. An' 'e's got nothin' say t'me. We're *estraniato,* in th'genel'mun's lex'con. Don' list'n to'im."

"Well, he's got a few things to say to *you,* now," Halliford says.

Rachel pulls at his sleeve. "Ben."

"Can' b'lieve he bother you," Junior says. "Can' trus' thing he says. Th'money I took's mine."

"No," Halliford says, through the rising pressure in his chest, just managing enough air to say it. "That isn't what he has to say to you at all."

Junior waves one hand; it looks like a greeting. "'E's crazy. Pare'noid desert. Mak'n things up. Oh, well. Heard all thousan' times. *Donnaiolo, donnaiolo.* Brok'n record. 'S'all bullshit."

"You've — " Halliford stops.

Rachel has grabbed his arm and squeezed. "Not *now.* We'll talk about it in the morning. Now I mean it." She turns to Angela. "You're both drunk. Go to bed. We'll talk tomorrow."

"We're paid up f'this week," Angela says to her.

Rachel sobs, suddenly, and Halliford puts his arm around her, leading her to the stairwell. He looks back at his daughter, who's standing there with her ex-husband lying on his back again, at her feet. "I can't believe you," he says to her. "I don't even recognize you."

Angela says nothing.

"Tell him he needs to talk to his father."

"Did someone die?" she asks, sounding sober now.

"No."

"Go to sleep," Rachel says, crying. "Everyone, please."

The night feels endless. There seem to be more alarms than usual out in the dark, some other catastrophe playing itself out in the city's streets. Halliford imagines he hears an argument in the other room, a low muttering, quick and intermittent. He walks out into the hall, clears his throat, steps into the bathroom, runs water and takes a drink. Back in the hall, he believes he hears her in the other room, sobbing and then cursing. But he can't be certain. It could be something else. Could even be laughter. He stops and listens. It is laughter. Drunken giggling, and it goes on, becoming slightly louder, and it's clear that both of them are trying to stifle it in themselves, growing more hysterical with the effort. Then he hears Rachel give forth a sound of distress in the bedroom where their daughter was born. He hurries to her.

"I've never been filled with so much hatred," she murmurs. "I wish I could stop it."

He holds her, murmuring, "My darling," meaning it more, it seems, in this new circumstance, than he ever has. They lie there hearing the sounds from the room down the hall. The sounds slowly diminish, and finally there's only the small creaking of the house, and the stirrings of the wind at the windows, a storm coming up, thunder in the far distance. He's exhausted. She's quite still, but her sighing tells him she's awake. He remembers the hurrying last few years of just the two of them, drawing away from people, their daughter far off, the days blurring, and how he felt content with it all; they were fortunate because they enjoyed each other. Yet, thinking about it now, here in the dark, it all looks like a long loneliness. He thinks of Junior's remark about his parents' trackless expanses, which end up shutting others out. She murmurs at his side, one breathed word. "Awful." It's as though she has been thinking these things with him. He reaches over and pats her shoulder, sighs, lying back. And the sudden realization comes to him that seeing Angela's features in the face of the *Magdalene* might actually have been a kind of inkling, as if the world itself had broken through his self-absorption, forcing him to see her life apart from his own. That the thing he had resisted all the time was the one necessary and rightful thing: To bring his daughter to the point of no longer needing him. Them. Him and Rachel. And even though his objections to Junior at the beginning have been borne out, they still comprise aspects of that crucial failure; they certainly contributed to the tensions that followed. And all of it seems bound up in this new desolation. He turns in the bed, breathes and again feels the pressure in his chest, the pure stress of the hours to come. The thunderstorm breaks over the house, and is loud and full of lightning flashes, and then slowly moves off, like a memory of the world's possible calamities. Toward dawn, he hears movement in the hallway, and then a rushing. He gets out of the bed, and realizes that he's been asleep, and that Rachel's not there.

He finds her with the other two down in the kitchen. Rachel is in the gray light of the window seat with Angela sitting next to her, hands to each side of her face, hungover, sleep in her eyes. Her former husband is leaning against the counter. There's coffee on the table. Rachel, seeing Halliford notice it, says, "I only made the coffee."

"No, thanks," he manages.

"Before anyone was up," she says. "They just came down."

"Dad?" Angela says, and then stops.

He says, "Honey." And can't speak for a second. He looks at Junior. "Have you talked to your father?"

"No."

"I waited for *you*," Rachel says.

"What *is* it, Dad?" Angela demands.

He concentrates on Junior. "Does the name Rosetta mean anything to you, son?"

Junior's face whitens, but he says nothing, standing there as if waiting for further explanation.

"Will you please tell us," Angela says.

"Rosetta lives in Tuscany, and she's expecting," Rachel says, flatly. "She's fifteen."

Junior shifts his weight slightly, but says nothing. Shows nothing.

"Fifteen years old," Rachel says.

"Dad?" Angela says.

"Junior needs to call his father," says Halliford.

"This is ridiculous," Junior says. "I told you. He's all bullshit."

"He said you're using Angela. And us. You're supposed to be under arrest."

Angela stands, and moves to face him. He's quite still. For an instant, somehow, accusation and admission pass between them without the slightest change of expression. Then she walks out of the room. They hear her on the stairs.

Junior remains very still, seeming almost poised, then faintly tensed, as though expecting something to come at him. He looks first at Rachel, and then at Halliford.

"You better call your father," Halliford says to him. "Right quick."

There's a long, increasingly painful silence.

"He's already set things in motion. You better call him."

"Motion."

"That's right."

"I don't have to do anything, here."

"I think you do. He's talking about extradition, son."

"Don't you dare call him that." Rachel rises suddenly. "Don't call him *son*."

"I'll go back to New York," Junior says, almost placidly.

"I'm pretty sure your father has the means to compel you," Halliford tells him. "You're in a whole lot of trouble, boy."

"Boy," Rachel says, sneering. "Boy."

"No matter what you think you can do, you can't stay here," Halliford says.

"A felony in your country," Rachel says, "is a felony in this one, too." Then she spits the phrase: "Statutory rape. I talked to the police yesterday and I'll be talking to them again today."

Junior turns and starts out of the room, but he's met by Angela, who has lugged his duffel bag down, and thrusts it at him. "All packed," she says. "Sorry the shirts aren't folded, and I'm keeping the books."

"Can we talk?" he says to her.

"What was she," Angela says, "fourteen when you met her?"

He looks down.

"Go."

"I don't even get to explain."

Angela doesn't answer. She stands waiting for him to come past her.

"I won't go back to Italy," he says. "There's nothing he can do."

"Just don't ever come back *here*," she says, low. "I should've *known*."

"I'm taking the car," he says. "I paid for it."

"Take it." She walks toward the stairs. "You think I care about it? Go! Just go! Now! I don't ever want to see you again."

He hesitates. "Is this what you really want?"

Without stopping or turning to look back at him, she shouts, "Get *out!*" She goes on back upstairs, holding on to the handrail, crying.

Junior hesitates again, then steps out the door, closing it quietly behind him.

Rachel goes to the window in the living room, and Halliford joins her there. Outside in the grayness, the lowering sky, Junior throws the duffel bag into the passenger seat of the little red Mazda. It seems impossible that the bag is all he brought with him. He walks around, gets into the car and starts it, and guns the engine, running it loud, for what seems too long a time. At length, he backs out, and pulls off in a white trail of exhaust and noise.

Rachel sits down on the sofa, as if lacking the strength to keep standing. He sits too, and takes her hands.

A moment later, Angela comes back down and into the kitchen. They hear her moving around in there. She comes out with a bottle of the amarone, and three glasses, held by their stems.

"I want to celebrate," she says in a shivering little, quick voice. She sets the glasses down. They watch her open the wine, and pour. Her hands shake; some of the wine spills. Halliford holds on, saying nothing. She sits across from them in the lounge chair. "Here's to money," she says.

"Angela," he begins, but his breath is gone.

She holds up one hand. "Come on. I mean it."

"We're so sorry," Rachel tells her. But there's no emotion in her voice. It sounds nearly involuntary.

"Nothing to be sorry about." Angela drinks the wine, staring beyond them out the window. "Everything's fine. The sun's coming out. See? Just fine." Her eyes well up. "I thought love — " She stops.

"Well, I'm a bit hungover. What's hilarious is the money never meant anything to me. It was never about the money."

Halliford can't look at her. He brings one hand up to his own eyes, presses them with thumb and index finger, then looks again. There she is, his girl, his only, grieving, hurt. "We love you," he manages to say.

Rachel says, "You're lucky to be rid of him."

Angela says, "Love you both." She gets up and moves to the stairs. "I'll try and take a little nap now," she says, low, then sobs, and goes quickly up and out of sight. They hear her door close.

"Did you see the look on her face?" Rachel says. There's little emotion in her voice. She seems almost calm.

"I saw."

"And him when you said that girl's name. Oh, I never hated anyone or anything so much. What did our girl — our poor girl — ever see in him."

He starts toward the kitchen, and hearing the sobs coming from the room upstairs, he hesitates.

Behind him, his wife says, "Thank God they didn't have time to get remarried."

"Should you go up to her? Or me?"

"Give her a little time." Rachel rises and comes to him. The two of them go on into the kitchen, and she sits while he starts heating the coffee. It's all like a heart continuing to beat in the pain of hours. He turns, holds on to the counter, gazing at her. It strikes through him again that this is all part of the one circumstance. That the thousands of physical miles of distance are nothing, and the loss is more than the end of a journey and years in beautiful Italy with a stranger. How awful, if his daughter's decision to leave the marriage and return here was only the beginning of her disaster. And the money blinded him to it, to its effect on his bright girl's spirit. Now, no matter what's happened before, there's all the suffering to come. The end of love, again, the grieving and the humiliation. Again.

"It was always gonna happen." Rachel's voice is still flat, like that of someone making an observation about the day's news. "I expected it. I heard what his mother said."

He's amazed at her composure. And he can think of nothing at all to say. He sits down across from her. The house seems too quiet. "Remember that day she fell in the yard right outside that window in the living room, and I let her stay home from school?"

Rachel gazes at the tabletop, and is silent.

"I remember thinking *that* was a terrible thing. She was humiliated and hurt and I'd only made it worse, lumbering around in full view of everybody in my pajamas. The very next day, she had to limp over and get on that school bus with everyone looking at her. I watched it from the door. I hid and watched it. I felt so bad for her, Rachel. And there was absolutely nothing in this world I could do. And that — that was so small compared to this. And I didn't know *then* how we would ever — " His voice breaks.

She sobs suddenly, and covers her mouth. She looks terrified.

"Oh," he says. "Lord. It's okay." He reaches across to take her hands again. So she has been holding it all in. His poor darling.

She gently pulls her hands away, and folds her arms tight, as if having caught a chill. "You keep dwelling on things lately. You have to stop going over everything."

They're quiet for a time. Two people sitting in the kitchen of a nice house, while a clear morning warms to a springlike day, crows calling in the bands of sun and shade outside the window. She pulls a napkin from the ceramic holder on the table, and starts daubing her eyes, sniffing. Finally, he says, "What happens now?"

She shakes her head.

"We can't ask her to move after this."

"Don't," she says. "We — " She stops, exhales, touching the napkin to her eyes.

He waits, heartsick, watching the tears drop down her cheeks.

"Agh. I don't know," she says. "Maybe we could travel?"

"What?"

"The three of us," she says.

That night, he lies awake, thinking about what they might do together. There isn't any reason they can't accompany each other. A family trip. He conjures possibilities, Costa Rica, England, the Far East. He drifts, and, in a dream, returns to Florence. The ancient city shines like an idea of itself, brighter than he can believe. He and his wife and daughter walk again around the high rim of the Duomo. They're alone. This fact worries him, nags at him. The world below brandishes its colors, and the colors shift and dissolve. The railing is too low. They are keeping back from it. He's trying not to look down. He hears himself say, "Be careful," and then wakes, breathes, feels the startlement of being where he is, and then relief. He turns and puts his hand on Rachel's hip. She stirs slightly, but sleeps on.

A MEMORY, AND SORROW
(AN INTERVAL)

For Brother Bobby

ONE EARLY DARK in the winter of 1966 my twin brother, Bobby, and I were force-marched in a freezing drizzle with a lot of other young men to a building the air force was pleased to call the Dining Facility, for an institutional meal of fish sticks and French fries. This was in Illinois, at the old, now defunct Chanute (pronounced Sha-noot) AFB, a training base 130 miles south of Chicago. The base was old when we arrived there, having been built in 1917, upon America's entry into what was then called the Great War. Air power was new in 1917, of course, and President Wilson saw the importance of it. Chanute had been in operation since. And by the winter of 1966, twenty-five thousand men a year were being trained there for duty far and wide — anywhere in the world, from stateside, as it was called, to overseas bases in Europe or Southeast Asia.

Bobby and I were at Chanute because, at twenty years of age, we had been on the verge of being drafted. The air force was our father's suggestion. He had served in the infantry in 1944 and he knew all about being a foot soldier in a war, which, he told us, hadn't substantially changed since Caesar. He said, "Getting drafted means the army, and the army means the infantry. I know that getting drafted, you'll serve just two years, and enlistment means you'll serve four years, but let me tell you, four years in the air force is better than *one minute* in the infantry, slogging through a jungle carrying a rifle and getting shot at. You just don't want that, believe me. And I don't want it for you, either."

We had joined a day or two later. And in fact most of the guys with whom we signed up had made the same choice for the same reason.

So, on this early evening, a Friday in late January, we had been marched through the freezing drizzle and were all fairly drenched, trying to get warm, sitting side by side and across from each other on long benches, like picnic benches, eating the fish sticks, which tasted fishier than fish should ever taste, and wondering aloud where the government might see fit to send us when we were through with tech training. We all knew Vietnam was a possibility, but that was distant, almost unreal, like the possibility of getting into an auto wreck, or suffering some other misfortune that happened to other people. Also we knew that, being in the air force, if you weren't flying you would most likely be manning an office with telephones, or working maintenance, managing equipment. Generally out of the line of fire.

Because it was Friday, we would have a day and a half of relative freedom. On Monday, Bobby and I were scheduled, at last, to begin a nine-week training course in survival and survival equipment, after which we would be sent out "into the field." We had been waiting more than a month for our course to begin, long days spent being force-marched reasonlessly from one end of the squadron area to the other, drilling, doing calisthenics, tending to our barracks, polishing and performing maintenance tasks, and working KP (kitchen patrol). Drudge work all day, with attendant harassment from the training instructors, or TIs, as they were termed by the air force.

The TIs called us all *draft dodgers* with what felt like an added element of derision beyond the usual expected hazing involved in military training.

No matter, really, that it was Friday. We were, all of us to a man, tremendously unhappy to be in freezing Illinois in January.

But one of the most miserable among us was a tall, Spanish-dark, nineteen-year-old kid from Vermont named Simpson. And in fact he had good and sufficient reason for his particular misery: one week *after* he'd been sworn in to spend four years in the air force, his mother had won a fortune in some state lottery, enough money to have paid for him to enter college and be classified as S-2, thus avoiding the draft. He saw this as his particular bad luck in the middle of lucky circumstance; he was wealthy, but he was also stuck at Chanute.

And he was obsessed about getting out.

The first time I ever really noticed him, he was perched on the top bunk of room 16 in our barracks, a room he shared with a guy named Weinberg (who in fact, temperamentally at least, seemed a good fit for him — we called Weinberg *Whiner* for his perpetual complaining about everything). Several of us had gathered in 16 because it was the room furthest from the front of the barracks, and the barracks commander's room. It was past midnight and we were telling stories — or, more accurately, we were listening to Bobby tell jokes. He and I knew plenty of them, being from a big family of storytellers (our father and his four brothers), but Bobby was better at it than anybody, including me. Simpson, from that top bunk, scooted closer to the edge of it and interrupted the joke telling with an announcement. "Listen. I've got a surefire way to get out of this shit."

We all looked at him. Five or six of us.

"It's simple. You know what I'm gonna do? I'm gonna let myself fall knees-first off this bunk. I'll break my kneecaps and then they'll fuck'n *have* to let me out."

We waited. I don't think anybody really believed he would do it. The whole thing seemed a bit clownish. Finally, Bobby said, "What if you do it and you end up in the base hospital for six weeks and then they put you back in line waiting for your course to start?" We watched him slowly lose the courage. Finally he flopped back and let one leg dangle over the side. "Goddamn it," he said.

But the next morning he was still talking about finding a way to make the armed forces, as he called the air force, *see* that he wasn't right for them. "It's all such a waste of taxpayers' money," he announced, as though he had just encountered the fact of it in a newspaper. "They've already spent so much money keeping us here while we wait and wait and fuck'n wait."

This was true.

All the tech courses were backed up. Every one of them. The nearly six weeks Bobby and I had been waiting was *below* the average wait times for others, in other schools. Poor Simpson had been marking time for more than twenty-two weeks to start his fifty-three-week course in the missile school. Indeed, later that same day, the top sergeant called out to him in the dayroom meeting, "Hey, Simpson, good news, buddy. You only got eight weeks left to wait now." Simpson responded very quietly: "Oh, well pardon me, while I go out of my fucking mind."

We thought he was already well on his way there.

So that winter Friday we were eating our fish and someone remarked that in England this food we were eating was called fish and chips.

Bobby said, "More like chips and shit." And laughter went up and down the table.

"I hope they send me to Italy," someone I didn't know said. He was a big, blocky, boy-faced guy with a unibrow, and teeth the color of yellow corn. "There's a base in Vicenza. That's for me." He looked at Bobby. "Tell us a joke, man. I hear you're a fountain of them."

"Hard to tell me one I haven't heard," Bobby said.

"Yeah?"

"Try me."

I thought of someone challenging a gunfighter with a reputation for being fast on the draw.

The unibrow guy shook his head. "I can't remember them."

It was a good-natured exchange. He went on talking about Italy. And then Bobby interrupted him, indicating me. "Our dad got wounded over there. Near Cassino."

"My whole family on my mother's side comes from there," the other said. "Well, Sicily."

"I want to be somewhere close to home," Weinberg said. "If it's possible."

"Where you from?"

"Baltimore."

"Andrews," Bobby said. "Us, too." We had dreamed of being sent to Andrews, where the air force would then simply be a job we went to. We might even do something with "Operation Bootstrap," as it was called, where you got an education toward becoming a commissioned officer. We might even make the air force a career.

"There's Bolling, in DC, also," Unibrow said.

"I heard that's closing," said Weinberg.

Simpson was across from me. He reached over suddenly and took hold of my forearm. "Listen, will you tell everybody I've been acting crazy? Will you do that?"

I pulled away. "Cut it, will you, Simpson. Nobody wants to be here."

He reached the other way, to Bobby. "Hey, Bausch."

Bobby was listening to a joke Unibrow was telling, about a foul-mouthed parrot. The only one he could ever remember, he said. I knew Bobby knew it, because I did, and I knew he would laugh at it, too, in his generosity. I turned back to Simpson, who was mumbling, chewing his fish, staring off. I saw the muscles of his jaw working. "Can't," he said, low, chewing. "No fuck'n chance." Then he looked directly at me again, swallowed and burst forth, "Don't you understand?" It was as though we'd been arguing with him about it, and he'd been going over it all in his thoughts. "They have the power to get us *killed,* man. Dead like this *fork* I'm holding. Or this *fish* we're eating. The government. The fucking *giant.* Ordering us to where we can *die.* And there's not a thing we can do about it. And it'll all be for nothing. It'll be that we *died* to save the fucking world for twelve-hour cold capsules and dog food! This ain't even a real war, man. It's just a lot of *murder.* Just *slaughter.* Meat wagons."

"Cool it, Simpson," Bobby told him. "We all know this."

Simpson stared, hands pressed to the table on either side of his plate. "But we've gotta *do* something. Somebody's gotta stop it, don't they?"

The question was too rhetorical to draw an answer or response from anyone.

"If I do something," he said to Bobby, "will you tell everyone I've been acting crazy?"

"Yeah, okay. Sure. Whatever."

He got up and walked over to the doorway leading out of the

building. Some of us followed him. He braced himself, standing a few feet away from it, swinging his arms back and forth, and then got up on his toes like a ballet dancer and marched fast, head forward, into the cylindrical hinge mechanism at the top. He went down, commenced pretending that he'd been dazed, and said, "Oh, I've been acting crazy. Tell them, Bausch. Tell them how crazy I've been acting. I just hit my head on purpose. You all saw it. Tell them, Bausch."

Bobby said, "He's been acting crazy."

"There," Simpson said to the gathered few airmen. "See? I'm very crazy. Go tell the TIs."

No one did anything. And then a TI came strolling in from the cold. He saw Simpson and stopped, and looked around at all of us. "What the fuck's this?"

No one spoke.

He looked at Simpson, who said, "They'll tell you, sir. Ask any one of them. I've been acting crazy. I just purposely walked into that door thing."

"Acting," the TI said.

Simpson simply stared helplessly back at him.

"You've got a welt starting on your head, there, Airman — " He paused and looked at the name in sewn letters above the left pocket of the other's fatigue jacket. "Simpson. Be careful, there, buddy — a big enough bump makes you qualify as being out of uniform." He laughed a little and went on to the noncommissioned officers' part of the facility.

"Goddamn," Simpson said, getting up and brushing at his pants. "It's coming for us."

"Shut up, man," one of the others said. "Jesus."

"I can't. I'm crazy. And it's coming for us."

We all stood there, watching him move back to where his plate was, with his unfinished dinner on it.

I got a piece of blueberry pie from an array of pie slices and made my way back to sitting across from him. The welt was already a bruise starting in the middle of his forehead.

Seeing this, I thought of something that took place in the first week of being at Chanute. I was in the common latrine of the second floor, standing at one of the sinks, shaving, trying to decide what I might say that wouldn't be mere complaining in a letter home. Out the eye-level window to my left, I saw what looked like a dusting of snow drifting on the air, and then realized it was ashes from the waste dump behind the base hospital a half mile off, out of view. I looked past the water tank in the near distance, at the vast sweep of black Illinois farmland — flat as a table all the way to the level horizon. I decided I would go back to my letter writing and just describe what I was gazing at. As I returned to my shaving, I heard a fighter jet take off from the flight line only six hundred or so yards away, a powerful roar, and abruptly I had the realization that I was part of the mightiest military force in the history of the world, that America was an empire as the Romans had been during Pax Romana. Something like a shiver of pride ran through me. It was pride. I thought of a Roman soldier twenty years old, experiencing an ordinary day, an ordinary soldier who would certainly be far stronger and tougher than anyone I knew — but here was the roar of that fighter jet fading on into the distance. I looked at my own hand, with the little Gillette razor in it, imagining how it would be to hold a sword, and in the next instant the whole chain of thought dissipated like the cloud of breath on a cold window. I finished shaving, and then wrote my letter about the scene outside and the fall weather in Illinois.

Now, looking at the welt on Simpson's head and hearing the fright in his voice, I thought of the ordinary Roman, and looked over at Bobby, who was smoking a cigarette and listening to another guy tell another joke I knew he had already heard. Bobby would be polite again, and laugh anyway. He did so, as always, then glanced at me and said, "What?"

He had seen into me. I looked down, forcing a smile. "Nothing."

"No — come on."

"I just thought of something that occurred to me in the first week we were here."

"A joke?"

"In a way." Then I told him about my odd little dream about empire and the Romans.

"Yeah," he laughed. "Not much centurion material around here, right?" He made a slight eye-roll in Simpson's direction.

I laughed. "Right." Then: "Nor me either, for sure."

"Nor me." He laughed. "No chance."

He turned back to the ones across from him at the table and began telling them about the farmer who had a constipated cow. I knew the joke, and watched, admiring his artfulness as he told it in a wonderful down south country accent: the farmer being given a big suppository pill for the cow, and told to insert it in the animal's rectum, and then going back to the farm and walking around her five times and finally stopping and holding the pill up and addressing her: "I'monna walk aroun' yew one more time, and if I cain't find this rectum thing a yours I'monna shove this up your ass!"

The noise of the laughs in the too-bright light and pride in Bobby's gift felt like a kind of respite. There were all these others around. We were out of the cold, and warm at last, and fed.

But then here Simpson was, oblivious to everything, worrying his one thought: he had no control over his life and he could be killed and it would mean nothing. And there was a fortune waiting for him at home. "Shit," he said. "I don't want to die even if it *would* mean something. My head hurts."

"You probably gave yourself a concussion," I said. I saw his lips tremble.

Sitting to his left was Weinberg. Squat, acne-scarred Weinberg, or Whiner, who was so unlikely looking as a soldier or an airman, with his round-framed glasses and double chin and pudgy features. He was hunched over, listening to something that I now noticed was being imparted, all along the row. He turned to Simpson and then looked at me and leaned across the table. "Somebody killed himself in Fifty-Ninth Squadron today."

This was going up and down the rows.

Guy just off guard duty. Whole bottle of aspirin. Found him under his bed.

I saw all the color leave Simpson's cheeks as I was turning to look down the table for Bobby. Someone was telling Bobby the news as I watched.

"Well," Simpson said in a defiant tone. "I'm not gonna do *that* for Christ's sake." It was as if he were rejecting somebody's suggestion.

I watched Bobby, who was now following the talk, much of it exaggerated and probably wrong.

More than a hundred aspirin; whole bottle; stomach bleeding; guy drowning in his own blood; blood everywhere; crawled under his bunk to die.

Gradually, we made our way back out into the cold. It had stopped raining, but the air was even colder than when we'd arrived. I was with Simpson and Weinberg; Bobby had gone off with a couple of others, who were still talking about it all. I'd wanted to go with them, but got sidetracked in the crush. I would catch up with Bobby, or he would catch up with me in the next few minutes. I looked at Simpson, and saw the distress in his face, and felt proprietary toward him, and toward Weinberg, too, who was so clumsy and out of it. They were leaning into each other, talking about the suicide. Like me, they were scared boys of the empire. I recalled how tense Weinberg had been on our rough flight to Chanute from Texas, where we'd undergone basic training. He was across the aisle from me, and when the plane took a sudden drop of what we later learned was a thousand feet, he screamed, "I'm a virgin!" at the top of his voice, with great umbrage, as if to alert God or Fate about that fact. And the merciless ribbing that followed, and that was ongoing, had left me feeling sorry for him in that way people who have been the object of mockery feel for someone else in the same circumstance. Now, watching him and Simpson in their white fear of suicide, as if suicide were a fate like falling out of the sky, I sought to change the subject.

"Hey," I said. "There's a guy in my barracks who says he played for the Turtles."

Simpson looked at me. "No shit."

"His brother drove here from Chicago and brought him his guitar. I heard him playing that Beatles song this morning. 'Day Tripper.'"

"Wasn't the radio?" Weinberg said in a shaky voice.

"It was acoustic, man."

"How's a guy get enough aspirin to kill himself?" Simpson asked us, as if we hadn't left the subject.

In truth, there had been talk of possible suicides from the beginning, through basic training in Texas and on into tech school; rumors of guys trying to cut their wrists, or taking a lethal dose of something, or threatening to jump from the roofs of barracks buildings. It seemed that everybody, including the TIs, had remarked at one time or another that infantry training involved mostly physical stress, while in the air force it was mostly mental. Our first day at Chanute, a TI had said: "If any of you pansy-assed draft dodgers get to feeling like it's too much and you decide you wanna check out of it all and off yourself, don't make a mess in the barracks. Go out in the field and get your blood on the fuck'n grass."

The news from Squadron Fifty-Nine had reached into us. Though nobody knew for certain that it was true.

"Wouldn't it take a long time to swallow that many pills?" Weinberg asked now.

"I'm not even close to thinking about doing anything like that," Simpson said. We went along the flight line in the wind and cold, and the several dozen others were around us, trailing along. I looked for Bobby.

Darkness in the Midwest is an entirely different matter than in Virginia, mostly because of the tablelike flatness of the land I spoke of earlier; so much more of the sky is visible; you can see a storm coming from ten miles away. You see many more stars on a clear cold winter's night, and when there's snow coming, as it was on this night, the moon shines on it all and makes it look like a prodigious advancing wall of blackness on a field of bright gray.

"Look at that," Weinberg said. "Goddamn, I wish I'd never done this. I wish I'd've just let myself get drafted, or run to Canada." His voice was tight with dread, and I thought he might actually begin to cry. He was shivering; but then we were all shivering.

We went on, toward the central square, which looked like a town square or plaza: stores, including the commissary and the pharmacy; a barbershop; a bank; the base library; the Airman's Club;

and the two theaters, named, unoriginally and colorlessly enough, Theater One and Theater Two. (Like the dead designations of the Nazis I'd been reading about in the William Shirer book *The Rise and Fall of the Third Reich,* which, when we first arrived, had been so violently taken from me, along with other books — Joseph Heller's *Catch-22* and T. R. Fehrenbach's *This Kind of War.* Right from the start it was communicated that books are the enemy: "Are yew some kina comyoon-ist?")

The moonlit night was closing down even in the square because of the approaching ceiling of clouds and snow. And the whole population of trainees seemed to be gathering anyway, some of them waiting for the theaters to open, some waiting for a place in the Airman's Club, and some — more and more by the minute — queuing up at the row of a dozen phone booths across from the commissary. I looked at the lines forming, everyone huddling, shivering, moving to keep warm, waiting to hear a voice from home, so far away for the first time — as Bobby and I were — and it seemed that I could feel, in the freezing air itself, the loneliness and the wanting to be elsewhere.

The lines stretched all the way across the street. I stopped there, not sure how I wanted to spend the rest of the evening. I might go to one of the movies; I wanted to see what Bobby had in mind. But I couldn't find him in the shifting throng. There wasn't much to do, of course. We were all crammed together in this self-contained little city in Illinois. And the fact that remained in the troubling background was that our kind were dying in larger and larger numbers in a place whose names we couldn't pronounce.

Nobody but Simpson had spoken about it directly. Now it seemed that the talk all around me was solely about Squadron Fifty-Nine and suicide. Poor Weinberg gave forth a little gagging noise, wondering aloud if some drill instructors were worse than others, and maybe that was a reason. Maybe the kid, whoever he was, had just been troubled in some other way that had nothing to do with the air force and war. Simpson slapped his hands together to work some heat into them. "Well that is definitely not an option for me, no matter what, even though I'm certainly and definitely out of my mind. I'm telling you. I really am. I'm out of my fucking mind. That's a true fact."

I didn't want to think about it anymore. This was the weekend, a day and a half of what would be like freedom, some kind of freedom.

Suddenly, though, looking at the mass of darker sky looming over us, I had an unwelcome sense of the enormity of the government the way Simpson had spoken of it — as indeed a massive *thing* out in the winter dark, skulking toward us. Simpson coughed, holding his fist to his mouth, and the sound of the cough, the physical bodily fact of it, a human cough, made me feel the real horror — that there was no life in the government at all; it was indeed a *thing,* all right, essentially lifeless, as if made of gears and wires and parts, completely blind and indifferent to us. I had a few seconds of sickening agitation, feeling my little life in the workings of a gigantic *apparatus.*

I paused, drew the cold air in, looking at all these others in their confused, purposeless commotion. And, turning in a small circle, I scanned the faces, looking for Bobby. Abruptly they were all essential to me, even as I felt hemmed in by them. The first flakes of snow had begun to waft down out of the now starless dark.

To Weinberg and Simpson I said, "What do you guys want to do?"

"I want to go home," Weinberg said, almost crying. "I wish I could go home." He wandered off in the direction of the commissary, where he would buy bread and canned meat for his time alone in the barracks. That way, he wouldn't have to go out again into the cold. Simpson followed him, muttering about his madness that wasn't serving its purpose.

Weinberg would be killed instantly only two months later, in a pipe-bomb explosion on the streets of Saigon. I don't know what ever happened to Simpson. He got transferred to another squadron, and I never saw him again.

That night I let them both go, and turned again in the crowd, and Bobby came toward me from the dark, saying my name. Someone had killed himself in another squadron. We were all brothers; I had felt that, I realized now, as something so obvious that it didn't need mentioning. But here, now, was *my* brother. And I was worried about him in an awful forlorn way as if I had already lost him. The possibility of that loss struck so deeply into my soul that it stopped my breath. I had the fullest, most awful awareness of where we *were* in that moment, not so much away from home, though that was at the base of it, but standing alone together in the wide, terrible, dangerous world of manhood, full of killing and violence, and that would require a toughness I simply did not have. I thought of how it would be to lose him, who knew me, and knew where I was tender and where I hurt, and knew what I was afraid of, and understood all of it because he was so much the same. He came toward me, and said something about hating the cold, and a trace of the same tremor was in his voice that I had heard in Weinberg's. For a hard minute it was as if he *were* Weinberg, and I was nowhere near, nor anyone to help him, or speak to him with the love and understanding of a brother.

And I knew I would never forget that moment, or us in it, as long as I might live.

I don't even remember what we did later that night, whether we went to one of the movies, or hung out at the commissary, or walked over to the Airman's Club to drink the twenty-five-cent beer and watch television or talk, or simply wandered back to the barracks, to read, or watch someone play guitar, or sleep. I don't remember anything else about that weekend, and so of course it is lost forever. I remember my twin brother walking toward me out of the cold dark, his face obscured by the hood he wore, and his flight cap pulled down so it made a shadow over his eyes. I remember that as he came out of the crowd of others, and spoke, I experienced an ache like grief, and at the same time an inexpressible relief at his presence, attended by fear about what the world might do to us, about what the future would do. I wanted time to stop forever.

That was fifty-seven years ago. Bobby's been gone since October 9, 2018. Every time I've heard a good joke or learned something interesting or seen something wonderful or even something awful — maybe especially something awful in these years — I've had the thought that I must tell him about it. Every time, in every instance, he stands in my mind. And, every time, I hear myself say, low, "Aw, Bobby . . ."

And the terrible not-voice — not that voice — the silence, *that* silence, opens again, the empty place simply widening all the time, never really lessening, but only continuing to expand awfully, like some inner Sahara, the far border of which I realize, over and over again, grows ever more distant, is so mercilessly itself, limitless, impossible to reach. We had all the years of each knowing the other was in the world; we had the laughs and the worries and the stories, and the shared enthusiasms and the sorrows and shocks, along with the riches of celebration, and I know that; I understand all that. And I know, too, that this is the blight man was born for, as the poet said. Nevertheless, mourning keeps its awful appointments without fail.

Oh, my lost brother! How I miss your heart and light.

ISOLATION

CHRISTINA STANDS IN her robe at the bedroom window, watching dawn rise over the trees and the river, and the towering shadow-shapes of the buildings beyond. The street below is empty, all the cars parked, nothing moving. It looks like an abandoned city. It's been twenty-nine days, and still, each morning, the sight of her neighborhood from this height is a shock.

Her husband, Bret, turns in the bed, and coughs, then snores. He's had the cough for three weeks, but there's been no fever. It's his garden-variety cold, he has told people on the phone. He emphasizes this: No fever. No pressure in the chest. Just the cough and the nose running, a cold. "Christina had it a while back and got over it."

Weeks of coughing, though last night there was a little less. He's getting better. It really is just a cold.

She goes quietly into the kitchen, makes a cup of coffee, then takes it to the living room, with its wide window overlooking the balcony and the park. She sits on the sofa across from the window, and holds the cup to her lips, breathing the aroma, feeling the heat rise to her face. There's no one in the park, and it will be that way all day; the sky is a gray, facetless screen, and it will be that way all day.

She hears him cough in the other room.

Just a cold, and she has already suffered it. He did catch it from her. She sips the coffee and thinks about throwing herself off the balcony.

Less than a mile away her lover, Gavin Bauer, awakes and cries into his pillow like a little scared boy, and this is the way the fever has affected him. The day ahead stretches on like unbridgeable distance. He's not an essential worker. In his fever, the phrase makes him think of Nazis and the war camps. He saw it in a film about the war. The phrase was used. *Essential worker.* He dries his eyes with the sheet, drifts slightly, dreams of gas jets in some narrow hallway, three men standing side by side with their backs to him. A braided rug with things moving in it, all this seeming perfectly reasonable and connected, strands of some profound unfolding narrative. He comes awake, and can't quite remember what it was, exactly, and experiences the desolate feeling of having mislaid something crucial. At length, he hauls himself out of bed and dresses as though he'll be going out. But he's got nowhere to go. His throat hurts.

His apartment building overlooks a normally busy street near a stairwell down into the subway. The street and the sidewalk are mostly deserted this morning. You see people with masks, and now and then you see couples, without masks, walking in the gray cold. There's been no sun for days.

He's lived alone since shortly after 9/11. A lot of marriages were damaged and ended up in crisis that year. He's done the research. His own wife went away with an old high school boyfriend, and after that shattering experience, he had determined to remain single. There were other women who were interested in him and tried to show it, but he simply ignored the overtures. He didn't want another relationship, though he was lonely. *Lonely* was the word. He often thought of an epigram he had seen somewhere from a blues song: "The Bible don't say nothin' 'bout the lonely; it don't call them blessed."

He and Christina were thrown together, as people say. And he loved her at first sight, having never believed in love at first sight. He used to make fun of the idea. Something about her frank gaze, her soft jade eyes, the way she had of tilting her head when she concentrated—this, he had learned, was the result of an anomaly in her vision, something about the muscles of the eye. He did not even look at her figure or her hair, not at the beginning. It was the tremendously interesting face, the dark eyes, and the voice—the voice, too. Her canny wit, her quickness with words.

Neither of them meant for it to happen.

They're both employees of the Social Services Department, but they did not even know each other until this past fall, when they were assigned to the same case—an abused boy named James

Lupino and his dope-addict parents. The problem wasn't violence, which would be simpler, but neglect, sometimes looking like mere absent-mindedness.

They spent several long afternoons outside courtrooms waiting to file petitions and to testify, and she would draw absently in the margins of her notepad. But the drawings were wonderfully exact depictions of figures in motion, faces, objects. It fascinated him, the little cross-hatchings of pencil lines that made shadows and crevices in faces and figures. She told him she had once worked for the news, doing renditions of court scenes, and then added with a small smile that she didn't draw much anymore.

"You should never stop," he said.

"I keep a little side room as a studio, at home. Sometimes I do portraits in watercolors and pastels for friends." She put one slender hand to her cheek. "And other people. For a price."

They got the boy, James, away at last, after having spent weeks accomplishing it, interviewing neighbors, and going through all the necessary steps attendant upon keeping the parents from any further control. When it was done, and James was in a friendly foster home, the two of them went for a celebratory drink. But he knew by then; they knew. The affair commenced without much thought, almost as if it had been arranged from the beginning.

Gavin Bauer is a collector of old clocks; he keeps most of them in a storage cubicle he rented at CubeSmart on Fifty-Fifth Street upon moving to New York, after his wife ran off. He used to have them displayed in a big room of the house they lived in across the river. They lived there for sixteen years. He has a daybed in the storage cubicle, too. He and Christina have spent their times together there, after drinks in a café near the Museum of Arts and Design, across from the entrance to the park. The first time, he gave her a kind of tour in miniature of the several dozen different types of devices he'd put on the walls and set on the tables, dressers and chairs in the little space, including several cuckoo clocks and pendulum mantel clocks. His extensive knowledge of the history and the seemingly numberless designs and types — the intricacies of their construction — delighted her. She felt happy appreciating something he loved. He described how the advent of portable spring-driven devices, the first wristwatches, during the Renaissance, increased interest in time itself, and brought about in the populations what scholars say was a heightened awareness of death, doubtless manifested in Shakespeare's absorption with the fleetingness of life in that gravedigger's scene in *Hamlet*. She saw the light in his eyes as he went on speaking about these things. She had the thought that his enthusiasm made him beautiful.

The first case of Coronavirus in the U.S. was identified in Snohomish County, in the state of Washington, that day.

He keeps thinking about how there were people who died of other things during the horrors of 9/11. He can't decide why. It's like an earworm. He remembers someone who suffered a fatal duodenal ulcer on that very day, an event having nothing at all to do with the passage of those terrible hours less than a mile away. He theorizes that it must simply have to do with the present public catastrophe. People all over the country, all over the world, are going on as best they can with their lives, in their private existences. They all have their other troubles, as well. He sympathizes with everyone. Yesterday he took his first delivery of groceries, three bags of food ordered online.

There are no pretexts, no excuses anymore. The Lupino boy is with the foster parents, and anyway everyone is in lockdown. The druggies, the biological — what he thinks of as accidental, catastrophic — parents are among the disappeared. Almost eight weeks now. That tragedy is also unfolding.

He makes peanut butter and honey toast, pours himself a glass of milk and sits in his small living room with the plate of toast on his lap, watching news on TV. Trying not to think about her. The news is that the orders to shelter in place will probably go on through the summer. He has no shortness of breath. He isn't coughing and though he feels very tired, he believes this to be the result of the restless nights. The sore throat is a thing that has been with him, recurring, since he graduated from college, twenty-three years ago. But the fever is worrisome.

Christina's thirty-nine years old. When she was two, she had eye surgery. It was meant to cure a misdiagnosed lazy eye, as the condition was called. It gave her the particular charming cast to her expression, and it also introduced her, quite early, too early, to serious pain. She has a clear memory of being held down while a doctor, a woman, kept jabbing her arm trying to find a vein, and then a big man took over, and he couldn't find the vein either. Her father, who was in the room, said, "Can't you prick her finger?" And the big man said, "This is easier for us." She saw her father go to the window of that high room and look out, and then turn around and come back. "This is over," he said, loudly. It startled the two people still working on her through her crying. "I'm taking her out of here." And he did. She can't remember whatever he went through or said or what the hospital people said; she remembers him carrying her wrapped in part of his coat out of the building, and she remembers crying harder because it brought him closer, made him hold her more tightly against his big chest.

Her marriage has known heartache, like any marriage: sorrow, childless years. Several mishaps, as she and Bret call them. She still loves him. They have been through so much together. They went through the loss of his mother in their first months, and of her father, three years ago now. Bret held her, then, and she cried into his chest, receiving the memory, like something primal, of the distant day she was carried, two years old, out of the hospital, the whole world surrounding her and nobody gone.

Bret walks in now from the bedroom, coughing. He wears only his jeans and a T-shirt with the Yankees logo emblazoned on it. "It's always worse in the mornings," he says. "This damn cough."

"You didn't cough much in the night."

"I know. Maybe once or twice. But not like before."

"No."

"You're up early. Hope the coffee's good."

"It's lovely."

He goes on into the kitchen. She hears him set a bowl down, and open the refrigerator. The French doors leading out onto the balcony are to her right. He comes in with his cereal and sits in the lounge chair where his books are stacked. He's an editor at Little, Brown. Working from home, now, and thinking of quitting. There are manuscripts beside the chair. But his mornings are reserved for pleasure reading. It's always been that way. He reads novels and books of stories while she reads the news, or, as he still calls it, the bad news. He's mostly rereading Dickens, these days, a favorite. And some Trollope in the evenings. But also the Roosians, as he has called them teasingly as long as she's known him. Tolstoy and Chekhov. He's widely read, and she's always been quite proud of him. Proud of their lives together. She would not have believed anything like what has happened to her would happen to her. And it feels exactly like that: an unimaginable eventuality. She loves her husband.

But she has never felt anything like this.

This morning he's reading Akhmatova. He holds the book in one hand while eating his cereal with the other. With each bite of the cereal, a little of the milk runs down his chin and he puts the spoon down in the bowl and wipes his chin with his fingers, then picks up the spoon, and the whole process begins again. When he has to turn the page, he puts the spoon down. The spoon makes its little clatter in the bowl. She never noticed this before, all the years. Such heartache. There he is, a man she knows to be good and gentle, sitting there being himself, confident in her and in their lives. Worried about business and the health of friends and family. Guiltless. Unmindful. Unaware. Unaware of everything, anything.

Somehow this fact makes him appear stupid to her.

She and Gavin had agreed to call it off just before the lockdown. Actually, he suggested it. They were walking in the park along its eastern edge, and they stopped at the base of a big sycamore tree. He kissed her, and then seemed to falter, reaching to put the flat of his hand against the trunk of the tree.

"Are you all right," she said, standing back to look at him.

"You make me weak," he told her.

"Oh, yes."

She kissed him and they held on for a moment. There were still some people walking nearby along the avenue. Several wore masks. The two had come from the little café across the street, down from the boutique hotel where they had spent most of the early afternoon. The first time they had taken a hotel room instead of going to the storage facility and the antique bed among the clocks.

"We ought to stop this," he said suddenly.

Something dropped in her heart; it felt like a physical something, a stone. She looked at him, at the strange light summer sky blue of his eyes, the kindly cast of his features, his mouth with its little mole just under the lower lip.

"I feel like we've finally really begun." She indicated with a tilt of her head the street going up to the hotel, from which they had just come.

"In a way, that's what I mean. We can't start that."

"A storage unit makes it doable?"

He shook his head. "We have to quit."

"Don't," she said.

"We have to. I feel wrong."

"I'll leave him," she got out. But, shifting her weight slightly to keep standing, she knew what she had just shown him, reaching to put her own hand on the tree trunk. She looked up into the skinny branches, which had just begun to bear leaves. "Please."

"Let's take a week," he said.

"I will leave him. I'll find a way." She saw the sorrow in his eyes.

"A week," he said. "Fourteen days."

"Why that?"

"I don't know."

"Do you think you've been exposed?"

"I don't know anyone. But how can you know? How can anyone know?"

"Is it just that?"

"It's an excuse to take some time," he said. "I'm sorry."

"I don't know if I can do it," she said, too loud.

They looked around themselves. There wasn't anyone near.

A week later, in the apartment, she went into the bathroom and ran water, and called him on her cell phone. Bret was asleep in his chair with a manuscript on his lap.

"I can't do this. I have to see you. I feel like I'm starving."

"I walked to the park. To our tree," Gavin said. "There were still people out."

"I've been thinking of drawing something. Us, disguised somehow."

They laughed softly, miserably.

"I don't think we should do this, calling each other."

"I just called you."

"I can't do it, hearing your voice. We have to try and be quiet with each other for a while."

"But *why*?"

"Because you still love Bret and you're tearing yourself up about all of it and I can see it even when we're being good to each other."

In the other room, Bret woke because part of the manuscript had slid off his lap to the floor. She closed the phone and went in to him. "I fell asleep," he said, leaning down from the chair to pick up the pages. It was a novel by a woman about a man writing a novel about a woman who was writing a novel about a man. He told her this, and she forced a smile. Then he went up to her, put his hands gently on her shoulders and said in a tone obviously meant to be reassuring, "You look sad." Then: "It'll be okay."

The lockdown came three days later.

She has always liked her husband's face, with its rugged angles, and the way the muscles of his forearms move, his shirt always rolled to his elbows, as now, late morning of the fifth week. He's compact, sharp featured; he has soft, light-brown hair that he brushes straight back. He wears a tie when he's dressed for work, even working at home, but by midday it's nearly always pulled undone, as now. He's in his chair again, surrounded by the books. But he's looking at another manuscript, a biography of Cole Porter. He's playing some of the songs, wearing earphones. He looks like a man at work even when he's relaxed. Intense in the best way, her friends tell her, because he's thinking about you. None of them know. It's been four days since she's been able to talk to Gavin. The cases are rising fast, as is the number of deaths. She looks at her husband now, the man without the slightest idea, and she's become afraid for the other, not hearing from him, receiving no sign from him. It seems to her that there's no way anyone out moving around in the city can escape being infected. She sees a couple walking a big dog on a leash as if there's nothing stalking people in the air or on all the surfaces, and her mind begins to buckle. The sensation is of a kind of interior avalanche. She goes out on the balcony. It's sunny today, and breezy. She looks down. Then she steps back, her knees trembling, and makes her way inside.

He's talking with a friend on his cell about how it's not as bad as the 1918 flu. "We know so much more," he says. "We've got all this science and they've already got the genome. They didn't even know it *was* a virus back then. And there was a world war on. You can't do social distancing in a war, or on a troopship."

She walks around him to the kitchen, puts coffee on, then opens her phone and taps in the number. Gavin answers after what seems a long time. His voice is low, almost guttural. He talks and coughs and she cries a little and aches.

He tells her he has been sick with a cold. Just a cold. "A cough, slightly sore throat."

"I can't stand this," she says, low. She hears him trying to stifle a cough.

"Nothing for it," he says in that rasping, low voice she can barely recognize.

"Do you have a fever?" she asks.

"Little."

"Oh, God, babe."

He manages to get to an ER. The doctor, wearing a protective suit, a mask and gloves, asks him to describe his symptoms, which he does through another coughing fit. The doctor listens to it, frowning, then listens to him breathe, takes his pulse, measures his blood pressure, his fever, his oxygen level. "I think you have it," the doctor says. "But your oxygen level's still good, and your blood pressure is fine. My advice is to go on home and stay there, and do what you'd do for the flu. Plenty of rest, lots of fluids. I'll write you a prescription for benzonatate and Zyrtec, and you can take Tylenol, too, for the headache, sore throat and fever."

"Thank you," he says to the doctor, who is already turning away to another patient.

He stops at the pharmacy on the corner, and then walks unsteadily on to the apartment, holding a scarf tight across his face. He manages to stay wide of other people, who number far fewer than at any time in his experience. There's no coughing now. At the apartment he lies down after taking the two medicines and the Tylenol, and then has another coughing fit. It hurts deep in his chest. His headache grows worse, and it still hurts to swallow. There are three unanswered calls from Christina, and one message: "Are you all right? Please, please text me. Something to let me know. Something about work maybe. Please. Anything."

He has never, all his life, felt so tired.

Lying on his back he texts her. "Lupino boy sick. they worry. ER. On med. Oxygen level good. Sent home. Being careful. Try not worry."

He sends it, and then puts the phone down and tries to sleep. Does sleep. He experiences terrible fever dreams that disappear as he surfaces from them — another whole world rampages down in his being somewhere, a frenzied upheaval and commotion; he sees a muddy river in flood with animals being swept by him in a churning, dizzying rush. He wakes, coughing, and can't quite call it up, can't remember exactly, can't tell any of it even to himself. He coughs again, deep, beyond breath, feels lightheaded, and the weight on his chest, lying there, gasping.

That he can gain the balance and strength to sit up amazes him. The room has gone dark. He reaches for the lamp on the side table and can't find the switch. Out the window, daylight is sinking below the spires and towers in the distance, shadows encroaching on the impossibly quiet city. He stands, steadies himself, makes his way toward the kitchen.

And then wakes up on the kitchen floor, unable to recall how he got here. There are no bruises or sore places; it's as if he simply decided to lie down on the cool hardwood. He manages to get himself into one of the straight-back chairs at the small table, with its salt and pepper shakers in their little rack, and the serviettes in their tin holder. The room spins again, out of a depthless cough. His phone buzzes where he left it on the couch. He doesn't have the inclination to try his strength to go pick it up, and now his coughing drowns out the sound of it.

Later, he finds himself back on the couch, in front of the TV. He doesn't remember getting himself here from the kitchen. With concentration, he can recall taking the benzonatate again, and forcing himself to drink a whole glass of water; he also took three Tylenol. The fever is 102. On TV there are people arguing in a courtroom, and music plays; the closed caption reads *Melancholy music.* It doesn't sound melancholic to him; it sounds circus-crazy, and then he sees the notation *Happy music* with a little musical note next to it. He realizes the scene has changed, and he comes to know that hours have passed. There's only the streetlights outside, and the window lights winking in the buildings. A wide panorama of sparkling as far as he can see, sitting on the sofa staring dizzily and half-asleep out the window, sitting in darkness, coughing, trying to breathe.

She hasn't slept in two days. This morning the sun comes up and she watches it again, and goes out on the balcony in the warming air and looks down at the empty street. It will be sunny today, and unseasonably warm even for April. She goes back in and makes tea, and takes a Xanax, then enters her little studio. She pulls the half-finished watercolor up and over the stand, and tries with a pencil to draw his face from memory. It's absurd. She turns the drawing into an old, old man, then pulls the watercolor back over it. In the living room again, she tries going to sleep on the sofa, with the light falling on her from the window. There's no sound of traffic. It's too quiet.

All day there will be the same silence over the city. This thought makes her shiver, and she gets up and starts to call Gavin. But then closes the phone, hearing Bret stirring in the other room.

A couple of days ago, Bret started an old jigsaw puzzle and then abandoned it. She sits over it for a time, drinking more tea. Finally he comes through from the bedroom, makes his cereal and sits in his chair eating it. He's reading Trollope now. *The Eustace Diamonds.* "Listen to this," he says, then reads, " 'We will tell the story of Lizzie Greystock from the beginning, but we will not dwell over it at great length, as we might do if we loved her.' Isn't that great? How could you not read on? That's the kind of audaciousness I seldom see any- more. All these so-close-to-the-vest exercises in restraint."

"I'm sleepy, hon," she manages.

"Sorry."

"No, that really is interesting. I'm just so tired now. I haven't been able to sleep."

"I know. Sleep as long as you can, dear."

They are quiet. She does drift slightly, rainy street images com- ing to her, and then trees in too-bright sunlight. There's the small clinking of the spoon. The work he has to do is piled on the side table next to his chair.

"I might put a mask and gloves on and go get some groceries," she says.

He doesn't look up from his cereal. "We've got what we need."

"We need milk."

"I ordered two gallons."

A moment later, he says, "They're talking about this going on to August."

"Oh, let's not talk about it," she says.

"Yeah. Discouraging. Christ. August."

"I'm sorry," she tells him.

"No, I agree with you. Let's not. It does no good."

The day is long. She watches more TV news, and then can't stand to watch it. Finally he says, "I've been wearing these clothes for three days. I'm gonna get squeaky clean."

"Okay."

As soon as she hears the water running, she opens her phone and taps in the number. Gavin doesn't answer right away. When he does, she has an instant of thinking it's someone else, and she tells him so. "Are you all right?"

"I'm trying to be." He makes a gasping sound and then coughs. And she presses the phone tight to her ear. This is not an ordinary cough. It's worse than any Bret suffered even in those first weeks of winter sickness. This is a cough that yields no relief, comes from no discernible paroxysm, but seems instead only a frail, awful welling up of the fluids of organic dissolution.

"Oh, please," she says.

"Can't talk," he tells her, hacking. "Take care of yourself."

Her husband is in his chair and she's on the sofa with a blanket over her legs. He thought it would be a good thing to watch a different movie each evening after they eat, taking turns choosing. This will be the first night of this new arrangement, and since it's his idea, the first one is his choice. "Let's keep it lighthearted, don't you think? Comedy?" he says.

"Yes, please," she manages.

He turns the TV on, to Vudu, and rents *My Man Godfrey*, with William Powell and Carole Lombard. The movie opens, with its scene of the big car pulling up to the shanty-shacked dump by the East River. "Want some popcorn?" he says.

"No, thanks."

"I love you."

"I love you, too," she says.

He's still coughing with the cold, intermittently blowing his nose. His cough sounds shallow, but it reminds her. They watch for a time, and then he pauses the movie to ask if she knows that Powell and Lombard had been married. He does this kind of thing a lot. Pauses what they're watching to tell her something about whatever it is, the history, the interesting sidelights. And they're always interesting. She has never minded it.

"Lombard decided Powell was too old for her, and then went with Clark Gable. They were friends through all that. I mean, think of that."

She only nods, feeling ill.

"Can you imagine keeping that kind of friendship after such a thing? I mean Powell actually suggested her for the role." He coughs, long and deep, to the bottom of his breath. His normal cough. It's the lingering of his garden-variety cold. It still frightens her. "I mean," he manages to say, clearing his throat, "can you imagine?"

"I can't imagine," she says. And begins to cry.

She cries for hours, it seems. Nothing he does reaches into where the pain is, though with obviously increasing dismay he continues to make the effort; there's something arid in his voice, but his touch is soft, his eyes tender and moist, watching her, eyebrows knitted, straining to see if there might be something to read in her face, some sign of a way to console her — or perhaps it's to explain to himself what this bottomless distress means. She can't bring herself to think about it. He puts his arms around her, and murmurs that he loves her, that it's all right, don't worry, try not to worry, and she tries to collect herself, for him. She's unable to look at his face, but for an hour or so she's quiet, still with the little sharp intakes of breath. They sit on the sofa and he watches her. The movie plays and ends with neither of them paying much attention to it, and then she can't keep from sobbing again, looking through tears at the heartless walls of the apartment, the bookshelves and the paintings, the manuscripts piled on the side table next to his chair, the windows looking out on the flickering night. "Let's get you to bed," he says. "It's this lockdown. It's got everybody upset and frantic."

"Yes," she manages, still sobbing.

He guides her into the bedroom, and she lies down in her robe. As he starts to unbutton it, talking about making her more comfortable, she puts her hands over his. "I'll just stay like this now," she says. "Please?"

He pulls the blankets up over her shoulder. "You all right now? You won't be too warm?"

"Just need some sleep," she gets out.

He goes into the living room. She hears him moving around, pouring a drink for himself, sitting in his chair. He puts the television on. News of the rising number of cases. The uncertainty of the coming summer. After only a moment, she's half-asleep, and doesn't dream, though as she emerges from it there's the sense of rising out of a nightmare. She begins crying again, silently, both hands clasped over her mouth. She hears him talking. He's called someone from his work, another editor.

"I'm not exaggerating," she hears him say. "I never saw her like that. She's sleeping now, but I'm afraid there's no rest in it. It's exhaustion. My poor, scared darling. I didn't know what to tell her. I should've been more gentle. All I could do was keep telling her not to worry. I should've tried to help her understand the science some way. I mean, they've got the genome already. I should've repeated that it'll pass. I mean, it will pass, right?"

THE LONG CONSEQUENCE

O N THIS CLEAR, cool daybreak in early June, Norman Sanger gazed out the picture window in his living room and felt that the scene before him might as well be a form of ethereal mockery aimed at him from the natural world. He was a painter, and often thought in terms of color and nuances of color, and it was a beautiful morning. But there in front of the house was his son's ratty old Thunderbird — askew, muddy, wrecked.

You couldn't look past it.

Seated on the couch with his second cup of coffee, he heard the boy's mother moving around in the kitchen, preparing her own cup. She'd just come downstairs, though she'd also been up most of the night, and he knew she would want to talk when she came in. He decided he felt too weary for it, so he carefully set the nearly full cup on the side table, leaned back and closed his eyes. He would fake being asleep. Almost immediately, though, without any awareness of the fact, he began to drift.

When she entered, she set her cup down on a side table and looked at him half-lying there, so disheveled, drooping that way, chin on his chest, the flesh at his neck piled upon itself, making him look so much older than he was. Going over to him, she touched the side of his face where, only an hour or so before, she had slapped him.

Her touch startled him a bit, and he opened his eyes, blinking at her. "Oh. Hello again."

"Sorry," she said, straightening, stepping back slightly.

"I accept your apology."

"Now you." She stood there, arms folded. Her eyes were red.

"I'm wondering what the exact province of this apology is."

"You get more flippant when you get scared, Norman. I said I was sorry. I meant for hitting you that way. And also for waking you just now."

His slight sidelong smile had always delighted her, though others had often misunderstood it. Actually, that was how he looked when he concentrated, and even in passes that troubled him his countenance could show a trace of the mordant smart aleck, full of perfectly honed self-deprecation. People sometimes took him for a crank. But he was nothing of the sort; in truth, deep down, secretly, he was tender, even in some ways wounded, in hiding. She had been aware of this since they were first together.

"I'm sorry, too," he said now.

She touched his cheek, then sat across from him. The house was quiet.

"We're both sorry," he said. "Everybody's sorry. *This* is sorry."

"Stop."

They'd been married almost thirty years. Of course, he knew her secret self — or selves — too. She'd been raised by people who wanted her to shine and yet expected her to fail at every turn. This showed up mostly in her continually plaguing worry about what others thought. Which was especially true this morning.

"I wonder if I'll ever finish anything anymore," he said. "After this."

"God, Norman. Stop."

In his studio, a room away, was another in a private series of nudes called *The Camilla Pictures;* it already had the shades of color and shapes of soft curves and bone structure, the contours of musculature and fine hair, and there were only the final touches to do on the heart-shaped face.

It was youthful still, and lovely.

But he was well past deadline on the project for which the university was paying him; he had only done sketching for a planned mural about music in Memphis, which would be twenty-five feet long and six feet high, taking up most of the back wall in the high-ceilinged lobby of the new student union. He'd sketched many of the famous dead of rock 'n' roll, R & B and jazz in action, playing their music and consorting with each other, and then the university president had decided she wanted the luminaries to be interspersed with ordinary citizens going about daily life in the river city. The kind of ordinary people those giants of entertainment came from.

But the faces and actions and relaxations of the so-called ordinary people weren't coming to him; nothing about the new sketches pleased him. Hence, the indulgence of a pause on that work to do the new portrait of Camilla.

And even that was out of the question now. Not today.

"Did you look in on him?" she asked, meaning their son, Josh.

"No."

The boy's live-in girlfriend, Maya, had left him and moved in with a young man she used to date, who was also a former heroin user. Josh had helped *her* break free of it, and they had been living together, planning to get married.

"We have to get back to being able to talk about everything," Camilla said.

"Well, okay. But what I said stands. He's an alcoholic mess at twenty-two, this — this *boy*. And now he's a felon."

"But you didn't have to throw it at him. And why can't you accept that if no one was hurt it might be nothing."

"Here we go again," he said. "You want to just slap me now and get it out of the way?"

"Well, just don't call him *boy*. He's not a child."

"That's right. So, he'll be tried as an adult."

"Can you quit talking that way?"

Quite patiently, he recited: "Leaving the scene of an accident is a crime, and he was DUI doing it. And if he hit someone —" He stopped. "Aw. Christ."

Once more, as in the long night, she felt the tears come. "I wish you'd just stop it."

Sanger said, "Let's just not get mad at each other again, okay?"

"But you have to see he's so — sad. His heart's broken. And it breaks *my* heart to see him like this. So sick with worry about her. She probably *is* using again."

Norman Sanger nodded, but without the slightest trace of sympathy. "We've been through this. Maya cheated on him. Maya took him for the proverbial ride. Maya left. Maya's a heroin casualty and I'm sorry about all of it. But none of it is a license to come unraveled. To sit crying in his booze at Tracks and then get in a car and *drive*.

Christ, he was only with her for — what? A month? Turns out she's just cheap. She's a ruin. And she's with the other guy now. So, as I said at least four times last night, whether she's using or not is no business of ours. Or Josh's."

They heard stirring upstairs. They paused, and it grew quiet again. Perhaps their son was listening.

"Let's go into the kitchen," Camilla said.

They made their way in there and sat at the table in the light from the window seat. The backyard was in shade and Sanger saw the blue-green outline of the house on the grass, which shimmered with dew. It was strangely, depressingly itself, somehow almost insistent.

"I hate this," she said, low. Then sighed. "The longer we don't hear, the more likely it is that nobody saw it, or reported it."

"It'll be reported," he told her, "and we're already *accessories after the fact.*"

"Oh, you're so negative and you make it all sound like a cop-show murder mystery. I wonder if you're not *relishing* the whole thing — your opinion about him, vindicated."

After a long silence, he said, "Jesus, kid. I'd just rather you hit me, okay?"

She couldn't look at him. Finally she sighed out the words "I'm sorry" and reached over to pat the back of his hand. "That was wrong," she said. "Look, can't we just — talk to the people, whoever they are, and pay for the repair, and then can't that be the end of it, if nobody got hurt? Lots of these fender bender–type things happen all the time."

"This was more than a fender bender. Take a look at that car out there."

"But he's *okay.* He got home unhurt. And he says he'll make it right."

Sanger's exasperated exhalation was tinged with exhaustion. "We can't keep subsidizing Josh Kendall Sanger and his heroin-addicted lovers and friends. There's got to be an end to it. Oh, Camilla, sweetheart — how in God's world — " He shook his head and looked down at his hands. "How did we, you and I, end up here?"

"Please," she said. "There's been good, too. We were so proud he helped her get clean."

"I'd bet you this house, and everything we have, that she's using again."

Camilla was silent, looking out the window.

"Anyway, it's all irrelevant now, isn't it."

"Well then," she said, "let's — we just have to help him stay away from her. And we'll get him to make everything right with this — this accident."

"Listen to yourself. Are *you* on something? The damage on the car alone's gotta be at least three or four thousand dollars."

"So, all right, then, what do we do this morning?"

"Like I've said. We get him in the good car and try to retrace whatever he can remember about coming home. And if we find where it happened, we try talking to the people whose property he damaged. And then we exchange insurance information. Like that."

She said, "And then — it gets reported and then he goes to jail."

Sanger shrugged.

This caused a rising of heat at the back of her neck. "You think that's where it's all headed, too, don't you."

And he shrugged again. "That's where it's *certainly* headed if we don't do anything."

A sudden, loud cough in the doorway startled them both. Their son cleared his throat with a liquid sound, and mumbled, "Didn't mean to scare you." He looked directly at his father. "I thought I told you guys already. I don't remember where." He had slept in his clothes. They were soiled and wine-stained down the front. His hair was wild. He scratched himself at his middle, an almost comic gesture, as if he meant it that way, shuffling to the counter, where he brought a cup out of the cabinet. He was twenty pounds heavier than his father, and much of the extra weight was in the paunch at his middle. "I really don't have the slightest idea," he said. "I took some people home and got lost trying to come back. I don't remember getting here. I think it must've happened somewhere close because — " He paused, emitting a small, gasping breath. "Well, I woke up on the front lawn." He paused again. Sanger saw the stains down the front of the shirt, and the distended belly. "And anyway," the boy went on, "ah — the car door was open and it felt like it was all part of one thing. I must've pulled up and parked and then got out and sort of fell over out front for a while. I'm sorry." He poured some of the coffee his father had made into the cup and took a drink of it.

"You do remember," Sanger said, "that we heard you come in. Right? We tried to find out where you'd been and what the hell you'd got yourself into. Surely you remember that much."

"Sorry. I do. Uh, some."

A moment later, Sanger said, "Yeah — well, we're just gonna have to drive around and look."

"Not today, if it's all right. I'm pretty miserable."

He tilted his head slightly, and studied the boy. "Are you really so pathetically *oblivious* that you don't actually know you've committed two *felonies*?"

"Norman," Camilla said. "Not that again. We get it."

And now he raised his voice. "Apparently you *don't* get it. We have to get to the bottom of it *today*. If *they're* riding around looking and they see that car sitting out there, we've got leaving the scene and a DUI, both. Can't either of you really take in how *serious* this is?"

Josh leaned against the counter heavily, the arm supporting him making one shoulder higher. "Please, I get it. Can you please stop yelling? That's what I remember from when I got in last — this morning. Yelling."

"But you didn't hear a word, did you."

"Norman," said Camilla.

"*Did* you."

"Please, Norman."

"We're gonna go around *today*," Sanger insisted through a tight mouth. "To look for where you left the scene of your DUI incident."

"Not me," Camilla said. "I'm staying here."

"All right." He reached across the table for his cell. "We'll just call the authorities and get to the bottom of it that way."

Josh moved suddenly and retched into the sink. He turned the water on, let it run for a few seconds, then leaned down to take it straight from the tap. He spit and wiped his mouth. "Sorry. Oh. God." He coughed. "I'm sorry."

"Go put on something clean," Camilla said in a shaky voice. "We'll all go."

The boy started toward the stairs.

Sanger called after him: "And for Christ's sweet forlorn sake take a fucking *bath*."

He and Camilla quickly dressed and then sat side by side on the couch. He held still, trying not to let his mind run. She breathed the odor of the shaving lotion he'd put on, and thought of neighbors, friends and acquaintances who had sons Josh's age; the sons were all doing wonderfully well, *they* were all finishing college. Two had already been married. She murmured, "The Magnussons' son, Brad, is a father now, as of yesterday morning." She wiped her nose and sniffled. "Little baby girl."

"No comparing," he said. "Okay? Let's cut that out. That way madness lies."

They waited.

Josh came downstairs wearing jeans and a T-shirt. The jeans had designer tears midthigh and just below the left knee. The T-shirt was black with bright yellow script across the chest: *Supertramp*. "Oh," he said, seeing how his parents were dressed. He went back upstairs.

"Jesus Christ on a raft," Sanger muttered.

"Well, we didn't *say* anything about dress."

"Do me a favor," he said, low.

She didn't wait for him to continue. "I know, I *know*. But we *didn't* say anything."

"The mistake, darling, is thinking it's our responsibility in the *first* place."

"Norman Sanger, I've been telling *you* what to wear for twenty years."

His face registered both an admission of the fact and weariness at the mention of it. "And here," he said, quietly, "is our problem:

these mitigating explanations the two of us feel by turns compelled to make for this — this lummox."

"Don't," she said, holding tight inside, breathing very shallowly, hands clasped in her lap.

At last Josh descended the stairs again, wearing dark blue slacks and a white shirt. His father looked him up and down. "Corduroy?" he said. "In June?"

"Okay," Camilla said quickly. "Come on now, this is fine."

They went out to the car. Sanger walked around it again. In daylight, you could see the damage was even greater than it had appeared to be. There was a long scratch across the passenger door, smeared with what looked like sap and muddy grass. The left headlight was broken, and the right one was cracked; the grille had what appeared to be flecks of black paint on it; the right front fender had come loose and the left was crushed inward, and had scraped much of that tire's tread away; indeed, the edge of it was in the way of the tire, but loose enough to allow the tire to turn while being scraped with every revolution. "I don't know how you got this far," he said. "The tire's about to burst."

"It was plenty noisy," Josh said, without making eye contact. Abruptly he stepped off the sidewalk and heaved up into the grass the coffee he'd had. Camilla moved to his side and put a hand on his back.

"Jesus Christ." Sanger turned and started down the street, then stopped and looked back. "You came from this direction, right?"

"Let's take the other car and drive around," Camilla said.

"So he can throw up in *that*?"

They said nothing.

"You couldn't've come far with that tire like it is," Sanger said.

His son shrugged stupidly. "I don't know."

"Well, take a guess."

Slowly, uncertainly, Josh moved past him, and went on down the street. Sanger saw the unhealthy stooped shape of his back under the white shirt; it was the slouch that had come to seem the boy's natural posture.

"Straighten up a little," Sanger demanded. "Will you? For Christ's sake."

Camilla let go a small sigh of frustration. Their next-door neighbor Lenora Adderley walked out on her porch in a bathrobe. She bent down to get her newspaper and then stepped to the railing. "Trouble?" she called. "Somebody hit you?"

"Nothing," Sanger said to her. "Fender bender."

"I hit something," Josh said. "I crashed into somebody's lawn."

"It's nothing," Camilla called to her.

"Pretty morning for a walk, anyway," said Lenora. "Maybe have some coffee later?"

Camilla waved to her. "We'll see. I think I may be coming down with a cold."

"You sound a little rheumy. Well, sorry for the fender bender." Lenora went back inside with her newspaper.

"She knows I've been crying," Camilla muttered. "I wish she'd mind her own business."

"You can tell her that over coffee," said Sanger. He was not quite aware of having said it and Camilla hadn't really heard it. He turned to his son. "You sound like you're bragging. Do me a favor and don't brag."

"I didn't mean to," Josh said. "Believe me."

They walked on, and reached a place where the curb was marked with wide black streaks, obviously tire marks, part of a tree branch lying on the grass there, its leaves still green. "You came this way," Norman Sanger said.

"Looks that way. It did feel like all one thing."

"Yeah, it's *been* all one thing from the beginning," his father muttered almost to himself. They didn't hear him. Camilla frowned a question at him. "Forget it," he said.

They got to the end of the block.

"I think we should go get the other car," she said. "This is ridiculous."

"You saw the skid marks. It's close. Christ, why don't you two go on back."

"I can make it," Josh said in the tone of a wounded fighter valiantly offering to continue.

"Take him home," Sanger said to Camilla. "Really. Get him out of my sight. I'll see what I can do. And if I don't find anything, I'll come back and we'll *drive* around."

"Come on," Camilla said to her son, angry now at both him and his father.

Sanger turned to go up the hill toward the road that led to the highway. He stopped and watched them go on for a few paces, Camilla supporting the boy, helping him along. Again, Josh stepped to the grass and spit, and retched. She stood back with her hands on her hips and watched, shaking her head slightly. She didn't look Sanger's way. He turned and went on, out of their view. At the house on his left, a man was pushing a hand mower back and forth while two teenage boys trimmed the hedges on either side of the lawn. Norman Sanger had a moment of actually hating the man *and* his boys. He looked back at the end of his own street and experienced a spasm of wishing that this trouble might in fact *be* bad trouble. And as he was trying to sweep this from his mind, going on away from the man and his lawn and his helpful sons, he crested the hill and saw, parked in front of a house at the far end of the street, two police cars, a fire truck and an ambulance, their repeatedly sudden red and blue lights flashing into the sunlight. Slowly he approached, keeping to the other side of the street. Two sections of the corner of a wrought-iron fence on the other side of the house had been flattened, and a small sapling was crooked to one side. There was a wide gash in the lawn where the red earth looked intentionally upturned, as with the blade of a plow. He felt suddenly sick, crossing the street slowly. No one seemed to be paying any attention to the damage. Two police officers stood with a fireman outside the front door, which was wide open, showing from this angle a blank, unadorned gray wall, and you saw the outside daylight dying on it, going in. Sanger felt his own morbid, fearful curiosity as a kind of invasion of the privacy of whoever lived in the house. The fireman standing there had his hands shoved down in the pockets of his yellow protective suit. A stretcher had been placed just beyond the tear in the grass.

Sanger breathed out a gagging exhalation. "Oh, Jesus Christ." He walked closer. A cop in a dark blue uniform with brass buttons up the front got out of one of the cars and approached him. "Do you have business here, sir?" An undertone of aggressiveness sounded in the voice.

"No business here," Norman Sanger said. "I was on a morning walk and — and I saw all this. What happened here?"

"Can't say," the cop told him.

Another car pulled up, and two men got out. One, another uniformed one, hurried into the house. The other, a completely bald plainclothesman in a light gray suit and blue tie, walked over. Sanger realized that the uniformed cop had signaled the man.

"Says he was out for a walk," the cop said.

"Out for a walk, huh."

"That's right." Sanger wiped one hand across his mouth, and shifted his weight slightly, unpleasantly conscious of the unease these motions betrayed.

The other man stared.

"What happened here, Officer? This is my neighborhood."

"You know the folks who live here?"

"No, sir."

"Have you ever talked to them or seen them going in and out on one of your walks?"

"I've actually never walked this way before. Thought I'd go a different way this morning." Hearing the slight shudder in his own voice, Sanger cast his gaze down at the sidewalk. "Just — curious, I guess."

"Followed the sirens?"

"No, sir. I don't remember hearing any sirens."

"Where's your house?"

"Couple — couple blocks. Back down that way. Look, Officer, can you say what this — were there any injuries in this — whatever this is?"

The other seemed to study him. "I'm Detective Burton. And you are?"

"Look," Sanger said. "You don't want to talk about all this and I accept that. Thank you."

The detective took a small notepad out of his jacket. "Your name, please."

"Man, I don't want any involvement here. I was just on a walk — and I was curious."

"This is a crime scene, sir."

Sanger felt the strength go out of his legs.

"A homicide, in fact."

He stood there, stricken, all the blood in his body dropping. He saw the gash in the lawn, and the sapling bent almost to the ground, the crashed-through fence.

"You all right, sir?"

The capacity for speech had left him.

"Sir?"

"That's — " he managed, and then had to take a breath. "That's terrible."

"You don't know these folks."

"I told you — no."

The uniformed cop said, "Well, I'm going on inside."

Sanger used this as an opening to start away. It felt exactly like an attempt to escape.

The detective said, "You know anything about drug traffic in this neighborhood?"

He stopped. "Drug traffic — I don't know anything about this place at all, or this block. I took a walk."

"You have teenage children?"

"What?"

"Anyone who might know something about drugs in the neighborhood. Anything at all."

"I've got a twenty-two-year-old son in junior college." Sanger felt his breath leave him. "I don't know anything about drugs."

The other indicated the house. "There's a meth lab in that basement, sir. And paraphernalia for heroin use, and a dead man with a pruning knife in his left eye. Forgive the brutal image."

Sanger couldn't speak, or return the man's gaze.

"Just meant to say, you know — looks like there *are* drugs in your neighborhood."

"Well, like I said, twice now, I've never come this way before."

The detective raised his hand placatingly. "I get it, sir. I get it. I'd like your name and number, though, if you don't mind. Just in case I have to ask you anything else. We'll be canvassing this whole area."

Sanger managed to give him what he wanted.

"Thanks."

"Can I have *your* full name?" he heard himself ask. He hadn't known he would do it, and then felt it as a ploy, a misdirection. He feared that his guilt was showing in his eyes.

"Samuel Burton," the detective said, bringing out a card and offering it.

Sanger took it.

"It's upsetting, I know." Burton's tone was faintly mollifying now. "We don't know much yet. Neighbor discovered it this morning — all this." He indicated the broken-down fence and the torn lawn, then tilted his head at the house. "Door was wide open, so he went in to see what was what. Claims he didn't know this was a meth house."

Two more cars arrived.

"That'll be lab people and the coroner," Burton said. "Sorry to've troubled you. We'll get to the bottom of it all. If you *do* think of anything, or if anybody in your house does, please let me know right quick."

"I will." Sanger tried not to hurry, feeling watched, walking away. When he made the turn and was back on his street, he saw Camilla standing over Josh, in front of the house. Josh had his forearms resting on his upraised knees. He had been sick again.

Sanger walked up to them. He had to pause, and gather the strength to say anything. He couldn't look at his son.

"Well?" said Camilla. "Did you find it?"

And now he did look at Josh. "You tell me the truth, now. Have you been using meth?"

"What?"

"Norman," Camilla said. "Listen — "

He turned to her. "No. Both of *you* listen."

"Dad, what's happened?" Josh said.

And he told them all of it.

The boy's face whitened, and his hands went up to his face, covering his eyes.

"Have you ever set foot in that house," Sanger said, in the tone of a flat statement.

Josh frowned at him. "How can you ask that?"

Camilla was crying. "Oh, God."

"I don't remember seeing anything," the boy went on. "I don't know anything about it."

"Well," Sanger said. "Here's what we *do* know. We know your car knocked down that wrought-iron fence and put a tear in the yard, and we know the sap of the front-yard tree is all over your car door."

Josh stared. His eyes were wild.

"Everything all right?" Lenora Adderley called from her porch.

"We're fine," Camilla called back to her.

They went into the house. Camilla moved to the living room couch and sat there, hands clasped tightly at her chest, rocking slightly, still crying. "Nosy witch."

Josh started upstairs. "She's just trying to be a good neighbor," he said.

"Stay here," Sanger demanded. "For Christ's forlorn sake."

The boy came back down, moved unsteadily to the chair across from the sofa. His father paced, saying nothing for a moment.

"I don't even remember," Josh said. "I swear. I sort of — I just — I came to, with part of the tree in the window. And I remember backing out of there, and that's all. The next thing I see clearly is waking up out front. With the car still running."

"And you've never been in that house."

"No. I told you. Never."

"You never knew or had dealings with anybody *in* that house."

Josh shook his head. He was someone expressing frustration at a thing he couldn't change or affect.

Sanger felt the need to press him. "And you don't do meth. And you're not on heroin. You haven't visited with Maya there and done heroin."

"How can you *say* that? Maya won't even see me. And she's clean. They're both clean."

"Are you in touch with them?"

"They're *dead* to me. Okay? Leave me alone about them. Jesus. I'm trying to forget them!"

"By drinking yourself to death. Is that it? Let's get to the bottom of *all* of it."

"Norman," his wife pleaded. "No."

"How do I know you're telling me the truth?"

And now she broke forth, sobbing. "For God's sake, Norman. You heard him."

"Yeah," Sanger said. "I heard him. That's right. Over and over. I heard him."

They spent the rest of the morning clearing out space in the garage for the car; they moved it in there. Camilla saw the way her husband and son worked together to accomplish this. The whole thing was done quietly, with little talk. They were all in cahoots now, and she concentrated on the fact that DUI and leaving the scene of an accident were relatively small offenses, which could be lived past; it was unlikely that anyone from the meth house saw anything or had been in any condition or would be willing to admit being there at all, given what had been found in the basement. The idea sent a reasonless rush of elation through her, and she sought to quell it. It was all so confusing. She had the thought: *How awful to be glad of a homicide.*

As she started across the hall to head into the kitchen, she saw, out the front-door window, a man in a light gray suit standing at the garage door. He was leaning up to look in the row of windows at the top of it. She hurried into the kitchen, where her husband and son were sitting at the table with sweating glasses of ice water. They weren't talking. They hadn't touched the water.

"Norman, someone's out front."

"Oh, Jesus!" The boy stood.

Sanger simply stared, mouth partly open. The doorbell startled all three of them. Camilla hurried, trembling, to answer it.

When she opened the door, the man there nodded politely at her. A uniformed cop stood just behind him. "Yes, hello. Mrs. Sanger?"

"Yes," Camilla got out.

"I'm Detective Samuel Burton. Is — is your husband around?" He leaned up a little to look beyond her.

"He's here. I'll — I'll get him."

"It might help to talk with you, too. Actually with all three of you. We've been canvassing the area, you see, as I mentioned to your husband we'd be doing? And we just spoke to your next-door neighbor, and she mentioned you and Mr. Sanger have a son who had an accident. Crashed into someone's yard, I believe was the phrase?"

Camilla couldn't speak.

"Can we take a closer look at the damage to that car in your garage?" Burton went on. "We were just looking at it, me and the sergeant, here, through the windows. Neighbor said you moved it in there?"

Camilla could only nod, helplessly. She heard Sanger coming up behind her.

"Hello again, sir," Detective Burton said. "Are there any guns in the house?"

"No guns," Sanger said. "I'm a painter."

"We need you to open your garage door."

"My boy didn't do anything," Camilla said. "Please."

Sanger took her arm. "My son's opening it now."

The uniformed officer had already started toward the opening garage door. Sanger and the detective and Camilla walked over together. Both policemen walked around the car, as if they were going to buy it or rent it.

Finally Detective Burton said, "I'm afraid we'll have to ask you three to come with us."

"Are we being arrested?" Sanger asked.

"Let's say you're being detained."

Moments later, the three of them were crowded together in the police car, with Camilla in the middle. Josh held his mother's hand. Sanger had the thought that this was all there was of them now — this pitiful huddle of crammed-in bone and flesh in the backseat of a car. At the station, two plainclothesmen took Josh down a hallway into another room. Detective Burton led Sanger and Camilla into his office, and indicated the two hard-backed chairs opposite his desk. It seemed arranged specifically for them — the chairs quite close, so they could reach one another.

"Neighbors," Burton said, then made a tsking sound. "That's the most fruitful resource we have sometimes. Anyway, these little interviews can take a while. You wanna go get some coffee or something?"

"We'll wait," Sanger said in a tone so placating that Camilla turned to glance at him. He looked back with his sad eyes; the distress in his features made her own distress worse. She reached for his hand and held it tight, trying to imagine strength flowing into him from her.

"Anyway," Burton continued, "we have a witness at the scene tells us they saw the driver of a car that plowed into the front yard of the place. Says the driver got out of the car and staggered around to look at it, then started to run, but then came back and crawled in, and they say it looked like he went to sleep a little. They didn't want to talk to us, they said, because they suspected it was a drug house and didn't want any involvement. But they got a good look at the young man."

Camilla squeezed her husband's hand again, meaning this time to signal him somehow not to speak. But Sanger gave forth a little cough and then said, "So, then — our son's under suspicion of — of having something to do with what you found there."

"Well, let's say he's a person of interest. You are, too, of course. Both of you, because you hid the car that way. That really wasn't acceptable, you know."

"My son would never do a thing like kill someone," Camilla burst forth. "He just wouldn't. He's the sweetest boy. A good-natured, sweet man." She let go of Sanger's hand, and reached into her purse for a handkerchief. "He'd had too much to drink and he drove the car through that fence and into the tree, and he left the scene because he was — he was scared and he's a little immature. But — look, he'd had too much to drink. He's recently had his heart broken. He does have a drinking problem. It's an illness. And we didn't know what to do and we needed time to think."

"I understand all that," Burton said. "Really. Right now, the boy's only a person of interest. That just means we're talking to him. He's not charged with anything yet. Nobody's charged with anything."

"He was too drunk to do anything but drive away," Sanger said as evenly as he could. "He passed out on our front lawn, with the car running and the driver's-side door open. On *our* lawn."

"He wouldn't lie about a thing like this," Camilla said.

"Well," said Detective Burton. "Let's just wait and see what we find out."

They waited a long time. The others in the room went about their business. Burton left them there for periods of time; they watched the clock. It occurred to Camilla that she and her husband were now objects of indignity, the sad parents who didn't know their own grown child well enough to say with any certainty what his recent history outside their house really was. She looked at the side of her husband's face and saw a mark in the skin, a new blemish she couldn't recall having noticed before. How odd that the sight of it made her feel his weakness, and, awfully, his separateness from her, too. He could have been a stranger sitting there with his horror-struck expression.

The detective stepped over and sat at his desk again, and gazed at them for a moment. "Okay, good news. According to the coroner, the killing took place around eleven o'clock, and your son's DUI event, we'll call it, was just before dawn. And there's no sign of him having been in the house, no fingerprints, nothing like that."

"Then he's free to go?"

The detective stared for a moment. "We've decided not to pursue the DUI, or leaving the scene, because there's this horrendous other thing with that house. Okay? For you all, it's just a dumb coincidence — well, in your case, a lucky one. But we *are* gonna cite him, of course, and he'll have to attend some classes."

"Yes," Sanger said. "Of course."

"And you understand that you're both liable for a citation as well, for putting that car in the garage. But since he wasn't involved in the other business, I'm not gonna charge you. I think you've been through enough."

"Yes," Camilla sobbed, wiping her eyes. "You're very kind, sir."

"And I will take the risk of offending you both by saying that you ought to make him go to a rehab center."

"We *have*." Camilla sobbed again, loudly. "Twice. We *have*."

Burton was still for a moment, and then, while she wept, opened a drawer of the desk and appeared to attend to something there. Finally he took out a sheet of paper and smoothed it, then pushed it aside. "Well," he said. "Your boy'll be released in a few minutes. You can wait in the lobby for him."

They left him at his desk making notes, going on with his work. There were several people sitting in the high-ceilinged entrance hall, which smelled of cleanser. They took two chairs under a wide window looking out on the street, a sunny sidewalk crowded with people.

"We've loved each other," Camilla said, low, putting her handkerchief to her eyes, still weeping. "We gave him a happy home to grow up in, didn't we?"

He looked at the people walking past. They appeared content, not even hurrying. "Our lonely, sick, sweet boy," he said.

"Oh, Norman."

He was silent. A woman and a young girl were seated along the wall on the other side of the entrance. It was clear they were waiting for someone who worked in the building. The girl was talking about her seventh birthday, and how that's the best birthday. She got down from her chair and turned to lean on her mother's knees. "Isn't that the best birthday to have?"

"It's a wonderful one to have," her mother said.

Purposely, Norman Sanger recalled an article he had read somewhere called "Nurture and Nature: Unequal Partners," which expressed the view that nurture had far *less* to do with the development of character than most people supposed. Some natures, the article said, were simply present at birth, like fate, and nothing could change or affect it. This was an oddly consoling thought now. He was appalled by the realization that, when first he had come upon the scene at the meth house, he thought Josh *was* involved, believed his son actually could've been mixed up in the whole thing. He turned to Camilla. "You remember the first time we caught him in a lie?"

"I don't remember any such thing."

"The dishonesty, Camilla. You remember it. He was seven."

"Stop it," she said. "Just stop it." She looked at the mother and daughter, and sought the memory of Josh's seventh birthday. But the idea of future horrors arose in her: what would things be like when he was thirty or thirty-five?

"We helped him hide the car. We helped him with the lie. We've been lying to ourselves so long we don't even see it."

"No, stop it. It's okay now. It's going to be okay."

He put his arm around her, mostly to quieten her, but also feeling the need of it for himself. She leaned into his embrace, attempting to breathe evenly and calmly, for his benefit. She couldn't stop crying, and he kept patting her shoulder. "There," he said, "there." But he was far away, resolving that he would return to work immediately on the mural for the university — it was something that needed doing, something with which he could busy himself. It would simply be working out tableaux of life in the city. Except that now he saw himself painting the scene of the meth house with the fence crashed through and the gash in the yard, the downed sapling, the open door going into the awful, dull, light-dying gray gloom, the stretcher, and the emergency vehicles parked in front with their roof lights flashing. He sought to dismiss the images, but couldn't shake them, couldn't stop seeing them.

"We're safe now, aren't we?" she said, still sniffling. Her voice startled him. "Maybe it'll be okay now?"

"Yes, my darling," he managed, "we'll work it all out. We'll find a way through."

But there was no conviction in his voice. And she had a nerve-shaking sense that the worst of it all was really only beginning.

THREE FEET IN THE EVENING

T HE CENTRAL HALLWAY at Long View Senior Village shone now like a calm lake with sun on it because each day a staff member ran a buffer over it. Cleanliness had been Ms. Gable's first priority from the start of her time as head nurse and administrator there. Soon after her arrival, which was at the height of the pandemic, the whole place began to smell faintly of cleanser. And it was true that the number of cases had indeed begun slowly to subside — though probably other, still unknown factors contributed to this. Over the harrowing previous months, as the numbers of the sick and dying kept climbing, Clement Dyson and three other men had, by a kind of terrible default, come to form what she now called her prize quartet — Dyson, Sid Bishop, Silas Borgman and Harold Slocum. *The four who remain,* Dyson called them.

At times, she seemed not far from eligibility for a room at Long View herself, at least in terms of temperament, though she was only in her fifties.

Dyson mentioned this to the others one fall morning — in a gently teasing way since she was standing right there. This was in the solarium, which resembled a big family room: two sofas, six wing chairs, a TV, a wide, low coffee table, and an upright piano no one used. "You could move right in," he added.

She gave a small companionable chuckle. They all liked the lilt of it. "I might could take you guys up on that one of these days."

"You could be happy living at Long View," Slocum told her.

"What 'long view,'" Dyson said, and made a spitting sound. "Long View. Some view."

The solarium windows now looked out on a road that had been widened and tarred, which ran in front of a massive, obstructing three-story red-brick house with a circular drive and two fat shrubs in front. The house was ugly and it was brand-new and it was empty. And it blocked what had once been the "long view" — a dappled open field of wild iris, tickseed and purple passionflower, ending in a distant green glimpse of the Mississippi.

And in any case Long View Village itself, for all its new polish, had been earmarked for demolition in the coming year. A new facility was under construction in Bartlett, and would open in the fall of '24. It would also be called Long View.

"Long View," Clement Dyson repeated. "It's just a stupid name now. There's no 'long view' *here,* anymore, and there can't be one *there* because Bartlett's — what — fifteen miles from the river? Long View, hell."

"Come on, now," Ms. Gable said. "Let's just focus on what's right about today."

She'd brought in from home her own tea set, a light blue porcelain pot and five cups, on a flower-printed aluminum tray. She had placed Dyson's birthday gift on the tray. This was his eighty-ninth, and, perhaps in honor of the day itself — who could say for sure? — a daughter whom he had never met or seen was coming to pay him a visit.

"Well, anyway, apart from the names of things," Ms. Gable said, "how do you feel this morning? I know it's a bit nerve-racking but at some level, you must be glad too?"

"This visitor doesn't know me from Adam and Eve," he said. "She wants something from me, though I can't imagine what."

"Maybe something about one of the books," Borgman said. "A long-ago royalty payment."

"Not a chance, Silas."

"Well, I guess we'll see," Ms. Gable said. "Won't we."

In a past life, as he called it, he'd published three "slender" — also his expression — volumes of poetry, a couple of which had actually been rather well received. He'd written the first one, called *Times Ten,* while teaching Shakespeare and the Elizabethans at Tennessee State, during his first marriage. But that marriage ended badly, and since then he'd been living mostly elsewhere — a lot of elsewheres, he'd say — as though it were some kind of requirement. Indeed, *The Great Elsewhere* was the title of the second book (the third one, published almost forty years ago, had been called, simply, *Poems*).

"You never can tell," Ms. Gable said to him, pouring tea into Sid Bishop's cup. "Maybe there's some money waiting for you from somewhere."

"I gotta say," Bishop told her. "It really is like you're one of us. Might as well move in."

"What would I tell my husband?"

"He'd be welcome here, too."

"I don't think the ladies here would take to it. And I can't say I'd blame them."

"Miss Terrier might pitch a fit," Slocum said.

"Now, now, Mr. Slocum, that's not nice. You know her last name is Terry."

"That's *Miss* Terry," Dyson said. "And she's pretty fierce about insisting on it."

Slocum glanced back toward the entrance to be certain Miss Terry was not in earshot. "I think Ter-*rier* fits her better."

"Reminds me of my sister, Grace," Dyson said. "Who went to her reward almost thirty years ago now. Even sounds a little like her sometimes with the religious stuff."

Miss Terry was ninety-three, and still in relatively good health. She had a way of snapping at you, and always seemed to be impatient about something: the wait for tea in the mornings or the arrival of dinner or how dinner was prepared, or the heat or the cold or the too-hard mattresses. She'd never been married, and she described herself as a former minister of the Gospel, though none of them knew what sect or religion she'd belonged to; she no longer went to church. No one ever came to see her. She didn't like the company of these rough men, and most nights she led a small group of the surviving ladies in prayer. (Lately, everyone was devout about something.) Clement Dyson had occasionally joined them. In the distant past, he'd spent a month at an abbey in France — it was when he was writing the group of religious poems that would appear in *The Great Elsewhere* — and, as he mentioned to Borgman, he actually liked the words of some of the prayers. *St. Michael the Archangel, defend us in the battle. Be our protection against the wickedness and snares of the devil.* He had even spent time alone with one or more of the women — tea on an afternoon, or brunch of a Sunday. The other men teased him about being a ladies' man. A fake priest. They considered him the luckiest among them for the life he'd led — the cities he'd lived in and all the women he'd been with — and for today's turn of events, too. A visitor. A daughter.

"*Miss* Terry's all right," Ms. Gable said now. "I wanna be like her when I grow up."

"You're never gonna be that closed down," Dyson said.

Silas Borgman agreed, then said, "But I'd say our young friend here does have Old Soul Syndrome. I bet hubby does too."

Bishop, who wore a hearing aid, said, "Gimme that again."

"I said Ms. Gable has Old Soul Syndrome."

"*Is* having an old soul a *syn*drome?" Slocum asked.

"Syndrome," Bishop said. "What about it? The first time I heard that word was in a public message about some disease or other." He'd spent forty years in the broadcast business, selling time, for ads.

"We're saying Old Soul *Syndrome,*" Borgman told him, loud. "It's a syndrome."

"Well," said Ms. Gable, filling Borgman's cup. "You're all welcome to speculate about my Old Soul Syndrome while you drink this very healthy herbal tea."

Harold Slocum smirked, deftly fiddling with his dry Zippo lighter, turning it over and over in one hand, then flicking it open with his thumb and snapping it shut, like a sort of nerve-tic. He hadn't lighted a smoke of any type in eighteen years. "I think the idea's nonsense," he said. "Calling it a syndrome. Makes it sound negative. Like Sid said. A disease." He was the youngest among the four, only seventy-six, though he looked much older from years of alcohol abuse. He often talked about those days, *high tales,* Ms. Gable called them: the many different jobs he'd held, the benders, the general craziness. He'd led an eclectic life. She jokingly called him "Hocum." Hocum Slocum.

"I agree with you, there, Harold," said Dyson. "It's nonsense."

"I'm pretty sure it's a thing," Borgman put in, "I'm sure I read about it somewhere."

"Probably in a Sunday supplement, right?" Dyson said. "And we all know how scientific those articles are."

"It wasn't a Sunday supplement. And what a snob thing to say. It takes smarts to be an electrician, too. There's plenty of really smart people who ain't authors. I never read the damn Sunday supplements."

"Oh, well," Dyson told him. "I did." Then: "Sorry, Silas."

"Anyway," Borgman said. "I think it's a syndrome."

"It's nothing of the kind," said Bishop.

"You all," Ms. Gable said. "You'd argue about whether a clear blue sky is blue."

"That's a fresh one," said Dyson.

She gave forth the soft lilting laugh. "I think I just made it up."

"How is it you're always so jolly, anyway?"

"Don't know. Now, please drink your tea."

"I'll have some more," Silas Borgman said. "Miss Scarlett."

Since July she'd had an idolatrous five-foot-high picture of Clark Gable in her office. It covered the whole wall behind her desk. She was not related to the actor (she scarcely knew the movies) yet she enjoyed the assumptions some people made about her when they saw it. Miss Terry, particularly, always glowered at it whenever she went by. But she wouldn't speak of it, or acknowledge it — probably, Dyson had said, for fear of offending Ms. Gable about her family. The picture was in fact a joke birthday gift from Dyson, and the others had chipped in.

They all thought the world of her.

She took good care of them, saw to their meals and their medications and the hours of what she called "self-actualization" (it was "alone time" to them) and social activities. Games like poker, bridge, gin rummy, and movies (TCM). On occasion she would even sit through a movie with them and the ladies who, after prayers with Miss Terry, would gather at the TV, which Dyson described as the one remaining view of the world outside.

And of course with gentle consistency, Ms. Gable encouraged

them to spend time outside in the cleansing air, the defending breezes, weeding the garden she'd put in, or walking around on the grounds, or even playing some croquet.

Plus she agreed with them about the eyesore blocking their view. "It's just the city's idea of development and progress, you know. And we're powerless in the face of it."

"Yeah," said Dyson. "And that's our status in any case. Powerless. I wanted that view of the flowers and the river. I wanted the actual long view in my goddamn last days."

"Please don't talk that way, Mr. Dyson. Last days. You could live another ten years."

He smirked. "An outside guess."

"Well, anyway," said Slocum, shutting the lighter with its little metallic clank. "Who wants to look at a fancy big-assed empty house all day? And I wonder if there'll be a solarium in the Bartlett Long View? I want a solarium just like this one — with a nice view."

Ms. Gable said, "You're all beginning to sound like spoiled babies."

"That's us," Dyson said. "Second childhood. Which *is* a syndrome. Surely you remember the ancient riddle — what has four feet in the morning, two feet in the afternoon and — "

She interrupted him. "Oh, I know that one. Yes. It's a man. The answer is it's a man."

Sid Bishop had spoken over her, and now he repeated himself. "Gimme that again. Was that a joke? What about feet? Is it dirty?"

"It's the riddle from Oedipus," Dyson said.

"Who?" Bishop said. "Never heard of him."

"I swear," Ms. Gable said, turning to leave them. "You guys're a trip. I've got work to do."

"What about Mr. Dyson's birthday present here?"

"Oh." She frowned slightly.

"Forget it," Dyson said.

She waved this away. "Don't be silly." And something shone in her dark eyes, which were usually so benevolent and cheerful. There seemed the faintest doubtful air about her as she crossed to the table and the gift. Dyson was reminded of the forlorn faces of

those pillowy rounded women in some of the Renaissance paintings. But then he thought of the impending visit from the faceless
daughter, and felt a sudden urge to complain about the racket of
Slocum's dead Zippo.

He looked out the window and muttered, "They're just gonna
keep ravaging the whole country, building these goddamn big, vul-
gar, ostentatious barns. Tract mansions."

She took the gift and held it for a moment in both hands as if to
shield herself. "Well?"

Crossing his arms, he sat lower in his chair, brooding.

"Come on," she said as though talking to a child; and when he
didn't move, she sighed and put the gift down gently in his lap.
"People've gotta live somewhere, Mr. Dyson. Try not to be so negative. Especially today."

"I'm not in the mood for observance," he said. "Or for any other
visitors but you."

She smiled briefly. He saw the small gap in her straight white
teeth, which was part of her charm. It always pleased him to see it.
She said, "You're sweet. But in heaven's name, why be so glum? This
is a good day. Something good's happening. And on your birthday."

He said, without inflection, "That's a coincidence. She wants
something, that's all."

They were all regarding him now.

"Look. I moved to Paris and then to Nice before she was even
born, *fifty-three years ago.* And I had two other marriages, and a son
from the last one, and *he* hasn't spoken to me in twenty-four years."

"Are *they* in touch with each other?"

"You think I know that? I don't know. And that's the reality of it
all, okay?"

"There you go," Sid Bishop said. "And that's true, too. Thank
you, Ms. Gable."

Dyson spoke up. "You just quoted Shakespeare, Sid. You said
the exact line Gloucester speaks after his son Edgar tells him, 'Men
must endure their going hence even as their coming hither; ripeness
is all.'"

Sid Bishop gave him a look. "Shakespeare said, 'Thank you, Ms. Gable'?"

"You know what I meant. It's from *King Lear.* And here we are, we four, quite ripe."

"How do you carry all that in your head?" Silas Borgman asked.

Dyson muttered, "And certainly we're also, aren't we, having to endure our *going hence.*"

"What's the matter with you, anyway?" Bishop said. "And don't mumble."

"You guys, I swear." Ms. Gable moved to the door. "I'll get the donuts and biscuits."

They watched her go. Borgman took a sighing breath and spoke in a low, confiding voice to Dyson. "She's got a very damn good sense of humor, however old her soul happens to be. To put herself out like this with us. She's a good sport. And I really wish you'd go easier."

Bishop said, "Christ, come on. Speak the fuck *up.*"

"I'll try to go easier, there, Silas."

"Just quit being so damn cranky," Borgman said.

"Ah, leave it alone, can't you."

"Happy birthday, asshole."

"Hey," Ms. Gable said from the entrance. "That's no way to talk."

"Forgive me," Borgman said.

"I think we can get some ice cream too. Will you all have some?"

"I will," said Dyson. He looked at Borgman and offered a side-long smile. "Okay, Silas?"

Dyson's father had owned a chain of jewelry stores. He was already elderly when Dyson was born, and so the boy's childhood memories all included the incremental processes of decline. His mother died a month after his first birthday. There was the grown sister, Grace, already married and living with her husband in Colorado, but by the time Dyson had entered his tenth year she was home, serving as a surrogate parent, observing in him the kind of cloying, secretive concupiscence she thought she'd detected in her ex-husband. She

believed the boy needed the sort of moral training that the old jeweler had been unable, at his great age, to provide. Her efforts mostly
took the form of increasing restrictions and tirades. He left home,
steeply against her wishes, the day his trust fund became available.
He traveled to Paris, thinking he would live there and write. He was
already composing verses, and he might've stayed longer, except
the old jeweler died, at almost a hundred years of age, and his sister gave up the stores. So he decided to go back home for college.
By the time of his graduation from the University of the South, he
was publishing his first poems in magazines and dating the young
woman who would become his first wife. She was a small, quick-
tempered, reticent girl, and he wrote many poems to her and about
her, and dedicated the first book to her. *For Maureen, for the laughs
and the passion.* But the laughs had died out quickly enough, and
the passion followed not long after; to the people they knew and
moved with, they were the fiery couple always going to extremes
with each other. She was unknowingly pregnant when he left her
for his second journey to France. He sent money, and then when
the divorce was final — when he found out she'd betrayed him with
a neighbor while they were still together — he ended any other communication with her. He knew she married the neighbor. A dentist,
named Thomas Benson.

Over the years there followed two more divorces and the son who,
when Dyson left that marriage, wasn't quite old enough to remember him. He'd paid the alimony and child support as was stipulated
in the decree, but otherwise preferred the distance. Mostly he'd
traveled alone, and lived quite consciously for what he'd thought
of as his moment, his one life as an artist, often through the women
he came to know. Various entanglements and affairs. He'd believed
he was cultivating an inward rage and tribulation to fuel the work.
And in the end all of that had failed him. He could admit this much
to himself. It was all the product of idle fancy and ego. He despised
it now. He'd outlived the few people he'd seen as friends, or who saw
him that way. He'd earned much of the enmity and bad feeling — or,
more accurately, indifference — toward him over the last twenty-five

years or so. His books had been out of print for a longer time than that. He had only the first book, *Times Ten,* in his room, published in 1958 when he was twenty-two. And he remembered that even then, even in the freshness of those early days with Maureen, he'd lain awake in the nights while she slept peacefully at his side, imagining himself with other women. *Times Ten* had won a prize from a now defunct university press, and he'd misplaced the small glass crest somewhere along the way to here. Anyhow he maintained that he didn't know where the rest of that other life could be; it was all gone and done with by the time he turned sixty, and he'd spent so many years traveling in the world, staying for periods in Nice, and Paris, and the Loire Valley; in Venice and Milan, and in Vienna; and then in Guadalajara and down to Santiago, and San Jose; always planning to use for his work what he saw and lived through in those places. But the work dwindled so steadily, and he'd come to believe it was the constant mobility that was killing the will to do it. So he went back to Mississippi, and taught Shakespeare in a high school in Corinth for the eighteen years leading up to coming here. He'd told Borgman in their first weeks of acquaintance that although going back to Mississippi hadn't rekindled his will to work, he'd derived anyway some pleasure from sending a few farm kids out into the world with a little of the Bard in their heads.

"What kind of teacher were you?" Borgman asked him once.

"The feared kind," he answered. And that had contained its grain of truth.

These days he lacked the will to think much about any of all that. What had been left to him was the simple peaceful view of a spacious field of wildflowers beyond which a continent-running river flowed with the last changing seasons.

And now that was gone, too.

The telegram from his daughter was quite simple and direct: *Coming to visit you. STOP. Tomorrow after six. STOP. Marilyn Dyson-Benson.*

"Well, I gotta say I still think it's a good development," Borgman said now.

"Her mother got remarried," Dyson said. "And had an apparently normal and happy life with the man she cheated on me with. I wasn't the only cheater."

"Well, then. See? Maybe she's just — only coming to see *you*. Her father."

"Yeah," Dyson said. "But no. No. They hate me."

"Damn, you're a hard-heart," said Slocum. "No offense."

"Fuck you, Harold. No offense."

"Christ, man." Silas Borgman made a sudden gravelly sound in his throat. "I'm ninety in a month. Fuck'n ninety. Don't seem possible."

Dyson sighed. "Time's gone by us all like a thief."

Ms. Gable, having just returned with the tray of donuts and biscuits, said, "Mr. Dyson, you should write a poem about that, since you *are* our resident poet."

He scoffed. "No, no. Not you, too, Ms. Gable. I haven't written a word — not even a letter — in years. And I just mouthed something so automatic, shopworn and clichéd that it doesn't bear repeating."

"Well, then let's just say that, as Miss Terry's our resident chaplain, you're our resident philosopher."

"I'll accept that. Since the first question of philosophy is whether or not to kill yourself."

After a brief pause during which the others made sounds of disapproval or amusement, she said, "Come on, now. Let's just stop."

"Yes *let's*," Dyson said quickly. "Exactly that. Let's stop."

"I mean let's stop that kind of talk, and you know what I meant." This time the pause was silent.

"And — well, but all four of you are up and about," she said. "Right?"

"Ambulatory," Borgman said. "Yes we are."

"Yeah." Dyson shrugged, looking off. "Ambulatory."

"Why don't you open your gift?"

"Let's put a candle in a donut and light it," Bishop said.

They all agreed; Borgman even giggled about it. But it took a while to find candles in the central kitchen, and then they couldn't find matches, either. Ms. Gable located a small can of lighter fluid and filled Slocum's dry Zippo, which, to their great surprise, worked

perfectly as if it had never fallen out of use. They lit the candle —
a tall one so thin that it looked like a baton with the donut stuck to
the end, a skinny torch. They sang "Happy Birthday," and Clement
Dyson opened his gift, a new annotated *Hamlet,* with critical essays
and the play itself. He looked at Ms. Gable. "You picked this?"

"We all did," she said.

But the others indicated her. "She chose it. We chipped in,"
Bishop said.

"Well, it's very nice," said Dyson as he bit into a donut. "Thank
you all."

"See?" Ms. Gable said. "So now go out, and enjoy the morning
air. Come on. Go get some air. It's such a pretty day."

It was indeed true that the four of them were "up and about." Dyson
had type 2 diabetes, and arthritis, and he suffered from mild neu-
ropathy in his feet, but he could still walk around, and for longer
walks he had his blackthorn walking stick. Though Borgman had
geographic atrophy in both eyes and was legally blind according to
the DMV, he could see well enough to walk from place to place on
the grounds, and to go for outings on those rare occasions when his
son visited with his minivan; Bishop still limped from a hip injury
he'd suffered almost sixty years ago in Pleiku, but he would proudly
tell you it was no worse than when it first happened. He did have the
hearing problem, and his hands were crooked with arthritis. Slocum had a bad stomach and angina. And sometimes he would lose
his way telling one of his high tales. This wasn't anything as serious
as Alzheimer's — Hocum Slocum himself called it "old timer's" —
but they all supposed it might be the decades of alcohol abuse.

Now they went out and walked carefully along the packed pea-
gravel lane leading to the east edge of the grounds. On this end
there were oaks and maples, through the trunks of which you saw
the blue road that wound on to the city center.

Because of the cold snap in late September, many of the leaves on
the trees had begun to turn. The leaves were dropping, carried aloft
swirling in the chilly breezes, and there was a faint smell of creosote
from the railroad track a mile away. They went back around the

building, to the west, where the low hedge was. Beyond that, they saw the big, odd-faceted, grotesque obstruction of the new house with its two verandas, one atop the other, its Dutch gable cedar roof and its two-car porte cochere.

Dyson stood and stared at it, hands in the pockets of his saggy brown slacks.

"It ain't gonna move, Clement," Slocum said. "No matter how long you stare at it."

"You know why they can't sell it, Harold? Because it's ugly. It's all kitsch."

"It's all *ritsch*, you mean. I bet they're charging more than a million for it."

"I needed that view," Dyson said. "The flower field and the big river. It's just gone."

"Well, Long View — this place — is gonna be gone, too. Nothing for it."

They returned to the solarium and ate some of the biscuits with the softening butter from the dish. Presently the new young assistant, Pru Janetz, came in and started taking the empty plates away.

"Where's our friend?" Borgman asked.

Pru said, "Oh, Anna got called away."

"Anna," said Dyson. "Called away."

"Yeah."

"Who called her away?" Dyson said.

She shrugged. "Something with her son."

He followed her down the hall. Pru handed the plates over to the kitchen staff, and turned to him. She had a way of thrusting her pelvis at you, just standing there, one hand on her hip. She was clearly unaware of this, and there was something rather childlike in her face and voice that softened the effect. She was just a girl recently out of high school, working a job she didn't like but didn't mind much, either. Yet, seeing her perfect feminine lines, he was surprised yet again to find himself indulging in the old habit of considering women's bodies as types — *versions*. Preferences. And, turning slow in the well of memory, he experienced an abrupt sense of disorienting abhorrence, and looked at the floor. It went through him that there were two grown people out there going on with their lives, and surely there were also grandchildren and conflicts and milestones. He had known nothing of it. And now he *would* know. With a gloomy stir of reminding himself, he understood that he would know at least some of the history today. He would doubtless have to hear it. And he was certain that he wouldn't be able to endure it: the life histories, the tender changes, the fault lines and little victories; sorrows, hurts, losses. He didn't want any of it.

To Pru Janetz, he said, "What's this with Ms. Gable's — with Anna's son."

"Well, you know, he's repeatedly been a lot of trouble."

"No I didn't know."

"Oh, maybe I shouldn't've said anything."

"Nothing to worry about," he said.

She shrugged again, and went over to the hallway down to the rooms for patients who were not ambulatory.

Slocum walked up. He'd heard the exchange. "Didn't know Ms. Gable *had* a son."

Neither of them said anything. They watched the other two come along the hall.

"So what's the deal?" Borgman asked.

"Something with her son and trouble."

"Medical?"

"Just that he's been a lot of trouble. Repeatedly, she said."

They all returned to the solarium, and took their usual places, facing the windows. Several of the women were watching figure skating on the TV. Or, Dyson saw, it was a movie about figure skaters. "Shit," he heard himself say. "Wonder what trouble."

Bishop was chewing on a beef jerky. "Well," he said. "Whose birthday's next? How much time — " He stopped.

No one answered.

"Time," he broke forth, chewing. "When I worked in radio I sold time, man. Imagine that. I was *selling* it. *Time.* That's what I did. I sold *time.* Wish I could buy some of it now."

"You know what?" Dyson said. "It's been all our shit from the beginning."

There was another silence.

"Think of it."

Borgman said, "What the hell are you talking about, Clement?"

"Forget it."

They were quiet again. Dyson shifted in the chair, leaning forward. "That woman listens to all our talk about us and our histories. Harold, you didn't even know she has a son."

"Well, there's a lot she doesn't know about *me*," Harold Slocum said. "And we know her husband's a plumber. She's talked about that. Hey, what is this, Clement?"

"Ah, hell. Forget it."

"I think we're all a little nervous because of this visit from your daughter."

"I still really believe that's a good thing," Borgman put in.

"Well, what happened with them, anyway?" Slocum asked. "How come neither of them ever came around?"

Dyson raised his voice. "Because they hate me, okay? I played around. I didn't stay. I went around, you know?"

"Shit," Bishop said. "I'd hate you, too."

"You're thinking about this one who's coming to see you and not Ms. Gable," Borgman said. "Ain't that right?"

"I wouldn't know," Dyson answered. "Why don't you tell me what *you* think?"

Miss Terry came toddling in, wearing her bathrobe tied tightly at her middle. She had forgotten her slippers. She looked down, and seemed suddenly confused. Dyson saw her blue feet, and he stood, intending to help her not to fall. But two of the women rushed over. "I don't want noise right now," Miss Terry said. "Stop all this noise." She pointed to the TV. "Turn that thing off." Then she looked over at Dyson and the others, and raised a hand to point at them. "Woe unto the world because of offenses! For it must needs be that offenses come; but woe to that man by whom the offense cometh!"

The two women turned her, and one of them, tall, hunched,

skeletal but clear-eyed, looked over. "Sleepwalking," she said. "It's been happening a little." They walked her back out to the rooms beyond Ms. Gable's office.

"Jesus Christ," Borgman said.

Twilight had begun, the earlier dark of the fall, and there was no moon. The diffused radiance and sparkle of West Memphis shone beyond the gigantic shadow of the empty house. All four men were convened again in the solarium. Ms. Gable, who had returned only a few minutes ago, brought in a small silver tray with a bottle of Canadian whiskey on it, and four glasses. They all knew the fourth glass was hers. It was a special-occasion drink, for Dyson's birthday. She'd also brought a can of Pellegrino for Slocum, who drank six or seven of those every day.

Dyson poured a healthy amount of the whiskey and offered it to her, smiling.

"Oh, that's too much for me," she said.

"Okay." He drank it down.

"You don't want to be drunk when your daughter arrives," Ms. Gable said.

He gazed at her. "No. Actually, I think I *do.*"

She paused, then took the bottle and poured the other three glasses, the last, only a small sip, for herself.

"Courage," Dyson said. He poured himself another. "How's your son?"

"My son — " She gave him a look. "My son — my son's fine."

Out the window, they saw the beginning of the last of the day's light, the sky a darkening carmine shade. They watched a crow sail over, and then another. A white car pulled in slow, and parked. It was five forty-five in the afternoon.

"That's probably your visitor," Ms. Gable said, taking the last of her drink. "Do you want me to bring her back here for you?"

"We'll adjourn," Borgman said, standing. "Come on, boys."

The others stood and began moving toward the door, where Ms. Gable waited.

Dyson said, "No — look. Stay, please. All of you."

She remained where she was, and they were all paused, watching her. "Well?" she said.

"You, too, please. I really can't be alone with this person. I don't even know her."

"This ain't our business," Borgman said. "It don't feel right."

"Are you my friends or not?"

Silence.

"Shouldn't this person meet my friends?" Dyson said to Ms. Gable. "Shouldn't she meet you and the boys and Miss Terry and the others and see firsthand that I'm okay here? What my life is here?"

Borgman sat back down. And the others followed suit.

Ms. Gable said, "All right then."

She motioned for Dyson to accompany her. They walked without speaking along the shining hall toward the front entrance. The image of them reflected up from the floor. Dyson saw this and quite suddenly the silence was nearly unbearable. "Tell me about your boy," he said.

"Excuse me?" She stopped.

"You were called away."

After a few more seconds, they were walking again. "Why don't you tell me about your daughter?" she said.

"Because I'm completely ignorant about her whole life."

"Well, then there'll be so much to talk about."

He heard something in her voice. He took her elbow, lightly. She looked down at his hand.

"Mr. Dyson."

"I'd like to hear about your boy."

"Well," she said, "maybe this isn't the place." They went on, and then they were waiting for the shadow figure in the parking lot to get out of the little car.

"I'd bet she's as nervous as you are. And she's trying to gather her courage."

"She and her brother both. They hate me."

"You don't know that, now. Look, don't ruin this chance." Again, he heard the something in her voice, the slightest tremor.

"Hey," he said, and nodded at her. "Hey. Come on, Anna. Tell me."

She stared for a few seconds, then sighed out the words, "He crashed the car. The second one. The second time. He was texting and he was drunk." She looked down at her hands. "He's on opium. Or morphine. Codeine. What all else." Now her voice had tears in it. "This is the first job outside the house that I've had since I was twenty-nine and left nursing. I wouldn't even be here if things — " She halted, tilted her head slightly, gazing at him, sniffling. "I don't regret my working here."

"I'm so sorry," Dyson managed.

Her embarrassed nod caused an ache in him, and he saw, in her fleeting smile, the little gap in her teeth. He took a breath, resisting the urge to touch the side of her face.

"You've been so good to us in all this hell," he told her.

"No."

"But you have, Anna. You never made it seem like it was a job to you."

"Don't," she said, still sniffling. Then: "I really don't mind the job. And — and you must remember to try and be open to whatever your — your visitor needs."

"Still worried about *us*."

"Well, maybe she doesn't want anything more than to know you."

"Don't worry," he got out. He saw the car door open.

"Plumber's income's just — not enough, you know," Ms. Gable said. "The pandemic took so much business away. We're at our wit's end." Now the tears were running down her cheeks. "I'll go inside now. I'll be in the office."

"No, don't leave."

"Mr. Dyson — " she began. "Clement."

But he interrupted her. "You won't stay?"

"It's best if you're the one person to greet her here. I'll come into the solarium in a little while." She took his wrist briefly. "And — and please. Don't say anything about this to the others. I shouldn't have said anything to you. Or to Pru. I told her in confidence, I *thought*."

"I won't say anything," he told her. "Of course not. And I'm so, so sorry."

"Nothing to be sorry about." She wiped her eyes with the heels of her palms. "You don't need — none of you need my troubles."

"But we *do*," he said. "We should've paid more attention. Should've been able to see *you* apart from our petty concerns." As the words left his lips he experienced a fleeting sense of another context for them, and tried to suppress it.

"No. Really, it's all right." She stood straight, hands at her sides. "Now, you just pay attention to this person who's come all this way to see you."

"All the way across time," Clement Dyson got out. "We'll talk more about — "

She took his wrist again. "Please. No. Don't."

"But you *can* — you can talk to me about it when you get low. Please."

"Say that to *her*," Ms. Gable said. Then she hurried back into the hallway and was gone. He turned as the glass doors opened, and a woman entered, too slender, almost frail seeming, and when she put the hood back he saw her close-cropped white hair, her sharp chin. She had blue eyes, a flat nose, thin lipstick-darkened lips. She didn't look like anyone he had ever known. She said, "I'm here to see Mr. Clement Dyson, please."

"Hello," he managed, his voice quavering. "That would be me."

FORENSICS

EARLIER, AT A MURDER SCENE involving hoarders in a decaying old house on Maple Street, Detective Casado happened upon a prosthetic leg with a gray woolen sock and a tan suede shoe on the foot. He had been pushing his way through a chest-level dune of old newspapers and magazines, and, seeing the frayed strap where it would attach to the knee, pulled it out of the mess. The fact that it turned out to be merely one more piece of junk amid horrors unstrung his nerves, burdened as he already was with the increasing desire to quit this job, find something else. It flickered in his consciousness all day as he labored in that hellish, packed, detrital place, raking through the rubble, advancing by inches, thinking of his hands and his breath and decay, this macabre excavation, wearing a gas mask. Coming upon what his therapist had called "imprinting sights." ("It's just a phrase I use, Elijah.")

A random prosthetic leg.

It felt as if something had tipped over under his heart. And the experience worsened an already existing anxiety scenario — a what-if. What if, having decided definitely to go, there wasn't anywhere for him to go *to*? At forty-eight, police work was all he knew; it was essentially the only working experience he possessed.

When his wife, Mae, called him there, he went outside in the blustery cold, as much for the fresh air as to speak to her. He sparingly explained where he was, and her tone in response seemed nearly facile. But that was her pattern, attempting to distract him with other matters, her own work as a loan officer at Tennessee Trust, or something concerning their lives away from all work. "Evelyn Tooey called me out of the blue today," she said. "After fourteen years. She's Evelyn Draper now. Evelyn Tooey-Draper. Evelyn. Do you remember her? She started with me at the bank. She moved to California. And she's back."

"I can't think right now, Mae."

"But after fourteen years. Imagine."

"I'd like to be able to do that," he told her. "I'd like to be able to imagine anything but what I have to deal with right here." He looked at the street — parked cars, lawns, houses, bright winter sky beyond — and he saw in his mind's eye what was behind him in the rotting house. "I've gotta go, Mae. Really."

"I'm sorry," she said. "But I called to tell you something good. Her husband's the new superintendent of schools for Shelby County. She's doing real estate and she had a call about showing a house but she's gonna call me back in an hour and we'll talk about getting together and really catching up."

The words didn't quite register. "Okay, but I've really gotta go now, honey. There's so much left to do."

"You poor thing. But listen. The new superintendent of schools. Maybe you could get a job teaching."

"Oh, I see." He stopped, and took a breath. "Well, then let's see about it, kid. Because this — well. Jesus. This."

"I feel like it's all gonna change now," she said.

"I've really gotta go, honey."

They were calling him back into the morass.

Now, arriving at his own small, mortgaged house with the river oaks in the backyard and the mimosa and magnolias in front, he saw the lights on in all the windows — the whole place lit up like Christmas. He hurried inside, almost as if being pursued, and closed the door on the winter, leaning his back against the warm wood. Mae smiled at him from the entrance of the kitchen. "Hi, honey," she said in her most studiedly cheerful voice. "You're home. You made it again. And I've turned every light on."

"I saw that. That's sweet. That's very sweet." He had often remarked in company that he could never be one of those men who claimed his wife didn't understand him.

"Bad day, huh," she said.

"The worst."

"Imprinting sights?"

He nodded. "Too many."

"Well it's gonna change. I've got good news. The Drapers are coming for dinner."

He stared. "Oh, Mae. Tonight?"

"When Evelyn called back — I wasn't sure she would — but she did and we talked, and she said — casually, offhand, not *about* anything, really — that the city's worried about teachers leaving in droves because of the pandemic."

He said nothing.

"There's bound to be openings, Elijah. And you taught survival back when you were in the air force."

"I was twenty-two. Sea survival with a one-man raft. Not much use for that here."

"But it *was* teaching experience. And you have a BA in English. You could get a certificate and teach."

He had been dimly holding on to that very idea for a while — finding something at a high school, a possible escape.

"It's perfect, Elijah, really. And imagine really being able to quit." She was drying her hands with a paper towel, and he saw the fluid motions of the muscles of her forearms. *Flexor digitorum*. He knew the term from forensics. He was so weary of it all.

"I'm in no shape for a job interview," he got out.

"That's the point," she said. "It's not a job interview. It's a nice relaxing meal. Nothing formal. We're having salmon and spinach salad. Time for me and Evelyn to catch up and — and the husband's gotta be looking for teachers. Imagine. You could have a regular job and be home on weekends."

"But, honey, right *now* I could crawl into bed and sleep till morning."

"Tonight's the only time they had this week."

There seemed nothing left to say for a moment.

"You were so discouraged when we talked today, Elijah. And Evelyn seemed so eager for us to get together again, and then she said that about teachers leaving and I just thought, *Well, of course.*

Superintendent of schools. This is perfect, you know? Anyway, a nice dinner'll take your mind off it all."

Not true. The particulars of the scene were riding through him: two men of indeterminate age, seated facing each other as in some bizarre stare-down, both partially decomposed, ensconced unreachably in one of the overstuffed rooms of the house, which was crammed to the ceilings with pile upon pile of magazines and newspapers, chaotic aggregations of junk — car parts, radios, bric-a-brac, lamps, cabinets, musical instruments, wall sconces, ornaments, and mail, thousands of pieces of mail going back decades. "Junk mail," one of the forensics people said, actually chuckling. "Think of it. Mail junk. Junk. Everywhere."

"Aw, Christ," Casado had said. "Leave off with the jokes, man, will you?"

Now, to Mae, he said, "Sweetie — what this day was. There was a whole automobile in there, in pieces, scattered. A 1927 Ford car. And nine violins, honey. Nine. Five guitars, a stand-up piano, piccolos, a clarinet. All littered everywhere, under stuff and on top of stuff. Jesus. The piano was on its back, with the keyboard gone. The keys were buried in a dozen places amid all the mess. And I found an artificial leg, I saw this strap and pulled it up, and Jesus, a random — "

"Stop, please," she said. "Remember what the therapist said. Memory is thought, and we've got to work at thinking better thoughts. Replacing the imprints. You made it home. Concentrate on that. Go change, and get relaxed. Fix yourself a drink."

He hung his coat in the front closet and walked down the hall past his stepson Christopher's closed door, from which music was streaming, and into the bathroom, where he washed his hands, brushed his hair and cleaned his teeth. It all felt remedial. He got out of his suit and donned jeans and a sweater, and put on clean socks, retrieving his loafers from the closet. When he went past the boy's room, the music seemed louder. In the living room, at the portable bar, he poured some Jameson into the bottom of a glass, picked up the day's newspaper and let himself down into the lounge chair by the hearth. She was still in the kitchen. He heard the ice-maker dropping cubes into the ice bucket. He put the drink down, folded the paper and went to her. She was standing in the bright light, and had begun seasoning the salmon, which was laid out over parchment paper on a cookie sheet.

"Looks good," he said.

She smiled. "It'll be fine. You'll see."

He kissed her cheek, and put his arms around her. "How do you study math while listening to the Velvet Underground?"

She gave no answer.

"What can I do to help here?"

"I've got this," she said. "Go relax a little."

"How was your work today?"

"Light traffic."

He opened a bottle of chardonnay, nestled it down into the bucket of ice, then took it into the living room, to the portable bar. He was beginning to feel a little better. The first sip of the Jameson stung with a familiar bloom of flavor. He took another sip, then poured more, and sat down. There had been another corpse, only thirty feet or so from the first two, under an enormous collapsed mountain of newspaper circulars and waste in a narrowed hallway. This one was in a much later stage of decomposition. The hallway had evidently become clogged in the way that he imagined arteries might clog, until it all gave way and buried the little someone nobody expected to find. One of the forensics men on the scene suggested that possibly the other two corpses had argued about the smell. "Looks like an accident followed by a murder-suicide?" he said.

Casado asked, "Where's the weapon?"

"Somewhere in all this shit."

"Do we know the sex of the one in the hallway?"

"Not yet. We can't even get in there yet."

Now, in his living room, the detective took another sip of the whiskey and again made the effort to put away the imprints of the day. He picked up the newspaper and looked at the sports page. The University of Memphis basketball team was undefeated, ranked second in the country.

Christopher walked in from the hall and flopped down on the sofa. Someone without one care in the world. "Hi, Elijah. You all right today?"

"Tired," Casado heard himself say. "You gonna eat with these folks?"

"Mom says I should just take a plate to my room."

He sipped the drink. "Well, but you'll stay out and meet them?"

"Mom already said so, sure."

"How can you study to the Velvet Underground?"

Christopher shrugged and smiled. "Helps me concentrate, no kidding." He was sixteen, just coming into the sense of himself: gifted athlete, first-team football, basketball, baseball. A star, and acting like it a little. Casado had not been able to keep up as well as he wanted to. Mostly he felt a kind of brittle remorse about it, but there were no signs from the boy that anything was particularly amiss. Perhaps a little more often he called Casado by his first name. But then occasionally he did the same with Mae.

When Casado first met her in the summer of 2005, she was a recent widow, unknowingly pregnant, her husband lost in a freak accident out in the Gulf Stream. The husband had been first mate on a charter fishing boat off Cape Fear. A summer job. One morning as he and the boat's captain were trying to reel in a big marlin, the fish suddenly flipped over and sounded, and the line caught the young man's wrist at the glove, pulling him over the side. Another of the mates dove in immediately afterward, and saw him already small in the vastness, struggling to pull the glove off, a shape becoming rapidly miniature, receding into the darkening green. The body had never been found.

Elijah Casado had lately been dreaming about it.

His stepson said, "I'm not that hungry, and I've got math."

"I don't know if I can eat much, either."

"We always say that and then we scarf it down like there's no tomorrow."

"That's true, isn't it."

Because the boy had been a preemie, born at thirty-three weeks, he had breathing problems as a baby. His parents would put him in one of those wind-up swings at the foot of the bed so they could hear his sleep-breathing while they made love. Casado consciously called up the morning light on the bed, and Mae turning to him. He tried to fix this in his mind, the way the light fell on her dark legs, the way it had felt breathing into her murmurings.

Of course the scenes of his workdays back then required that he develop powers of savoring the good moments, but at that time, somehow, such scenes were more like harrowing puzzles, and what he saw seemed only itself.

"Shouldn't you be studying now?" he said.

"Taking a break."

Mae came to the entrance of the room, pulling off her apron. "I saw their light out the kitchen window. They're here. Get the door, will you, honey?" She went down the hall. He saw her calves. *Soleus.* It struck him that he loved her exactly as he had at the very beginning, when he was simply trying to help a neighbor get through, a woman he liked immediately while assuming she could never be interested in a cop.

He sipped the drink.

There didn't seem to be enough air in the room. Gazing at the amber highlights in the whiskey, it occurred to him that this, too, was an imprinting sight of a kind. The therapist he had seen was an older man named Brill, a former policeman, with dark eyes and a calming offhand manner. Brill seemed convinced the trouble was temporary. He believed in medicine, and prescribed Xanax. But the drug only made Casado drowsy. And his problem anyway wasn't nerves, but a discouragement so deep it drained and weakened him. "If it continues, I recommend you change jobs," Brill had told him.

Well. Yes, of course.

The Drapers looked younger than he had expected they'd be. Evelyn was delicate featured and quite small, with the slightest touch of guardedness in her gaze, as though she expected hazards. She was only dimly familiar. Her husband stood more than a foot taller than she; he was round faced, chinless, with wide shoulders and a thick neck. She introduced him as Archie, handing her coat and hat to

Christopher. The hat looked like a small orchid with a net attached. Her husband took his coat off, too, and held it out. "Actually, out in the world, as they say, I go by Archibald."

Christopher set the coats and the hat at one end of the couch.

The superintendent of schools startled the boy by offering to shake hands. "Hey, young man," he said in the animated, loud tone of drink. "I saw you play night before last. Our girl's a senior at Bartlett. Cheerleader. I bet you know her."

Christopher said. "What's her name?"

The man seemed almost puzzled. "Draper."

"He's asking what her first name is," Evelyn said. She leaned toward the boy. "Allison. Her name's Allison. Allison Tooey-Draper."

"Do you know her?" Draper asked.

Christopher pondered a moment, then repeated the name. "Allison." He shook his head. Then: "I don't hang with the cheerleaders that much."

"We never miss a game," Draper said. "You're a damn good player." He turned to Casado. "He's a damn good player. Twenty-seven points the other night."

"I missed that one," Casado said.

"My dad works a lot of nights," said Christopher.

"Oh, right. Police work. Yeah. That's gotta take up a lot of time."

Casado indicated the open bottle of chardonnay on the drinks cart. "Some wine?"

"Oh, I'll just have a glass with dinner," Evelyn said quickly.

Her husband pointed at the whiskey in Casado's glass. "Actually, I'd rather have whatever that is you've got there."

"Archie, no," she said.

"It's just one drink, honey." He laughed. "Well, three."

"Four," she muttered.

"You've never had the slightest gift for math." He leaned toward her. "Evvie." Then, to Christopher: "She hates it when I call her that. Take my advice, son. Always keep them off balance. That's how you win." He turned to Casado. "What's that you're drinking?"

"Irish."

"Oh, I always loved the Irish. Are you Irish?"

"He's talking about the whiskey, Archie," his wife said, cheerlessly.

"I know that," he said, still looking at Casado. "Jeez. I was making a joke."

"So," Casado said. "Irish, then."

"Yeah, please. With ice. I like it with ice."

Casado poured the whiskey. They all sat down. He thought of building a fire exactly at the moment Christopher said, "You want me to make a fire, Dad?" Mae had been letting the boy do it and he was by now the expert.

"Might be nice."

A while later, she entered, and gave forth a flourish of hugs and holding Evelyn by the upper arms, her own arms extended. "Let me look at you. How long's it been?"

"Fourteen years" Evelyn said. "Well, we were in Mendocino thirteen years. We got back last year."

"A year ago."

There was a moment of silence freighted with the fact that it had taken a year for Evelyn to get in touch.

"Life just becomes so — busy, you know."

Christopher had the fire going.

"Think I'll have some of that chardonnay," Mae said. She looked at Evelyn. "Remember our chardonnay lunches?"

Evelyn said, "I'll just wait for dinner, if it's not too much trouble. I'm the DD tonight, you know."

"DD," Mae said. "That's a new one, isn't — "

"Oh, come on, Evvie," Draper broke in. "One drink won't affect your designated driver status." He had been absently watching the boy build the fire. He got up from his chair and poured another Jameson for himself. "This whiskey's so good," he said, low. "Touch more. Hope you don't mind."

"I'll wait until we sit down to eat," Evelyn said with a definiteness, only glancing his way.

"Come into the kitchen with me?" Mae said.

"You gonna be trading secrets, there, girls?"

Without answering, the two women went on into the kitchen. There followed an uneasy quiet, Christopher poking at the fire, though it was roaring, and Evelyn's husband helping himself to still another glass of the Jameson. A moment later, he turned and sipped, and said to Casado, "So, you're in homicide."

"Right."

"What's the docket look like?"

"The docket?"

"Whatever the term is — what's the most pressing thing you're looking at?"

Casado stared at him. "I try never to bring that stuff home."

Silence.

"You know, we work pretty hard to think of it as 'out there.'"

"Yeah, but you can tell me — it's just us boys, right?"

Casado rested his elbows on his knees. "I just don't like talking about it at home."

The other was unfazed. "I've always been fascinated with murder cases, you know, and I seem to have embarked upon writing this novel. I've been reading a lot of them, you know, whodunits. And I thought, hey, why not write one. And man, here *you* are, actually living it."

Casado kept still.

"Must be just the most interesting — "

"No," Casado told him. "In fact it's — well, to be honest, there's a dull, persistent repetition in it, pretty much. And we never mention it at home, really."

"You're kidding."

"Most of the cases I've seen — the thing is, for all the movies you see, it's mostly just — most of the time it's just depressing."

"You mean you're bored."

"I think I'm just tired. It's been a long day."

"Oh? Okay, well — if you don't mind this once. What was it today?"

Casado looked down. "As I said — "

"Oh, right. You don't want to bring it home."

For a few seconds there was only the sound of the flames crackling in the fireplace.

"Hey, champ," the superintendent of schools said suddenly to Christopher. "Who're your favorite players?"

"Larry Bird and Magic Johnson."

"Really? But those guy're ancient history now. What about LeBron? Or Steph?"

Christopher shrugged. "I don't really follow it all that much."

"Well, you don't have to — putting up twenty-plus points a game."

The boy gave him a small, embarrassed, brief smile. "Yes, sir."

"Well, I'm gonna have just a little more of that Irish, if it's all right."

"Sure," Casado said.

He and his stepson watched him waver slightly as he stood to pour another drink. The neck of the bottle clinked against the glass. When he sat down he gave forth a long sigh of satisfaction, and took a sip of what he'd poured. "So," he said, leaning back. "What should we talk about?"

Casado said, "Do you still teach, even with your present duties?"

"Oh, I'm out of the classroom, are you kidding? Haven't been in one for years."

"Well, I've been thinking of maybe teaching."

Draper sipped the whiskey, and then, tilting his head, stared for a bleary-eyed few seconds. "What would you teach? Detective work?"

"No. I was hoping — " Casado hesitated. There was nothing to do but say it. "I have a college degree in English. I was hoping for something in K through twelve."

The superintendent of schools nodded, not quite returning his gaze. "Gotta be so damn interesting. All these crime scenes." He made a smacking sound, looking at the whiskey in his glass.

Again, the only sound was the fire.

"I hope you guys are hungry," Mae called from the kitchen.

"I read that murders increased during the pandemic," Draper said. "Fascinating."

Casado nodded, heartsick, watching him sip the drink.

"What's it actually *like*? I mean, is it possible to visit a crime scene, just for research?"

"Excuse me?"

"You know. Research."

"I wouldn't know about that."

"I'd love to *see one*. It must be awful sometimes, huh."

"It can be pretty — well, but it feels good when you catch the bad guys."

"You really think about it that way? The bad guys?"

"Not really. A lot of the time it's just — lives gone wrong. Bad luck, rage, cruelty and sloth combined. Madness, drunkenness, envy, spite, hatred. Even fear, sometimes coming down from child-hood, you know. And bad people, sure. Evil people."

For a moment, the other was silent, staring. He shook the ice in his glass. "And you're thinking you want to teach."

Casado nodded. "I think I'd be a good teacher. In fact I — I know I'd be a good teacher."

Another silence. The words had sounded unpleasantly earnest as he said them; there was too much of the aspirant in them, the petitioner. He cleared his throat. "I taught survival on a hitch in the air force when I was just a kid. I liked it a lot."

Draper swallowed and coughed, and then laughed a little to himself. "Survival."

"That's right," Detective Casado said thinly. "Survival." He cleared his throat again. "Mae says Evelyn mentioned that you've got a lot of teachers leaving."

"That's the truth of it. Yeah."

Another silence.

"But then, you know, we've got applications stacked to the ceiling."

"Really."

Draper reached clumsily across and made as if to pat the other's knee. "You'd probably stand a good chance though. What with your experience."

Casado looked into his hazy, apathetic eyes.

"I mean all the shit you've been privy to. And, you see, there's a good reason Evelyn got in touch with Mae again. Like I said, this novel I'm working on — "

Mae came in. "Dinner's — " She hesitated, clearly worried about interrupting them. "Dinner."

Christopher led Draper into the dining room, and Casado followed. He had finished his whiskey and he brought in the bottle of chardonnay. The salmon fillet was laid out on a platter with a row of lemon slices across its length. It was already sliced thick. The spinach was in a big bowl, and Mae had let Evelyn help her prepare avocado with tomatoes. Christopher put some of the spinach and a small piece of salmon on his plate, and then excused himself.

"Oh," Draper said. "You're not gonna eat alone, are you?"

"He likes to eat in his room," Mae said flatly.

"You sure it's not because of us?"

"She just said that he likes to eat in his room," Evelyn told him.

"Yeah, I heard. Just — checking."

They sat at the table, the two couples facing each other.

Casado lifted off one falling-apart slice of the salmon and passed the platter to Evelyn. After taking a very small piece from it, she handed it to her husband, who clumsily took three. "I'm not all that fond of salmon," she said softly. "Sorry."

"I'll have your portion and mine, too," Draper said. He poured some chardonnay for himself and looked across at Casado. "Tell me, what's the worst case you ever had to deal with."

"Archie," Evelyn said, low. "Mae says they don't talk about it here."

The superintendent of schools looked at her, chewing. "Yeah, but it's okay to exchange views a little. We're professionals."

"I think I overcooked the salmon," Mae interjected.

"It looks so delicious," said Evelyn. "I wish I liked salmon more."

Draper scoffed. "That's a silly-assed thing to say, sweetie." He sipped the wine. "So." He looked across at Casado. "Come on. What's the worst. Just tonight."

"Actually, you know, they all begin to blur. Tough to think of one."

They all ate for a time in a perfectly awful silence, no one looking at anyone. Draper poured more of the wine for himself, and his diminutive wife made a low sound of disapproval. Casado broke a piece of bread and buttered it. "Anyone else?" he said.

"I'll have a piece," Evelyn said.

He passed it to her.

There was more silence. Mae looked over at Casado and gave a scarcely discernible shrug as she smiled. Evelyn was concentrating deeply on her salad and her piece of bread. Draper reached and took more of the salmon.

"Well, then," he said. "Today. Can you talk about that. Just a little."

Casado looked at him. "Today was a slow day."

"What's a busy day like?"

Evelyn quietly demanded: "Stop it, Archie. Just quit."

"There's a house on Maple Street," Casado said. "Do you happen to know where that is?"

"Vaguely," said Draper. "Maple Street, sure. It's a long street."

"This is near the end of it. By the interstate. Three men lived there. Hoarders. Three of them. You know that term? You know what a hoarder is?"

"Elijah," Mae said.

"I believe so," said Draper.

"Elijah," Mae said, a little louder. "Won't you have a little more salmon?" There was a straining in her voice. "And you, Archie?"

Casado went on: "You know what we found there today?"

She put her fork down and quietly left the table. Evelyn watched her, then turned to her husband. "Look what you've done."

Draper was calmly, sloppily eating. The silence lengthened. Finally she said, "I'll go see if Mae's all right."

"What did you find?" Draper said, still chewing.

"Forget it," said Casado. "Look. Tell me about *your* job, okay? What grade levels are lacking most in numbers of teachers."

Draper waved a hand across his face. "Hell, I don't think that's even vaguely worth talking about. You think I want to talk about that stuff? Numbers? Available classrooms? Look, here's the deal. I'm writing this novel and I need some expert eyes on it. You know what I mean? Some expertise into normal police procedures and all that."

"You're not getting that kind of stuff from your whodunits?"

"Well sure—but I thought if I could get the feel of it the way it really goes down—get some expert opinion about the way I'm describing it all."

Casado said, "You—you want me to read your novel."

Another wave of the hand. "Expert opinion. Sure."

"I don't write novels."

Draper simply gazed back.

"I deal with killings, you know. Murders."

Silence.

"Death."

He leaned back and stared.

"And I'd very much like to stop doing that," Casado said.

The superintendent of schools seemed to let down, drooping slightly, looking at his empty glass and his plate. "Well, you can apply. Like anybody. Hell, you can put in your name and a vita and see what happens, you know. It's individual schools. See what they need. I don't really have that much say in all that."

Casado nodded—dumbly, he felt. There wasn't anything left to talk about.

The superintendent of schools said, "I thought—you being an expert and all—" He didn't finish. His small wife walked in and stood over him. It occurred to Casado absurdly that with Draper sitting and Evelyn standing, they were exactly the same height. "Archie," she said. "Time to go."

The next few moments were a kind of flowing confusion of the two getting their coats and murmuring apologies until at last they were gone. Mae shut the door and turned to lean against it as Casado had earlier. "Oh, lord," she said. "Let's not even talk about it. Let's go to bed."

"I'm sorry," Casado said.

"Forget it, Elijah. *I'm* sorry." She looked like she might begin crying, but she held it in.

"They're gone," said their son from the hallway. "Thank God." He didn't wait for a response, but returned to his room and closed the door. Casado and his wife heard the music start.

"I'll get the dishes in the morning," he said to her. "Please."

They went past the boy's door, on into their bedroom, and quietly got into their pajamas. They didn't speak. After standing side by side cleaning their teeth at the bathroom mirror, they crawled under the blankets of the bed and lay close. Her warmth, the mint on her breath, the faint flowery smell of her hair, soothed him, aroused him. He reached and turned the light out, lay back and turned to her, and, surprisingly, she kissed him with more than a goodnight kiss. They began making love. Completely unexpectedly. There was something powerfully urgent about it, like a kind of defiance of all the forces of negation and torment surrounding them. When it was over they were quiet, breathing slowly, holding on.

"Well," he managed. "We have this — *us,* the two of us — you and me together. Don't we."

"I'm sorry," she said again, softly.

"Stop it," he told her. "You thought I might get a teaching job."

"You still can. It can happen. The county needs teachers."

They were quiet again, each aware of the other, and the silence drew down on them, toward sleep. In the flow of his thinking about the evening, there was now again the intrusion of the prosthetic leg, the gray sock, the suede shoe, the flesh-colored plastic and the strap at the top. He touched her side, wanting a little more talk.

"Baby," she sighed, without quite waking. Turning on his side, facing away from her, he made an effort to drift off himself, and finally, for a space, he was nowhere and nothing. It seemed only a wink, but it was hours. He came to himself quite suddenly, and realized morning had arrived and that he had been dreaming again about her lost first husband. Once more the image came to him of the young man wrenched into the sea, becoming the smallest struggling shape being pulled out of sight into the green depths. It terrified him.

She lay quite still, dreaming whatever she was dreaming. It seemed a peaceful slumber. He experienced a moment of blazing gratitude for her. Gently, with great care, he removed himself, put on his pajama bottoms, walked around to her side of the bed and, bending slowly, kissed her hair, her cheek. Then he made his way soundlessly to the front door, feeling the necessity of making certain that it was locked and that the porch light was off. The dead bolt was engaged and the porch light was indeed off. It was another day; he could not help but think of it as the *next* day. A slight draft from the threshold brushed across his bare feet, a freshet of cold air from the winter on the other side.

BROKEN HOUSE

I think, growing up Catholic, taking it seriously, compels you to live on a great many levels . . . At a certain point, there's something touching and gallant . . . about the situation of being a kid and having to deal with eternity and all these absurd and monstrous concepts.

— Robert Stone, *The Eye You See With*

PART ONE

I.

This story begins far away and long ago at a place called Saint Agnes of Rome Catholic Church and School in Point Royal, Virginia.

Nineteen fifty-nine. September. The air turning incrementally cooler. Birds flittering and singing in the trees, whose leaves were just beginning to show color. Sunny days with fragrant breezes fresh as the proverbial first morning in Eden. And beyond all this, far beyond the processions of fleecy clouds in bright skies, another Russian satellite circling, circling.

They were far ahead of us in space, and they had the bomb now, too.

The TV newscasters spoke of the Soviets and communism in grave tones. People had started digging fallout shelters. In school the previous spring we'd had drills about ducking and covering. People felt spied on. I associated the word *communism* with disease, as in *communicable* disease.

Each morning, I hoped for overcast skies, fog.

I was fourteen years old. One of seven boys from Bradley High School who'd been accepted as a future acolyte and were gathered in the church sacristy around Father Llewellyn Burns for our first training session. Back then, religious training for public school children was offered on Saturday mornings. *Confraternity of Christian Doctrine. CCD.* The classes ran from eight to ten, followed by an hour for confessions. The new altar boy candidates were allowed to be late for the first class that fall to attend this session. I hadn't yet been to confession that week, and anyway I believed I was in peril of eternal fire.

No doubt this sounds a little comic now, even silly.

It was nothing of the kind back then. In fact it remained just under the flow of my thoughts, as did the relatively recent awareness of the concepts — I almost said "twin" concepts, for they were equally powerful — of sex and death. Abstractions, at that young age, yes, certainly; but they were tangled up in my mind, and I recall their pressure, even as I clowned and jostled with everyone in the tightly huddled group around the priest.

Father Burns said, "All of you, *shut up*."

And in the following silence, after looking at each of us in turn, he began showing the instruments of the Mass, explaining the function of each, one by one: the cruets for water and wine, the consecration bells, the pall, the paten and finally the chalice. I was standing across from him as he brought it out with its long stem and its rounded reflection of us in it. "When the celebrant," he began, then paused and took a breath, seeming impatient with himself. "That is, when the *priest* — when the priest says the Latin words *hic est sanguis meus,* the wine in this holy vessel, through the miracle of transubstantiation, becomes the actual sacred blood of our lord." He looked around at us, and slowly, holding it out with great solemnity, went on: "It is made out of pure gold, and only the priest may touch it."

In that instant someone reached past my ear and took hold of the lip of the holy vessel, index and middle finger inside and thumb actually rubbing the outside. "Is that *gold*?"

The priest lashed out backhanded, just missing my head. I turned, and saw a boy whose name I didn't yet know holding his hand to his face. He was about my size, with bronze-hued skin, his hair and eyes pitch-black. The other boys were laughing at what had just happened, and another, whose name I did know, Derek Moss, said, "Way to show you're paying close attention, there, cuz."

Father Burns clipped him with a swiping motion across the top of his head, as if swatting at a fly there. "That's enough from *all* of you. Study your Latin for the next lesson. Now get."

"Where do we go?" Moss asked.

"Don't be idiotic, boy — go back to the class."

The class was taught by Sister Mary Margaret, who was past seventy and looked to me like a man with her wispy chin whiskers that caught light at certain angles. When we latecomers arrived, she had already done seating arrangements, and was just preparing to start a slide show. She waved impatiently for us to take our seats, and then got the slides going. The first three were of grotesquely sated-looking people in attitudes of lazy revelry, women lounging in purple tangles of satin or silk, their fleshy arms and necks showing under the leering gaze of surrounding men, almost everyone eating or drinking, leaning back holding up clusters of grapes, or tearing at some sort of meat. There were two or three such pictures, in bright colors, each appearing after a small ding. As I recall them now, I think of paintings from the Renaissance. A voice from what sounded like an echo chamber spoke of living only for the pleasures of the flesh. This was followed by a representation of Judgment Day: a mass of sticklike figures with indeterminate half-formed faces tumbling into a fire pit, screeching as they fell, the screeching mostly female it seemed. Each previous slide had shown for what seemed a long time, but this one's duration was even longer than the others, and a deep voice said, "Listen to the screams of the damned as they are hurled into the unquenchable fires of hell," followed by an even deeper voice, evidently representing the voice of God: "Depart from me, ye curse-ed." The last word spoken as two syllables. *Curse,* and *ed,* and reverberating dramatically before the next little *ding,* and the shift to the last slide, which was an image of the glorious saved, all in white robes, kneeling at the base of a jewel-studded throne upon which a white-maned old man sat staring sternly out at us. The throne was enclosed by an oval luminescence radiating like sunlight or the blast of an explosion.

I thought of the atom bomb.

The boy who had touched the chalice leaned toward me and murmured, "So, I guess heaven's a monarchy, huh."

I thought he might have just committed a sin. But then I felt a strange sense of release, as though I'd been granted a better way of seeing it all.

He nodded at me, smiling. "You know?"

I gave a nervous little confused smile back at him, and saw a small sickle-shaped scar, like a drawn line in dark clay, just under his lip.

He murmured: "I guess God's a grouchy old man."

Sister Mary Margaret, having shut the machine off, said, "Quiet!" She finalized the class roll. When she got to the chalice boy, she said his name. "Phillip Chorros." And she repeated the surname. "Is that Spanish or Portuguese?"

He shrugged. "Don't know. My father's from Phoenix."

"Appalling," she grumbled. "You don't know. And you say 'Sister' when you speak to me. You say, 'I don't know, *Sister.*'"

"Oh, right," he said, and left the slightest pause. "Sister."

She ignored this. "I happen to know the name *is* Portuguese." And then she launched into the story of Fátima, where the Virgin appeared in repeated instances to three little Portuguese girls, first on May 13, 1917, and then on the thirteenth day of the following five months, the last being October 13, the day of the famous Milagre do Sol (Sister Mary Margaret used the Portuguese, then translated it: "Miracle of the Sun"). She looked around the room. "The sun moved," she continued. "Think of *that*. It actually came closer. It got brighter than it has ever been. The whole village saw it. It's documented. Milagre do Sol. And think of this. The Virgin Mary gave the oldest girl, Lúcia, a horrible, horrible vision of hell—the very ground opened up, a wide gaping hole right at the girl's feet, and she saw something far worse than what we just looked at. And then the Virgin said to her that this was what awaits sinners, and she predicted that a country called Russia would rise up in the world and breed Godless Communism. She predicted the rise of the Russians. And she gave a sealed envelope to the girl with a message in it, addressed directly to the Pope. A message that'll be revealed to the world in 1970. The Pope—Pope Benedict the Fifteenth at the time—read it when he got it, and he wept. He cried. The Pope cried. And each of the ones who have followed him, the Piuses, eleventh and twelfth. And our beloved John the Twenty-Third. They all shed tears seeing what it said. So think of *that* the next time you're tempted to get into some mischief."

Mischief.

The word seemed—and seems now, too, doesn't it?—rather wildly out of context. How could *mischief* warrant the grave voice of the slide show? That doomful voice that was also somehow—though I had no word for it at the time—tinged with the faintest note of delectation, saying, "Listen to the screams of the damned," and then the second voice, so deep, so dramatically pronouncing the word *cursed* as *curse-ed*.

The atom bomb, Godless Communism, curse-ed.

And mischief?

As the class was dismissed, Phillip Chorros leaned over and said to me, "What in the world is it like inside *her* head?"

I whispered, "She looks like my elderly uncle Steve." I had made it up, trying to be funny.

And he laughed, then muttered: "Evidently no prophecies of the Nazis or the six million or a whole other world war my dad got wounded in."

I felt an immediate affinity for him. "My dad, too."

"Did your dad go batty?"

I had no answer, because I hadn't quite understood how he meant the word. I had heard my mother use it jokingly about her sister, my aunt Constance.

"Yeah, the old man went batty," Chorros said, and with his index finger extended he made the familiar circling motion at the side of his head. "The gift of a war that keeps on giving."

My name is Vance Bourdin (pronounced *Bour-dan*), professor emeritus of history here at Western Illinois University, which affords me some residual respect, along with a small office in the library. My wife, Angela, is also retired. When I met her she was a resident psychologist at Dalby Community Clinic, which no longer exists (it has been transformed into a shopping mall; and sometimes, she says, she feels effaced in the way of that once-vibrant charitable institution).

The name Bourdin stems from a line of French Canadians who were deported from Quebec after the Battle of the Plains of Abraham in 1759. Most of those people wound up in New Orleans, but our branch settled almost four hundred miles north, in Memphis. I have relatives in Louisiana, I'm sure, but that connection ended with my great-grandfather Michael, who married a Creole woman in 1881 and, when the whole New Orleans branch of the family objected, told them they could all go directly to hell and dropped the letter *a* from his first name. Michel lived to ripe old age, as did his wife. And they never missed Mass, either.

Everybody's Catholic, of course.

Vance is also my father's name, and his father's as well, though neither my father nor I ever went by the name Junior. When I was small and we all lived close in West Tennessee, family members and friends called us the three Vances. Grandfather Vance died in a one-car crash at age sixty-eight in 1951, in Memphis, where he had been born and from which he never ventured. He grew up on the same land he farmed until the Depression and Memphis National Bank took it away from him. And then he became a general repairman and electrician in and around the city. I was too young to attend his funeral, but I remember my mother, Jean, crying on the phone when she learned of the accident.

My father went into the army in early '42, an athlete who had excelled in baseball, basketball and football. The day of his enlistment, he was six feet two inches tall and weighed 185 pounds. A little more than two years later when he returned wounded from France he weighed only 128, and was suffering from what was then called battle fatigue, or CSR — combat stress reaction. I was born ten and a half months later. He was alone in their bedroom a lot of the time when I was small; his wound took a long time to heal: a piece of shrapnel had gone through the rotator cuff in his left shoulder. I saw the Z-shaped scar several times. We still lived in Memphis, then, and Jean had close relatives of her own in Somerville, so there was plenty of help.

I have very little from that time, of course. My sequential memory only starts, really, from when I was nine, three years after we left Memphis and a year before we got our first car, a used, baby-blue 1951 Ford that we loved and took rides in just to go around and look at neighborhoods or countryside.

But along with the family stories I heard, there are of course fragments of memory that, though no specific time attaches to them, still make a pressure to be included here: they complete the background, so to speak. I remember the happiness in our house at the arrival of the twins when I was eight. And I have a recollection, roughly from the same time, of standing in the freezing winter dark of the backyard with Vance while he planted two maple saplings, repeating several times that we were doing it together, though I couldn't do much more than stamp the cold ground at the base of the skinny trunks. Yet I believe I must have sensed how important it was to him that the two of us perform the task. "There was a time over in France," he often said, "when I prayed for just that — my first son and me, planting."

My strongest memory of the event is the cold, and wanting to be inside.

But I recall nights lying awake, afraid, hearing faint whimpering sounds come through his snoring breath in the next room — almost a kind of wordless protest, but pleading, too. It seems now in reflection that a lot of nights were passed that way, though there's also the happy image of Jean greeting Vance as he returned from work, the two of them standing in a tight embrace, holding on to each other in the open door, so deeply in love, and the winter air coming in.

Phillip Chorros's father was a man whose wounds from the war were interior. They made him volatile and inclined to a brooding impatience. Instead of being at a distance, as my father had been in my early childhood, Chorros's was a towering angry presence, a disapproving fierceness. And whenever I saw the man I was glad of my own father.

His wounds, interior and otherwise, had somehow made him more introspectively kind, and they had strengthened him in his religion and devotion to his family. He was devout. They were devout. On their wedding night the first thing they did was say a rosary together. It was a point of humble pride for them. As a family we gathered to say it in the evenings. And each week, until my twelfth birthday, anyway, we watched *Life Is Worth Living* with Bishop Fulton J. Sheen. Of course I'm aware of the quaint sound of all this, but the fact is that love did reside in the little rooms of that house.

And still I remember being secretly fearful much of the time. Well.

I suppose it may be unnecessary to explain the rock-bottom reason for this, or to point out that it had little to do with the bomb. You've likely guessed something of its contours anyway.

I've already mentioned the two abstractions: sex and death. As we all know, the latter remains fixed in its ghastly redoubt from long before the former begins to stir in our consciousness. And so I'll simply report the unsurprising fact that just before I turned thirteen, I discovered something that every boy inevitably discovers about his own body: a normal privy act nevertheless considered by the church to be a grave offense — so grave that Onan, that scriptural bungler (the passage sounds like an accident: *He spilled his seed upon the ground!*), was struck dead by God himself for it.

I had learned about Onan during Sister Mary Margaret's CCD class. That woman saw evil everywhere she looked: rock 'n' roll was the work of the devil and was causing the corruption of a whole generation of children; the drumbeats and electric guitars and long sideburns all led to promiscuity, led to girls wearing revealing sun suits (*sin* suits, she called them) and boys touching themselves in the mortal sin of onanism.

In my particular case, I thought the word for any sin involving sex was *adultery*. In fact I almost confessed my sin as multiple acts of adultery. But I couldn't bring myself to introduce the idea. So I was going around hoping I'd be alive long enough to find some way to confess and be forgiven — and, as the prayer says, amend my life. In confession I had said I was guilty of impure thoughts and hoped that was enough. I had been going every Saturday to old Monsignor Drummond (he was probably sixty or so), who seemed mild. He told me such thoughts were sinful only if I indulged in them. But of course I *was* indulging in them, and I kept finding myself producing excuses for looking through books at home or in the library, continually, almost autonomically attempting to satisfy my consuming curiosity about it all. I couldn't sleep, and I dreaded the sun going down; I hated being alone because when I was alone I could think of nothing else. Indeed often enough there was nothing else in the mornings under the warm sheet. The whole of my waking and dreaming life was engulfed in mortal sin, and I watched others, especially Chorros, with secret wonder that they could seem so indifferent to the constant enticements everywhere (for one instance, the Sardo bath oil commercial on TV, which played without warning every single day: a beautiful blond woman in a shaft of silky light in her claw-footed bathtub, arm obscuring what you knew were her breasts, one bare leg up as she soothed herself caressingly with the oil).

This is all laughable now, and of course embarrassing.

Yet it was the ground upon which I was standing at the time: according to everything that surrounded me where I lived, I was in a state of mortal sin, experiencing a continual undercurrent of dread even as I clowned for everyone. And I was increasingly on the lookout for inklings of the same kind of inner turmoil in others. I had no way of expressing this then, and I saw no contradiction in it, either. I was simply living it, and going through life as I knew life. I had inherited something of my mother's talent for drawing, and there exists a self-portrait I did then; the boy in that drawing stares out with shadows under his eyes, looking as though he's bearing up under glooms of despair. Which he was. Though in the society of others I somehow managed to hide it.

I spent a lot of time alone. Jean and Vance were occupied with the twins, who perpetually got into things, never still for a moment it seemed (today they would probably be classified as having ADHD). Jean said to friends that I was studying, and sometimes I was trying to. I had to learn the Latin responses for the Mass — the Confiteor being the longest. *Confiteor Deo omnipotenti, beatae Mariae semper Virgini . . .*

2.

On November 19, 1959, nineteen other boys and I, including Phillip Chorros and his cousin Derek Moss, were instituted as new altar boys. The nuns and other priests were already calling us Father Burns's Crew. By then, I had taken on some of Chorros's mannerisms and figures of speech, which is doubtless a fairly common form of hero worship. Yet it was mixed, too, with a troubling sense of precariousness, as if something extreme were on the other side of each moment. He fascinated and repelled me at the same time; and, withal, I yearned to be like him. It's possible that in that early stage of the friendship I wasn't much more than somebody he liked talking to and being crazy with about the absurdity all around. In fact, all along — as will be increasingly evident — I had no idea what he was really thinking or feeling. The important thing to remember is that he was clearly everything I *wasn't;* he was unlike anyone, in fact: a vivid eccentricity emanated from him; it was like a heartbeat you could sense in the bones of his face. Comic, unpredictable and evidently free of the anxiety and the leaden thoughts weighing me down, he seemed always in some strange way quite comfortable in his own skin, while others, including his cousin, thought him weird. And he *was* weird. I heard Shipley and Moss both, at different times, say he was a little crazy. I'm sure now that it all had to do with his way of confounding expectations.

Once, asked to write three simple sentences on the blackboard for an exercise in English class, he wrote:

1. *Mr. Binglecrucker is a droopy little man who cleans floors at the Empire State Building.*
2. *He stumbled and fell headlong down the stairs.*
3. *As they stood him against the wall to face the firing squad, he cried havoc.*

When told rather passively by Mr. Manser, the English teacher, that the task was to write *simple* subject/predicate sentences, he wrote:

1. *Jane runs.*
2. *Jack runs.*
3. *They collide.*

I took all this down and kept it, and for a long time, for years, looking at it again could make me laugh. Whenever I was around him, in fact, alone or in company, my secret unease receded. Plus I had discovered the liberating pleasure of being able to amuse *him.* I had a facility for doing different voices and foreign accents; I was something of an impressionist.

Anyhow, I never laughed harder or more often than I did with Phillip Chorros, especially when he was laughing, too. And we were altar boys together.

That May, Father Burns decided to take us all on a Saturday field trip into the mountains of West Virginia to visit a place called the Abbey of the Holy Cross. The journey would start from the parking lot of Saint Agnes at sunrise. This was the first event where the whole crew would be together. Most were from Saint Agnes and so I didn't know many of them. Someone had brought up the possibility of having a Catholic president, but then the talk shifted to baseball. The news was about the U-2 fiasco and the failed summit. The Cold War possibly getting hot. Nobody was talking about that. I had been thinking about the Soviets, who had sent another Sputnik into orbit and just successfully launched the first unmanned space capsule. I moved across the lot in the direction of the few public school boys. I saw Chorros walk up with his cousin, and went over to them. "Hey," he said, grinning. But then Father Burns made us all gather in a circle, and we had a roll call.

"You boys're gonna see something of the monastic life today," he announced. "A little tour, by my old friend from undergraduate days Brother Edgar. He'll give us a look at the normal daily existence of the Franciscan monks who work and pray at the abbey. And I don't suppose I have to remind you that any deviation from exact discipline and orderly behavior will be punished. Do you understand me?"

"Yes, Father," we said in a ragged unison. Some of us weren't even quite awake yet. I looked at what I thought of as the Russian sky, the thinnest sliver of a day moon faintly showing in it. Phillip Chorros edged closer to me and said, "Let's all just stay up there in the mountains with the monks." I noticed a raised welt on his right cheekbone.

I pointed before I could think not to. "What happened?"

"Walked into a door," he said. "Sometimes I call it Dad."

I stared.

"It's not every day, you know. But enough to feel like it is."

I could think of no response, and evidently none was expected.

"I'm being punished for the venial sin of fibbing to my mother. Judged guilty before she could prove my innocence or I could explain. And you should see me when he catches me in a mortal sin." He stood there smiling at me as if the whole thing were a joke. "Let's hide at the abbey and be monks. Then we can avoid the occasions of sin."

The good sister had used the phrase in her most recent lecture, again about touching ourselves or others in a sinful way.

"Whatever Uncle Steve says," I got out.

A moment later, a school bus pulled up. On its sides were large red letters in script: *St. Agnes of Rome.* We all started climbing in. We ranged in age from twelve to fifteen. The fifteen-year-old was a public school boy named Michael Drexel, tall, skinny, with bright red hair and freckles. The twelve-year-old, also from the public school, had just turned twelve — a pint-sized kid named Reynolds, with quick bright eyes and pink ears, who reminded me of a rabbit.

I had known Drexel for a while. He kept an enormous collection of comic books. You had the feeling he collected them in order to make friends. He sat in the aisle seat to my right, having pushed in front of Chorros, who shrugged and took one two rows up across the aisle. We were all about eight rows back. "I've never been to West Virginia," Drexel said to me. "I wonder how long it'll take."

I might've given a half shrug. I was looking at Chorros, thinking of his father and venial and mortal sins.

"I've never seen a monk before," Drexel went on. "What does a monk do all day, anyway? My mother says it's all just praying."

Chorros looked back and grinned at him. "Well, not just praying. I spent time with one last month. A beady-eyed little guy who farted a lot, and each one smelled like fish. Bourdin was there. They actually smelled like fish, right, Vance?"

"Yep," I said. "Like fish. And they sounded like questions."

Chorros laughed, and repeated the word. "Questions, yeah."

I looked out the window and felt unreasonably glad.

Our driver was a loose-jowled, heavyset man named Boozer, whose appearance I quickly associated with, well, booze. He was shaped like a Bartlett pear. And I made the comparison softly but aloud within seconds. The others laughed again.

Father Burns had stepped up into the bus, behind the confusion of everyone finding a seat. "I want quiet," he said in a way that threatened consequences. His gaze seemed to glide over every face, but he was looking for one of us. He fixed on Drexel and held out one hand. "Bring me your bag."

Drexel went forward and gave it to him. The priest reached in and pulled out three Classics Illustrated comic books. He held them up one at a time: *The Count of Monte Cristo, Ivanhoe,* and *Crime and Punishment.* "This guy," he said, pointing to the Dostoyevsky, "predicted communism more than forty years before it happened."

It was as though he had just blamed Dostoyevsky for Sputnik.

Everyone waited for him to explain further. But he put the comic books in his own bag and said to Drexel, "You can collect these after today's trip."

Drexel came back, looking like he might start crying.

"Anybody else planning on reading and getting carsick?" Father Burns asked.

We kept still.

"I want quiet on this trip. I'll be watching you."

"I wasn't gonna read on the bus," Drexel said low to me. I had scooted down a little to be out of the line of sight from the front. "Anyway, reading is quiet, ain't it?"

"Do we understand each other?" the priest continued, still quietly.

We all answered, "Yes, Father."

He turned and sat down, and I saw his bald spot. Somehow it was like looking into him. I was very much afraid of him. And this had nothing to do with the now well-documented instances of unchecked sexual abuse by priests. That's not what I mean here at all. The fact is, I myself never encountered anything of the kind.

But there *was* evident and accepted maltreatment, generally.

In those days, people whipped or beat their children; it was a common occurrence, even an expected one (a paddle, a strap — a hand across the side of the head, or on the face hard enough to leave a welt; in our own house, we had the yardstick. "Don't make me get the yardstick," was the phrase). Father Burns was strict. He would smack you, or paddle you with a branch he kept for that purpose, or pull you by your ear or hair. Each action was available to him as punishment if you strayed from expectations, and you never knew exactly which punishment it might be or even how severe. For the altar boys he had a special penalty he called the Beltline. It was a form of gauntlet. He would make boys line up in two facing rows about eight feet apart, each boy holding a belt. Whoever had earned the penalty would have to race between the two rows while the swung belts whapped his back.

Probably it goes without saying that there were also the piercing, dignity-stripping things he would *say:* about your shape, or height, or coloration; how skinny you were (me, believe it or not) or how fat; how dark you were (Chorros) or scarred (Chorros again, with the mark below his mouth), or where you came from (again, me, Memphis, Tennessee). Chorros put it into perspective for me one day after we had served a six o'clock Mass together and Father Burns casually pointed out that my haircut made me look like someone had placed a bowl on my head and then trimmed everything around it. "He's rude, Vance. Pay no attention to it." *Rude* was the word. And this instance was especially wounding, since at the time we couldn't afford a barber. My father had solved the problem by purchasing clippers to cut our hair himself, and the look was exactly as the priest described it. The twins, Edward and Drew, didn't care about it because they were six. I wore a Washington Senators baseball cap wherever I could get away with it.

As now. On the bus. Headed toward the mountains. Twenty-six boys and two men.

Drexel, sitting next to me in his dejection about the comic books, folded his arms and put his head down, evidently deciding to try for sleep. He kept fidgeting restlessly. A lot of talking rose around us. For a while, I feigned sleep, not feeling like having to respond to anyone. The bus chugged on for an hour and a half in the hot rush of exhaust-smelling air from the windows, as cars and trucks sped around us and on. The different voices made a steady increasing confusion of sounds. And perhaps I drifted a little. Directly in front of Drexel and me were Moss and his friend Ethan Shipley, who was so broad across the shoulders that everyone called him Beef. He was a football player. Chorros and his cousin and Beef were a trio, and because Chorros and I were friends, Beef had appointed himself my guardian against the Saint Agnes boys, who in fact posed no threat at all. But that was Beef, with his way of inventing windmills to charge. They were all three going on now about the Russians, and I tried to tune it out.

The road began to climb, and soon enough the ascent grew steep. Boozer kept having to shift gears, which made a grinding noise. Out the windows we saw a pattern of miniature-seeming clusters of houses and farmland, a river winding through it all, and patches of packed forest which, at that distance, reminded me of the fur of a buffalo's back. The roar around me grew even louder. I was reaching to get Chorros's attention by swiping at his arm with my baseball cap, and Father Burns stood suddenly to glower at us from sleep-laden eyes. He looked directly at me, as though he had caught me misbehaving. "You!" he yelled, startling even Boozer. "Put that cap away!"

I shoved it into my back pocket.

He stood there taking us all in. And when he spoke again his voice was steely calm, though still loud, each syllable crisply enunciated. "I will remind you only this once. I expect the utmost of decorum and order." He adjusted his stance, bringing his shoulders back slightly, the gesture of someone who had just settled an argument. "Now. All of you. Look out at the glory of the beautiful country God has given us, this miracle going by your windows, and pray. And shut up."

He sat down. The only sound now was the chugging of the engine. Perhaps another forty minutes passed before the long hill turned to gravel and crested, revealing a big brick monument sign with raised black letters: *Abbey Of The Holy Cross.* Through the mottled shade of the woods beyond were several buildings set in a field of well-trimmed grass, the field bisected by orderly yellow paths made out of pea gravel. The main building was a long, brown-roofed brick structure with three horizontal rows of windows, one above the other; it had brown spires crowning either end and looked like a fortress, adjoined by a church with a white steeple. The church was smaller than the main building, yet looked like the pictures I had seen of cathedrals in Europe, with arched stained glass windows. I counted four gargoyles along the steep edges of the roof, though I had no name for them then. They looked angry; they seemed, in fact, demonic.

Brother Edgar was standing out where the front walkway met the plaza as our bus, now utterly silent inside, pulled in, engine chuffing and hawking. We filed out like soldiers at the command of Father Burns. "Come on. Get a move on. No dallying."

Brother Edgar opened his arms in greeting. "What a handsome group of lads!" He wore a brown robe with a hood draped down the back; the robe was tied in the middle by a heavy, woven blond cord. I thought of the heat. He beamed, and gestured for us to come close. "Welcome, all," he said, and when he looked at me he gave a wide, toothy smile. He was taller than Father Burns, looked younger and appeared distinctly less severe, less inclined to censure. His haircut reminded me of my own (which might explain the smile that had seemed so clearly aimed at me), and I received the notion that his relaxed goodwill might soften the hard edges of the priest, who shook hands and gingerly sought an embrace, then stood back slightly, looking around at everything. Apparently he had never visited the abbey and the two men hadn't seen each other for some time.

"We'll have grilled haddock for lunch," Brother Edgar said, "with fresh baked bread. I just saw them put a big batch into the ovens. Of course we bake it all day long."

"Crunchy on the outside and soft on the inside," Phillip Chorros offered.

Father Burns cuffed him playfully across the back of the head. "No speaking out of turn. You know better than that, Phillip."

Chorros stood still and straight, with a look of injured surprise on his face.

And at the risk of seeming portentous, I'll report here that I wouldn't understand the full meaning of that look until sixty years later.

In the next moment Brother Edgar clapped his hands together and said, "So. This old abbey was built just after the Civil War, and since that time things've stayed pretty much the same. We farm and harvest and cook and spin, just as always. There's almost a hundred of us, working and praying all day, each day. It's a community of prayer." He smiled that wide smile. "And of course there's a lot of work to do just keeping up. We raise our own stock, make our own clothes, our bedding, our rugs and towels, all our artwork, everything we eat — it's all produced here. We have two priests who say Mass for us and hear our confessions, and we celebrate Mass each morning of the week. I'm not ordained, so you call me *Brother Edgar*."

He led us along the pea-gravel path adjacent to the big building, past its arched entrance and on, to the church. As I've indicated, it was a good deal smaller than the main building, but to my eyes it seemed very imposing indeed with its gargoyles and stained glass. It was definitely larger than Saint Agnes. We filed into the echoing silence of the central aisle, and he murmured with a little nodding grin, "This is the nave." Then we moved quietly to the space where, with the same grin, he said, "And this is the transept." He paused, and glanced at the priest, then resumed. "This is the classical layout of any cathedral." A few steps farther on, he indicated the intricately carved Gothic altar. "That's the apse. You see, it all amounts to a kind of scale model."

"A miniature Notre Dame," Father Burns whispered.

"I prefer to think Chartres," Brother Edgar said.

"Chartres has no football team."

"All right, then I say a miniature Fordham."

"Well, they've got a team, if you can call it that with their record."

The fact that the two men could banter in this way or knew anything about football surprised me, and anyway the talk seemed out of place. I looked at the high ceiling and abruptly felt weighed down by actuality: bricks and mortar and statues and wood — and somehow my physical self, too — all heavily *on earth*. I looked at the figures in the stained glass windows: to the right, a depiction of Christ surrounded by angels; to the left, the Virgin Mary astride the globe with the serpent under her feet, the tinted light through the panes bathing us all like the grace of heaven, the power of God's love, meant to keep us strong. But the talk was so plain, and I was craven, a paltry flesh-container for an inner muddle of trembling. The confusion made me queasy. Everyone was quiet, and Father Burns was watchful. Finally he said, "Sit," in the tone of someone addressing a trained pooch. It seemed addressed at me. We filed into the first two pews. He and Brother Edgar knelt at the altar rail and prayed for a few moments, then spoke back and forth a little.

Then Father Burns rose slowly, turning to face us. He recited a prayer of blessing. His friend had also come to his feet and faced us, head bowed, his discomfort in that robe increasingly evident. When the blessing ended, he produced a handkerchief from the brown folds of his left sleeve, and dabbed it at his forehead. "It's only a little cooler in here," he said, low.

Father Burns reached over and took his arm above the elbow, a gentle squeezing nudge of encouragement or sympathy. The gesture seemed so completely out of character that it was as if I'd been shown something entirely new about this life, except that somehow I already *did* know it in my bones. I understood so little about anything then. And isn't it true that at that egocentric age, just turned fifteen, everyone around you seems rather one-dimensional and flat, only knowable in the narrowest way, like a figure in a story, your story?

Brother Edgar took us around. He showed us the kitchen where the bread was being made. "We sell to outlets in three states," he told us. Several other monks nodded and smiled at us as we filed by. We visited the little thrift shop where they sold secondhand clothes and some of the winter wear the monks themselves made. And we walked through the freezer room with the hanging sides of beef and pork and the hollow, headless carcasses of fowl — with that unappetizing, too-white, stippled skin — and on through there and out another heavy door and down a corridor, to a low-ceilinged room with big fans in the windows and a long counter where still other monks were filleting the halibut expertly, setting the strips side by side. In one large enclosure with ventilation spaces along the ceilings we saw wooden stalls and hay floors, where several cows stood docilely chewing. We breathed a heavy odor of manure. That space led through an exit into a wide dirt yard backed up to a hay-stuffed coop. This was a place for chickens to wander. There were many chickens moving jerk-headed and haphazardly in all directions until Brother Edgar, reaching into a bin, brought out some corn kernels and invited us to take some and spread them around. Chorros took a handful and tossed them, making a motion as if he were bowling. The chickens gathered quickly close, clucking, flapping their flightless wings and pecking at the ground.

At last we went around to the back of the building, where a falling-down log fence bordered a wide untrimmed field of knife grass. There were woods beyond. I brought out my cap and put it back on, and, seeing Father Burns notice it, experienced a moment's apprehension that he might single me out again. But we went along the slanting rails, following Brother Edgar toward the middle of the grounds, and a broken gate. A boothlike tool shed stood just on the other side, like a guard sentry box. He pulled it open and, dodging bees and swatting at flies, brought out a football. "Some of us throw this around in the afternoons in the fall." He tossed it lightly back and forth between his pale hands. Father Burns took a few trotting paces into the weeds, and Brother Edgar threw him a perfect spiral, which he dropped. He bent to pick it up, and now Brother Edgar ran a leisurely crossing pattern and caught the priest's pass. He turned to one of the other boys, a short, slight, pale kid from Saint Agnes, and said, "Heads up," tossing the ball underhand. The kid dodged it and another boy picked it up and ran a few paces, then lateraled it to Moss, who tossed it to Shipley. Father Burns and Brother Edgar moved back through the gate, to lean there and watch us in our haphazard game of maul-ball — that game where whoever got hold of the ball had to avoid being tackled by all the others. Chorros got the ball and threw it to me. "Go, man. You're the fastest one here."

I turned quickly and flipped it to Drexel, who hurled the ball high, tried to run under it and was lost in the rush of others. A heavy boy I didn't know caught it, then lost balance and sat down, hard. "Ow." He started crying. "Wilson," Father Burns said to him from the fence. "Walk it off. You want the Beltline?" The boy named Wilson got to his feet, and was tackled before he could take a step. "Wait a second," he yelled, tears still in his voice. "Can you all just please wait a second?"

But the whole thing was falling apart. There were too many of us, the grass was too high, and the sun was beating down, no shade anywhere. Some of the others kicked the ball around as if the game were soccer, but the rest just stood and watched.

"Keep playing," Father Burns said. "Don't be dullards."

"Tell you what, boys," Brother Edgar said. "There's an old, old beat-up house a ways through those trees. You can wander down there and tear that apart if you like."

"There's a lot of country to wander in," Father Burns said. "Explore a little."

The two men went up to the back entrance of the big building. Brother Edgar held open the thick double wooden doors and then followed the priest in. We watched the doors swing silently shut. I glanced around at the others. Phillip Chorros was looking at me.

"Well?" I heard myself say.

3.

Irony, as we all know, is lost on the young.

It was Chorros who led the way down the path into the trees, though when I stopped to pick up a stick, he stopped, too. We went along in the shade. Shipley and Moss, of course, and Drexel, who had stepped closer to me when I spoke (it was as though I had challenged him simply by saying, "Well?"), and all the others. I think we were just glad to be anywhere out of the sun. The path was packed dirt, and still it gave off little puffs of dust with each step. Soon we were in the tawny cloud of it. The air was breezeless, burning, not a leaf stirring, and the shade offered little relief. We kept on, twenty-six of us, many of whom I had never even spoken to. Reynolds was the youngest and smallest of the public school boys, and I had served with him once, but hadn't the chance to say anything to him because Father Burns, as we were preparing, called him "squirt" and chided him for not looking old enough, as if the poor kid were fraudulent in the first place for his appearance. "I've been twelve for three weeks," Reynolds said, almost defiantly. I saw that he was shaking and about to cry, so I picked up the tray of cruets for him and placed them next to the altar. After the Mass, he removed his cassock and was gone as though trying to escape. Now he stood right behind me with Drexel. He still made me think of a rabbit. His eyes were wild.

We came out of the shade to a clearing, a swale of weeds and grass, in the middle of which we all saw the surprisingly big, gray-ish clapboard farmhouse. Peelings of faded white paint stood out on it. It was indeed *old,* as Brother Edgar had said. It stood two stories high with a sagging, weed-engulfed porch along the front. The upper level had two dormer windows on either side of a row of three regular ones. There were also windows along the lower floor, two flanking the front door. None of us could believe how big it was. We were all looking back and forth at each other, astounded. Beyond the house was a wide sloping field in which several cows grazed. "Wait here," I heard Shipley say to the others as I started down the shallow hill with Chorros and Moss. So it was the four of us who went stealthily up to and onto the porch with its rotting boards, and looked through the coating of dust on the leaded windows. We saw empty rooms. A hallway. A staircase.

"Let's pretend this is France," Chorros said. "And we're in the war."

Moss said, "No, we're braves, a raiding party."

"I'll be Sitting Bull," I said. "Comanches."

"Sitting Bull wasn't a Comanche," Moss said.

"He was Lakota Sioux," said Chorros. "Hunkpapa."

"Tell them," his cousin said.

Chorros looked at Shipley and then back at me. "You know what my middle name is?"

"Naiche," Moss said. "Go on, tell them. It's Apache."

Chorros said, "My mother's name is Liluye. Everyone calls her

Lil. But her name is Liluye. It means 'Hawk Singing.' It's an Apache name."

We all stood quiet for a moment. I was stunned that I'd never learned this, that he had never said anything to me about it. Also, I was in awe: Chorros was an Apache by birth.

"Okay," Shipley said. "So, then, let's be Apaches."

"You can be Cochise," Chorros said to me. "I'll be Geronimo." To Moss, he said, "You be Mangas Coloradas."

"Red Sleeves! Yeah," said Moss. "What about Shipley?"

"I'll be Taza," Shipley said. "Son of Cochise." He smirked at me. "Rock Hudson."

I knew the movie.

We started back to the crest of the swale. We found the others crouching in attitudes of readiness, with their make-believe weapons.

"Hey," Shipley said to them. "Chorros is related to Cochise."

Moss said, "No, he isn't. His mom's an Apache."

"What's your dad?" Shipley asked.

Chorros put his hand to the welt on his cheek, as if to scratch an itch there. He shrugged. "Portuguese?" Then: "Okay, listen," and he explained quickly our scene: the raid. "Spread out," he said.

"The test for an Apache to be a grown man and a warrior," said Moss, "is running two miles in the desert with a mouth full of water that you spit out when you finish."

"Okay," Chorros said. "That's enough, Derek."

"Is someone in the house?" Drexel wanted to know.

"Anybody live there?" someone else asked at almost the same instant.

"It's empty," I heard myself say.

The others were picking up more stones or pieces of fallen branches, already focused on the attack, moving along the tree line in opposite directions, partially surrounding the place. We were like one of those flocks of birds you see shifting with perfect synchronization in midair, without the slightest sound or sign. Soon we were ranged in a wide half circle, all of us "armed" with something. No doubt our excitement was at least partly because we had permission for what was about to take place. All my fantasies from the movies about Indian attacks stood in my mind, and I was Michael Ansara, who played Cochise in the TV series *Broken Arrow.* There was a pause. We edged slowly, quiet as cats, forward. And then suddenly, to my own amazement, I let out a yell, and ran at the place. What followed was piercing whoops and calls as we swarmed onto the rickety porch all at once, from the steps and all along the front, and from both sides. After two fake shots with my make-believe rifle at imaginary defenders, I rammed the stick into the window to the left of the door, shattering it into a thousand pieces and what looked like a powdery shining dust. Within seconds all the windows fronting the porch were smashed, and other boys had climbed through them. I stepped through my own broken space and opened the door, and came face-to-face with Drexel. He had not used his stone. He dropped it and stood slightly aside as two boys I didn't know came lurching in, carrying a length of the porch railing. They began battering it against the wall to the right of the door. The plaster board fell away, revealing the slats beneath. I had become more observer than participant now, though I yelled with the others, our collective tumult seeming like one voice. Phillip Chorros came partway down the staircase — I could not believe he had got up there so fast — waving a piece of the banister at me; he turned and went back up, and I followed. We found four other windows to break. Drexel had followed me, and seemed to want direction; he was full of gleeful anticipation. "Pull it all apart," I said to him. And behind me Chorros shouted, "I am. That's what I'm doing." He had located a wire in the wall and was yanking at it. More boys were pulling down the drywall, and breaking through the slats. Broken glass was everywhere under our feet. Chorros and Moss, using part of the window frame, wedged a corner of one of the dormer frames loose — it made a cracking sound, almost like a gunshot — and they pushed it out onto the battered roof of the porch, where it tipped and then went over to the dry grass and dirt below. I moved back down to the first floor. Shipley stood at the base of the stairs, nursing a small cut on the heel of his palm. He took off his shirt and began wrapping the hand. I stepped into the hallway just outside the kitchen and saw a closed door to the left. In the room on my right were glass-doored cabinets full of stacked dishes, coffee mugs and small wineglasses. I saw this and quite suddenly everything seemed wrong: those things signified some sort of lived life in the rooms; this was not a broken-down old shell, but a dwelling.

Drexel must have got past me someway, for he and his friend Reynolds were already at the cabinets, pulling out the dishes and wineglasses and smashing them down. They were screaming bloody murder — as I'd heard my mother say more than once about the twins.

My mother.

In that moment she came to mind, and I felt very far beyond anything I had ever known. I could scarcely imagine finding my way outside. Opening the door across from me, I descended a narrow flight of stairs into the dim and musty cellar, really just to get away from this feeling and the noise, which seemed only slightly less loud above me. I sat on the bottom step and was visited by the unwelcome thought of secret places. I could not believe it, hearing the devastation continuing above. I stood quickly, as if to run back up into the noise. Before me in the half dark, beyond the dust-falling shaft of light from the open door at the top of the stairs, were rows of big glass jugs full of dark liquid. They were waist high, and the rows extended to a pair of dust-clouded basement windows at the far end.

I moved to the first jug and stood for a moment, seeing the shape of myself like an unfinished photograph in blurred reflection on its curved top side. With some difficulty I managed to unscrew the tight cap. It had been wax-sealed. A pungent odor rose; the liquid looked black in the dimness and it called to mind the cruets during Mass. I stood for a moment concentrating on the fact that we had permission to tear the house apart; this was *of* the house. I tipped the jug, holding the lip of it, and some of its contents spilled out. Wine. I kept pouring. The thought of waste occurred to me. Perhaps the wine had all gone bad. Setting the jug straight again, I took a step back and, looking around, saw a length of metal pipe, a random steel bar lying loose — some sort of construction support or fitting — on the cement floor just under the stairs, as if put there for my use. I walked over and picked it up, feeling the solid weight of it, then moved back, holding it like a baseball bat, and swung it at the open jug. The jug shattered in a shocking disintegration with a flood of the wine. I turned, gripping the pipe so tightly my fingers ached, and smashed another without opening the lid. The popping sound it made startled me, but was also strangely pleasing. I waded into the row, swinging the pipe, glass breaking and liquid splashing and pouring all around me. There was something of a fit about it, and I realized I was crying. This surprised and frightened me. I waited there a moment, sobbing, trying to dry my eyes with the tail of my shirt, afraid one of the others might see me that way.

I had an image of the kitchen space above, the wineglasses and dishes in the cabinets, the way the glasses shattered, one by one, as they hit the floor. The end of the metal bar was stained with wine, and the wine looked like blood. I dropped the thing as though it had become red-hot. It made a loud sound against the cement. The commotion went on above me. Standing in that shard-strewn, soaked space, I willed myself to recall exactly Brother Edgar's words of permission, then climbed the stairs, feeling, for some reason, the need for stealth. Opening the door an inch, I looked into the narrow hall. The house seemed empty, though there were still thumping sounds nearby. I went through the broken glass of the kitchen space, out the back and around, to find Chorros, Shipley and Moss using one support post like a battering ram against the last one holding up the porch roof. I went to the others, who were standing a few yards away. This was the last stage of the attack. We were not imaginary Indians now; we were like a group of grim quiet witnesses observing an execution.

Chorros saw me. "Cochise!"

I went up to him, and he gestured for me to take hold. Drexel was there too now, again with that look of anticipation. He got in front of me, holding on, and the five of us made the final charge, slamming into the last supporting post. It gave way, and we jumped down and turned to watch the roof come against the house like a gigantic shutting eyelid — somehow it happened that slowly; it was even somnolent seeming, dust rising from it, more glass breaking.

The silence went on for what seemed a long time. I couldn't look at anyone.

"Well," Shipley said finally, unwrapping his cut hand to put his shirt back on. "That's it."

We watched the dust rise from what was left.

At length, everyone began slowly to move away. Some boys paused and picked up stones and threw them, or simply turned and looked at the dust that was now settling back on the grass. When we got to the edge of the trees, we stopped to look again at it all. It was an oddly subdued moment, shaded with a touch of pride in the accomplishment, I suppose, but also, for me anyway, a dim, unexpressed sickness at heart. And I thought I saw it in the faces of some of the others, too. In fact, no one seemed as thrilled as we had been, or thought we would be.

The wine had soaked my shoes, and the smell of it in that heat was repellent. We went back along the path, still in a quiet that might have seemed reverent, though there were little bursts of horsing around and chasing back and forth in the trees. I was one of the last to come out into the field behind the main building of the abbey. I had seen a black snake slither off the path and had gone off the path to look for it a little, thinking of the one in the garden of Eden and feeling more confusedly guilty by the minute. Chorros came with me, expressing the idea that we might scare the others with the snake. For a silent moment we stood in the deep green shade and I wanted to tell him the whole of everything — everything, even my rotting interior life with its libidinous longings, my obsessed mornings with only myself and mortal sin. But then something else moved in me as I stared into his dark, friendly, laughing eyes. He was a kid, like me. He must have been dealing with the same thing. Yet it was also possible that this wasn't true; he had always seemed so self-possessed, and I could not go past the notion that he might not be afflicted, as I was. I hadn't known about his mother being an Indian.

"Why'd you never tell me you're part Indian?" I heard myself ask.

He shrugged. "She likes her name. Nobody's sure about any of the rest. What's it to you?"

"I don't know," I said. "I just thought I knew you better."

"What you don't know about me — " he said quickly, then stopped himself. We stood there. "What anybody knows about anybody," he added in a low mutter.

Now *I* shrugged.

He ran on ahead. I looked up at the sky through the interstices of leaf and branch, and tried to pray for strength, for relief from the inexpressible regret and confusion I had begun to feel.

When I came out into the still-blazing afternoon I saw Father Burns holding Phillip Chorros tight by the arm, talking grim-faced through his teeth, with Brother Edgar trying, unsuccessfully, to calm him.

"Tell me what you think you were doing!" Father Burns insisted. "Tell me!"

I went up to Moss, who was wringing his hands and muttering, "Jesus. Jesus."

The others were all gathered around, coated with the dust and dirt and grime of how we had spent the last two hours.

"Really, Llewelyn," Brother Edgar persisted.

When Father Burns saw the wine stains on my tennis shoes and once-white socks, the splatter stains on my jeans and the dark band on the bottom cuffs, he started toward me.

Brother Edgar said, "Llewelyn, *please.*"

Several of the Saint Agnes boys pointed at us, and declared that it was mostly "those guys" — Chorros, Moss, Shipley, Drexel and me.

"Llewelyn," Brother Edgar said. "Now, listen to me, *please.*"

The priest had stopped, but he was still glaring murderously at me. He pointed as he turned back. "Look at him. Look at the shoes, Edgar. Look at those jeans. Do you see that?"

"We'll figure it out," Brother Edgar said, rather forcefully. Then: "Really. Please, now. Let's stop this."

A little later, after we had stood and petted the horse brought out for us to see, one of the other monks led us back to the main building's great room while Father Burns and Brother Edgar went off to assess the damage to the old house. The great room had tall, also leaded windows, and the monk introduced himself as Brother John, one of the abbey's main chefs. He was a gaunt, deep-eyed, kindly-looking man with no hair and, strangely, no eyebrows. The light from the windows shone on his forehead. He put Mercurochrome and a Band-Aid on Shipley's cut, and produced a clean pair of white sweat socks for me, along with several pairs of jeans from the thrift store for me to try. It astonished me that I had not given a moment's thought to the wine spilling all around my shoes and pants legs. To my relief I found one pair of jeans exactly the baby blue color of my own — and they were Levi's, too, like mine. They fit me a little loosely around the waist but were the perfect length. I also tried on two different pairs of tennis shoes, but they were not *Keds,* nor quite the right fit. "Well," Brother John said, "I guess you can try the washing machine."

"Thank you, Father," I said.

He corrected me with a gentle smiling nod: "Brother."

He had also single-handedly set out lunch. We all lined up quietly for a plate, and made our way along the buffet. I didn't take very much. I looked at the cornices and the walls and baseboards, thinking about how it would be to come there and live, out of the worries of the world.

We sat at facing banquet tables. Brother Edgar and Father Burns came in and took their place at the head table. Derek Moss, with his brown cowlick and his green smile, sat next to me, and on my other side was yet another boy unknown to me, but whom I had seen pulling at the stair railing until it snapped. That snapping sound was in my head as he turned to me and mumbled his name. "Rodney Cleese."

I told him mine, speaking low.

He only got the last part of it. "Nice to meet you, Dan." It turned out he was a friend of Shipley's.

"I don't get it," Moss said. "What's the deal."

Chorros, sitting down on the other side of him, said, "Brother Edgar was joking."

We were all surreptitiously watching the priest and the monk.

The bread was amazing, crisp on the outside and soft on the inside, just as Chorros had said it would be. And the fish was seasoned in a way that reminded me of my father's steamed hard-shelled blue crabs. I hadn't thought I would have any inclination to eat.

I avoided looking at the two clergymen.

"It's the Beltline for you guys when we get back, for sure," Rodney Cleese said. He explained how the punishment worked. This was the first time I had heard it described in detail.

Chorros, to whom this was evidently also the first explanation of it, looked at Cleese and said, "What'll we do, Rodney? Take turns? All of us? We all did it."

At the head table, Brother Edgar murmured something insistent and placating to the priest, who ate quietly and intently without looking at anyone.

Brother Edgar leaned close and said something else, low.

"Well, they didn't have to take you at your word!" Father Burns thundered.

There followed an utter silence. Perhaps a full minute went by, with only the sound of the forks against the plates.

During the dessert of chilled strawberries and cream, we learned that along with supplying bread for restaurants and shops in the community, the abbey was a supplier of wine for the churches of the regional parishes. The house had been built in 1892, and had belonged to a farmer named Danby, who worked a sharecrop arrangement with the abbey until the Great Depression forced him and his family to move on. This from Brother Edgar, who went on to say he often imagined the sad family leaving the place, like the Joads, having to head out in desperation to make their way somewhere else in the world, far from home. The phrase *far from home* struck through me. We had torn apart someone's home. And the fact that the farmer lost the house in the Depression reminded me of my grandfather Vance. The others seemed to be feeling something of the sadness, too, sitting there looking around at each other. But soon I realized they were mystified by Brother Edgar's mention of the Joads. Phillip Chorros shook his head and sighed. "*The Grapes of Wrath,* guys. Henry Fonda in the movie. He played Tom Joad." No one said anything.

Brother Edgar smiled. "You know the film?"

"And the book," Phillip said.

Father Burns said, "I've never read *The Grapes of Wrath,* nor anything else of Steinbeck."

"I thought everybody read that one," Brother Edgar said.

"No," said the priest.

We had been given the lesson about the house because Father Burns demanded that we know what we had destroyed. Brother Edgar finished by saying, with a quick ameliorative glance at his friend, that the house was in fact used sometimes, though not often, as a meeting place.

"Well," the priest said. "These punks have put an end to its use as anything but scrap wood. And what about the wine."

"Only six jugs were broken. There's forty-four left." Brother Edgar looked directly at me, forgiving me with a little of that smile.

After the meal, and a glum tour of the rooms and a novena in the church, we all went out into the clear, hot, late afternoon. The bus had pulled up, with Boozer behind the wheel. He looked sleepy and disheveled. Father Burns took Brother Edgar's handshake and embrace, and then ushered us onto the bus, past Boozer's stare of curiosity bordering on wonderment. "What'd they get into, Father?" he asked as the priest got on and glared at us. "They look like they've been through a war."

"They tore down a house."

Apparently thinking this was sarcasm, Boozer smirked. "That's what it looks like."

"Well," said Father Burns. "That's what it *is.*"

The bus driver glanced back at us again, and I saw a near laugh begin on his face before he turned and started the engine.

Father Burns was still standing, one hand on the first seat back. He stared until we were quiet. Out the window I saw Brother Edgar approaching the arched entrance of the abbey; he was small now in the distance. He would wait until we pulled away.

"Chorros," Father Burns said. "Shipley, Drexel, Moss, Bourdin."

We waited. All the other boys were looking around at us in our different places on the bus.

"The Beltline," Father Burns said. "As soon as we get back." He glared another moment, then sat down, and Boozer ground the gears.

All the way back to Saint Agnes of Rome, the other boys sang to the tune of what I later learned was Chopin's "Funeral March," "Cheer-up, Chor-ros, the worst is yet to come," repeating in perfectly annoying unison the same notes, substituting the names: Drexel, then Shipley, then Moss, and finally me. And, without pause, as if it had been rehearsed, back around to Chorros and on to me again. Over and over. And Father Burns, in the front seat, tolerated it. In fact, he fell asleep. His head listed to one side and stayed that way. Boozer drove on, concentrating on the road, his face unreadable in the big rearview mirror.

The dirge went on. And then died down, and after a few minutes of discordant chatter, began again, as if rehearsed. I couldn't tell who started it up.

We got to the church. Boozer pulled the lever to open the door, and we all began to exit, gathering near the steps leading up to the arched entryway.

"Over here," Father Burns said, moving to the terrace opposite, which led down flagstone steps to the football field/baseball diamond.

"I'm gonna stay and watch," Boozer said, and winked at Chorros going past him.

"Get polio," Chorros said, low.

"What'd you say?" asked the priest as Chorros stepped down.

"Nothing."

Father Burns slapped the back of his head, not even slightly playful this time. Chorros looked crestfallen rather than stung; the muscles of his jaw moved. "Over here, all of you," the priest said. He led everyone over to the middle of the field, in the slightly cooler late afternoon shade of the church building. "Well, this isn't symbolic or anything," Chorros said through his teeth, indicating the steeple shape blocking the brightness.

"Belts off, all of you but the *condemned*." Father Burns emphasized the word.

I watched the others comply. Little rabbit-like Reynolds and one St. Agnes boy had no belt. The priest looked at Drexel. "Give Reynolds yours." And then, turning to Chorros, indicating the other boy: "And you, too, Phillip — go on. No exceptions. The same with you." Chorros pulled his belt off furiously, cheek muscles still clenching, his face chalk white around the lips. He handed it to the other boy. Drexel held his belt out to Reynolds, who seemed to cower away from it.

"Take the belt, squirt," Father Burns said.

Reynolds did so, head down, and then slowly took his place in line.

"Now," the priest said. "You all know what you're supposed to do."

Suddenly Moss turned back toward the incline to the parking lot and vomited loudly into the grass. Father Burns pulled him roughly by his arm to the steps and made him sit down. Then he returned to us. Drexel had begun crying without sound, tears running down his face. For a few seconds everyone watched Moss, who had got up and timidly returned to the original spot as if worried about worse consequences. But he got sick again. We all stood there.

Father Burns waved him away as if dismissing a thought. "Go back and sit down," he said.

There were two facing rows, now, and he moved to set everyone the correct distance apart, with enough room to swing the belts. The two lines stretched about fifteen yards.

"Remember, hold them by the buckles. You hear me? We don't want any blood."

They were already in compliance.

"Okay." He paused. "Who's first?" His face was almost passive.

It got very quiet. Boozer coughed, and hawked into the asphalt. The grime and dust still clung to us. Chorros was shifting his weight back and forth, arms swinging.

"Okay, then. Phillip," Father Burns said.

And it was Boozer who said, "Go!"

Phillip Chorros burst forward, taking the first thwack from his own belt. He ran fast, and the belts swung. Not many missed him. It seemed to take forever. Finally he stumbled by the last pair of boys and turned. He stood holding one arm at the elbow, and defiantly stared right at Father Burns. He was not crying. His eyes were burning into the priest. I thought of Apaches running two miles in the desert with a mouthful of water.

"All right," Burns said. "Excellent. An excellent run." He actually clapped, twice. Then: "Next. Mr. Shipley."

And Shipley bolted into the gauntlet almost before anyone could get set. Several boys missed him, and he kept slapping at the belts as if they were flies to be swatted away. He made it through like a running back barreling through tacklers, and stood glaring revenge up and down the two lines, holding his cut hand where the Band-Aid had come loose.

Father Burns said, "Watch the dirty looks, there, Mr. Shipley, or I'll make you go through again."

Ethan Shipley looked down.

"Now," said the priest. "Mr. Drexel."

After a painful period of quiet sobbing and deep breaths, Michael Drexel started through. But he fell only a few paces in, after being thwacked several times, and the boys there closed on him, swinging their belts. It went on for several awful seconds.

"Hold on, HOLD ON, THERE!" Father Burns yelled. "BACK OFF."

They did so, and Drexel, who had gotten himself to all fours, breathing and crying, sputtered, "I didn't do anything. Everybody did it — we all did it. Brother Edgar said we could."

The priest walked over. "Okay," he said.

Drexel kept crying. "He told us we could if we wanted."

Father Burns leaned down to take hold of his arm. "You shouldn't have *wanted*."

Drexel sobbed, but said nothing.

"Get up, son. You've had enough." The priest walked the boy out of the gauntlet, behind the others on that side, and over to where Moss sat crying silently in the grass. I looked at Chorros, who still stood in that defiant pose, one arm held at the elbow, legs slightly spread — someone who would not bend for anyone or anything.

A few feet away, Shipley sat with hands clasped over his upraised knees, facing away from it all; he, too, would not bend.

"Okay," Father Burns said, "Mr. Bourdin," his face showing a little strain now.

I swung my arms forward and back as Chorros had, steeling myself, certain that I would be like Drexel, crying pitiably in front of everyone. But then it occurred to me that in fact I did not have to do this at all. I'd run a 10.9 hundred-yard dash in gym class only that spring, missing the state record by two tenths of a second, and nobody on that field, not even Shipley, could run with me. Looking at Father Burns with his impatient, relishing, sallow face, and at the others, waiting with their belts held tight and ready, I swung my arms once more, paused, then turned and bolted. The priest yelled my name twice, the second time louder than the first, and I heard some of the others shouting, too. I glanced back and saw that they had become a gang, chasing me. I heard Father Burns shout. I think he was trying to call everyone back. I went across the long parking lot, up the hill and on, winding down the path to Dempsey's Rec Center, with its asphalt basketball court, where many of us had often played. I was gasping for air but still sprinting. I almost fell, pitching forward as I reached the court and then crossed it, and leapt the creek, where I did go down briefly to all fours when I landed on the opposite bank. I clawed at roots and dirt, scrabbling up and into the woods.

I have no idea how many of them kept after me. Hearing the yelling, I knew some of them had. I ran all the way home, slowing now and then to a trot, but then sprinting again. I had outdistanced them all. I saw our street as I came down to it from Blue Hill Road, the shadows of the houses on the lawns, and there was our house, my father up on the roof, where he had been fixing the drains from bad thunderstorms and wind earlier that week. "Hey, Vance," he said as I approached. He was a shadow up there, moving to the ladder. "You look like you've been through it. What's happened?"

As he turned and carefully reached with his foot for the first rung of the ladder, tottering only slightly at that height, I thought of what he had been through in the war, the CSR and the stressful life after, working so hard all those days before we could even buy a car, the long walks in the freezing cold down to Hammer's Mill Road to catch the bus to his job in town. For the first time in my life, I saw him as a person, separate from me, much stronger than I would ever be, but with worries and bad memories and hurts; it went through me, an interior mistral of fright and sorrow, and then I thought of what it might mean to him if he knew what had just taken place, that I had run away like that. I felt sorry because he didn't know what a coward he was raising. He was the good man who led us in the rosary each evening, and he had been through hell, and in the nights his sleep was still disturbed by whatever caused those little sighing cries in his breathing.

He got down and stood appraising me.

"Well? So, what's the deal?"

"Nothing," I said to him.

"Is that plasterboard dust?" He took hold of my shirtsleeve and then swiped at it. But the dust was in the threads now, and was only the gray shade of coloration. "Your shoes. What's that all over your shoes? Come on, boy." He laughed softly. "What do they — what the heck went on at that monastery?"

"We all sort of tore apart an old, old house," I managed, being careful to use Brother Edgar's words. I smiled. Then I explained the whole thing about battering the house, excluding the business about the Beltline. I told about breaking up the wine jugs. Only the fact of it. "But Brother Edgar said we could go tear it apart," I said. "We thought he meant it, so we did."

"Must've been quite a shock for the poor guy," Vance said.

"Yes, sir," I got out.

"Looks like it might've been a lot of fun for you guys, though." He smiled. "Did you run all the way home?"

"Yeah." I managed my own nervous smile.

We went into the house. He sighed. "I bet it'll be a funny story for them one day. Tell your mother. Hey, sweetie," he said to her, "guess what Vance ran all the way home to tell you."

She was sitting at the kitchen table with coffee and a cigarette. I heard myself say, "I don't think I want to be an altar boy anymore." I was almost in tears. Thankfully they took it as part of my being still a bit out of breath from running.

My father said, "No, hey — tell her what happened, though."

"Why don't you want to be an altar boy?" Her hair was tied in a bun, and a strand of it hung down. We had no air-conditioning and it had been a long day.

I couldn't answer right away. I shrugged. "I don't know."

"Hey," my father urged. "Come on. Tell her what happened."

So I managed to repeat the story. It was a little like I was reciting it. But then I heard myself embellishing things about the depredations of the other boys, the bad language and the destructive habits. I even said some of them smoked, though I had only heard about it in Father Burns's threats. I made it sound as though they were all hoodlums — and saying this about them, recalling the way they had sung with such delight that dirge about what was coming to us, and the fierce glee with which they had wielded those belts, and how they had clustered around Drexel and lashed him repeatedly until Father Burns called them off — I believed they *were* hoodlums.

"You look like you've been in a dust storm," she said. "Go get cleaned up. Then we can talk about the altar boys."

"It's funny about the old house, though, right? Poor guy's making a joke and they take him at his word. Imagine the shock."

She looked at me. "And that's why you want to quit the altar boys?"

"Not really," I said. "I've been thinking about it."

"Well," she said, with a glance in my father's direction. "It's your decision, son." A small smile creased her lips.

In the bathroom, I looked at my face in the mirror, hearing my twin brothers playing in the other room. They were making the sounds of battle and struggle. For the first time in a long while, it felt uncomplicatedly good to be alone. I took off my clothes, turned the water on and suddenly thought of Father Burns coming to the house or calling to report that I had run off, maybe even to exact his punishment. I hurried through the shower, got into clean clothes and made it downstairs.

The call didn't come until the next morning. Sunday, when we were getting ready for going to Mass; they were in their room and I was waiting in the living room, so I was the one who answered the phone.

"You all right?" In his tone I heard everything of the previous afternoon.

I said, "Yes," with as much coolness as I could muster.

"We were worried. The other boys were worried, too."

"Yeah," I said, low, and wanted to say, "I *bet* they were."

After a pause, he said, "Well, they were." It was as though I had spoken the words. And then I thought I might actually have done so. Abruptly I felt like we were equals, and he was just another one of the mob that had chased me.

"I'm fine," I said with a definiteness.

"Well, then, you'll serve for the six o'clock morning Mass Thursday?"

"I have to concentrate on school, Father."

Silence.

"I can't be in the altar boys anymore," I blurted out, my heart beating in my throat. The shakiness in my voice made me angry with myself. But I couldn't draw enough air to say more. I had a sudden urge to tell him I was moving to Kansas or someplace.

"What you did was brave," he said. "I thought I should make sure you knew that."

Now the silence was mine.

"Can I speak to your dad?"

"He's not here now," I said.

"How about later today."

"No." My voice was more steady now.

"I think I understand. Sometimes — sometimes we have to resort to measures to keep that many ruffians in line. But I think, if I were you I'd reconsid — "

I interrupted him. "I have to go."

"Have you talked to your dad about what happened?"

"No, Father."

"Will you?"

"Don't know," I said, and felt an instinctive desire to worry him.

"Well, we'll miss you."

"Please tell Brother Edgar I'll always remember him," I said.

"Right — hey, why don't you write him?"

I heard anxiety in his tone, and experienced a pleasant sense of possessing the upper hand. I said, "I think I will." Then: "Goodbye, Father." And I put the phone down.

"Well, you told him you were leaving," said my mother, later. "I'm proud of you."

Of course I saw him at Mass some Sundays that summer. We never made eye contact. At Mass I watched him, and would glance at my father as the sermon went on, usually leading from whatever that day's gospel was to the bad news about the communists.

"I don't like his sermons," my mother said afterward. "He's too bleak. I'd like not to be thinking about the Russians and the bomb all the time."

I kept wondering if any of the altar boys might have told their parents or would tell them about the Beltline. I worried about it, but should've known that this was not at all likely. Not then. Not as things were in those days. After all, I had kept it from my own. And as I've pointed out, such severe experiences were a normal element of life growing up. In any case, I was determined to avoid the Saint Agnes altar boys if I could; I told myself that it was because they made up the gang that had chased me, but deep down I think there was also an element of shame: they had witnessed my flight.

Chorros and Moss kept serving Mass on Sundays. After that summer ended and through the next few months and the turn of the year I rarely saw them outside of school. Chorros had been signed up for afternoon music lessons by his mother and there were few opportunities to spend time. His cousin and I did speak once about the summer. We were on the basketball court down at Dempsey's. Late October, an Indian summer afternoon. Moss said, "Man, I got to tear down a fucking house, and didn't have to get whipped for it. Good thing I upchucked, huh? That Beltline thing, man. I'd much rather be sick."

I had wanted to ask him if he ever thought about the house as a place where a family had lived. The question, of course, was completely unaskable. Not with him. I was just glad he didn't mention my running away. I changed the subject quickly.

The presidential election was dominating the news. Kennedy was hitting hard about the recession and the U-2 incident and America "going soft." Nixon, evidently without much help from Eisenhower, was claiming the "important element" of having been vice president.

Words and phrases resounded: *new frontier; Peace, Experience, Prosperity;* and *missile gap.* But I didn't give any of it much thought. Jean and Vance had voted Democratic as long as I could remember, and they were going to vote Democratic again. They had lost when Stevenson ran in '56, and I assumed they would lose again.

But Kennedy won, and when he took office that January, my mother and father and I watched the inauguration.

"Imagine," Vance said, sitting next to Jean on the sofa. "A Catholic in the White House."

"He's so dashing and handsome."

"Just like a movie star, huh."

She smiled and leaned to rest her head on his shoulder. "Like some people I know."

Kennedy used the word *renewal* in that speech, but the spring and early summer proved to yield much of the same kinds of trouble: the Bay of Pigs happened and the Berlin Wall went up; the Russians put a man in space and brought him back. We were so far behind. I found myself paying less attention to the news. I had begun to entertain the idea of renouncing the life of the world, of perhaps becoming a monk, like Brother Edgar, though also — I suspect in a secret I kept even from myself — I was just too scared and depressed to think much about any of it. The civil rights movement was intensifying and I attended to that some as a sympathetic observer, like someone watching a movie on television. The week of the Bay of Pigs fiasco, Chorros came to school with a bad violet-colored lump on his forehead. "I was in on the Cuba thing," he said to me. "Castro's boys roughed me up." Then he shrugged. "Nah. I ran into that door again." His flat tone shut down any other talk about it. The gym teacher, Mr. Dupree, said only, "You all right?"

"Just fine," Chorros said. We were learning wrestling. I lost twice to a boy named Curtis, and the third time I let go of the moves Dupree was trying to teach us and just held on. I wound up pinning him with my chin pressed to his chest. "Bourdin's started a winning streak," Dupree said, and then laughed to himself. "Unorthodox but effective."

Chorros had the moves to perfection and he won so quickly that Dupree asked if he might want to be on the wrestling team. "No," Chorros said. "Not even if it would break up the Yankees. Not even if it ended the Soviet Union and killed Castro."

"Okay," Dupree said. "Why don't we let go of the attitude."

"Just being emphatic," Chorros said.

4.

I read the books, practiced what I could of *The Spiritual Exercises of Saint Ignatius.* Often now I felt isolated, even when I was clowning with Chorros and the others. That summer I played basketball with Moss and Drexel and Shipley, and sometimes Chorros, too, who played a strange, spastic-looking game, almost studiedly so; you couldn't tell if he was simply awkward or if he might be clowning. He had long arms and they seemed sometimes to move without his knowledge or intention. And running, he looked like a moving bundle of sticks. "This is a stupid game," he said. But he played hard. And with aggression. He seemed almost angry at what he couldn't do. But he would joke about it. And we sat in the shade of that wraparound porch at Dempsey's talking about Maris and Mantle; the home run chase. We went on about the Russians in space. Moss and Chorros spoke of Chorros's father, who had been in a fight in a bar in DC, and come home with a broken hand, and contusions on his face. "Eyes all swollen shut," Phillip said. "He looked like Carmen Basilio after Ray Robinson." I didn't know the names, and he patiently explained that the two had fought for the middleweight championship back in '57, and he would never forget Basilio's face, what a mess it was after, though Basilio won the fight, as apparently his father had.

"I wanna be a boxer," Moss said.

Phillip Chorros grinned. "You and Shipley."

The Maris/Mantle run at the Babe was something he followed with a kind of fanatical concentration. He would look at box scores and do the math to figure the changes in batting averages, and he was keeping close tabs on the pace of each man's home run numbers compared to Ruth's. All this while claiming no real interest. "I suppose I can see the anthropological value of it," he said. "And this is good math practice."

We played basketball in the hot days. Shipley came to the park on the Fourth of July with some cherry bombs. Chorros said, "Let's just do it to hear the noise. I don't want to blow anything up."

"Can you imagine," Moss said, "if we'd had these at the abbey that time?"

"I can think of times I wish I'd had one of them. Just one." He had a split lip.

Moss said, "For your dad, huh."

"No. Not him. Not at all. What the hell."

We blew the cherry bombs up in the creek, impressed with how they went off anyway, even in water.

One rainy Saturday afternoon in late August I was watching the Senators play the Yankees on TV, waiting through the rain delay, and when the game was canceled, I turned the channels, wanting distraction. I found a movie: Gregory Peck as Father Francis Chisolm the missionary priest in *The Keys of the Kingdom*. The film was about the priest's whole life, with stirring music. In a scene where you see Father Chisolm, grateful for some miraculous turn in his labors, standing on a hill looking into light saying the Magnificat — . . . *because he who is mighty hath done great things for me, and holy is his name* — during that scene, I began thinking about becoming a priest. Remember, I was just sixteen.

I said nothing to anyone at first.

At those morning Masses I stayed far in back, watching Father Burns or Father Drummond go through the steps of the ritual with the altar boys doing their part. I imagined myself as the priest, and yearned to go there, to be old enough, everything accomplished, all the tangles of mind and emotion settled and solved. When Father

Burns was the celebrant and I came to the railing and knelt to receive communion, he seemed to have no memory of me, not even really to see me, murmuring the words, *"Corpus Christi."* Once, Chorros was serving, and we looked at each other.

I don't recall exactly how Jean got wind of my thoughts of a vocation, but she went to the library and did some research and sent out for the pamphlets of several seminaries, researching the various orders. The first pamphlet we received was accompanied by a letter from a Father Gillette, who knew that Father Burns's parish was Saint Agnes of Rome and who remembered him from a class at Gonzaga University twelve years before. So I took it upon myself to write Father Gillette, thinking how friendly Brother Edgar had been. I said I'd been thinking I might enter a monastery but that perhaps the priesthood made more sense because I wanted to help others. I got a very nice letter in response, explaining in some detail the aspects of receiving "the vocation," as he called it, learning to cope with and understand the feelings, being aware that no shaft of light or bolt of lightning is involved. He advised me to pray for guidance. I wrote him back and said I was certain. He answered right away, telling me that he hoped I would remain devoted to God and that if, in two years, I still felt called to serve, he would be glad to hear from me.

Naturally, my parents told the rest of the family.

And so I was now the incipient priest, which made me the star of every visit. Everybody wanted to know about it or had a story about their own youthful sense of "having the vocation." Aunt Constance told me she had dreamed of being a nun right up to the time she met Whitey, her eventual husband. The whole thing made me uneasy, and as summer drew to a close I found myself taking some trouble to avoid Chorros and the others. I didn't want them to know; I was certain they would make fun of me.

One early Wednesday morning in September Vance decided to attend Mass with me. As we were headed there in the Ford we saw two nuns walking along Oak Lane. A storm was gathering in the low sky so he stopped and offered them a ride. They were young. One of them wore round-rimmed glasses and looked scholarly, the other had dark brows, lovely light brown eyes and a very white smile. This one said, "We decided to take a little walk and I guess we went too far." Her voice had an alto fullness like Jean's.

"We're on our way to the six o'clock Mass," my father said.

"Oh, how sweet."

"Vance here's been walking to Mass every morning," he said in an ingratiating tone I had never heard him use. I saw him watching the road, his face flushed and somehow child-proud, eyes wide, as if he were no older than I. He went on, "This boy's planning for the priesthood."

Now it was my turn to blush. The one in the round glasses said, "Oh, that's just marvelous. You must be very proud."

"Awful proud," my father said. I nearly sank down in the seat.

She gave a satisfied sigh. "I have a younger brother studying for the priesthood. He seems very happy. And I believe there's another boy in the parish — one of Father Burns's altar boys. Or, as we call them, his crew."

"That's wonderful," my father said. He glanced at me and I gave a little shrug, thinking of the Saint Agnes boys who had chased me.

The one with the alto voice patted my shoulder. "And how old are *you*, young man?"

I told her. She was very pretty, with perfect skin, and I had an abrupt unwanted awareness of her femaleness beneath the black cloth of her lap. I put the thought away with a slight shake of my head, looking out the windshield. It had gone through me like a draft from hell.

"Doesn't seem like sixteen years," said my father.

"Well, how proud for you."

"Whole family's proud of him."

I looked at his hands on the wheel, the fine brown hair on his wrists, and loved him, and felt suddenly that I had been lying to him and to everyone else. It was the strangest, sourceless sense of falsity. I concentrated on the houses gliding past, feeling completely discouraged and at sea. We were coming to the church. The rain was starting. They talked about all the Russian nuclear tests and Hurricane Carla, in Texas. "I wonder if this rain is coming from that."

"Probably the outer edge of its path," Vance said.

"Imagine," said the one in the glasses, "this gentle storm has probably reached us from the Texas coast."

The other said, "Oh, Sister, you have the wildest notions." Her laugh was lovely. I struggled to put away the idea of loveliness.

We pulled up to the entrance of the nuns' residence. They thanked us, hurrying out and then rushing up the sidewalk to go in. The rain was really coming down now, with thunder and lightning, so we pulled around to the church parking lot and waited for it to let up. Finally we had to hurry in, and we got fairly soaked. Father Burns said the Mass. And Phillip Chorros served.

When I knelt for communion, he gave me a little half smile, as if there were some joke between us.

Later that same day, at school, I was in the cafeteria with Moss, and mentioned seeing his cousin at morning Mass. Moss took a moment of staring silence. "You were at the six o'clock Mass?"

"Yes," I said, embarrassed. "With my dad."

"Really," he said, shaking his head a little. "Well, anyway, I found out my mom thinks he's crazy." He lifted one shoulder, a half shrug. "He's my cousin, and I tell you I don't have any real idea who he is these days. He's keeping off to himself a lot."

In the fall, Chorros left school and went to Arizona. According to Moss, it was flight. Running away from Chorros Senior. Drexel, with his collection of comic books like bargaining chips for friendship, had already moved with his family to Buffalo in the late summer, but his little friend Reynolds seemed to be everywhere, scurrying down the hallways from one place to another like the rabbit he resembled, always with more papers in his notebook than he could comfortably carry. He never spoke to me and he always appeared to be going away.

I missed Chorros, missed his presence. It was almost as if I missed his example. And in a way I was following it: keeping to myself more.

I did go out for the basketball team, perhaps only because Moss and Shipley had. Being on the basketball team with them kept me in the circle of those who had gone to the mountains and experienced the abbey. I don't believe this was conscious, though. The abbey was there, a common memory we never spoke about. Concerning the basketball, there was actually something of an inertia about going out for it. The sport had been a solitary refuge for me and I had discovered I possessed a certain talent for it. The hours of shooting alone had given me what Mr. Dupree said was a dead shot from fifteen feet and he jokingly called me "Deadeye."

Moss took it up. When he saw me in the halls he would nod and say, "Hey, Deadeye."

I always gave a sidelong smile in answer. I wanted to ask about his cousin. Except that you didn't ask that sort of thing of Moss, or really of anyone in those days. I'm sure Moss would've thought it weird. In the way of those things, we had all gone apart. Once, as we were leaving the gym, I almost asked him if he still liked me. It was ridiculous. The fact is, I had never much liked Moss.

In January, two days after my seventeenth birthday, the pope excommunicated Fidel Castro. My father reported it to us at the breakfast table, holding open the morning paper, as if he were talking about a weather event. It was the first time I knew about the concept: *excommunication,* and it obsessed me for weeks; *excommunication:* a public sentence, a consignment to hell. I kept turning it in my mind.

Basketball ended, and I had done well. Bradley High had a winning team. I averaged 18.7 points a game. I kept going to Mass and communion each morning, and I began spending a lot of time in the library, reading: Thomas à Kempis's *The Imitation of Christ* and Dom Eugene Boylan's *This Tremendous Lover.* Even sections of Aquinas's *Summa Theologica.* And everything I could find of Fulton J. Sheen and Thomas Merton.

The spring went by that way. Basketball practice each afternoon, the games, and many afternoons in the library poring over books, neglecting all else, including homework — especially math homework. In the classes I still clowned or daydreamed, and when baseball season arrived I made that team as a second-string outfielder and a pitcher. In classes, failing math, I made up imaginary statistics for imaginary players. I liked looking at the numbers and was as thorough with these made-up figures as Chorros had been with the real ones. The world went on around me without my noticing it much, beyond weather. Chorros was going through whatever he was going through those thousands of miles away. I imagined him moving among friends who didn't consider him weird, no longer having to worry about his father's temper. I wished this for him, thinking I would never see him again.

He and his mother returned in the summer. The parting from Chorros Senior had evidently been a trial separation.

I was down at Dempsey's, where I spent most days, shooting baskets with Shipley, and Moss walked up with Chorros. It stunned me to see that I was now taller than he was.

"So how was Arizona?" Shipley asked him.

"I got through a school year," said Chorros, smiling. "I got to spend time away."

We played that day into the evening hours and when I started home, Moss, who had his father's car, asked Shipley and me if we wanted a ride home.

In the car, Chorros, riding shotgun, turned and gave me a look. "So you're the high scorer for the basketball team."

"No," I told him. "Guy named Cawley. Twenty-one points a game."

"I ran track," Chorros said. "I got down to eleven point four in the hundred, I won a medal for the best time."

"Hey man, think of it," Moss said. "You still wouldn't've caught Bourdin."

In that moment all four of us were silent, as if the old house with its shattered windows and collapsed porch roof were another passenger in the car.

"Wonder where Drexel is now," Chorros said.

Shipley said, "His family moved to Buffalo."

"Did he ever get his comic books back from Father Burns?" Moss wanted to know.

"I thought Burns gave them back that day," Chorros said.

I hadn't thought of Drexel for quite a while.

Moss asked if I wanted to go over to Shipley's with them, and as much as I wanted to I decided to go on home. Chorros said he wanted to be let off, too. His mother wanted him home for reasons we all sensed. The house looked fairly derelict, and there was only one light on upstairs. I watched him go on up the sidewalk and in.

Moss said, "Weird."

"He's the same," said Shipley.

"What?" I said.

"Where's the old man. Anybody know where the old man is?"

"They separated," Moss said. "Now she's back. We didn't hear anything of him or see him at all while they were gone."

We pulled away and were quiet for a time, going down Blue Hill Road. "Hey, Bourdin," Shipley said. "Where'd *you* get to, man? This ain't you. You're like a — a zombie these days. What's up?"

"Nothing," I said. "I'm fine."

They dropped me off and took their time pulling away. I wondered what they might be saying about me.

In the middle of that October, 1962, I came home from school and found my mother on the phone, her face white and frowning. "I know," she said, nodding a greeting at me and then turning away slightly. "I know. But it could be anything, right? More Berlin, maybe."

"Is that — " I began.

She whispered, "Constance."

Aunt Constance. I waited. Constance still lived in Tennessee. She and Jean exchanged letters and cards often, but long distance was a sign of something momentous.

As though in answer to my thought, Jean said into the phone, "Well, 'highest national urgency' means real trouble of some kind. It's scary."

After she hung up, she turned and embraced me. We stood that way awhile, silent. Her pregnancy with the baby girl she would name after Constance had made her large around the middle. A late-life child, she had told others. She was thirty-nine. I stepped back and her hands went to the rounded place as if it were something to carry in her arms. "The president's gonna make a speech tonight. Highest national urgency. That's what your aunt says."

That evening, we watched it. Even the twins, who had recently turned nine years old. Jean rested her head on my father's shoulder. "Everything we've already been through," she murmured, then sighed.

The phone rang. My father answered it. "Yes? Yes, he's here. Can I say who's calling?" He waited a second, then handed the receiver to me. "It's Phillip Chorros," he said.

We had rarely ever talked on the phone except to arrange for going places or doing things. "What do you think of this?" he asked.

"Don't know," I said stupidly.

"I'm calling everybody."

I waited.

"I think maybe it's the end of the world. So does Derek. Shipley's dad is talking about moving to Canada. So what do you think. You think this is the end of the world?"

"I don't know."

"Are you scared?"

It occurred to me that actually at that moment anyway I felt very little fear. The whole matter of it was too unreal. "I guess everybody's scared," I managed.

"You don't sound scared."

"I'm scared," I said, beginning to feel it.

He went on. "Old Father Drummond said we shouldn't think of the end of *the* world, but the end of our — the end of *our own* individual world." He halted. "Our own lives. I served the Mass at the eleven on Sunday. I took Derek's place. Derek had a fever. I didn't want to but I couldn't get out of it." His voice shook a little. "I can't figure anything out. There's something —" He halted. "I'm — I think —" Again he left a pause. "I believe in God, you know? But I can't figure —" He stopped.

"I believe in God, too," I said.

"Well," he said with a note of impatience, "I've gotta go. Never mind." And he hung up.

I went into the bedroom that I shared now with the twins and knelt at my bed to pray that nobody would drop the bomb. The twins were still out in the living room watching TV. I had been reading about the stigmata and the saints who had experienced them — Francis of Assisi, Catherine of Siena and others. The time, that very time, that day itself, felt extraordinary, and I closed my eyes, thinking of miracles and visitations. I had wondered why the angels who appeared to the shepherds on Christmas night said, "Be not afraid." And why the shepherds *would be* afraid, since this was clear proof that everything was true and they would never have to worry or doubt again. I had my hands folded tightly, my head bowed, eyes closed, thinking of this and thinking of the stigmata and the end of the world, and suddenly the feeling came to me of a nearby presence, or presences. Numen, or Shekinah, as I believe it is called, though of course I didn't know the words then. The world was on the brink of the atomic destruction we had all been warned about every day and I felt the strongest inkling of an imminent vision, an angel or a communication from *otherwhere;* my own Fátima. It was close; it was at hand. I felt the rush of blood to my face, the stirring in my veins.

I bolted out of that room as if ten thousand devils were after me.

My mother was in the hallway, carrying a wicker basket of laundry — she had already gone back to what her day required. I almost knocked her over.

"What in the world?" she said.

"I'm sorry."

"You look like you've seen a ghost or something." I was taller than she was now, and her motion to look past me into the room, lifting slightly on her toes, made me aware of this like new knowledge. I was still such a little boy inside, even reaching my full height. "Why're the lights out?" she asked.

"I always turn the lights out when I leave the room," I told her.

She shrugged. "Really." And then looked past me again. "Well, dinner'll be ready in about fifteen minutes. We're late tonight. Your father's cooking steak."

"Yes, ma'am."

"Then we'll be saying our rosary. No more TV tonight. I've already told the twins."

"Are you scared, Mom?" I heard myself say.

She smiled. "Don't be afraid, honey. You'll see. This old world's been around so long. It's not going anywhere. We'll all feel better as soon as we say our rosary." She balanced the basket against her hip and with her free hand brushed the hair from her brow, still smiling. It seemed that she knew for certain we would be all right. I was about to be seventeen years old, and standing in that dim hallway with all the accumulated dread weighing on me, I felt suddenly convinced that she *did* know.

And I felt the church, too, its centuries, like a strength.

Watching her go on into their bedroom with the basket of clothes, I marveled at her ability simply to get on with the rest of the day. Later, lying awake in bed, the twins moving restlessly but deeply asleep in their bunks, when I heard once more those small half-whimpers in my father's deep snoring, I had the thought that Jean was somehow stronger than all of us. Vance seemed to be talking. "Huh-no," he breathed out. There followed a deep, snoring inhalation, and then the whimpering, spoken sigh. "Huh-no."

The next morning, walking to school, I looked at the placid, cloudless blue sky and replayed Jean's voice in my head about this old world not going anywhere. And even so, I couldn't help envisioning mushroom clouds and missiles. It was difficult not to feel the impending end of everything. I wondered what it must be like on the streets of Moscow.

I saw Chorros with Moss in the central hallway. They looked at me and seemed to be waiting for me to say something.

"My mother says this old world will keep going on."

"Maybe it shouldn't," Phillip said, and walked away.

Moss shook his head. "Weird," he said. "I think he *wants* bad news."

The vice principal of the school, Mr. Muth, held a general assembly in the middle of that week to go over procedures during nuclear attack. We filed back to our classes quietly and waited for a drill, but there was no drill.

In art class our teacher, Mr. Eberley, set up a still life for us to draw with pastels — a blue bowl with three green apples in it next to an intricately decorated teacup on a saucer. Tranquility itself. Most of us understood that it was meant that way: something harmless and even nourishing on which we could concentrate. Apples, tea. Everyone worked quietly. Phillip Chorros was at the left end of my table. In his version of the still life two of the green apples had melted over the edge of the plate like Salvador Dalí's famous clocks, and the other one was glowing. He had somehow managed to make the light emanating from the skin of the glowing one seem the reason for the melting, and, looking at it, you thought immediately of radiation.

"That is a fail, Master Chorros," said Mr. Eberley.

"I like it, sir."

"Put it away and do another. That's morbid. Dalí was not morbid. He was making a statement about the persistence of our perception of time, the illusion of it and the elastic and, yes, sometimes oppressive nature of it."

"I feel only the oppression, sir."

"Just *stop* that." The word *stop* — pronounced so vehemently — caused a small bead of spittle to catch in his mustache. He wiped it away with the back of his hand. "Keep your puerile and morbid perceptions to yourself in my class. Redo this. Or you fail."

Chorros said, "Yes, sir," but with an edge of disdain.

The art teacher walked away.

The second still life, produced very quickly and brilliantly, was a perfect image of the apples and the teacup and the plate, except there was a minute crack in the cup, and a worm hole in one of the apples. Mr. Eberley, collecting the work as class ended, said nothing.

The back-and-forth of the missile crisis went on through the week. Each night, walking out on our street, I concentrated on Jean's assurance about "this old world," while I looked at the cloudless sky with its numberless stars. I thought of the story from Fátima, and abruptly recalled the fateful date about which Sister Mary Margaret had spoken with such certainty. Nineteen seventy. If the Pope, whoever that might be, would not reveal the contents of the letter until 1970, it followed that we couldn't be at the end of the world in 1962.

I couldn't believe I had forgotten the letter. After all, Sister Mary Margaret had said the several Popes had wept. I thought about being ready to die and go to heaven — a depraved boy who had recently thought of sex looking at a nun riding in the backseat of his father's car. Finally, I gathered the courage to go back into the house and ask Vance about the letter. He looked puzzled — and curious, too. He said, "Let's ask your mother." We went into the living room, where she was folding clothes, sitting on the couch with the TV news on. A Russian ship and an American navy ship were closing on each other in the Atlantic, both armed. On the coffee table before her were a cup of coffee and a lit cigarette in an otherwise clean ashtray. As though the world weren't on the brink of total destruction. She pondered my description of the old nun's story, then frowned and looked at Vance. "Ever heard of this, honey?"

"Well," Vance said, shaking his head, "Sister Mary Margaret *is* getting on in years."

"I think she's getting on in being cracked." Jean looked at me. "Forget it, son. I never heard of a letter or anything of the kind."

"Why would she tell us that?"

"She's an old lady with too much time on her hands and a big imagination."

"But that's a sin," I said.

"Oh," my mother said, "I'm sure she *believes* it. She's not lying if she *thinks* it's true."

A little later, I went out into the cold again and looked at the sky, shivering as I walked.

I had managed with great effort that whole summer and early fall to keep pure and even to govern my thoughts. I'd attended Mass every morning and gone to confession often, sometimes more than once a week. I decided to go that Saturday of the showdown out in the Atlantic. I walked to the church alone, and found forty or fifty people, grown-ups, lined up in both side aisles all the way to the front, waiting. It looked like the lines at the theater to see *West Side Story* the year before. I decided to go on home.

Through that week I kept thinking about people my parents'

age and older who apparently did *not* believe this old world would go on. I watched Jean and Vance being who they were, though they did keep tuned to the news, and read both newspapers. But we didn't talk about it. The twins asked some questions, and Jean answered them much as she had answered me. Otherwise, we simply went through the week. She had some false contractions. My father painted the room that would be the baby's. At school, during lunch, Phillip Chorros grabbed the microphone for announcements at the front of the room and said, "Study Russian, everybody, so when those bastards conquer us we'll know what the hell they're talking about." Mr. Muth and two other teachers escorted him out of there, but perhaps because everyone was feeling anxiety about the possible end of everything, they only warned him about the language and gave him detention.

When the crisis finally ended and we were saying our nightly rosary in thanksgiving, my mother wept again. And once more that night, unable to sleep, I heard my father's distressed sleep-sounds, this time with occasional spoken words: "There," I heard. "No, there." And then, "Oh, let me," and, once more, "Huh-no." I imagined him living through — or reliving through — something terrible under his skin where no one could help him. And for a while again I was afraid of sleep, and filled with anxiety about twilight, when the twins and I would have to turn in, as my father always put it. "Time to turn in, boys." The rosary actually helped, and often, having said it with the family, I would lie in my bed with my own set of beads, saying it myself. I remember feeling a little less uneasy when my parents stayed up for favorite TV programs in the evenings, or my father watched a baseball game while Jean sat in her chair knitting or reading one of her novels. Some nights, because he wanted me to love the sport as he did, he would let me stay up and watch a game with him. I always felt buoyed when a game was tied, because that could mean extra innings; it could go on into the night, and was therefore a possible reprieve.

At school, the crisis over, we experienced a reckless new energy, a kind of repercussion. Mr. Muth held another assembly, and had three different clergymen offer a prayer of thanksgiving. The Catholic one was Father Llewelyn Burns. There he was, with that raspy voice and the muddy green eyes. His tone was gentler somehow — well, less harsh. He spoke of faith, and gratitude. I looked for Chorros in the crowd, but couldn't find him.

In art class, those weeks, he kept drawing pictures of torture — burning saints and impaled martyrs, skeletal figures on the rack or tied to stakes being whipped, or hanging from trees. No matter what Eberley assigned as a theme, Chorros's drawings were of terrible physical suffering. And somewhere he'd gained comprehensive knowledge of human musculature and bone structure; the depictions were stunning in their faithfulness to the grisliest features of bodily harm, muscles and tendons and limbs in attitudes of appalling stress. Eberley took them without comment.

Near Christmas, he asked us to draw something relating to the holiday. Chorros stared at his sketch paper for a long while, then, with great alacrity, clearly inspired, drew a picture of Santa Claus as an aged, exhausted, pallid fat man sitting naked on a bench, looking disconsolately over his deeply sloped left shoulder at us, the flesh of his buttocks drooping over the back edge of the bench. A lighted cigarette dangled from his snowy beard, smoke trailing in a bluish strand from it, his fur-lined red suit dirt-stained and heaped on the floor. You could suppose this was a department store employee, except that two tight-mouthed, impatient-looking elves with very pointed ears stood to one side, evidently waiting for him to get on with the routine. It was a brilliantly belligerent piece of work. No cartoon, but a perfectly rendered line drawing of a figure so depleted by his life that he lacked the energy to keep sitting upright. Mr. Eberley, when he put his paperback novel down and walked over to see it, said, "You'll get no credit for that. Draw something else."

"But it's Santa," Chorros said. "He's just a little tired."

"Redo," the art teacher demanded. "Or you fail."

Chorros moved the drawing aside, patiently took another sheet of sketch paper and started something else. I watched, fascinated, until Mr. Eberley said, "The rest of you, get to work. This is not a joke class."

I had been trying to draw a manger scene, but couldn't render the Virgin. The face looked mannish, a little like Sister Mary Margaret's. Of course Chorros's drawing made my effort seem embarrassingly earnest, not to say trite. I put it aside, and started a snowy street scene with an ornament on a streetlamp. Chorros's new picture, done in less than twenty minutes, was of the same fat figure dressed in only the red pants this time, standing with his bare back turned, the folds of flesh there looking like loaves of bread hanging from just under his shoulders. He was decorating a Christmas tree with the same two elves, everything quite appropriate for the season except for Santa's flabby back and the pants sagging just enough to show the top of his ass. At the heels of his shiny black boots there were broken ornaments scattered, a big cockroach peering out from the hull of one shard, which was perfectly shaded to show the reflection of the nativity.

Mr. Eberley said, loud, "You have no respect."

"Yes, but I have talent, sir. Way more than you."

Mr. Eberley glared, his face turning bright red. "What did you just say to me?"

Phillip Chorros gave a seemingly innocent smile, but his voice trembled with rage. "I said I have talent, sir. Way more than you. And really, what *do* you have, sir? You have Mickey Spillane."

Mr. Eberley grabbed him around the middle and pulled him from the table. He lifted and then dragged, and then lifted him again to the doorway, and pushed him out into the hall. Eberley came back toward us, looking apoplectic — I thought he might collapse — but then he spun around and went out again. Chorros had evidently started away. Several of us rushed to the doorway, and saw the art teacher going up to him, the boy standing there, defiant, arms at his sides. Eberley took his shirt at the shoulder and walked him toward the main office. Phillip didn't resist. We went slowly back into the room, where others were passing the two drawings around, saying nothing; it was as though we were looking at some sort of evidence after a crime. Except that the evidence was inspired. The bell sounded the end of the period, and Eberley hadn't returned. I stayed with several others until he came into the room again.

"Go," he said, his face white as the walls. "Get out. All of you. Now."

They expelled Chorros, and I didn't see him again for a time. I kept expecting to run into him or his cousin at Mass, or at Dempsey's. I might have called his house, but I feared having to talk to his father. And I wasn't getting down to Dempsey's much anyway. My little sister, Connie, had arrived and we were a family of six, crammed into that little three-bedroom house on Oak Lane. Because the house was so small we heard the baby all night, each night. Connie had colic. Vance and Jean were dealing with it, heating formula "in the wee small hours," as he put it. I was responsible for taking care of the twins. I would pour them cold cereal in the mornings after getting in from Mass and communion. My mother called me her angel. I didn't feel like an angel. I kept having erotic dreams, and my curiosity about sex and my yearning to experience it were no less boundless. Because no one in the house was getting much sleep, my dreams were fairly bizarre and feverish. Often when I got up and dressed to go to Mass, I had not really been asleep. And I kept thinking of Chorros and his cousin, who also seemed to be gone.

I found out from Moss, when I did see him, that Phillip had gone to Phoenix again with his mother and was finishing high school out there. They had left his father for good. I asked for an address, and Moss didn't have one, of course. But two days later he gave it to me. I carried it around for a time. But when I sat down to write a letter, the whole thing seemed false. And eventually I lost track of the address.

5.

I graduated from high school that spring, and had decided I didn't want to drive yet — which was all right with my parents, who of course never drove during those years before we got the Ford. Perhaps a month after my graduation Jean sat me down to read me a letter from the Sacred Heart Seminary, which was signed *Yours in Christ, Father Gillette* but began with *Dear Applicant*. (I saw this aspect of it later.) Jean had read it, and put off telling me about it, not wanting to ruin the good feeling of my graduation.

"Honey, it's not good news," she said, a tremor in her voice. She read Father Gillette's letter: scholarly aspects of life in seminary, very keen competition, my grades not nearly at a level, etc., and perhaps it would be a good thing if I were to attend a junior college for a year or so, to prepare myself. She nearly broke down crying as she read. When she finished, she wiped the heel of her palm across her nose, sniffling. "You'll do well in junior college — you'll see. It'll all work out."

"It'll be fine," I said, surprised by the prodigious sense of relief I felt. "I'll go to school."

So I applied at Blair Junior College and started early, with a remedial class in math, in July. I saw Moss several times down at Dempsey's. And Shipley was in my remedial math class until he simply stopped coming. Moss said he heard that Shipley had boosted a car to go on a joyride. He brought it back, but was arrested anyway. I asked Derek Moss if he had heard from his cousin. "Nope," Moss said. "And he hasn't heard from me, either."

I had to take a language in the fall, and signed up for Spanish. I recognized a Saint Agnes boy, who looked at me and then looked away. So I dropped the class and took French. I kept thinking of calling Moss. When we played basketball at Dempsey's we talked a little about some of the other altar boys and about Father Burns. Even about Sister Mary Margaret and her story of the ominous letter to the Pope. But the subject of his cousin just never came up.

I didn't see Chorros again until November, a little more than a year after the missile crisis, when the horror unfurled in Dallas. Father Burns said a memorial Mass at Saint Agnes that Sunday the twenty-fourth, and Phillip Chorros was one of the altar boys. He had cut his hair so short it looked like a dark stain on his skull. He gave a sidelong smile and nod, holding the paten under my chin as Father Burns put the host on my tongue. The priest's sermon was about retribution, the wages of sin, the sickness of present times. On the way home, my father said, "He laid it on the line today."

"I thought he was morbid," Jean said. She had the baby in her lap. The twins were silently taking everything in.

"These are bad times," my father said.

She began to cry. We had all been crying off and on since Friday, and we went home and watched the funeral procession through the hours — the drums sounding, the marching cadres of soldiers, the dazed, weeping crowds lining the way, the dark wagon-hearse drawn by the six caparisoned white horses, followed by the riderless black one being led, nearly prancing, along Pennsylvania Avenue, with the backdrop of the Capitol dome, and, on either side, the federal buildings in their neoclassical splendor, and the winter trees and the widow and the two surviving brothers and the world leaders inside the shining limousines in the bright cold sun of that day. And Chopin's funeral march being played. (*There* was that melody in its beautiful sepulchral entirety!) Other than the television with the drums and the tolling bells and cadenced sound of the marching booted feet, and the solemn music, the only sound in the house was little Constance's babbling and complaining. The Chopin was played at least twice more. Remembering the refrains of that dirge on the bus heading out of the mountains, I saw again the old beaten-down house in the swale, and recalled how I felt helping to tear it apart. I received an image of myself destroying the wine jugs in the basement. It all seemed like a sin now, and I wanted to talk to Chorros. I had just seen him and he'd smiled, but something about the passage of time since we'd been classmates was getting in the way.

"What'll we do?" my mother said, blowing smoke from her cigarette. "Who in the world is Lyndon Johnson?"

"He's the president," said my father. "We'll pray for him."

I didn't see Phillip Chorros again until the following July. I was nineteen, and going to night school again at Blair, after a short span of working in a pet store in Falls Creek. One afternoon I walked into a record store in Adams Morgan, and there he and Moss were, the two of them crowded into one of the booths listening to the Beatles. The Gulf of Tonkin incident was in the news; Vietnam was heating up. We talked about the draft, and being in school. We went on about the music, the British Invasion, as everyone was calling it. "They're playing our own music back at us," Chorros said. "I think it's cool."

"Hey," Moss said suddenly to his cousin. "Why don't you take Bourdin to the ball game?"

"The Yankees are in town," Chorros said to me. "Are you a Senators fan?"

I had not been to a baseball game since the summer of '62 with my father, who had been a fan of the team that migrated to Minnesota two years before that. The expansion team was a hodgepodge of journeyman players, and they lost far more often than they won. But they would be playing the Yankees. I said to Chorros that I was indeed a Senators fan.

"Well, I've got this extra ticket, and Derek's got a date. He says."

"I could go," I told him. "Sure."

The next morning on his way to work, my father dropped me off at the apartment complex where Chorros and his mother now lived, in Arlington. She had made sandwiches and iced tea for us. Phillip called her *Lil,* as if they were old friends. She looked at me with her sad, dark eyes and I saw the lines of worry on either side of her mouth. I thought of her life with a man gone batty from the war. "We've just got back here from family out west," she said.

Chorros said, "Tucson."

She nodded and said, "We got tired of desert living. Are you in school, Vance?"

Chorros broke in and volunteered that he wanted to study history. He hadn't entered college yet, but would soon. He was working part-time as a mechanic at a garage in Seven Corners. "Well, college," he said to me. "How's it feel?"

"I like it," I said, though in fact at the time I had no liking for it at all.

"I think Phillip should be an artist," his mother said to me. "What do you think?"

"He *is* an artist," I said. "Yes."

She turned to him. "See?"

"I've gotta get myself in college," he said. "Or I'll end up in the infantry."

Lil said, "You're already registered for classes in the fall. Don't talk like that."

"I'm still thinking about going north," he said, nodding at her. "To that — retreat."

"Are you talking about Canada?" I asked.

He shook his head and smiled. "No."

"I don't want anyone to go anywhere anymore," Lil said.

"I still might study art," he said. "Or art history, maybe."

I told him I had no idea what I would do.

It was soon time to leave for the game. We got on the old DC Transit bus that came down that street in Arlington every day on its way into town. As we were chugging and bouncing along in the bus, which rattled and coughed like an old horse, I thought of the trip into the mountains. I believe he was thinking of it, too, because he gave me a look and muttered, "Moss doesn't know what he's missing."

"Is he taking courses?"

"Sure. He's going to Montclair."

"I'm at Blair. Taking English and history."

He grinned. "The whole thing for me's more about not having to go to war."

I nearly said something to him about the reason I was in school: still believing, at least partially, that I would go through with the plans for seminary. Instead I repeated for him what my father had said to me on more than one occasion: "You don't want to end up in the infantry lugging a rifle through the jungle and being shot at."

The bus stopped and three elderly men got on, wearing New York Yankees baseball caps.

"Although, I don't know," Phillip Chorros said. "Sounds like it might be an adventure."

I said nothing.

"Getting expelled from school here was a lucky break, you know. I like Arizona, and my uncles, Lil's brothers, run an auto repair shop there. They taught me to work on cars. I'm a qualified mechanic, man. I could build an engine."

"Isn't that what your father — " I stopped. His father was an auto mechanic.

Chorros didn't hesitate. "Yeah. He's up north somewhere. Maine or New Hampshire. We don't hear from him. I mean, he's the reason for our Arizona trips, mostly. Running from him. I wish I could say I miss him. But when we got back he stayed drunk most of the time." He shook his head. "The heartbreak's all Mom's." Then he sighed. "She actually still misses him."

"You don't miss him, even a little?"

He seemed to ponder this. "I guess. Maybe some."

"But you think lugging a rifle through the jungle might be an adventure." I thought again of the ruin of the old house, doubtless because that adventure had been our own little make-believe war. I wondered if he might've just had the same thought. But he said nothing.

As the bus pulled by the street two blocks from the stadium, he turned to me and said, "Your dad's still around, right?"

"Yeah."

He shook his head. "Mine just went batty, man. I was scared to be around him. I really thought he might kill somebody. I worried about it all the time."

We left the game in the seventh inning because the Senators were behind seven to nothing and the Yanks' ace, Whitey Ford, was pitching. We got back to the house and had more iced tea, and ate some cookies Lil had baked, talking about the still-powerful Yankees, and then Vance picked me up and that was that.

Over the next few days, Chorros would call, or I would. Nothing much to do, nothing much to say, it seemed. He'd decided that indeed he was going to head north, to the retreat.

I said, "What sort of retreat is it?"

"Just — I don't know. A retreat for guys like me."

"Artists?"

"Sure."

Before the end of that summer I stopped hearing from him. I saw Moss at church, and he told me that it was not a retreat, but seminary.

"*Sem*inary," I said. "Why wouldn't he say something to me about it?"

Moss shrugged. "I don't think he knows what he's doing minute to minute."

There seemed nothing to say to this.

"I'm getting married," he continued. "And you never even met her. She works for my father and she's three years older than I am, so she'll really be my old lady. We're doing the ceremony at her parents' house in New York."

"Well, when you talk to Phillip," I said, "will you tell him I said hey?"

"He's in seminary, man."

Night school and late-night studying had put an end to my trips to early morning Mass. That fall, my father required gallbladder surgery, and afterward he developed an infection. Things were uncertain for a while. Jean and I said rosaries each night and murmured prayers all day long. Vance used the time in the hospital to study real estate (we learned that he had been secretly studying it for months) and when he was finally well, he got his license and a position with a firm in Herndon. Gradually, then, the nightly rosaries dwindled, and finally ended. If you asked any of us to say exactly when, we wouldn't be able to agree about it: we missed one night, then another; then, a week later, still another. Like that. We bought a new car, and there was even talk about getting a bigger house. Vance was making more money. I remember having the thought that this was the reason the nightly rosary lapsed, along with a couple of other family habits: we seldom ate dinner together anymore since Vance had appointments showing houses at times outside the normal eight-hour day. As I said, I had stopped going to morning Mass.

By the late sixties, I had stopped going to Mass at all.

There was no single defining event, really, no turning point. The whole house just fell (if, given the story I have been telling, I may be allowed the metaphor). Anyway, I began to drift from my childhood, as we all do, of course.

And as I must do now, in fact.

PART TWO

I.

I left home for good in the spring of '65, when I transferred to George Washington University from the community college. I had decided I would major in history, thinking of answering Kennedy's call to service in something like the Peace Corps. I still envisioned now and then how it might be to live in a monastery like the Abbey of the Holy Cross. I had read Thomas Merton's *The Sign of Jonas,* a journal of his first year at the Abbey of Gethsemani in Kentucky, and the idea was inviting; but as Father Drummond had said to me in confession, there was nothing to be gained in thinking of it as refuge. Finally, like the priesthood, the idea of entering the monastic life seemed unreasonable. And indeed this was the last of my stages of pious intention, if this isn't too brutal a thing to say. I played basketball with a regular group of boys at Dempsey's, though I still was rather a loner otherwise; a boy named Brian took a liking to me, but he had a mean streak that unnerved me. I learned from Moss that Shipley was in some kind of trouble, but no one else I talked to had any specifics. And I often thought of Chorros, off in seminary; he had left me behind, and I felt the irony of it a little, as you might feel if someone you didn't know won a prize for something you'd once pursued yourself. I finally did write him, twice — the fact of my previous plans conjoining with his actual journey seemed an important thing for him to know — but I got no answer. Finally it was as though his studying for the priesthood was the sign and indication of my own stalled condition. I had no idea what I might finally end up doing in life. When I imagined working in real estate, like Vance, I felt anxiety; I had no interest in selling houses. I had begun reading history and the professor I had was a former newspaperman who had been questioned by HUAC. He had strong opinions but also plenty of facts to support them. I was finding out how much of the curriculum I'd been exposed to in high school was untrue. It all reminded me of Sister Mary Margaret's apocryphal letter from the Blessed Virgin to the Pope. For a time, then, it seemed the whole world was made of lies. And I could not understand — though I tried — how a man like Thomas More, about whom I had been read-ing, could go to his own execution rather than simply tell one lie when so much of everything else was built on lies.

Remember, I was twenty.

I had taken a small efficiency in Adams Morgan, and most Sun-days were now given to basketball on the Ellipse or in the nearby high school gymnasium. I had begun missing Mass.

That fall semester, on the first day of classes, I was walking along Logan Circle outside Gelman Library, and I recognized Phillip Chorros heading in the same direction on the other side. I hurried over there, and when he saw me approaching I thought I perceived a slight inclination to shy away. There was something drawn back about his demeanor.

"Hey," I said.

"Damn," he said with a small smile.

"Are you going *here* now?" I asked him.

He said, "I'm on my way to class."

"Weren't you — ?" I began. "I mean, Moss said — "

He interrupted. "I left after the first month." He seemed a little embarrassed about it.

"Did you get my letters?" I asked.

"Letters?"

"I wrote about the — that I had plans for seminary, too."

He seemed unsurprised. "Well, most Catholic boys do, don't they? At some point?"

"I was serious."

"So was I," he said. Then he grinned. "Apparently not the right choice for either of us."

I said nothing.

He started off, but in fact we were headed to the same class. An American history class. "Well, Cochise," he said as we got ready to enter the room. "Look at us." And immediately our old relation was renewed.

He had developed a strong abhorrence concerning the dep-redations of the US government where Native Americans were concerned, which was no surprise to me. And he wasn't shy about bringing it all up in that class. The recent big hit movie from those years was *How the West Was Won*. He and I talked about it and we pointed out to anyone who would listen that it was a cheesy piece of tawdry, racist Technicolor propaganda. Some of the professors at GW back then disliked him, as his high school teachers had, without being able to ignore him. Again, not surprisingly, he knew more than some of them did. Certainly he knew more than I did. His mother was Liluye, and they were Christian Apaches. She was back in Tucson, helping one of her brothers at the auto shop, the other having been drafted and sent off to Vietnam.

Chorros still attended church. I went with him once or twice.

Of course, whenever I was visiting at home I went to Mass with Jean and Vance and the kids. Christmas of '65, they were all excited about the new house they were thinking of buying, nine miles from Oak Lane, in Seven Corners. They took me on a tour of it — a tall Colonial, with three living levels. It was on a corner lot within walking distance of the shops and the theater at Seven Corners. We went back to the Oak Lane house and celebrated the season, and on Christmas Eve, after the children were in bed, I had a beer with them. We said nothing about the priesthood. Drew and Edward were altar boys, part of Father Burns's crew. They seemed glad of it. I refrained from saying anything about the priest's idea of discipline; I hoped it wouldn't come up.

My father and I went out back and looked at the two maples, which were taller than we were now. "In a way, I hate to leave," he said. "We've been so wonderfully happy here."

The next morning, tossing a baseball back and forth with the twins, I asked, "Do you guys get along with the other altar boys?"

Drew appeared momentarily confused.

"I talk to that little guy, Reynolds," Edward said. "Now and then, anyway. He's weirder than Phillip Chorros was."

"*Chorros.* You guys know about *him*?"

"They *still* talk about *him*. The artist weirdo who went to be a priest."

I said, "But he left seminary, you know. He's in classes with me at GW. We hang out all the time. And he's not that weird. He's just talented."

"Well," Drew said. "They talk about him. The Apache." He pronounced it *Apach-ay*, with a flourish, as he tossed the ball.

"You guys'd like him. He's cool."

They said nothing, tossing the ball to me and then to one another. For a while there was just the sound of the ball smacking into the gloves.

"Are Mom and Dad disappointed in me?" I said.

Drew frowned. "Why would they be disappointed?" It sounded like a challenge, and I left it there.

Chorros had gone with a new girlfriend to visit the girlfriend's family in South Carolina, and then on to Tucson to visit with his mother and uncle, so I didn't expect to see him until January when we all returned to GW. I looked forward to telling him about the fact that he was still being talked about among the altar boys at Saint Agnes. The first afternoon of the semester, I went straight to the place we had agreed we would meet, a place called Ben's Kitchen on N Street. I confess that I went there also hoping to see the girlfriend, who was a delicate-looking slender blonde named Michelle. I felt drawn to her wit, her gift for cracking wise, and her fluid way of moving, her flawless face and greenish-blue eyes the color of a thrush's egg.

Ben's Kitchen was blaring with Dylan's "Like a Rolling Stone." I walked through to the back and found Michelle alone in a booth, crying. She reached for me, taking both of my hands. "He's leaving, Vance. He's quitting school, going back to Tucson. He says he's going to enlist. He went to the dorm to pack. He just flew in to pack up and go back. I can't even get him to talk about staying. Don't leave me here alone."

"Come with me," I said.

It was a cold day, and snowflakes pitched back and forth in the inconsistencies of the wind and the city air. She walked with me across the quad to his dorm building, a tall, dark brick structure that looked soot stained. I went inside. The light above the entryway was out; the bulb had been shattered, its pieces all over the floor. She came in behind me. The glass crackled under our shoes. Chorros came down the stairs with his duffel bag packed. Of course it was all he owned in the world.

His uncle Trace had been wounded in Da Nang. A mortar round had hit the barracks he was in; one fragment had nicked his shinbone, and the other had lodged dangerously in his lower spine. He was coming home to Tucson in a body cast. "I just came here to get my stuff. I'm gonna be there when he gets back. And I'm gonna enlist, too. This fucking stupid crime of a war!"

"Hey, I'd bet nobody in your family, including Trace, wants you to quit college."

"This isn't about what anybody else wants."

"But it's a mistake to — " Michelle began.

"The *mistake*," he interrupted, nearly at the level of a shout. Then he paused, and his voice became almost a whimper. "Is believing any of the shit. But Trace is closer than a brother. And I'm not gonna hide in school anymore."

"Hide," I said. "What the — "

He broke in. "I've been hiding for years, Vance. Putting my faith in — " He stopped. Then shouldered the bag, already headed out the door. "I'm going to find out about it all," he said. A cab had pulled up. "Write me if you want to."

"Yes," I said.

But he had been talking to Michelle. She wept as the cab pulled away.

He never wrote back. To either of us. And he never called. We were just without him. We were lonely a little; it was something always at the back of our talk, our exchanges with others, hanging out. We didn't speak about it, but when we were in each other's company things seemed calmer somehow. And we ended up together. This was in our last year of college. She was also studying history. She said I reminded her of Phillip, and she liked to hear me tell stories.

2.

Now, it's necessary that I glide over a few other matters — trusting that you'll understand why I don't wish to dwell on them as I have others.

In 1968, just out of college, I got drafted and sent to Saigon, where I worked in an office that was never bombed, nor set upon by any of the surrounding mayhem. That part of the city was teeming with soldiers and hectic with commerce, things being peddled on the street, bars crowded every night, women dancing on tables and people trading drugs, jewels, trinkets and sex. My office was in a falling-down building where you could see the slats in the walls, and seeing this made me feel as if I had been forcefully returned to that old house behind the abbey. It was depressing, yet I seldom went out, and I started going to Mass again in the little makeshift chapel provided by the air force.

While I was over there, Martin Luther King and then Robert Kennedy were killed. We were locked in a war thousands of miles away from home, and home itself appeared to be coming apart. Phillip Chorros showed up in DC at the time of the Chicago riots. His uncle Trace was recovering from his wounds and had managed to convince him that he should finish school before enlisting. Michelle wrote that he was more committed to earning a degree than ever, even with the confusion all around, and that he had no patience and no time for what she called his earlier goofing. He had gotten, she said, "serious." She was seeing him again. The love of her life, she said about him in the letter she wrote telling me goodbye only weeks before I was set to come home. They went out to Las Vegas, where she would begin teaching in a high school and he would man a blackjack table for a while. I didn't hear from either of them after her postcard telling me where they were and what they were doing and how I could get in touch with them. But there seemed no point in that, or in much of anything else for a time. I came home and lived alone in DC for a couple of years, then finished graduate school in California, at UCLA. There I met Dora, who was from

DC, and getting ready to return, as I was. She was starting out as a journalist for a local Baltimore paper.

I think I loved her right away. This bright, talkative, funny young woman with steely gray eyes and a way of measuring you with a look, as if she were going to say something withering, but it was almost always a joke, and the joke was almost always at her expense. I argued with her at first (I have no recollection now about what). We agreed on all sorts of things, especially the war. She flew to Baltimore the week before I left for DC. But I saw her shortly after I arrived, and we started going around together. I'd rented a room in Adams Morgan. Whenever I visited with my parents on a Sunday, we all went to Mass.

The first time I took Dora to dinner with them at the house on Oak Lane was just before they moved out of it. They had at last decided it was time. The house was full of boxes — either packed, or empty and waiting to be packed. My father took her out back and showed her the two maples. It was a crisp fall day and the leaves were bright with color. "Vance and I planted these when he was just a little boy, and it's one of the reasons I'm gonna hate leaving here." The trees were very tall now, and the breeze shook the burnished leaves down from them.

At the table a little later Jean brought up my devoutness at the time of the missile crisis. Dora said, "My father was stationed in Turkey then, at one of our missile sites aimed at Russia. He got sent home right after it was over."

I knew he had divorced her mother when he was assigned to duty in Germany, and that she was not presently on speaking terms with him.

"We all felt sure it meant nuclear war," Dora said.

Jean said, "Everybody felt that way. We just kept praying. Vance told us about the huge crowd waiting for confession at the height of it."

After a slight pause, little Connie pointed at me and said, "He was going to be a priest." She had her brown hair in pigtails tied with pink ribbons for the occasion (Jean's work). "Weren't you," she continued, addressing me. "You were going to be a priest."

Dora smirked. "That's kind of hard to imagine with this guy. He's such a cutup." Then, in the following polite silence: "Most everyone in my family's always been sort of atheist, especially my grandfather, who was adamant about it. I have to say sometimes I actually hope there *isn't* a heaven, because if there is, that would mean the other place exists, too, and if *that's* there, then *he's* there."

The twins laughed. "We're altar boys," Drew said. "And Vance was, too."

"I think that's beautiful. Wish I'd had that, growing up. I remember talking to some friends about the Bible and finding out that the New Testament *wasn't* just a more modern translation of the old one." She laughed. "They had to explain it to me. Which they did, of course, with a lot of mockery. I was mortified. Ever since then, I try to keep quiet when the subject comes up. I mean I wish I knew more."

"Well," my father said quietly, "we've always been believers in this house."

"Right," said Dora in a faintly helpless tone.

Another silence followed. I saw my father watch Dora sip from her glass of iced tea. It struck me that we were all watching her.

She smiled at me. And then, as if asked, she said, "My father was in the marines."

"So he's — retired now?" Jean asked.

"He went off with some baroness or other. They're in Europe somewhere. We're not — we're not in touch."

"And your mother?"

"Oh. She gets along fine now. She runs a little styling shop in Orange County, California. She did Doris Day's hair one afternoon and has her autographed picture on the wall above the cash register."

"Doris Day," Jean said. "I love her movies."

Edward, the quiet twin, said to me, "You didn't tell her you were an altar boy? Didn't tell about tearing down a big old house up in the mountains with Phillip Chorros?"

She said, "Oh, I love that story. I call it 'the tearing-down-the-mansion story.'"

"They got in a lot of trouble for it," Drew said. "The altar boys still talk about it."

"It must be something to be part of a legend," Dora said with an edge of affectionate sarcasm.

"It was no mansion," I told them.

"Well, the legend — at least for me — is not so much the old farmhouse, but this Chorros kid who was so talented the art teacher got jealous, and had him kicked out of school."

"Where is Phillip now, I wonder," Jean said.

"He turned up at GW," I said. "You knew that, didn't you? We hung around together for a while. He did finish up his high school, at some private school out there, and then he went to seminary."

"What?" Jean said.

"Didn't last a month," said Dora.

"Father Chorros," Drew said. "Wow."

"The last I knew he was living in Las Vegas," I told them.

"Your Michelle went with him," my father said. "Right? Did they get married, do you know?"

"Haven't been in touch with either of them for a while."

"You better not," Dora said with feigned severity.

After dinner, she and I went for a walk along Oak Lane. "They're very nice," she said about my parents.

"I'm glad you approve."

"Well?"

We went along a few paces. A slight breeze stirred the leaves of the trees lining the street and I thought how it sounded like whispers urging me to say something.

"I didn't mean to offend anybody with that crack about hell," she said.

"No offense," I got out.

She picked up an oak leaf, and turned it in her hand. "Such a pretty deep, polished red."

"I really don't think anybody was offended," I told her.

She let the leaf fall. "Well, that's good, then." She took my hand. "Your dad seems pretty sad about moving."

"He's a sweet sentimental man who's seen and actually been through hell."

She was quiet.

"I hope I didn't, um, offend *you* by saying that."

"Stop it, Vance. That's nothing to tease about."

"What makes you think I was teasing?"

She shrugged. "Sounded like teasing. Because *I* was worried about offending."

"I was dead serious. I *do* hope I didn't offend you."

"Are we having a fight?"

"I love you," I said. "What do you think?"

We walked on. "I guess we're not having a fight," she said.

A week or so later, after I had asked her to marry me, and she had accepted with a smile and a kiss, my mother called me and, when I answered, simply began with a question: "Are you still going to church, son?"

"Hello, Jean."

"Well?"

"Yes," I lied.

"Dora doesn't go with you, though, does she."

I waited a beat. Then: "Sometimes."

"She doesn't believe in God, son. I hate that word *atheist*. It's always seemed evil to me."

I said, "Don't worry."

"Do you think you can change her mind or something? Because that almost never works. I mean, I've never seen it work. Remember us saying the rosary each night."

"Jean, what're you telling me?"

"I don't like it when you call me Jean. I'm your mother."

"All right. Mother. What're you telling me?"

"I know it's none of my business, son, but I'm worried about you going with Dora."

"I asked her to marry me this morning," I said.

For the few seconds of silence, I thought she might've broken the connection. "Will she convert, then?"

"We've agreed we're going to raise the children Catholic."

She left another long pause, punctuated finally by a low, exhausted-sounding sigh. "Son," she began. "You — "

And I interrupted her. "That's the deal, Mother."

So Dora and I went through the rigmarole of the prenuptial meetings with a new curate named Freiz, who was very kindly and iron-jawed, with a thin, tight mouth — the only part of his face that moved when he spoke — and on the fifteenth of June 1969, less than a month after Jean and Vance did finally move to the new, larger house, in Point Royal, we were married.

From the beginning, perhaps because of my experience with Michelle, I was prone to doubts about us; I kept falling into the habit of supposing her to be less than completely *with* me. And of course this made her unhappy. But we worked through most of it, finally. We were good together; it seemed we were a little like Jean and Vance had always been, and whenever we visited with them in their new home we all went to Mass together. Dora would put on a good show, even managing to seem interested. The far end of the back lawn at the new house afforded a lovely view of the Shenandoah Valley, and we could all stroll down there to a row of skinny pines beyond which you could see the softly corrugated, distant line of the Blue Ridge Mountains. Jean liked the rural feel of the place; my father, I think, missed the old house. I did too. Jean told me she felt wrong for having reacted about Dora as she had at the beginning, and that she and Vance had been conflicted about her after that first dinner. "She just rubbed us the wrong way. And of course we couldn't have been more wrong."

I remember waking in the nights and kissing Dora as she lay sleeping, touching her fine hair and her cheek. And now and then thinking of Phillip and Michelle, wherever they were. I would lie there in the dark, propped on one elbow, gazing at Dora almost in disbelief as she slept, and knowing that I loved her and that we were happy, and I wanted Phillip and Michelle Chorros to know about it. I wanted them to see how glad we were, Dora and me.

She left suddenly in our eighth year.

We had moved to Illinois, to teach at Western. Both of us in the History Department. She didn't like the teaching, though, and quit soon after we got there. When my mother developed a lesion in her thigh bone and required surgery, I drove to Virginia, and while I was there, Dora packed up what she required to live alone, as she put it, and moved out. I had no inkling anything was wrong. We talked on the phone, so even as she was moving things out of the little house we had rented and was headed out of my life, we spoke about my mother's surgery and the biopsy results, for which, because it was bone, we had to wait several days. The house when I got home was empty of any sign of Dora. She'd gone to her mother, in California, and we had only one conversation after that.

"What in God's name's come over you," I remember saying.

"I'm so sorry, Vance. I can't be married and happy. I couldn't keep it up."

"Keep *what* up, Dora? It's been almost nine years."

"This." Her voice was as detached as that of someone announcing departures and arrivals at an airport.

I had no words.

"I wish it was different." And now she began to cry. "I'm so sorry, Vance."

"Come home," I said. "Honey. Nine years."

And she resumed as if I hadn't spoken. "I think I had an inkling of it all the way back when your father took me out and showed me those two trees that time, in the backyard at the old house. I saw the trees and thought of time and time and time, and you and me in it, and I started to feel trapped. Even then. I'm so sorry. Please, just forget me, like none of it ever happened. Like I never existed. I'm so sorry, Vance. You're the one who's a sweet sentimental man."

I have very little more from that year. There were nights that went on and on in the sound of the clock. I lived alone a long time, thinking it might be for the rest of my life. I wondered now and then if my love of her had been a form of idolatry. A sort of infatuation about the *idea* of love, as my earlier life had been about the *idea* of holiness. For a time I worried that perhaps I lacked some essential intellectual or spiritual quality everyone else possessed, something of which, when people got close enough, they felt the absence, without quite being able to put their finger on it.

One thing I did do, which likely would surprise no one: I took a journey by myself up into the mountains of West Virginia to look upon the abbey, and Brother Edgar if I could, and the old wreck of a house. I'm not sure what I expected to find — the whole thing emerged as a kind of idle quest, really; it was past, and perhaps it no longer even had to do with me. But I believe some part of me must've been seeking to recover something. Anyway, I went.

The trip seemed far shorter than I recalled. The abbey itself hadn't changed at all. But there were wide fields beyond it, and no sign of life around it. No cattle, no monks working outside. I drove in and stopped. And waited a moment, thinking someone might come out. Finally, I walked up and knocked on the big entrance door, and in a surprisingly short time, as if he had been waiting for me to knock, a monk answered. He was round faced, with a thin mouth. His hair was cut very close.

"I'm looking for a Brother Edgar?" I said.

He frowned and thought a moment, then shook his head and beckoned me into a small office to the right of the door. A woman sat there, looking like a gathering of heavy limbs supporting a broad chest and shoulders, and a leonine head of dark red hair.

Indicating the monk, who was moving off, she said, low, "I should've got up and answered the door. But my ankle." She moved to show it to me in its Ace bandage. "We saw you drive up." She moved her ankle back out of sight. Then: "He's on a vow of silence. Self-imposed penance."

I explained again that I was looking for Brother Edgar.

She frowned. "Brother Edgar, Brother Edgar. Why, I believe he left a while ago. Two or three years, anyway. It was before I came to work here. I'm one of the first woman residents. There are several of us now. I'm Sister Grace Marie."

I excused myself and went out, and walked around the place and onto the field in back. The woods were there, but there were houses built in among them. A neighborhood. I went along a gravel path in the direction I thought must be the right one. It was just houses. Ramblers, all alike. Pretty lawns, parked cars. There was a slight dip in the path, and then a road, and I was sure I was standing near the place. The very spot. I actually felt a sudden, strangely breath-stealing bereavement, standing there in the birdsong and sun-mottled shade, thinking how much of our actual lived life is fugitive.

3.

I taught history until 2008. I met my present wife, Angela, in 1993 when she came to be guest lecturer for the psychology department. She resembled Dora, with her bright wit and soft eyes — in fact, this kept me from asking her out for quite a while. But I liked her, and found myself somehow more myself when I was with her. Her laugh is as charming as any I know. She's a very lovely, insightful, kindhearted woman, interested in others, sometimes to her detriment (we all know the type: the one who thinks of herself last). We live in Hamilton, Illinois, on the Mississippi River. She still sees patients privately now and then, and we've been married almost twenty-two years.

Now and then she fusses with me about my emotional registers, as she calls them. I can still be very much the brooding, ruminative type; she dislikes having to worry about me when, on occasion, I slip back into my cave of quiet, which is another of her expressions. I tell her I don't know how I can learn to be other than I am. She says she prefers the smart aleck in me, the one who describes wrecking an old house by mistake, or the absurd scenes in an art class taught by a man who hated artists *and* art. We've had no children, though I helped raise her son, who's living in Nice, France, now. We visited him and his family there last year, and walking along the beach with its heavy smooth blue stones and the marketplace on the other side of the wall, the sea shimmering with sunlight and sparkle, I thought of my grandfather Vance, who never left Tennessee.

Though it was only a desultory kind of casual occupation born of simple curiosity, I searched off and on through the years for the altar boys. Angela called them "the lost boys." It is likely that the haphazardness of the search is why I never had much success. The revelations about the pedophilic clergy had been surfacing for years by then. And how strange to have come down the decades from being that sex-obsessed boy hoping for holiness in a literally fallen world, knowing so little beyond the nun's tales and the admonitions of the priests. I wondered about the other altar boys, especially

Chorros — probably at least partly because Michelle had gone with him (though I never looked for Dora). No, it was Phillip Chorros. Something unspoken, that kind of youthful adulation that persists through years. Once, in DC with Angela, I went to the Vietnam memorial and looked along the black wall for names. Angela was annoyed with me about it and I suppose she had a point.

But as I say, there was always the sense of a kind of nagging incompleteness about those years at Saint Agnes and just after. Those strange times in my youth.

I had finally let go of it, indeed nearly to the point of forgetting, when my mother called to say she had run into someone in Target whom she had known back then, Ethan Shipley's aunt Lena. Aunt Lena relayed the news that Ethan had been killed only a month before, in an auto accident. That was 2013, and knowing this, for whatever reason, got me going again. One search on Google turned up a retired naval officer, P. N. Chorros, who had served for twenty-five years and presently lived in Pensacola, Florida. In my muddled, haphazard way I had searched for artists and painters by that name. But on this particular occasion I simply typed in the name and looked at the several variations that came up. Phillip Nicholas Churro, Phillip Church, etc. I found myself more and more keen to know what had become of him. I had no quarrel anymore with the way things had turned out where Michelle was concerned; my life had given me the time with Dora when it was good, and the years with Angela. Nevertheless, I thought about them. You could say it was something like the feeling a man has upon waking from a dream just as someone else in the dream says, "Here's the answer we've all been seeking."

I wondered if he might have died, like Shipley. Or if he and Michelle might have divorced, or *she* might have died.

Finally, one afternoon I looked again at this naval officer in Pensacola and decided it couldn't hurt to write him, just on the off chance. Though if I'm to be completely honest I must say some part of me felt it as a kind of last gambit, to fill a need; I had reached the age when you want to go back, and to know. To recover something of the fascination, the aliveness. So I sat down and wrote a short note, introducing myself to someone who in any case by now was a stranger.

I received an answer within the week.

Dear Vance

So great to hear from you, and yes it is me. What a surprise. How long has it been? I was stationed at Ft. Myer in Alexandria for a couple years back in the early eighties and wondered if you were still living in the area. But I was recovering from a brain injury and not much good to anybody. I wonder if you'd like to come see us. We're at 24 Perdido Beach Blvd. Well you know that. You wrote us here. We've been here fifteen years. Much to catch up on. Where everybody's gone. Don't know where Shipley ended up. Last I heard he was working as a short-order cook after a couple years in the pen for petty crimes. Remember wrecking that old house? Well, let's see about getting together.

Your old friend,
Phillip

I wrote him back immediately, without mentioning any of the history, of course — including the history involving Michelle, or the art either. It was more or less a flat summary of things, some of which I've just provided here, including the fact that Shipley was gone. And I did express interest in a visit to Florida — why not? Angela and I had been talking about going down there to have a look at it as a possible place to spend retirement. And so in the way of such matters an idea took form, and soon Angela started on reservations, and was in touch with Michelle. I heard Michelle's voice again, on the answering machine one afternoon, and didn't recognize it. It was cigarette deep. I found it hard to imagine that voice coming from the girl I'd known all those years ago.

Before long Angela and I were on a plane south.

Obama was still president, of course, and we were, and are, enthusiastic supporters. I didn't think to ask Phillip Chorros what

his politics were but as Angela and I sat looking out at the blue dis-
tances, she told me Michelle had said something about having run
for councilwoman on the Republican ticket. Together we specu-
lated about how things would go if, being a retired military man
now, Phillip Chorros turned out to be the kind of unimaginative
rightist Republican we had seen emerge in recent years. I simply
couldn't picture it from the boy and the young man I'd known. If
anything, given my history of devotion to an idea, it would seem
that I'd be the candidate most likely to become ultraconservative.
Perhaps I'd narrowly evaded it. I recalled Graham Greene's line that
some of the greatest saints had more than a normal capacity for evil
and the most vicious men have sometimes narrowly evaded sanctity.
I laughed a little, thinking of it.

"What," Angela said.

"Just thinking about my time as an altar boy."

Phillip and Michelle were at the airport together to greet us. She was
still slight, still in possession of the fine intelligent features, but her
hair was a dark auburn and tied back in a chignon. I had forgotten
how tall she was; Angela stood just at shoulder height, facing her.
They embraced, nonetheless. They had worked together to arrange
everything and had become friendly. Chorros was trim looking,
gray at the temples. He wore a mustache, which was lighter gray,
and his eyes were clear; the wrinkles at the corners spoke of laughter. He took my hand into both of his and squeezed. We started
through the airport, exchanging small talk about the flight and the
weather.

Their car was a Tesla, and I remarked that I never thought I
would ride in a car without an engine.

"Post–Industrial Age," he said, smiling. "So, what's it like being
emeritus at a university?"

During our few phone calls we had not gone much beyond
accounts of places lived in and traveled to, and respective careers.
"At Western," I said, "emeritus is mostly honorific. You have use of
an office, and an email account."

"You still get some kind of stipend?"

"Well, TIAA-CREF, you know. And I still teach an occasional class. What about you?"

"It's been five years, for me. Lots of time to do whatever we want. Michelle's become a real gourmet cook. You wait. She's had her own local cooking show here for a couple years now."

The women were talking about Angela's work. And Angela told a story about a curiosity she had encountered in her first year as a therapist. It was a favorite, and she was good at telling it: the time she worked in the mental ward and a patient was assigned to her with a psychotic terror of talk, any talk. "She actually got over it," Angela said. "But at first you couldn't get her to say anything, and if you spoke to her she would scream and cower. So I was at a loss for, you know, words. Any words."

"I remember thinking I'd go to hell for saying certain words," I said.

And Phillip Chorros snickered. "Oh, life at Saint Agnes."

I continued: "That could've ended with my being just like your patient, hon, now that I think of it."

"What *do* you say to someone with that trouble?" Michelle asked.

Angela chuckled softly, a little shyly. "The first thing I said was, 'Well then, why don't we both just shut the fuck up.'"

Michelle laughed, then coughed. We waited. "She actually got better?"

"I think the humor might've actually helped," Angela said, nodding. "And maybe a little shock at hearing a doctor use that word. A little shock, anyway. I mean she looked surprised that I'd said it, yelled again because of the sound of speech, I guess, and then laughed at it, surprised again, maybe by the laugh and the sense, and we sort of went on, slowly, slowly, from there."

Michelle laughed through this. It was a deeper-sounding laughter and I noticed the trill was absent. I thought of the cigarettes. To her husband, I said, "You still drawing and painting? I mean, does that figure into doing whatever you want to do?"

He smiled. "Sure."

We got to their house, a sprawling Craftsman with a flagstone façade and an American flag flying from a corner of the roof. We went up the stone steps, across the pavilion-like porch. He opened the door and walked through to stand holding it for us, as I imagine my father might have done, showing houses. To the left, just off the foyer, was a wide staircase leading in a curve up to a balustraded landing. A big flagstone fireplace and hearth spanned the right side of the expansive living room. Paintings and drawings adorned the walls, of course, but only three were by Phillip, small ones, of his now grown children. Watercolors. They were perfect. Through the large bay window looking out on the redwood deck was a narrow stretch of switchgrass on either side of a blue-gravel path, then sand, and the wide emerald shoreline. It was a beautiful view of the sea.

"I expected more of your art on these walls," I couldn't help saying.

"Oh, that's downstairs, in the studio."

Michelle opened a bottle of white Capri, and poured us drinks. There were two wonderfully adroit arrangements of finger food on the coffee table, which was the size of a door — fresh fruits, crackers, different cheeses, and dainty cuts of salami folded and shaped to look like roses. We sipped the Capri, and talked. "Our oldest son studied art history at Colgate," Michelle said. "I think I told you that, Angela. But did I add that he can't draw a lick?"

"I think so," Angela said, with a soft laugh.

Michelle looked at me. "And he lives in LA now, works at a gallery on Wilshire Boulevard."

"After a stint dealing blackjack in Las Vegas," Chorros said. "Just like his old man at about that age."

Michelle spread some Brie on a cracker and offered it to me. I took it, smiling, and caught myself wondering if she might be thinking about when she and Phillip left DC for Las Vegas that first time, while I was in Saigon. It crossed my mind, anyway. I took a little more of the wine.

"Our second son joined the marines right out of high school," Chorros added. "He's stationed in Quantico. And he is, uh, also completely devoid of artistic talent or interest."

"They both take after me," Michelle put in. "Our daughter's the one who inherited the talent for drawing and painting. She's the one most like Phillip."

"Then she's brilliantly talented," I said.

"We're gonna need a second bottle of Capri, darling," Phillip said to his wife.

She went to a wine cabinet just at the entrance to the dining room, and brought out another bottle.

"Our daughter Miranda's a mom," Phillip Chorros said. "Mother of four. Two marriages, two by each husband. Michelle probably told you."

"And Miranda lives close," Angela said. "I think that's marvelous."

Michelle nodded, smiling. "Fort Walton Beach. So we get to see those grandkids pretty often."

"And you have a son in France," her husband said to Angela.

"Yes. We don't see him as often as we'd like to."

"Do you see your relatives from Arizona?" I asked Phillip. "Your uncle Trace?"

"Trace lives in Maine now."

"He's been here for a visit," said Michelle. "A while back. He married a younger woman, and they have three small children, so travel is difficult."

"My parents are gone," Chorros said. Then, after a pause: "Separately, and within a couple months of each other, back in '05."

For a few minutes, they talked about their grandchildren.

"For some unknown reason," he said, "my sons never got into the kind of trouble I did, growing up."

"So they never tore down a house by mistake," I said.

He paused a moment, looked at me and then poured more wine, seeming to concentrate on it. "Right."

"I'm sure you've told them about that episode."

He nodded distractedly. "Of course."

"Did you ever see Mr. Eberley again?"

He frowned, thinking, then repeated the name.

"Twelfth-grade art class." I felt now as though I were pressing him. I took another sip of my wine, and smiled.

"Oh, right. Eberley," he said. "Eberley. You know, I was ridiculously hard on that poor man. I was pretty ridiculously hard on a lot of those people. And, the fact is, they weren't the real target."

I waited, expecting more, and when he didn't go on I said, "I always thought I was going to hell."

"Oh, I was a believer," he said. "Devout. Very deeply. Well, you know I tried seminary."

"I applied for that," I told him. "I told you about it. Wrote you too, but you never got the letters."

"But I don't recall you ever mentioning that you were thinking of the priesthood."

"Well," I said, "I thought of saying something more than once. But it felt so private."

He left a pause.

"So we're with a couple of failed priests," Michelle said, then looked at me. "I do remember how religious you were."

"I came to think I *needed* the vocation," Chorros said. "I mean I actually sought it. And it caused a bit of trouble between Michelle and me. I mean I wasn't exactly the most *active* boyfriend. I actually thought I could maybe — well. But it just wasn't there."

Now I left the pause.

"A lot of Catholic boys go through that though, don't they?" Angela said.

"I believed everything they told us," Chorros broke forth. "Then one day it all looked — " He paused, took a sip of his wine, then sighed. "Well."

"I just — fell away," I told him.

And in the lengthening silence that followed, it was as if he and I, two very different men, had come to that elegant house on the edge of the sea from our mutually exclusive experiences, no more familiar to each other than Angela and Michelle. I thought of his grown children, whose lives had been so different from his own. Angela asked about the details and difficulties and excitements of putting on a food show and dealing with grandchildren. We concentrated on the finger food and enjoyed the wine, going on politely about the ocean, the weather, the hurricane seasons. Finally Michelle excused herself to go prepare dinner, and Angela went with her. Chorros took me into the living room. The first thing I saw were five tall, exotically feathered spears in a big, barrel-like ceramic vase. He spoke of them briefly; they were from some South American tribe. Along the wall opposite the stairs were artifacts and art from West Africa and Sri Lanka, Egypt and Afghanistan, and I saw painted porcelain faces in a row across a side table. "These I brought back from Tokyo," he said. The whole room was like a section of a museum. It made me feel parochial with my years of teaching in one place and my little office with its walls of books. He opened still another bottle of Capri, and we went out on the back deck. He offered me a cigar. We sat smoking quietly for a little while, looking at the pelicans hunting low over the water. A school of dolphins swam by, their phosphorescence trailing just along the surface; they leapt wonderfully in a kind of balletic consonance. He talked about leaving the job in Vegas, and then of his journey to the navy and becoming an officer, and some more about the many places he had traveled. He had gone back to Africa several times, and he loved Spain. He told me he had voted Republican until Obama. He wanted to tell me that. About Obama, he said, "I thought it was time we had a Black president."

"That's the only reason?" I asked.

He thought a moment, blowing smoke. "I admired McCain, but I knew some things about his views. I think he might've had us bombing people like it was 1968. And anyway he picked that ignorant boob for a running mate. And then I couldn't stomach Romney."

"I've voted Democratic all along," I said.

He nodded and made a little scoffing sound, as if to say, "Sure, *you* would."

This irked me. I sat looking out at the mildly troubling shoreline, trying to think of something else to talk about.

"I cheated on Michelle," he said suddenly. It seemed cold; in fact, almost aggressive. "Not too long ago. Last year about this time I was in New York for a reunion, and the woman running the thing and I — well. And Michelle found out about it. Well, I told her. Recently. I mean it came out recently. I didn't think — never thought. But it just did, not too long after you and Angela agreed to come visit."

I kept very still, holding my cigar where I had stopped its progress to my mouth.

"Just a couple weeks ago, in fact." He shrugged.

I took a draw and blew the smoke, which sounded like a sigh of exhaustion or impatience.

"Being completely honest. Just felt like telling you, you know? I've got some heart trouble. And I had a brain bleed from getting T-boned in traffic when we were stationed at Fort Myer. We're — both all right about it now, you know, we've got through it. I told her that I wish *she'd* been unfaithful to *me*. Then we'd be even."

I took another draw on the cigar and almost coughed.

"I guess you've been faithful to Angela."

I felt a little as I'd sometimes half-consciously felt when I was with him back in DC, as if I were a person whose witness he required for some reason. I'd read somewhere that a particular kind of man will be casually intimate with his valet.

"Well?" he persisted.

"Yeah," I answered. "Pretty much."

"Pretty much."

"Nothing more than a brief grappling kiss at a party, when drunk. Eight or nine years ago."

"Did you tell her about it?"

"No."

"She still doesn't know, then."

"Right."

"You're a smart man."

"It didn't seem important enough to mention."

A moment later, he said, "How's *your* health?"

"Fine, no complaints."

"Lucky man. I've got some increasing short-term memory trouble."

"I've struggled with depression some," I told him.

A moment later, he said, "Is Angela your first wife?"

I looked at him. "No."

He waited.

"My first wife left me," I said, and almost pointed out that before *that,* Michelle had also left me. But then I couldn't be sure what he knew or remembered, and anyway I didn't want the embarrassment.

"When did you meet Angela?" he asked.

I told him.

A jet leaving a contrail went across the top of the sky.

"I never thought I'd marry again," I added. "When Dora left me. Her name was Dora."

"You never had any children."

"No."

He nodded, staring off, blowing smoke.

A moment later, I heard myself say, "When did you stop going to church?" And then fearing to cause him any uneasiness, I quickly volunteered my own story of lapsing. I heard myself say it might've had its seeds in the afternoon of the Beltline.

He watched me, wine in one hand and cigar in the other, both held near his face. He took a puff on the cigar and blew the smoke, looking at the sea again. "Actually the Beltline seemed small to me. I mean perfectly shitty, but *of the time,* really. Father Burns let you know where you stood. I actually liked the way he was. There were other things, things other than just — being tough or strict — like Burns was. Hell, my own dad was strict. Sometimes more than strict. You knew that." He stopped. Then: "Did you have much to do with Father Drummond?"

"I always went to him for confession. I'd wait in a long line rather than go to Burns."

"Did you serve Mass for him?"

"Only a couple early Masses before the trip to the abbey."

"He never came to your house, or took you aside."

"No."

"Well, you know, Drummond was one of them."

I waited.

"You've seen the stories, right?"

Now I sat forward, feeling a tightening in my throat.

He went on. "Drummond never came at you that way?"

"Are you talking about — do you mean — "

"Yeah," he said. "I *mean.* That's — that's exactly what I *mean.*"

We heard the women talking and laughing in the kitchen.

I shook my head. "Father Drummond. My God. I thought he was so much kinder than Father Burns."

"Father Burns, like I said, was just strict. I really — I actually *liked* him."

"God," I said. "You were carrying that."

He sighed. "I spent a lot of time scared and pissed off afterward. And yet it ended up making me more religious in a weird way. I think maybe it could've been some kind of denial. I was afraid I'd go to hell if I didn't — " He halted. Then: "When the — when he tried it, I don't know where I found the strength, but I — I pushed him away so hard that he fell down. And then he got all sorrowful, hauling himself up from the floor, all repentant and loud and — and begging me to help him ask for God's mercy, kneeling and grasping at me, saying he wanted us to ask forgiveness together, pulling at me. 'The two of us,' he kept saying. 'The two of us.' I was struggling to pull away and then Father Burns walked in and looked at him and the bastard let go and I ran out of there. And I never went near him again if I could help it."

"Old Drummond," I said. "My God."

"And then later, Father Burns asked me to say exactly what happened."

"And you told him."

"I said I didn't know what happened. But he knew. He helped me keep the son of a bitch at a distance. Never said anything, but he knew something. And I kept going to church, too, as you — you remember. I was Catholic, after all." He took a long drink of the wine. "Anyway."

"I'm so sorry," I said.

"I guess it was stupid to think you'd come here and we'd only talk about our lives since then. Idiotic, really, to think we might talk about tearing down an old farmhouse and messing around in high school and not come to talking about this."

"I never saw," I told him. "My God, I never had an inkling."

We smoked quietly and the laughter and chatter came from the kitchen.

"Michelle won't tell Angela," he said. "About the other — you know. And I hope you won't either."

"I wouldn't do that," I said. "Come on." Now I had an irksome sense of being an intruder. I crushed my cigar out in the ashtray.

Something popped in the kitchen. Michelle had opened a bottle of champagne. "You boys need anything?" she called.

"Everything's fine, darling." He gave me a look. "I guess I'm a little drunk."

I said, "What was that word Sister Mary Margaret used?"

He shook his head.

"Mischief," I said. "Remember?"

"Oh, yeah."

"It just doesn't fit. Does it. Doesn't have the *gravitas*." I emphasized the word.

He shrugged. "It'll do, I guess. I never had your sense of the subtleties in language."

"It was tormentingly lightweight," I went on, "for what we were talking about back then. What *they* were talking about. What we were *dealing* with. And it's especially lightweight when we talk about — "

He was pouring more of the Capri, and I had the sense that he'd stopped listening. I watched him relight the end of his cigar.

"Heaven and hell," I said. "Eternity."

"Wherever dear old Father Drummond is," said Chorros, "I hope it's eternity and he's burning in it."

"I was terrified of Father Burns."

He drew on his cigar and the coal glowed in the dark. I saw the silhouettes of more pelicans crossing in front of the moon, gliding above the water, and diving. "Father Burns was an honest priest, if you overlooked his natural brutality. Which was — " He paused for emphasis. "The brutality of the times." He stopped. Then: "And that guy never — I wish I'd told him the whole thing that time. Then I'd've been able to see what he'd do about it. I mean he'd have to do something about it, right? I think I ended up just giving him room to let it go on, you know? Like so many others let it go on. But man, I needed the church back then. I needed it to be a church."

I kept silent, searching for something to say.

"People *kill* for *religious* reasons," he continued. "You know? All this — all these — these assaults — they're blaming it on the celibacy rule. They see the celibacy rule as some kind of reason for it or cause of it — but look at it. *Look* at what that fucking idea *really* supposes *logically*. It logically makes all of us — every man and boy on this earth from infancy to death — into brutes being led around by our genitals and animal urges. I never had an urge to touch a child that way. You? You ever had anything *remotely* like it? And according to their thinking, that's what all men, not just homosexual men — which is its *own* horrible assumption — but all men end up being drawn to, when they're sworn to celibacy."

I said, "It's hard to understand the *recent* proliferation of it. I mean, back when we — "

He interrupted me, leaning close. "It goes all the way back to 1654, Vance. I read up on it. Sixteen hundred fifty-fucking-four. First official record of it."

I sat there gazing out at the water in the failing light, and the sparkle at the horizon. Some kids were running along the beach. A high female voice rose in a laugh. Chorros coughed, then drank more of the wine.

"Drummond never touched you, or fondled you?" he asked.

"No," I said. "In the confessional, he was so gentle. I — "

"Never tried to kiss you?"

I said nothing; I don't think I even breathed.

"Forget it," he said. His cigar had gone out again, and when he put a match to it, his hand shook. "I could never figure out why he picked me. Why me, of all of us. Was it because my mother was an Indian?"

I said, "Did you ever tell your mother or father about him?"

"Kept it secret for years. Never told anyone. Liluye went to her grave, still devout, not knowing. Aside from Michelle, no one else knows. My children don't know. I really don't know why I told *you*. I didn't think I would. But then you said you were thinking of seminary when I was. And I remembered that and just now I wondered anyway if he might've come at you, you know, like maybe he went after the ones who were most serious about it all. I know he went after poor Reynolds. I don't know where Reynolds ended up. But he was shell-shocked all that last year, walking around wringing his hands."

Again, we were quiet.

Presently, he crushed the cigar out. "You work a lifetime and travel thousands and thousands of miles — " He stopped. "And I was one who managed to get away. Drummond let me alone after that. But I suspected he went after poor Reynolds and I didn't do a thing. I drew pictures of torture and stupid caricatures of Santa."

"I thought they were brilliant drawings."

"They were desperate. And I got very devout — well, you know. And that's where it really started to fall apart."

"Nobody came near me," I told him.

"I've been carrying it a lot more lately. Reynolds and how many others. I keep reliving those confusions."

I said nothing.

"Do you know anything that can be done for despair?"

"Excuse me?"

"The wine only deepens it."

"Well, it's a depressant," I said, feeling as if I had uttered something so irrelevant as to approach obscenity. I tilted my head slightly to look directly at him. "Angela prescribed duloxetine for me."

He smiled. "I've been taking it for years."

We were quiet.

"I don't want to be that boy again," he said. "I don't want to go back."

"No, nor I."

"I've been forgetting things — forgetting what's right in front of me sometimes. Right in front of me and I don't have a clue or an inkling. Nothing. Not even on the tip of my tongue, you know? And all that long-ago shit is goddamned clear as hell."

"But isn't that the way of it?" I said. "The far past stays crystal clear."

"No," he insisted. "It's more than that. Short term — last week, yesterday, an hour ago. It's disappearing. Michelle had to explain to me the other day what a — to open a — that thing you use — hell. I can't even think of it *now*. A fucking — a can opener. There."

I waited.

"Can opener," he repeated, as though it were something he was going to have to recite. Then: "I don't like being this old. I can remember all the prayers. I have it all clear as hell. You believe that?"

"Oh, I believe it all right."

"It's not a good thing, having all the *back then* while being slowly effaced from the *right fucking now*."

I kept still.

"I believed them. The priests. I believed it all."

"Me, too."

Somewhere out in the harbor, a boat horn sounded. The gulls cried, and the waves made their low hammering on the shore. Now when he spoke his tone made it clear that he wanted to drop the subject. "So, your folks are still with us."

"Coming up on their sixty-seventh anniversary," I said. "And still happy with each other."

"And they still go?"

"Both of them," I said. "You know Father Burns is there?"

"You're kidding." This seemed to amuse him.

"He came back last year. He's Monsignor Burns now. My mother told me about it the last time we visited with them."

"I think about Brother Edgar now and then."

"Yeah."

"You think they might've been lovers?"

I looked at him. "I guess it's crossed my mind — half consciously anyway. Now and then."

"Father Burns," Chorros sighed. "In a way he saved me. And he was gay. No doubt. Him and brother Edgar. Two very kind men, even Burns. I mean, he'd seen the war and he thought we should be tough. He wanted us *tough*. He *believed* we were going to have to face the same thing, and it was his job to make us strong and ready for it. And didn't we? Didn't we end up having to face a war?"

"Well, he terrified me," I said. Then, after a beat, "Anyway, he's pastor there now."

We watched the moon shining in a bright avenue of light on the water. The agitation of the waves now looked to be turning luminescent. The beach was deserted, and I thought of the idea of God as light, the light shining in the darkness, as the book says.

At length, Chorros sat back. "I'd rather not ruin the meal by talking about this anymore, if it's all the same to you."

"Right," I said.

We sipped the wine. In the kitchen, I heard Michelle talking about what she added to bouillabaisse to make it more spicy. Her tone, I felt certain, was that of her TV persona. A moment later, Phillip Chorros confirmed it. "Michelle forgets that she's not on camera sometimes."

I said, "You hear from your cousin, these days?"

"Moss is dead," he muttered, shaking his head. "Funny. I don't know why I didn't mention that in our first phone calls. Moss is gone. Isn't it strange how all of us become permanent *present tense* when in fact we're so very definitely *of* the past. Think of it. *Is*. Moss *is* dead. He *was* alive, and he *is* dead. He's entered the permanent present tense of *was*. So he's out of it."

"Did he know anything about — "

Chorros was already shaking his head. "I tried to tell him once, but you remember how he was. Everything a joke. Always thinking up the next thing he wanted to tell you."

I said nothing.

"He went early. Lived in Pittsburgh with his wife and three kids. One early morning. Bang. Like that. And he never smoked or drank much either. He exercised, stayed trim."

"I'm so sorry."

"Eighteen years ago."

"God."

"Let's leave the book of the dead alone, shall we?"

"Okay," I said.

He sighed. "I can tell you I ran into Michael Drexel in Huntington Beach, California, about eight or nine years ago when I was stationed out there myself for a while. He served twenty years in the air force, and then retired and became a TV repairman, in the last place he was stationed. He seemed really very happy."

I took the last of my Capri, feeling drunk. "I'd sure like to see your studio."

He took me down there. It was a low-ceilinged rectangular room, cut out of a larger space, where boxes were stacked and an old lawn mower sat collecting dust. Just inside the entrance, he picked up a blond teakwood box from a small telephone table and smoothed one hand across the surface. "I made this in the first week of my retirement." Opening it, he took out a black pistol and held it toward me. I took it, felt the weight of it, and started to hand it back. "Careful," he said, taking hold. "It's loaded."

I watched him set it down in its red-cloth bed and close the box. He said, "In case anybody wants to come down here and steal my deathless art." Then he grinned and lightly slapped my shoulder. "Kidding. It's my service revolver. 'The Pistol,' we always called it. Beretta M9. Standard. Though I bought this the day I turned in my government-issue version. Just seemed wrong not to have it."

"It's really loaded?" I said.

"Sleeping with its belly comfortably full. Safety on."

"Jesus," I said.

He winked at me. "For any emergency." Then he indicated the rest of the room. On the wall and stacked along the wall were drawings and paintings of his children, of Michelle, of some of the sunsets he must've seen in various parts of the world, including his own seaside view off the deck. And some wonderful abstracts, from violent clashes of color and shadow to muted shapes inside shapes. He'd also done faces, many faces — African, Asian and Middle Eastern, most of them children and women.

"So marvelously true to life," I said, and could not help adding, "And interesting. So pleasing to the eyes. I was sure you had a great future ahead of you as a professional artist."

He shrugged slightly. "I was never gonna be anything but a craftsman sitting in an office somewhere with drawing pads and sketch pads and drafting tables. It's just a mimetic gift. There's no real vision, no real *being* here, man. Just a pleasant hobby that used to relax me. Or that I expressed rage with."

"You mean you don't do it anymore?"

He shrugged. "Nothing suggests itself."

"But all those people you made up, the Cossack, and the monk and Geronimo and — and Santa."

"Yeah," he said simply. And shook his head.

We looked through a few more of them, especially the ones of his daughter and the grandchildren.

"I was sure you'd be famous."

"Well, I've loved the sea."

Upstairs, we had what anyone would say was a charming dinner, prepared by a woman who had been a professional. Michelle had a lot to tell us about their first days together after he came back from Arizona. She went on about it and about their happy marriage, and I sensed that she was saying it all for his benefit, given what I knew about their recent history. But then, considering our own history, I thought it might be for my benefit, too. I rehashed the subject of our misguided calamity in the mountains of West Virginia by telling of my stop there those years later; but a note of the stale and rote seemed to sound in it all now, and I sensed that Chorros saw something almost boorish in my bringing it up. "I'd never want to go back there," he muttered. A little later I saw the dour cast in his demeanor as Angela and I were departing. We'd agreed to a plan, put forward a little urgently by Michelle, that we would come back for brunch. But to my relief, they canceled that next morning, explaining — well, she explained — that Phillip had forgotten an appointment for his yearly physical. She said they might call if there was a way to do something in the evening. But they didn't call.

Angela and I spent a day lying around the hotel. We had a couple of cold beers before turning in. I didn't say anything about what Phillip had confided to me. And Phillip and I never spoke about it again. He called several times, and he was very direct about present matters. "Michelle's watching me so close," he said. "I wish I'd kept my mouth shut. I wish I'd been like you." Then: "I'm getting too old for her." On another call, he grew angry at himself for not being able to remember the man who lived next door, and what day of the week it was. "Can't make it quit," he said. "Can't keep a goddamn thing five minutes." Finally the calls ceased. Angela heard twice from Michelle in the months that followed. Both times Michelle spoke of her husband's slippages, as she called them. She somehow managed to sound brave and cheerful on these calls, yet it was costing her; Angela could hear it.

I told her, finally, about Father Drummond. It was the afternoon we received the news from Phillip's daughter — who was simply calling everyone in the address book to spare her mother having to explain — that he had gone down into the basement where all his drawings and paintings were, opened the teakwood box, lifted what was contained there from its bed of red satin and sat at the base of the wall where you might expect him to prop some of his beautiful work. Evidently he intended to use the pistol on himself. No one can know what kind of stress storms through the nervous system and takes hold in the arteries and veins when such a desperate decision is reached. Phillip Chorros's daughter told us that Michelle had found him sitting there, in cardiac arrest, the unfired pistol in his lap.

4.

Father Drummond went back to Ireland in 1983. As far as I know, nothing ever came out about him. And as I had told Chorros, Father Burns did return to Saint Agnes. He's ninety-one now, my mother tells me. It's so strange to think that only sixteen years separate us. In 1959 he seemed a man from an unreachable province of authority and severity, worlds beyond me. And how had Father Drummond, in his sick desperation, seemed to Phillip back then?

Recently, my mother told me over the phone that Father Burns had given what he called his last sermon, a sad one, she said, about his difficult journey to acceptance, and how the revelations all over the world during recent years had been a source of helpless rage, sorrow and consternation to him. He went on to say that because of his failures as a man, he had thought of renouncing his vocation, but that his dear friend Brother Edgar had talked him out of it. "He almost broke down, son, talking about this friend, who's gone now, I guess."

I said nothing.

She continued. "He talked about an old punishment — some sort of gauntlet for disciplining altar boys who'd misbehaved. He said he used it routinely."

I remained silent.

"Vance, he told us he decided to stop using it one day when a boy turned and ran and all the other boys chased him. He lost his voice, talking about it, how that experience filled him with doubt. He said he'd been a coward about things for years, had kept quiet or refused to believe it, and then this thing with the punishment — and this boy who turned and ran and his keeping all of it secret in his heart for years. He got emotional, son. It was like a confession. Does any of this sound familiar to you? He gave the year as 1959."

"I don't remember anything like that," I managed to say.

"Well, I guess it must've happened just before you."

"Probably."

She added: "The poor man still feels bad about it. This was his last sermon. Imagine."

Again, I said nothing.

"So strange," she said. "And you were planning to be a priest. Think of *that*."

"Wouldn't you have felt proud?"

Now she was quiet a moment. "I think I might've been sad for you, a little."

She's just turned ninety-four, and will tell you that the habit of taking nine golden raisins soaked in gin every day explains her good health. Vance, at ninety-six, will tell you the same thing about himself. He's begun showing signs of slowing down, but just in the last year or so. He walks with a cane these days. The two of them will never let go of the Point Royal house, though the taxes on it are more than the mortgage ever was. We all still gather there at Christmas, the twins and their families; Constance, alone, as I was at her age; Angela and me. We go to Mass together at Saint Agnes of Rome, because Vance and Jean never miss it if they can help it.

Recently I drove over to Oak Lane to see the little dwelling — I say dwelling; I would hate to think of anyone smashing it — where we said the rosary each evening. I thought about how we were in those years, and had a moment of being suffused with the fervent hope that anyone who presently lives there has love as plentifully as we did then, even as I recalled nights lying in fear of heavenly wrath, hearing my father give forth those small cries in the darkness. The trees we planted in the backyard have grown tall enough to provide good shade in summer. I stood gazing at them and thinking of him stepping carefully down from the roof that day so long ago.

Then, remembering my flailing in the musty, wine-smelling basement of the old house in the swale, I experienced a kind of retrograde sense of what that actually must have been, though of course at such a young age I could not have possessed the capacity to express it — or understand it either. I believe now that in some nameless, half-conscious way I was battering at the whole edifice of the church itself, its requirements, its heaven and hell, where a little boy could be led to believe he might be cast into everlasting flames for entertaining a thought. And I freely admit the possibility that I'm supplying this aspect of the story out of subsequent will — an interpretation, so to speak, less truth than a trick of hindsight. And I never had any notion of what Phillip Chorros knew and lived with all that time.

I often think of him reaching past my shoulder and grabbing hold of the chalice. He was a daydreaming child, after all, astonished and impressed at the shine of it, reaching over out of the natural impulse of a born artist to touch something so bright. That is what stands out in my mind when I think of those days now. That boy, Phillip Chorros, late of this world, filled with wonder, so richly talented, putting his fingers and thumb on the gleaming chalice and saying, "Is that gold?" simply because, having heard nothing of the priest's explaining, he wanted to know if it was real.

A NOTE ABOUT THE AUTHOR

RICHARD BAUSCH is the author of thirteen novels and nine other volumes of short stories. He is a recipient of the Rea Award for the Short Story, the PEN/Malamud Award for Excellence in the Short Story, a Guggenheim fellowship, the Lila Wallace–Reader's Digest Writers' Award, the Literature Award from the American Academy of Arts and Letters, and the Dayton Literary Peace Prize for his novel *Peace.* Three full-length motion pictures have been made from his work. He is past chancellor of the Fellowship of Southern Writers, and his stories are widely anthologized, including in *The Pushcart Prize; The Granta Book of the American Short Story; The Best American Short Stories; Blue Collar, White Collar, No Collar: Stories of Work; The Ecco Anthology of Contemporary American Short Fiction;* and others. He is on the writing faculty of Chapman University in Orange, California.

A NOTE ON THE TYPE

This book was set in Agmena, which was designed by Jovica Veljović for Linotype in 2012. Inspired by the forms and proportions of Renaissance fonts, Veljović created Agmena with the intent of making the perfect text face for books. Agmena was awarded a Certificate of Typographic Excellence by the Type Directors Club in 2013.

Typeset by Scribe,
Philadelphia, Pennsylvania

Designed by Marisa Nakasone